THE
JUST CITY

Jo Walton comes from Wales but lives in Montreal, where the food and books are much better. She writes science fiction and fantasy, reads a lot, talks about books, and eats great food. She plans to live to be ninety-nine and write a book every year.

D1375839
C333779018

Also by Jo Walton

THE
JUST CITY

——

JO WALTON

corsair

First published in the US in 2015 by Tor, an imprint of
Tom Doherty Associates, LLC.

First published in Great Britain in 2015 by Corsair

1 3 5 7 9 10 8 6 4 2

Copyright © 2014 by Jo Walton
The moral right of the author has been asserted.

All characters and events in this publication, other than
those clearly in the public domain, are fictitious
and any resemblance to real persons,
living or dead, is purely coincidental.

All rights reserved.
No part of this publication may be reproduced, stored in a retrieval system,
or transmitted, in any form or by any means, without the prior permission in writing
of the publisher, nor be otherwise circulated in any form of binding or cover other
than that in which it is published and without a similar condition including this
condition being imposed on the subsequent purchaser.

A CIP catalogue record for this book
is available from the British Library.

ISBN: 978-1-4721-5076-9 (paperback)
ISBN: 978-1-4721-5077-6 (ebook)

Printed and bound in Great Britain by CPI Group (UK) Ltd., Croydon, CR0 4YY

Corsair
An imprint of
Little, Brown Book Group
Carmelite House
50 Victoria Embankment
London EC4Y 0DZ

An Hachette UK Company
www.hachette.co.uk

www.littlebrown.co.uk

This is for Ada, who took me to Bernini's *Apollo*.

Wherever you go, there are plenty of places where you will find a welcome; and if you choose to go to Thessaly, I have friends there who will make much of you and give you complete protection, so that no one in Thessaly can interfere with you.

—PLATO, *Crito*

The triremes which defended Greece at Salamis defended Mars too.

—ADA PALMER, *Dogs of Peace*

Yes, I know, Plato; but if you always take the steps in threes, one day you will miss a cracked one.

—MARY RENAULT, *The Last of the Wine*

If you could take that first step
You could dance with Artemis
Beside Apollo Eleven.

—JO WALTON, "Submersible Moonphase"

THE
JUST CITY

1

APOLLO

She turned into a tree. It was a Mystery. It must have been. Nothing else made sense, because I didn't understand it. I hate not understanding something. I put myself through all of this because I didn't understand why she turned into a tree—why she chose to turn into a tree. Her name was Daphne, and so is the tree she became, my sacred laurel with which poets and victors crown themselves.

I asked my sister Artemis first. "Why did you turn Daphne into a tree?" She just looked at me with her eyes full of moonlight. She's my full-blooded sister, which you'd think would count for something, but we couldn't be more different. She was ice-cold, with one arched brow, reclining on a chilly silver moonscape.

"She implored me. She wanted it so much. And you were right there. I had to do something drastic."

"Her son would have been a hero, or even a god."

"You *really* don't understand about virginity," she said, uncurling and extending an ice-cold leg. Virginity is one of Artemis's big things, along with bows, hunting and the moon.

"She hadn't made a vow of virginity. She hadn't dedicated herself to you. She wasn't a priestess. I would never—"

"You really are missing something. It might be Hera you

should be talking to," Artemis said, looking at me over her shoulder.

"Hera hates me! She hates both of us."

"I know." Artemis was poised now, ready to be off. "But what you don't understand falls within her domain. Ask Athene." And she was off, like an arrow from a bow or a white deer from a covert, bounding across the dusty plains of the moon and swooping down somewhere in the only slightly less dusty plains of Scythia. She hasn't forgiven me for the moon missions being called the Apollo Program when they should have been called after her.

My domain is wide, both in power and knowledge. I am patron of inspiration, creativity, poetry and music. I am also in charge of the sun, and light. And I am lord of healing, mice, dolphins, and sundry other specialties I've gathered up, some of which I've devolved to sons and others, but all of which I continue to keep half an eye on. But one of my most important aspects, to myself anyway, has always been knowledge. And that's where I overlap with owl-carrying Athene, who is goddess of wisdom and knowledge and learning. If I am intuition, the leap of logic, she is the plodding slog that fills in all the steps along the way. When it comes to knowledge, together we're a great team. I am, like my sister Artemis, a hunter. It's the chase that thrills me, the chase after knowledge as much as the chase after an animal or a nymph. (*Why* had she preferred becoming a tree?) For Athene it's different. She loves the afternoon in the library searching through footnotes and linking up two tiny pieces of inference. I am all about the "Eureka" and she is all about displacing and measuring actual weights of gold and silver.

I admire her. I really do. She's a half-sister. All of us Olympians are pretty much related. She's another virgin goddess, but unlike Artemis she doesn't make a fetish of her virginity. I always thought she was just too busy working on wisdom to get involved with all that love and sex stuff. Maybe she'd get around to it in a few millennia, if it seemed interesting at that point. Or maybe she wouldn't. She's very self-contained. Artemis is always bathing naked in forest pools and then punishing hunters who happen to see her. Athene isn't like that at all. I'm not sure she's ever been naked, or even thought about it. And nobody would think about it when they're around her. When you're around Athene what you think about is new ways of thinking about fascinating bits of knowledge you happen to have, and how you might be able to fit them together to make exciting new knowledge. And that's so interesting that the whole sex thing seems like a bit of relatively insignificant trivia. So there were a whole host of reasons I was reluctant to bring up the Daphne incident with her.

But I really was burning with the need to know why Daphne turned into a tree in preference to mating with me.

I went to see Athene, who was exactly where I expected her to be and doing exactly what I expected her to be doing. She fights when she needs to, of course, and she's absolutely deadly when she does—she has the spear and the gorgon shield and she knows everything about strategy. But most of the time she's in libraries, either mortal libraries or Olympian ones. She lives in a library. It looks like the Parthenon in Athens on the outside, and on the inside it looks like . . . a giant book cave. That's the only way to describe it.

There's one short stumpy pillar just inside, where the owl sits napping with its head curled around under its wing. Generally the spear and shield and helmet are leaning against that pillar. There's also a desk, where she sits, which is absolutely covered with scrolls and codices and keyboards and wires and screens. There's exactly one beam of sunlight that comes in between two of the outside pillars and falls in exactly the right place on the desk to illuminate whatever she's using at the moment. The rest of the room is just books. There are bookcases around the walls, and there are piles of books on the floor, and there are nets of scrolls hanging from the ceiling. The worst of it is that everything is organized—alphabetized, filed, sorted, even labelled, but nothing is squared off and it all looks like the most awful mess. I never go in there without wanting to straighten it all out. It bothers me. If I'm going to see her, often I ask her to meet somewhere comfortable to both of us, like the Great Library, or the Laurentian Library, or Widener.

As I said, we make a good team—but we generally make a team as equals. I don't tend to go to her as a suppliant. I don't tend to go to anyone as a suppliant, except Father when it's absolutely unavoidable. It's rare for me to need to. And with Athene, on this particular subject, it made me deeply uncomfortable.

Nevertheless I went to her library-home and stood in the beam of light until she realized it had widened to the whole desk and looked up.

"Joy to you, Far-Shooter," she said when she saw me. "News?"

"A question," I said, sitting down on the marble steps outside, so I wouldn't have to either hover in the air or risk treading on a book.

"A question?" she asked, coming out to join me. She lowered herself to the step, and we sat side by side looking out over Greece spread out before us—the hills, the plains, the well-built cities, the islands floating on the wine-dark sea, the triremes plying between them. We couldn't actually see the triremes from this distance unless we focused, but I assure you they were there. We can go wherever we want, whenever we want, but why would we stray far from the classical world, when the classical world is so splendid?

"There was a nymph—" I began.

Athene turned up her nose. "If this is all, I'm going back in to work."

"No, please. This is something I don't understand."

She looked at me. "Please?" she said. "Well, go on."

As I said, I don't often come in supplication, but that doesn't mean I don't know the words. "Her name was Daphne. I pursued her. And just as I caught her and was about to mate with her, she turned into a tree."

"She turned into a tree? Are you sure she wasn't a dryad all along?"

"Perfectly sure. She was a nymph, a nereid if you want to be technical about it. Her father was a river. She prayed to Artemis, and Artemis turned her into a tree. I asked Artemis why, and she said it was because Daphne wanted it so desperately. Why did she want to become a tree to avoid me? How could she care that much? She hadn't made a vow of virginity. Artemis told me to ask Hera and then said maybe you would know."

Grey-eyed Athene looked at me keenly as I mentioned Hera. "I thought I didn't know, but if she mentioned Hera then maybe I do. What's at the core of what Hera cares about?"

"Father," I said.

Athene snorted. "And?"

"Marriage, obviously," I said. I hate those Socratic dialogues where everything gets drawn out at the pace of an excessively logical snail.

"I think the issue you may be missing with Daphne, with all of this, is to do with consensuality. She hadn't vowed virginity, she might have chosen to give her virginity up one day. But she hadn't made that choice."

"I'd chosen her."

"But she hadn't chosen you in return. It wasn't mutual. You decided to pursue her. You didn't ask, and she certainly didn't agree. It wasn't consensual. And, as it happens, she didn't want you. So she turned into a tree." Athene shrugged.

"But it's a game," I said. I knew she wouldn't understand. "The nymphs run away and we chase after."

"It may be a game not everyone wants to play," Athene suggested.

I stared out over the distant islands, rising like a pod of dolphins from the waves. I could name them all, and name their ports, but I chose for the moment to see them as nothing but blue on blue cloud shapes. "Volition," I said, slowly, thinking it through.

"Exactly."

"Equal significance?" I asked.

"Mm-hmm."

"Interesting. I didn't know that."

"Well then, that's what you learned from Daphne." Athene started to get up.

"I'm thinking about becoming a mortal for a while," I said, as the implications began to sink in.

She sat down again. "Really? You know it would make you very vulnerable."

"I know. But there are things I could learn much more quickly by doing that. Interesting things. Things about equal significance and volition."

"Have you thought about when?" she asked.

"Now. Oh, you mean *when*? When in time? No, I hadn't really thought about that." It was an exciting thought. "Some time with good art and plenty of sunshine, it would drive me crazy otherwise. Periclean Athens? Cicero's Rome? Lorenzo di Medici's Florence?"

Athene laughed. "You're so predictable sometimes. You might as well have said 'anywhere with pillars.'"

I laughed too, surprised. "Yes, that about covers it. Why, do you have a suggestion?"

"Yes. I have the perfect place. Honestly. Perfect."

"Where?" I was suspicious.

"You don't know it. It's . . . new. It's an experiment. But it has pillars, and it has art—well, it has very Apollonian art, all light and no darkness."

"Puh-lease." (That wasn't supplication, it was sarcasm. The last time I used the word it was supplication, so I thought I'd better clarify. But this was sarcasm, with which I am more familiar.) "Look, if you're about to suggest I go to some high-tech hellhole where they've never heard of me because it'll be a 'learning experience,' forget it. That's not what I want at all. I am Apollo. I *am* important." I pouted. "Besides, if they think the gods are forgotten, why are they writing about us? Have you read those books? There's nothing more clichéd. Nothing."

"I haven't read them and they sound awful, and the only thing I want to get from high-tech societies is their robots," she said.

"Robots?" I asked, surprised.

"Would you rather have slaves?"

"Point," I said. Athene and I have always felt deeply uneasy about slaves. Always. "So what do you want them for?"

Athene settled back on her elbows. "Well, some people are trying to set up Plato's Republic."

"No!" I stared down at her. She looked smug.

"They prayed to me. I'm helping."

"Where are they doing it?"

"Kallisti." She gestured towards where Thera was at the moment we were sitting in. "Thera before it erupted."

"They're doing it before the *Republic* was written?"

"I said I was helping."

"Does Father know?"

"He knows everything. But I haven't exactly drawn it to his attention. And of course, that side of Kallisti all fell into the sea when it erupted, so there won't be anything to show long-term." She grinned.

"Clever," I acknowledged. "Also, doing Plato's Republic on Atlantis is . . . recursive. In a way that's very like you."

She preened. "Like I said, it's an experiment."

"It's supposed to be a *thought* experiment. Who are these people that are doing it?" I was intrigued.

"Well, one of them is Krito, you know, Sokrates's friend. And another is Sokrates himself, whom Krito and I dragged out of Athens just before his execution. If Sokrates can't make it work, who can? And then there are some later philosophers— Platonists, Plotinus and so on, and some from Rome, like Cicero and Boethius, and from the Renaissance, Ficino and Pico . . . and some from even later, actually."

I was suspicious, and a little jealous. "And all of these random people in different times decided to pray to you for help setting up Plato's Republic?"

"Yes!" she sounded wounded that I doubted her. "They absolutely did. Every single one of them."

"I have to go there," I said. I wanted to try being a mortal. And this was so fascinating, the most interesting thing I'd heard about in aeons. Plato's *Republic* had been discussed over centuries, but it had never actually been tried. "Where are you getting the children?"

"Orphans, slaves, abandoned children. And volunteers," she said, looking at me. "I almost envy you."

"Come too?" I suggested. "Once you have it set up, what would stop you?"

"I'm tempted," she said, looking tempted, the expression she has when she has a new book she very much wants to read right now instead of fulfilling some duty.

"Oh do. It'll be so interesting. Think what we could learn! And it wouldn't take long. A century or so, that's all. And it'll have libraries. You'll feel right at home."

"It'll certainly have libraries. What will be in them is another question. There's some dispute about that at the moment." She stared off at the clouds and the islands. "Being a mortal makes you vulnerable. Open. Love. Fear. I'm not sure about that."

"I thought you wanted to know everything?"

"Yes," she said, still staring out.

We didn't have the least idea in the world what we were letting ourselves in for.

2

SIMMEA

I was born in Amasta, a farming village near Alexandria, but I grew up in the Just City. My parents called me Lucia, after the saint, but Ficino renamed me Simmea, after the philosopher. Saint Lucy and Simmias of Thebes, aid and defend me now!

When I came to the Just City I was eleven years old. I came there from the slave market of Smyrna, where I was purchased for that purpose by some of the masters. It is hard to say for sure whether this event was fortunate or unfortunate. Certainly having my chains struck off and being taken to the Just City to be educated in music and gymnastics and philosophy was by far the best fate I might have hoped for once I stood in that slave market. But I had heard the men who raided our village saying they were especially seeking children of about ten years of age. The masters visited the market at the same time every year to buy children, and they had created a demand. Without that demand I might have grown up in the Delta and lived the life the gods had laid out before me. True, I would never have learned philosophy, and perhaps I would have died bearing children to some peasant farmer. But who can say that might not have been the path to happiness? We cannot change what has happened. We go on from where we stand. Not even Necessity knows all ends.

I was eleven. I had rarely left the farm. Then the pirates

came. My father and brothers were killed immediately. My mother was raped before my eyes and then led off to a different ship. I have never known what happened to her. I spent weeks chained and vomiting on the ship they threw me onto. I was given the minimum of bad food and water to keep me alive, and suffered many indignities. I saw a woman who tried to escape raped and then flogged to death. I threw buckets of seawater over the bloodstains on the deck and my strongest emotion was relief at breathing clean air and seeing daylight. When we arrived at Smyrna I was dragged onto the deck with some other children. It was dawn, and the slope of the shore rising out of the water was dark against the pink sky. At the top some old columns rose. Even then I saw how beautiful it was and my heart rose a little. We had been brought up on deck to have buckets of water thrown over us to clean us off for arrival. The water was bone-chillingly cold. I was still standing on the deck as we came into the harbour.

"Here we are, Smyrna," one of the slavers said to another, taking no more notice of us than if we were dogs. "And that was the temple of Apollo." He gestured at the columns I had seen, and more fallen pillars that lay near them.

"Artemis," one of the others corrected him. "Lots of ships here. I hope we're in time."

From the harbour they brought us all naked and chained into the market, where there were men and women and children of every country that bordered on the Middle Sea. We were divided up by use—women in one place, educated men in another, strong men who might serve to row galleys in another. Between the groups were wooden rails with space for the buyers to walk about and look at us.

I was chained with a group of children, all aged between about eight and twelve, of all skin colours from Hyperborean fair to Nubian dark. My grandmother was a Libyan and the rest of my family all Copts, so I was slightly darker than the median shade of our group. There were boys and girls mixed indiscriminately. The only thing we had in common besides age was language—we all spoke Greek in some form. One or two of the others near me had been on my ship, but most of them were strangers. I was starting to realize how very lost I was. I had neither home nor family. I was never going to wake up and find that everything was back as it had been. I began to cry and a slaver backhanded me across the face. "None of that. They never take the snivelling ones."

It was a hot day and tiny flies rose all around and plagued us. With our hands bound before us at waist level we could not prevent them from getting into our eyes and noses and mouths. It was a tiny misery among many great miseries. I almost forgot it when the boy chained immediately behind me began to poke at me with his bound hands. I could not reach him except by kicking backwards, which he could see and I could not. I landed one hard kick on his shin but after that he dodged, almost pulling the whole line of us over. He taunted me as he did this, calling me fumble-foot and clumsy-cow. I held my silence, as I always had with my brothers, waiting for the right moment and the right word. I could have poked the girl in front of me, who was one of the pale ones, but saw no purpose in it.

When the masters came we knew at once that they were something special. They were dressed like merchants, but the slavers bowed before them. The masters acted towards the slavers as if they despised them, and the slavers deferred to them. It was clear in their body language, even before I could hear them. The slavers brought the masters straight towards our group. The masters were looking at us and paying no attention to the adult slaves bound in the other parts of the market. I stared boldly back at them. One of them wore a red hat with a flat top and little dents at the sides, which I noticed at once, before I noticed his eyes, which were so surprisingly penetrating that once I had seen them I could look at nothing else. He saw me looking and smiled.

The masters spoke to each of us in Greek, asking questions. Several of them spoke strangely, with an odd lisping accent that slurred some of the consonants. The master with the red cap came to me, perhaps because I had caught his eye. "What is your name, little one?" He spoke good Italianate Greek.

"Lucia the daughter of Yanni," I replied.

"That won't do," he muttered. "And how old are you?"

"Ten years old," I said, as the slavers had instructed us all to say.

"Good. And you have good Greek. Did you speak it at home?"

"Yes, always." This was nothing but the truth.

He smiled again. "Excellent. And you look strong. Do you have brothers and sisters?"

"I had three older brothers, but they are all dead."

"I am sorry." He sounded as if he truly was. "What's seven times seven?"

"Forty-nine."

"And seven times forty-nine?"

"Three hundred and forty-three."

"Very good!" He looked pleased. "Can you read?"

I raised my chin in the universal sign for negation, and saw at once that he did not understand. "No."

He frowned. "They so seldom teach girls. Are you quick to learn?"

"My mother always said so."

He sketched a symbol in the dust. "This is an alpha, *ah*. What words begin with alpha?"

I began to list all the words I could think of that began with alpha, among them, either because he himself put it into my mind or because I had heard it from the slaver as we came in, the

name of the old god Apollo. Just as I said it the slaver came up.
"This is a good girl," he said. "No trouble. Still a virgin, she is."

This was technically true, for virgins fetch more at the market. Yet that very man had emptied himself into my mouth the
night before on the ship. My jaw was still sore from it as he spoke.
The master with the red hat turned on the slaver as if he guessed
that. "I should think so, at ten years of age!" he snapped. "We
will take her."

I was unchained and taken aside. About half the group were
selected, among them the extremely fair girl and the boy who
had been poking at me. I was glad to see a red mark on his shin
from the one good kick I had given him.

The masters paid what the slavers asked, unquestioningly. I
could see how delighted the slavers were, although of course
they tried to hide it. They had made more for each of us children than they would have for a beautiful young woman or a
strong man. We were roped together and led down to a ship.

I had grown up on the shifting shore of the Delta, seeing
ships only far out to sea, before the pirates had come in to attack
us. Since then I had seen only their slave ship. I could tell that
this ship was different, but not in what way. It had no banks of
oars and no great square sail, but two masts and a series of
stepped sails. I later learned that she was a schooner, and sailed
by wind and tide alone. Her name was *Goodness*.

On the deck of the ship a woman was sitting with her legs
crossed, a book in her hand. One of the masters unbound the
ropes from our hands and legs as we came aboard and we were led
up to her in pairs. The woman seemed to be writing down the
names of the children, after which they were led to a hatchway
and disappeared. My own master, he of the red hat, led me up
to her with my tormentor. "These two have saints' names," he
said. "Will you name them, Sophia?"

She looked up, and I saw that her eyes were grey. "Not I. You should know better than to ask, Marsilio. You name them."

"Very well, then. They were chained together. Write them down as Kebes, the boy, and Simmea, the girl." He smiled at me again as he named us. "These are good names, names that will stand you well in the city. Forget your old names, as you should forget your childhoods and your time in misery. You are going to a good place. You are all brothers and sisters here, all reborn to new lives."

"And your name, master?" Kebes asked.

"He is Ficino, the Translator," the woman answered for him. "He is one of the masters of the Just City."

Then one of the others shepherded us to the hatch, and we climbed down a ladder into a big open space. The hold was nothing like the hold of the slaver. It was surprisingly well lit by strange glowing beams that lay along the curving slope of the ship. By their light I could see that it was full of children, all strangers. I had never seen so many ten-year-olds in one place, and apart from the market, never so many people. There must have been more than a hundred. Some were sleeping, some were sitting in groups talking or playing games, others were standing alone. None of them took much notice of the new arrivals. There were so many strangers suddenly that those who had been chained by me seemed like friends by comparison. Kebes was the only one whose name I knew. I stayed beside him as we went in among the others. "Do you think the masters mean well by us?" I asked him.

"I hate them," he replied. "I hate all of them, all masters who-ever they are, whatever they mean. I shall never forgive them, never submit to them. They think they bought me, think they changed my name, but nobody can buy me or change me against my will."

I looked at him, surprised. Like a dog who had been beaten,

I had been ready to love and trust the first kind word I received. He was different. He looked fierce and proud, like a hunting hawk who cannot be tamed. "Why did you poke me?" I asked.

"I will not submit."

"I wasn't the one who bound you. I was bound beside you."

"I couldn't get at the ones who bound me, and you were bound beside me where you were the only one I could reach." He looked a little guilty. "It was a small rebellion, but the only one I could achieve at that moment. And besides, you got me back." He pointed at the fading mark on his leg. "We're equal. Tell me your name?"

"Simmea, the master Ficino said." I saw his lip curl as if he despised me. "Oh, all right. Lucia."

"Well Lucia, though I shall call you Simmea and you may call me Kebes where the masters can hear, my name is Mat-thias. And I will never forgive them. I may wait for my revenge, but I will get it when they do not expect it."

We had not even reached the city. The ship was barely out of the harbour of Smyrna. Already the seeds of rebellion were growing.

3

MAIA

I was born in Knaresborough in Yorkshire in 1841, the third child and second daughter of the local rector. My parents christened me Ethel.

My father, the Rev. John Beecham, M.A., was a scholar who had been at Oxford and cared as much or more for the classics than he did for God. My mother was a worldly woman, the daughter of a baron, and therefore entitled to call herself "the honourable," which she did on all occasions. She loved nothing so much as pretty clothes and decorations. Her recreations were embroidery and visiting friends, and her charity consisted of doing good works in the parish. My elder sister, Margaret, known as Meg, was so entirely my mother's daughter as to be almost another edition of her in miniature. My father had hoped to have the same for himself in my brother, Edward, who was born the year before me. Unfortunately, Edward's temperament was not at all like my father's. He was an active, energetic boy, but sadly unsuited to scholarship. My father frequently grew impatient with him. From the first I can remember, I was consoling Edward and helping him con his lessons.

I do not remember learning to read. Perhaps my mother taught me, as she had certainly taught Meg. I have been able to read for as far back as my memory stretches, so perhaps it is true what

Plato says, that we bring some memories from our past lives. If so, then all I remembered was reading. Certainly I remember clearly that when I first saw the Greek alphabet, when I was six and poor Edward was seven, it came to me immediately, more like recollecting something forgotten than learning something new. The shapes of the Greek letters were like old friends, and I only needed to be told their names once. But for Edward it was torture. I remember coaching him in it over and over. He would get hopelessly lost, poor boy. That was when we began to work together in earnest. He would always bring me his lessons as soon as he left Father, and we would go over them together until he understood them. In this way we both progressed together in Latin and Greek. Soon I was reading ahead of him in his books. I had already read everything in the house in English.

Mother and Father did not take much notice of me in early childhood. I was brought down daily to greet my parents in the afternoon for an hour after tea, and often that was the only time I saw them. Meg was four years older than Edward and five years older than me. Mother taught Meg herself and took her about with her. She had a splendid wardrobe which suited her very well. She was a fetching child, good natured, always smiling and laughing, with golden curls and pink cheeks. My hair was paler, and lifeless in comparison, it would never take a curl. Nor did I ever try to charm the company. I retreated into myself until my mother thought me dull and sullen. When Meg was already old enough to begin to play the piano and to sew prettily, Edward and I were still under the care of our nurse.

Edward had his lessons with Father every morning. I stayed in the nursery and read everything I could lay my hands on. Then in the afternoons, after I had helped Edward understand his morning's lessons, we took healthful walks on the moors. This went on happily enough until Edward was twelve and Father began to talk of sending him away to school. Edward dreaded it, and begged to be allowed to stay at home. "But your work is so much better," Edward reported that Father had said. "Your last Latin composition had only one mistake, and your last Greek had none." Edward then burst out crying and admitted to Father that they were both my work. Father forgave him but was bewildered. "Little Ethel? But how does she know enough to do it?" He called me in and tested me on unseen passages of Greek and Latin, which I translated with pride and without difficulty.

Thereafter Father taught both of us together, and if anything he paid more attention to my progress than to Edward's, because I could follow his mind, which Edward could not. The next year Edward went off to school, scraping through his exam. Father continued to teach me. By the time Edward went to Oxford it was almost as if Father and I were colleagues, both scholars together, spending all day poring over a text and discussing it. Father said I had the wits of a man, and it was a shame I could not go to Oxford too, as I would get more benefit from it. I said that I did not want to leave him, but that perhaps Edward could bring us some more books. Father had a great desire to re-read Plato, which he did not own and had not read since he was himself at Oxford.

The year after, 1859, my father died, quite suddenly, of a chill that went to his lungs. Edward was in his second year at Oxford. Our lives changed overnight. The rectory, of course, had to be given up. Meg, who was twenty-three, had been betrothed for some time to the son of the local squire. It now seemed best to everyone that they be married immediately and set up housekeeping. My mother, almost as a matter of course, went to live with her. The day after the wedding I was sent off to my godmother, my father's sister, Aunt Fanny, in London. Aunt Fanny had made an advantageous marriage and was now Lady Dakin. She could better afford to support me than Meg's new husband.

Edward frowned at all this, but was powerless. My father's

estate, such as it was, went to him. It was barely enough for him to live on and remain at Oxford. He promised me that when once he had graduated and found a living that would support us both, he would take me into his house as his housekeeper. He painted a rosy picture of the two of us living happily in some country rectory, him out hunting and me in the study writing his sermons. It seemed the best future I could aspire to.

Aunt Fanny was very kind and gave me a London season with her youngest daughter, my cousin Anne. It was not the kind of entertainment that was to my taste, causing me to continually twist about on myself with shyness, thrust out among so many strangers. I was not a success with the young men to whom I was presented.

Aunt Fanny and Anne constantly urged me to make the best of myself and to wear lilac and grey after three months, but I insisted on wearing mourning black for my father for a whole year. Indeed, I missed him bitterly every day. Also I missed my books. I had been allowed to bring only certain books of Father's, and I felt parched for anything new. At the end of the London season, with neither of us married and being no doubt desperate as to what to do with two girls, Aunt Fanny carried us off on a tour to Italy. We had a guide and a carriage and we stayed in *pensiones* or in the houses of friends. It was all very grand, and at least it afforded me new things to see and think about. Sometimes I could even tell the others the stories of the places we were visiting, which always left them a little taken aback and caused the guide to despise me.

Then in Florence I fell in love, as so many have before me, not with any personage but with the art of the Renaissance. In the Pitti Palace I saw a fresco that showed the destruction of the ancient world—Pegasus being set upon by harpies!—and the refugee Muses coming to Florence and being welcomed by Lorenzo de Medici. I was so overcome I had to borrow a handkerchief from Anne to mop my eyes. Aunt Fanny shook her head.

Young ladies were supposed to admire art, but not so extravagantly.

Indeed, poor Aunt Fanny had no idea what to do with me. In the Uffizi, she found the Botticelli Madonnas "papist." I realized as soon as I saw them how bleak was the notion of God without any softening female spirit. I believed in God, of course, and in salvation through Christ. I had always been a devout churchgoer. I prayed nightly. I believed in Providence and tried to see its hand even through the difficulties of my life—which I reminded myself were not so very much to suffer in comparison with the lives so many led. I might have been utterly destitute and forced to beg, or to prostitute myself. I knew I was lucky. Yet I felt myself trammelled. Since Father died I had never had the conversation of an equal, never indeed had any conversation that was not at best quotidian. I wanted to talk to somebody about the female nurturing element in God, about the lives of the angels visible in the background of Botticelli's Madonnas, and even more about the *Primavera*. Anne, when I asked her what she thought, said she found the *Primavera* disturbing. We stood in front of the *Birth of Venus* as the guide mouthed nonsense. We moved on to another room and to Raphael, who had painted men I felt I could have talked to. I was so lonely I could have talked to their painted selves, had I been unobserved. I missed my father so much.

In the San Lorenzo market the next day, while Aunt Fanny and Anne were cooing over some leather gloves, I stealthily moved to the next stall, which was piled high with books. Some were in Italian, but many were in Greek and Latin, among them several worn volumes of Plato. Even the sight of his name on the faded leather seemed to bring my father closer. The prices seemed reasonable; perhaps there was little demand for books in Greek. I counted my little store of cash, gift of my generous aunt who imagined I wanted to buy trifles. Instead I bought as many books as I could carry and the money would reach to. Of course I could not carry them inconspicuously, so my cousin and my aunt saw the pile as soon as I caught up with them. I saw dismay in Aunt Fanny's eyes, but she did her best to smile. "How like your father you are, dear Ethel," she said. "My own dear brother John. He would also spend all he had on books whenever he got the chance. But you must not let men think you are a bluestocking. There is nothing that they so dislike!"

The next day we left for Rome. I had decided to make my books last and read only one book a week, but instead I gorged myself on them. In Rome I saw the Colosseum and the ruins of palaces on the Palatine Hill. I read Plato.

Like everyone who reads Plato, I longed to stop Socrates and put in my own arguments. Even without being able to do that, reading Plato felt like being part of the conversation for which I had been so starved. I read the *Symposium* and the *Protagoras*, and then I began the *Republic*. The *Republic* is about Plato's ideas of justice—not in terms of criminal law, but rather how to maximize happiness by living a life that is just both internally and externally. He talks about both a city and a soul, comparing the two, setting out his idea of both human nature and how people should live, with the soul a microcosm of the city. His ideal city, as with the ideal soul, balanced the three parts of human nature: reason, passion, and appetites. By arranging the city justly, it would also maximize justice within the souls of the inhabitants.

Plato's ideas about all these things were fascinating and thought-provoking, and I read on, longing to talk about them with somebody else who cared. Then, in Book Five, I found the passage where he talks about the education of women, indeed about the equality of women. I read it over and over again. I could hardly believe it. Plato would have allowed me into the conversation from which my sex excluded me. He would have let me be a guardian, limited only by my own ability to achieve excellence.

I went over to the window and looked down on the busy Roman street. A workman was going past, carrying a ladder. He
whistled at a young woman on a doorstep who called something
back to him in Italian. I was a woman, a young lady, and this
constrained me in everything. My choices were so unbearably
narrow. If I wanted a life of the mind I could work at nothing
but as a governess, or a teacher in a girls' school, teaching not the
classics but the proper accomplishments of a young lady—
sketching, watercolors, French and Italian, playing the piano.
Possibly I could write books; I was hazily aware that some women
did support themselves in that way. But I had no taste for fiction,
and writing philosophy would hardly be acceptable. I could
marry, if I could find a man like my father—but Father himself
had not chosen a woman like me, but one like my mother. Aunt
Fanny was not wrong when she said that men dislike bluestock-
ings. I could perhaps keep house for Edward as he had suggested, and write his sermons, but what would then become of
me if he were to marry?

In Plato's Republic, as never in all of history, my sex would have
been no impediment. I could have been an equal to anyone. I
could have exercised freely, and learned philosophy. I wished
fiercely that it existed and that I had been born there. He had
written two thousand three hundred years ago, and never in all
that time had anyone paid any attention. How many women had
led stupid wasted unnecessary lives because nobody listened to
Plato? I was furious with all the world except Plato and my father.

I went back to my seat and took up the book again, reading
on faster and faster, no longer wanting to disagree with Socrates,
saying yes in my heart, yes to everything; yes, censor Homer,
limit the forms of music, why not; yes, take children into battle;
yes, by all means exercise naked if you think it better; yes, indeed,
begin with ten-year-olds—how I would have loved it at ten.
Yes, please, please, dearest Plato, teach the best of both sexes to

become philosopher kings who discover and understand the Truth behind this world. I turned up the gas lamp and read most of the night.

The next morning Aunt Fanny complained that I looked fatigued, and said that I should not exhaust myself. I protested that I was very well, and an outing would revive me. The guide took us to see the Trevi Fountain, a huge extravaganza which Anne admired, and then on to the Pantheon, a round temple to all the gods, built by Marcus Agrippa and since reclaimed as a Christian church. The dome leads the eye up inexorably to a circle of clear sky. I looked at all the Catholic clutter of crucifixes and icons down below and saw it as impious in this place which led the heart to God without any need of it. Surely the philosopher kings would have divined God in the Truth. Surely nobody could come in here without apprehending Him, even the pagans who had built the place. Surely behind the façade of the mythology they understood, perhaps without knowing what they understood. They had no saints and prophets. Their gods were the best way for them to comprehend the divine.

My thoughts turned to the Greek gods, and to the idea of the female principle within God that had struck me in Florence. Without in the least intending it I found myself praying to Athene, the female patroness of learning and wisdom. "Oh Pallas Athene, please take me away from this, let me live in Plato's Republic, let me work to find a way to make it real."

I am sure that the next instant I would have realized what I was doing, and been shocked at myself and fallen to my knees and begged Jesus to forgive me. But that next instant never came. I was standing in the Pantheon looking up and praying to Athene, and then without any transition I was on Kallisti, in a pillared chamber full of men and women from many different centuries, all as bewildered as I was, with grey-eyed Athene herself standing unmistakably before us.

4

SIMMEA

I have never known what year it was when they bought me in Smyrna, or even what century. The masters wanted us to forget our old homes, and when once much later I asked Ficino, he said he could not recall. Perhaps he truly could not. He must have been on many of those voyages, into many years. They gathered up ten thousand Greek-speaking children who appeared to them to be ten-year-olds. I have often thought since how much better it would have been for them to have gathered up the abandoned babies of antiquity—but then they would have needed wet nurses, so perhaps that would not have worked either.

We spent two nights on the *Goodness* before we came to the city on the afternoon of the third day.

My first sight of the city was overwhelming. The masters brought us out in groups to see it as we approached. Kebes and I were among the last to come out, when we were almost in the harbor. The ruins at Smyrna had impressed me. The city was intact, was new made, and it had been positioned for maximum beauty and impact. Coming to it from the sea I saw the great mountain rising behind it, smoking slightly, and below that the slopes of the hills cupping the city. The city itself shone in the afternoon light. The pillars, the domes, the arches, all of it lay in the balance of light and shadow. Our souls know harmony and proportion before we are born, so although I had never seen anything like it, my soul resonated at once to the beauty of the city.

Immediately in front of us lay the harbor, with the mole curving out before it. This reflected in miniature the balance of man-made and natural elements in the city and the hills. I stood in awe, moved beyond words by the wonder of it. Kebes poked me in the ribs. "Where are the people?" he asked. "And what's that?"

I looked where he was pointing. "A crane?" I suggested.

"But it was moving." Indeed, it was moving. None of us had ever seen a worker before. This one was the color of bronze, with treads and four great arms, each ending in a different kind of hand—a digger, a gripper, a claw, a scoop. It was easily twice the height of a man. I would have assumed it a kind of beast, except that it had nothing that could be considered a head. It was trundling along the harborfront ready to help us tie up, so we saw it very well as we came inside the mole. We were all asking each other what it was, and at last one of the masters came and told us it was a worker and that we were not to be afraid. "They're here to do the heavy work and help us," he said, in his strange slurred Greek.

Once the *Goodness* was tied up we were taken ashore in groups of fourteen, seven boys and seven girls. We were led off in different directions through the streets. I was glad Kebes was with me, and even more glad to be in the group led by Ficino. Whatever Kebes said, I already felt that Ficino was a friend. I looked about me eagerly as we went through the streets. They were broad and well-proportioned, and lined with pillared courts and houses and temples with statues of the gods. We passed the occasional worker, some the same as the first but others shaped very differently. We saw no people until we had been walking for some time, when we heard the sound of children playing. We walked for some time more before we passed the palaestra where they were exercising—the sound had carried in the empty city. "Where are all the people?" I asked Ficino boldly.

"You are the people," he said, looking down at me. "This is your city. And not all of you are here yet."

A little while after that, a young woman came out of one of the houses. She was wearing a blue and white kiton with a key pattern around the borders, the first I had ever seen. She was fair-skinned, and her fair hair fell down her back in a neat braid. "Joy to you," she said. "I am Maia. The girls should come in here."

I lingered on the threshold as Ficino led the boys on. I did not want to lose track of the only people I knew. I was relieved to see them turning into the next house along the street.

"This is Hyssop house," Maia said, inside. I turned and went in. Inside it was cool. It seemed dark after the street, and it took my eyes a moment to adjust to the light that came in through the narrow windows. I saw that there were seven beds neatly lined up, one beside the door and three on each side of the room. A chest stood beside each one. Beyond them lay another door, which was closed. The walls and floor were marble, the roof had wooden beams.

"There is hyssop growing outside, by the door," one of the girls said, a tall girl as dark-skinned as my grandmother.

I hadn't noticed the hyssop. Maia nodded, clearly pleased. "Yes. All of the sleeping houses have their own flower or herb." Her Greek was strange, extremely precise but with odd hesitations as if she sometimes had to think to remember a word. Most disconcertingly she pronounced her V as B. "Each sleeping house sleeps seven people—either girls or boys, never mixed. Now I will teach you about hygiene."

She opened the other door, which led to the most amazing room I had ever seen. The marble floor and walls were striped black and white, and at the far end of the room the floor dipped into a trench with gratings underneath it. Above that were metal nozzles projecting from the wall. Maia shrugged out of her kiton and stood naked before us. She pressed a metal switch in the wall and water began to jet from the nozzles. "This is a wash-fountain," she explained. "It is to cleanse you. Come on."

We moved forward hesitantly. The water was cold, pleasant on a hot afternoon. "Take soap," Maia instructed, showing us another switch and putting her hand underneath a jet that provided a single gush of liquid soap when she pressed it. I had never encountered soap before. It felt strange on my palm. Maia showed us how to wash with the soap and how it lathered up in the water, she showed us how to wash our hair under the jets. "There is no shortage of water, but you should not be wasteful of the soap," she said.

"It smells of hyssop," said the girl who had noticed the hyssop outside.

Then Maia showed us the four cubicles at the other end of the room, each of which contained a latrine-fountain—a marble seat, with a lever to pull to summon water to carry away our wastes. "There are four latrine-fountains for the seven of you. Be reasonable in taking turns," she said. "Tomorrow I will teach you how to clean yourselves with oil and a scraper."

I was becoming numb with marvels when she led us back into the bedroom. "There is a bed here for each of you." She turned to the dark-skinned girl. "What is your name?"

"They said I was to be called Andromeda," she said.

"That's a wonderful name," Maia said, enthusiastically. "Andromeda, because you spoke first and noticed the hyssop, for now you will be the watcher for Hyssop house. You will have this bed by the door, and you will come for me if you need me—I will show you where I live. You will be in charge of the house when I am not here, and you will take note and answer for the conduct of the others. The rest of you choose beds now."

We looked at each other. We had been splashing comfortably together in the wash-fountain, but now we were shy. I took a hesitant step towards a bed, in the inner corner. The other girls sorted themselves out with no squabbling—though two girls ran for the other corner bed, the girl who got there second retreated and took the next bed. "Now open your chests," Maia said. We did so. Inside were two undyed blankets, one linen and one wool. "Dry yourselves on one." I took out the wool blanket and dried myself. "Now put that one on the bed to dry. Take out the other." She picked up her kiton and shook it. "This is how you wear it." She demonstrated. It was much harder than it looked, especially making the folds. It took some of us a long time to develop the skill of tucking it in—a thing that is second nature now, but was difficult that first day. Maia gave each of us a leather belt and a plain iron pin to fasten our kitons. "These will change," she said, but did not explain further.

"The other blanket is your cloak," she said, and showed us how to fold the cloaks. "You won't need it before winter. They are also your blankets and towels, as you have seen."

"They are ours?" one of the girls asked, touching the pin. "Ours to keep?"

"Yours to use," Maia said.

"Who is our master?" Andromeda asked. "You?"

"You must obey all the masters, but you are not slaves," Maia said. "Ficino will explain later. Come on now. It is time to eat."

We were all dressed, and none of our kitons were actually falling off. Maia led us to our dining hall. "Our dining hall is called Florentia," she said. "A sleeping house is a small thing, though each has a name and a flower, and you might want to embroider hyssop on your kiton later, if you care to. But a dining hall is a very important matter. Each of them seats seventy people, mixed boys and girls, and each of them is named for one of the great cities of civilization."

"How many eating halls are there?" I asked.

"One hundred and forty-four," Maia answered at once.

I calculated in my head. "So there are ten thousand and eighty of us?"

"You're quick with numbers! What is your name?"

"Simmea," I said.

She smiled. "Another wonderful name. Well, Simmea, yes, there will be ten thousand and eighty of you, twelve tribes, a hundred and forty-four dining halls. And you will all learn about the cities of your dining halls and take pride in their accomplishments."

"And is Florentia a great city?" Andromeda asked. "I never heard of it."

"You will hear about it soon," Maia promised.

The dining hall was immense. It was built of stone, not marble, and it had narrow windows and a twisting tower rising from one corner. Inside it had a courtyard with a fountain, and stairs leading up to a big room with a great cacophony of children sitting on benches drawn up at tables. I was glad to spot Ficino and Kebes sitting eating among the others. They were both wearing kitons, but Ficino kept on his red hat.

Maia found us places, all together at one of the tables. Kebes saw me and waved a hand as I sat down. "We all take turns serving," Maia explained. I was hungry. A boy brought out trays of food and set them down where we could help ourselves. The food was amazing—it was bread and fresh cheese with olives, artichokes, cucumbers, and olive oil, with fresh clean water to drink. That first night I remember we had a delicious buttery ham that seemed to melt on my tongue.

It was when I was eating the ham that I looked up and saw the paintings. On all the walls of the room hung paintings, ten of them, all of mythological scenes, and nine of them painted with a wonderful delicacy of imagination that made me stare and stare. I did not see all ten that night, only the one on the opposite wall, which showed an old man with a long beard shaking snow from his cloak while beautiful young women danced around a frozen fountain and a wolf gnawed at a bundle dropped by a fleeing hunter. I had never seen snow before, but that was not why I couldn't stop staring.

"You're not eating, Simmea," Maia said after a time. I realised I was sitting there with ham in my mouth and not chewing.

"I'm sorry," I said, closing my mouth and swallowing. "But the painting! Who did it? What is it?"

"Sandro Botticelli did it, in Florence. Florentia," she corrected herself at once. "It's *Winter*. It's part of a set. *Summer* and *Autumn* are here too."

"Not *Spring*?"

"*Spring* is in the original Florentia," she said. "But I can show you a reproduction one day, if you like it."

"Like it? Of all the wonders here it is the most wonderful," I said. I had seen paintings before. There were two ikons in the church at home, one of the Virgin and one of Christ crucified. Botticelli left them in the dust.

After dinner we went off to bed. It turned out that there was a glowing beam in Hyssop House, which gave us enough light to use the latrine-fountains and then undress and get into bed. Maia showed Andromeda how to turn it off, using a switch near the door. I curled up under my two blankets and slept. The next morning Andromeda woke us, and we cleaned ourselves again in the wash-fountains before going back to the dining hall. There were even more children present, though the hall was not full. I saw Maia was sitting with a another group of girls who were staring around, amazed. We were served a porridge made of nuts and grains, and there was as much fruit as we wanted. I had seated myself where I could see Botticelli's *Autumn* as I ate, and I kept looking up at the rich leaf-colors and half-hidden faces.

At the end of the meal Ficino stood up, and after considerable hushing we all fell silent. "You are all gathered now, my little Florentines, ten sleeping houses gathered into this dining hall. You came from many different places, many different families. But now you are here in the city, and you are all brothers and sisters. Let your old life be to you like a dream on waking. Shake it off, as if you had come here fresh from Lethe. Imagine you had been sleeping in the soil of this island and dreaming all you remember, and that your life begins here and now. When you were under the soil the metals of the Earth mixed in you, so that you are all a mixture of iron and bronze and silver and gold. Soon you will learn which metals are uppermost in you, and what you are good for. Here in the Just City you will become your best selves. You will learn and grow and strive to be excellent."

He beamed around at us all. I saw that Kebes was looking down and frowning. Then Ficino spoke again. "We begin today. Those who can read to my left, those who cannot to my right."

I went to his right, and indeed, that was when my life truly began.

5

MAIA

A young lady from Queen Victoria's England does not expect to have her prayers answered, or at least not in such a direct and immediate way, and certainly not by Pallas Athene. My first thought as I looked at all the variously dressed people around me, united only in their expressions of complete bewilderment, was that throughout history everyone had wanted to know the truth about God, about the gods, and now there could be no question. There were gods, they did care about humanity, and one of them was Pallas Athene. She stood still, looking gravely out over the hall. She was half again the height of the tallest of the men, just as Homer describes her, with her helmet, spear, and an owl tucked under her arm. The owl was looking at me. I nodded my head to it. I should have wondered if this was a dream, but there was no doubt whatsoever that it was real. It was the most real thing that had ever happened.

Then Athene spoke. I had never before heard anyone speak Greek, though my father and I had sometimes read it aloud. I was so overwhelmed by the naturalness of the way the syllables sounded that it took me a moment to catch up to what she was actually saying.

"You have come from many times, but with a shared purpose. You all wished to work to set up Plato's Republic, to build the

Just City. Here we are. This is your plan, but you have all asked me for help. I suggest we discuss how to go about it and what we will need."

A long-haired young man in the habit of a Dominican monk stepped forward. "Are we dead, Sophia?" he asked. "Is this place the afterlife?"

"You are not dead," Athene said, smiling kindly at him. "You stand here in your mortal bodies. Some of you who were near death have been healed of your infirmities." She nodded to the Dominican. "You will age naturally. When you die here, in the course of time, your body will be returned to the moment you left."

How would that work? I couldn't quite imagine it. Would Aunt Fanny and Anne look around for me and find instead the corpse of an old lady? An old lady who had grown old in Plato's Republic? I found myself smiling as I realised I didn't care.

"And our souls?" a man in a toga asked.

"Your souls will also go back to that moment and be reborn from that time, not from this time."

There was a murmur across the room, as three hundred people said to themselves happily in their native languages: "We have immortal souls! I *knew* it!" I could only understand Latin and Greek and English, and I heard it in all three of those languages.

A white-bearded man in a Greek kiton, looking the very image of a philosopher, asked "Are they three-part souls as Plato described?"

"Would anyone prefer to return to their own time now?" Athene asked, either not hearing or ignoring the attempt to clarify the issue of our souls. "This would seem like a dream, soon forgotten."

To my surprise three men raised their hands. Athene blinked, and they disappeared. I was looking at one of them, a shabby man with a donnish look, wondering how he could possibly not want to stay, when he just wasn't there anymore.

"Now, we need to make plans," she said.

"But where are we, Sophia? You spoke of our own times. When are we?" It was a man in Renaissance clothes and a red hat.

"We are in the time before the fall of Troy. And we are on the doomed island of Kallisti, called by some Atlante." Even I had heard of Atlantis.

"Then what we make cannot last?" he asked.

The goddess inclined her head. "This is an experiment, and this is the best time and place for that experiment. Nothing mortal can last. At best it can leave legends that can bear fruit in later ages."

After that, with the big questions out of the way, we began to discuss how we would go about the work.

It soon became clear that we were united on many issues and divided on others, and that there were practical problems none of us had thought through. Plato's *Republic* was extremely specific on some issues and distressingly vague on others. It wasn't really intended to be used as a blueprint.

There were almost three hundred of us, from twenty-five centuries. There were close to equal numbers of men and women, which astounded me at first. I had never before met another woman who cared about scholarship. Now I did, and it was wonderful. Before long I realised that most of the women were much like me, young, and fortunate enough to obtain enough education to make their possible lives unsatisfactory. I met young women from every century, including several from my own and the century after.

"It does get better," one of them reassured me. Her name was Kylee, and she was wearing what seemed to me a man's suit, but cut to her form. "In the eighteen-seventies they established colleges for women at Oxford and Cambridge, and in America too. By the nineteen-twenties they began to grant degrees. By the nineteen-sixties they were actually nominally equal to the men's colleges."

"More than a hundred years from me," I said.

"And even in my time it's a wearisome business," she said. "It's not that I want to die, but not being allowed to offer to die for my country means that my country doesn't consider me a true citizen."

We young women from the Centuries of Progress were one clear group. The men of the Renaissance were another. The Neo-platonists made a third. This was Kylee's name for the group led by Plotinus and sharing a particular mystical interpretation of Plato based around numerology. They called themselves simply Platonists, of course. Plotinus was the white-bearded man who had asked the question about three-part souls when we first arrived.

There were also many Romans, who could have been considered a fourth group except that they never agreed about anything and so could not be thought of as a faction. I was delighted to find Marcus Tullius Cicero among them, and his friend Titus Pomponius Atticus. Atticus was charming; he reminded me a little of my father. How I wished my father could have been here—but he would never have prayed to a pagan goddess. When Atticus introduced me to Cicero, whom he called Tullius, I found he was less delighted to meet me. He was not among those who believed Plato on the equality of women. He was flattered when he found how much of his work I had read, and how high his reputation stood in my century, but he could never really consider me, or any of us women, as people to be taken seriously.

The difficulties and complications of actually putting Plato's ideas into practice were immense. But we had Athene, whom we all addressed as Sophia, meaning "wisdom." She had brought the workers—automata that could follow orders and build and plant crops and perform even more wonders. "They come from the future. They are here to labor for you," she said.

Very few of us had seen anything like them before. Kylee said they were robots, and "workers" was a good translation of that. She said they were more advanced than any such things in her own day.

We formed into committees to work on different aspects of the Republic. We came together to report on progress in formal sessions, which we came to call Chamber. At first we had just that one hall, where we all slept in drafts on the cold marble floor. It was lucky it was summer. We drank water from a spring, and had the workers dig trenches for latrines. Then we had them build a fountain, and bathrooms, and kitchens. Few of us knew how to cook, but fortunately the workers had some limited abilities in that area.

As we had, as yet, no philospher kings, and as we could acknowledge no leader but Athene, we decided that for the time being, when we did not agree, we would vote on an issue. Athene smiled at this. The first divisive issue that came to a vote was names. We voted that those of us with inappropriate names would adopt new names, and that we would do the same with the children who came to us, naming them from the *Dialogues* and from Greek mythology. Kylee and some others felt strongly against this, but in the vote after the debate, the majority carried the day. I adopted the name Maia, for my birth month, and for the mother of Hermes. Kylee took the name Klio, as being the closest she could come to her original name. We also agreed that we would have one unique name each. The Romans and others who had multiple appropriate names would limit themselves to just one.

For the first time ever I was fully engaged in life. I cared about everything. I read the *Republic* over and over, I took part in debates in Chamber, I served on committees, I had opinions and was listened to. It was marvellous. I woke up every morning on the cold floor of the hall, happy simply to be alive. I daily thanked God, the gods, Athene, for allowing me to be there and part of all of it. That's not to say that it couldn't be infuriating.

I served on the Technology Committee. We had long debates about how much technology to allow. Some of us felt that we should do it with the technology of the day, or that which Plato would have understood. But we already had the workers, and without workers we should have needed slaves. The workers needed electricity, which was produced from the sun. Sufficient electricity to feed the workers would also provide good lighting, and a certain amount of heating and cooling. "The advantage of that," Klio said, when she presented our recommendations to the whole Chamber, "will be to keep the library at a constant temperature to better protect the books."

Most of the older people and all of the famous ones were men, but most of the people who understood technology in any way were young women. Though we had nominal equality, there were always those like Tullius who would not accept us as equals. In addition I saw in other women and detected in myself a tendency to defer to older men—as I had always deferred to my father. We had grown up in slavery and bore the marks of our shackles, as Klio said when I talked to her about this, but we were to raise a generation in the hope of true freedom. The committee on technology was almost entirely composed of young women, with only one man, the Dominican, whose name was now Ikaros. Somehow, imperceptibly, because of this, technology came to be seen among the masters as feminine and unimportant. We voted to have lights but not to have heating and cooling, except for the library. We voted to have plumbing everywhere, but only with cold water, which seemed like the morally better choice, and what Plato would have wanted. We made up Greek names for shower-baths and toilets.

Ikaros served on several of my committees—indeed, he had volunteered for every committee as they were being set up. He had been accepted onto an improbable number of them, and served on all those that did not meet at the same time. He seemed to have boundless energy and enthusiasm, as well as being notably younger than most of the other men. He was also extremely good-looking, with a wonderful smile and long chestnut hair. Working together so much, we became friends. He seemed to be everyone's friend, moving through all the different circles charming everyone. He was even a favorite with Athene, who seemed to unbend a little when she spoke to him.

Plotinus and the Neoplatonists dominated the committee designing the physical form and organization of the city. They announced that Athene would bring in mature trees, and we voted that through. Then they proposed that there would be ten thousand and eighty children, divided into twelve tribes, each divided into a hundred and forty-four eating houses that would each be named after a famous city of civilization. We voted this through without dissent. A hundred and forty-four eating houses allowed everyone to get their favourite cities mentioned. The proposal was made that the eating houses be decorated in the style of their cities, which I thought a charming idea. There would be two masters attached to each eating house, as far as possible one man and one woman. "Are there any Florentine women here?" I asked Ikaros after a Tech Committee meeting. I hadn't noticed any in their group.

"Not that I can think of," he said. "Why, do you want to be attached to the Florence house?"

"I loved it so much. And it's where I found Plato. I never got to Greece, only as far as Italy."

"Talk to Ficino. He's bound to be the man who gets Florence." He sounded a trifle envious. Ficino's name was now formally Fikinus, but everyone went right on addressing him as Ficino.

We voted that we would all adopt the kiton, and those who knew how to wear one instructed the rest. The workers wove the cloth for them. I had lessons in how to don one from Krito himself, the friend of Sokrates. Once I was used to it I found it charmingly practical and comfortable. The kitons had an unexpected benefit—once we were all dressed alike, the factions among us were less immediately visible, if no less real.

On the women's committee, Kreusa, originally a hetaira from first-century Corinth, explained the use of menstrual sponges. We voted by acclamation that this method would be the usual and standard method of the Republic. We did not even present it to the full Chamber. Workers could easily harvest the sponges. We knew the men wouldn't recognize or care about their significance. We had agreed that the masters should not have children of our own, and Kreusa told us about silphium root, which had the ability to prevent conception. We agreed that it should be available to all female masters who wanted it.

I was the only woman on the committee to select art, on which Ficino, Atticus, and, inevitably, Ikaros, also served. Plato is very clear about the purposes of art, and what forms of it should be permitted in the Republic. We were divided on whether we should have only original art or allow copies. This was an issue on which passions ran high, and on which Ficino, Ikaros and I were united—the children should see only originals if they wanted to learn excellence. We should ask Athene to allow us to rescue lost and destroyed art to adorn the city. Copies, especially copies created by workers and more than once, would make them see art in entirely the wrong light.

Atticus and some of the others argued against us. "We have already decided that the eating houses will be copies of buildings in the cities they are named for," he said. "If the workers can build them, and if it won't harm the children to see a hundred and forty-four copies of architecture, then how can art be different?"

"It would be better if we could get the original buildings too," I said. "But it's not possible. It is possible to get the art."

"It might be possible to get some buildings," Ficino said. "Sophia isn't just wise, she's powerful as well."

"Were there enough suitable buildings that have disappeared?" I asked. "I don't know about Greece, but when I was in Rome it looked as if every brick and piece of marble was being reused in some other building."

Ikaros shook his head. "It's completely different. It wouldn't be better if we could get original buildings, because the real problem then would be that the buildings wouldn't be so suited to our purposes as the ones we will build. The design for the sleeping houses, for example, is elegant and ideal." He was on that committee as well, of course. "We want them to be identical and classical and useful, and that's how they are. We don't want the city to be full of repetition because that would teach the wrong lesson. The sleeping houses will all be the same; the palaestras where the children will exercise will be functionally the same, but have different decoration, for variety. And the same goes for the eating houses, temples, libraries, and practice halls. We want everything to be as well-suited to what we need it for as can be. Making new buildings in the style of old ones is best for that, for buildings. They won't really be copies, not functionally."

"Functionally?" Atticus repeated, frowning.

"The buildings for our city have different functions from the buildings in any existing city. Even if we had all the choice in the world, it would be difficult to find sufficient buildings with big eating halls and kitchens and rooms of the right size for classes," Ikaros explained. "Ideally they'd all be new designs by wonderful architects, but as it is, we've decided to take the features of the old buildings, in the styles of the cities the halls are named after, and have the workers reproduce them on our buildings."

"But why couldn't we do that with art as well?" Atticus asked. "The workers could just as easily reproduce that."

"But the original art best fits the Platonic purpose," I said.

"Plato says art should show good people doing good things as an example to the children," Atticus said.

"Yes, and also be an example of beauty, to open their souls to excellence," I added.

Ikaros looked approvingly at me. "Yes! And when it comes to art, the best is definitely the originals."

"Jupiter!" Atticus swore. "They won't be able to tell if they're originals or copies."

"Their souls will," Ficino said.

Eventually we won the day, which the three of us celebrated at dinner with cold water and barley porridge. Ficino and Ikaros shared memories of wines they had drunk together in Florence, and discussed how long it would be before the grapes the workers had planted could produce a vintage. We pretended to be mixing our water with wine, in best classical practice, and Ikaros pretended to grow a little drunk, whereupon Ficino reproached him by quoting Socrates on temperance, and Ikaros pretended to be abashed. I had never spent a pleasanter evening nor laughed so much.

Back on the committee the next day, it became apparent that Ficino and Ikaros wanted to save everything.

"The Library Committee is sending an expedition to the Great Library of Alexandria to rescue everything," Ikaros said. He also served on that committee. "Manlius and I are going. We're going to have it all, all the written work of antiquity, though we will of course control access to it. Why not all the art we can find?"

"We have to be selective and make sure it fits what Plato wanted," Atticus said.

"How could it not?" Ficino asked.

"Before we allow it into the city we need to examine everything to make sure it does," Atticus insisted. We all agreed to this.

We put together a complete program of art rescue through the centuries. It all had to fit the message we wanted the children to understand from it, and of course it had to be on classical themes. There was a huge amount of art potentially available from the ancient world—it was heartbreaking that so much had been destroyed. I entirely agreed that we should save as much as we could. There were many lost works available from the Renaissance which were also deemed likely to be worthy. Athene took the men of the Art Committee on several expeditions. To my astonishment and delight, they brought back nine lost Botticellis, snatched from the Bonfire of the Vanities.

"At first I pretended to be a Venetian merchant and tried to buy them, but Savonarola wouldn't listen. In the end we stole them and replaced them with worthless canvases we'd bought," Atticus said, laughing.

"Who ever met a Venetian who could only speak pure Classical Latin?" Ikaros teased.

"Look at the *Judgement of Paris*," Atticus gloated, taking it off with him to show Tullius.

"Does that show good people performing good actions?" I asked, quietly, so that Atticus wouldn't hear.

Ikaros grinned at me. "Some of these show mysterious people performing mysterious actions. But they do lift the soul."

"They certainly do," I said.

Ficino spread out another, smiling. "These will hang in the Florentine dining hall," he said.

"Do you have a woman master for Florence yet?" I asked. "Because if not, I'd really like to volunteer."

"So you can see these every day?" Ficino asked, looking proudly at *Winter*.

"Yes, and because, though I'm not a Florentine I loved Florence so much," I said.

"I'll think about it. I should find out whether there's anyone with a better claim," he said. "What would you think would be the best Florentine building to emulate as the eating hall?"

"Oh, it's hard to choose, because it was all so beautiful," I said. "Perhaps the Baptistry? It's a shame the Uffizi wouldn't really be practical, even though that would be the best setting for these wonderful Botticellis."

"The Uffizi is a symbol of Medici power and the loss of the freedom of the Florentine Republic," Ficino said, frowning.

"Then the Palazzo Vecchio," I said, at once. "That was for the Republic, and it's so beautiful."

"Much too big," Ikaros said, cheerfully. "Now for Ferrara, Lukretia has suggested we can do half of the castle."

"How about the Palazzo Vecchio at half-size," Ficino suggested, ignoring Ikaros and looking at me.

"I think that would be splendid," I said, as affirmatively as I could.

"Or maybe we should have something in three parts, for the three parts of the soul," he mused. "It's going to be so wonderful to see the children grow up and the best of them really become philosopher kings."

"I can hardly wait," I said. "It's wonderful to think we're getting everything ready for them. Did anyone tell you yet that the Tech Committee have decided to go with full printing in both languages for the reproduction of books? So everything will be available to all of us through the library. And first, immediately after the complete works of Plato, we're going to print the things Ikaros and Manlius rescued from Alexandria, so that all of us can read them."

"Excellent," Ficino said. "I shall volunteer to work on trans-lations so that I can see things early."

"New plays by Sophokles!" Ikaros exulted. "And the original works of Epicurus, and the Hedonists! I'm going to read them the second they're printed." He grinned. "I'm on the Censorship Committee, so I'll get to them before anyone."

6

SIMMEA

I learned to read, first in Greek and then in the Latin alphabet. Before the end of a year I was reading both languages fluently, though I had not known Latin before. There were many native Latin speakers among the masters, which made it easy to pick up. Even those who were not native Latin speakers knew it well, for, as they told us, it had been the language of civilization for centuries. I was soon speaking and reading both languages easily. I no longer noticed the slurring and softening accent so many masters had, or even the use of B for V. I had begun to speak Greek like that myself.

I began to learn history before they began to teach it to me, and I knew without examining it that this was the history of the future. We were living, they told us, in the time before the Trojan War. King Minos ruled in Crete and Mycenae was the greatest city on the mainland. Yet, although it had yet to happen, we knew all about the Trojan War—a version of the *Iliad* was one of our favorite books. We knew about the Peloponnesian War, for that matter, and the wars of Alexander, and the Punic Wars, and Adrianople, and in less detail about the fall of Constantinople, and the Battle of Lepanto. When I asked Ficino what happened after Lepanto he said it was after his time, and when I asked Axiothea, who taught us mathematics, she said that history got boring after that and was nothing but a series of inventions, the laws of motion, and telescopes, and electricity, and workers, and so on.

From the beginning, and by design, we rarely had a free moment. Our time was divided equally between music and gymnastics. Music came in three parts—music itself, mathematics, and learning to read, later superseded by reading. Gymnastics also had three parts—running, wrestling, and weights.

Gymnastics was fun. It was done naked in the palaestra. There was a palaestra shared between each two eating halls. Our palaestra was Florentia and Delphi, and it had rows of Doric columns for Delphi along the back and two sides, and exuberant Renaissance columns along the front, with a very elaborate fountain. I felt proud that Florentia had contributed the fountain. It was easy to love and feel pride in Florentia, that great city, with so many great scholars, writers, and artists. Ficino himself came from Florentia. When we came to dye and embroider our kitons, I embroidered mine with a running pattern of lilies, the Florentine symbol, and above them snowflakes, leaves, and roses, for Botticelli's three seasons, which remained my favourite pictures. Above those I put a pattern of interspersed books and scrolls, in blue and gold, which so many people admired and asked permission to copy that it became quite commonplace.

Our palaestra stood open to the air, naturally, and the ground inside was made of white sand, which the hundred and forty of us churned up every day and the workers raked smooth every night. I soon stopped feeling conscious of nakedness—we all took off our kitons when we went into the palaestra, it was just what we did. I learned to use the weights, both lifting and throwing, and to wrestle, and to run. I was good at running, and was always among the first at races, especially at long distances. I soon learned that I would never excel at wrestling, being small and wiry, but found it good fun when matched against somebody my own weight. Weights, once I had learned how to handle them, were a delight, though there were always people who could throw the discus further and lift heavier weights than me.

The odd thing about gymnastics was that we didn't really have enough teachers. Only the younger masters could teach it, and not even all of them. This oddity made me realise how few masters there were. There were two masters assigned to each dining hall, and just a handful of others. There were a hundred and forty-four dining halls, now completed with seventy children in each. That meant there were only two hundred and eighty-eight masters in all, or perhaps three hundred at most, to ten thousand and eighty children. I thought about the implications of this, and decided not to point this out to Kebes. He still muttered about wanting to overthrow the masters, but I was happy.

How could I not have been happy? I was in the Just City, and I was there to become my best self. I had wonderful food—porridge and fruit every morning, and either cheese and bread or pasta and vegetables every night, with meat or fish on feast days, which came frequently. On hot days in summer we often had iced fruit. I had regular congenial exercise. I had friends. And best of all, I had music, mathematics, and books to stretch my mind. I learned from Maia and Ficino, from Axiothea and Atticus of Delphi, from Ikaros and Lucina of Ferrara, and from time to time from other masters. Manlius taught me Latin. Ikaros, one of the youngest men among the masters, set us to read provocative books, and asked fascinating questions about them. Sometimes he and Ficino would debate a question in front of us. I could almost feel my mind growing and developing as I listened to them. I was twelve years old. I still missed my parents and my brothers, sometimes, when something recalled them to me. But little did. My life was so different now. Sometimes it truly felt as if I had slept beneath the soil until I awakened in the City.

In the winter of that year, Year Two of the Just City, just before I turned thirteen, I began my menstruation, and Andromeda, who was still the watcher for Hyssop, took me to Maia. Maia had a little house of her own near Hyssop, with a neatly tended garden of herbs and flowers. Maia made me a peppermint tea, and gave me three sponges and showed me how to insert them into my vagina. "One of these will last you for an hour or so on the first day, longer than that afterwards. You can probably leave the same one in all night unless you're bleeding very heavily. You can clean them in the wash-fountains, never in drinking water. If you hold it under the running water all the blood will wash out. Insert a fresh one and let the first one dry in sunlight on the windowsill. Store them in your chest when you are not using them. Never use anyone else's sponge or share yours with your sisters. Three should be all you need, but if you find you are bleeding too heavily and needing to change them often on the first day so that there is not a sponge dry when you need it, let me know and I will give you a fourth."

"These are marvellous," I said, and then went on, forgetting that I should not talk about my earlier life. "My mother used cloths that were horrible to wash."

"Mine too, and so did I before I came here," Maia said. "This way of managing menstruation is one of the lost marvels of the ancient world. The sponges are natural. They grow under the sea. Workers harvest them for us."

I turned the two clean sponges over in my hand. They were soft. "Am I a woman now?"

"You were born a woman." Maia smiled. "Your body will be making some changes. Your breasts will grow, and you might want to pleat your kiton so it falls over them. If they grow very big so that they flop about and feel uncomfortable when you run, I will show you how to strap them up."

"What will—" I stopped. "What happens here about

marriage?" I realized I'd never heard a word about it, nor even thought about it since I had come here. All of the masters lived alone, and all of the rest of us were still children.

"When all of you are older there will be marriages, but they will not be like the marriages you . . . should not remember!" Maia said. "No need to worry about it yet. Your body is not ready to make children, even if bleeding has begun."

"When will it be?" I asked.

Maia frowned. "Most of us think twenty, but some say sixteen," she said. "In any case, a long time yet."

Then she took down a book. "Long ago I promised to show you Botticelli's *Spring*," she said.

Spring was as marvellous and mysterious as the other three seasons. I tried to figure it out. There was a girl at the side, and a pregnant woman in the centre with flowers growing around her. "Who are they all?" I asked. "Are those the same flowers that are growing in *Summer*?" I glanced at the opposite page of text for help, and was astonished to see it was in the Latin alphabet, but a language unknown to me. I looked inquiringly at Maia.

"It's the only reproduction I have. Nobody knows who they all are, though some think she's the goddess Flora."

I stared back at the picture, ignoring the mystery of the text. "I wish I could see the original at full size like the others." I turned the page and gasped. It was Aphrodite rising from the waves on a great shell. Maia leaned forward, then relaxed when she saw what it was.

"I really wish you could have seen the original of that one," she said. "It's so much better than the reproduction. It fills a wall. There are strands of real gold in her hair."

"When will we be taught to paint and sculpt?" I asked, touching the picture longingly. The paper was glossy to the touch.

"We don't have enough masters who can teach those things,"

Maia said. "Florentia should have a turn next year, or perhaps the year after. Ideally, you'd have been learning all along. Meanwhile, I was intending to ask you if you would teach some beginners to swim in the spring."

"Of course," I said. Growing up in the Delta, I'd been swimming for almost as long as I'd been walking. I had won the swimming race at the Hermeia, as well as coming in second in the footrace. I'd been given a silver pin for these accomplishments, which had been the proudest moment of my life. Silver meant bravery and physical prowess. Only gold, for intellectual attainment, ranked higher, and nobody I knew had a gold pin yet.

Maia put her hand out for the Botticelli book. I took a last look at the Aphrodite and gave it back. She turned the pages and showed me a portrait of a man in a red coat. "We don't know who he was, some scholar of the time I've always thought."

"I love his face," I said. "Is that picture in Florentia too?"

"Yes," Maia said.

"Perhaps I'll travel there one day."

"It wouldn't do you any good. You know they haven't been painted yet." Maia smiled.

"Maybe I'll go there in the time when they have been painted. When I'm grown up and finished being educated, I mean."

"No." Maia looked serious now. "No, we've been brought here out of time by Pallas Athene for a serious purpose. We're here to stay now, all of us. We can't go wandering about in time on expeditions to look at pictures."

"Why not? Pictures are important."

"Art is important only as a way of opening the mind to excellence," Maia said, but she didn't sound very sincere. She took the book back and closed it. In the seconds I could see it I noticed that it had a circular picture of the Madonna on the cover, surrounded by angels. She put it on a high shelf with other books.

"Oh, please!" I said.

"You know I can't show you that. I probably shouldn't have shown you this book at all."

"How is it that we have the nine Botticelli paintings that we do have?" I asked.

"They were going to be destroyed and we rescued them," Maia said.

"Mother Hera!" I didn't often swear, but I couldn't stop myself blurting it out. "Destroyed!"

"Yes, some terrible things happened in that future you'd like to visit to look at paintings! You're much better off here. Now, go to bed, and let me know if you need any more sponges."

I bade her joy of the night and went off thoughtfully down the street. The city looked especially beautiful by moonlight. I raised my arms and murmured a line of a praise-song to Selene Artemis. But my mind was buzzing, not with thoughts of menstruation and marriage, which I had almost forgotten, but with Botticelli. The mysterious figures gathered around in *Spring*. The smile of his Aphrodite. The thought that our nine paintings would have been destroyed. Was that true of all the art in the city, I wondered? Had Phidias's gold and ivory Athene in the agora been rescued? How about the Herm I had been crowned before, the one with the mysterious smile? What about the bronze lion on the corner I always patted as I went by? I stopped to pat him now, and the moonlight found an expression of sadness on his bronze face that I had never seen before. His mane had fantastical curls, which I stroked, tracing the whorls. He seemed so real, so solid, so impossible to harm. It was my bleeding body making me sad for no reason, I told myself. My mother had talked about that. But it was true about the Botticellis, Maia had said so.

I gave the lion a last pat and turned to take the last few steps to Hyssop and my bed. All the art, saved, as we children had been saved? But saved for what purpose? Saved to make the city? A worker trundled past, unsleeping, off on some errand in the dark. Had they been saved too? And from where? I opened the door and wondered if I would ever have answers to these questions.

The next summer I taught eleven children to swim with no difficulty. The twelfth was Pytheas. He was a boy from Delphi, so I had seen him at the palaestra, and wrestled with him once or twice, but I did not know him well. I had noticed how beautiful he was, and how unconscious he seemed to be of it. He had an air of confidence that was not quite conceit. I had friends who disliked him because he was so lovely and seemed so effortlessly good at everything. I had been inclined to go along with them without examining why. Teaching him to swim made us friends.

As with the first eleven non-swimmers, I took Pytheas down the slope of the beach until we stood in chest-deep water. Then I had him lie back onto my hand, to learn how the water would support and cradle him. The problem was that he couldn't relax. It didn't help that he had essentially no body fat—every curve on his twelve-year-old body was muscle. But Mother Tethys is powerful; he would not have sunk lying back with my palm flat in the small of his back, if he could have found a way to do that. He tensed immediately, every time, and jerked back under the water. The exercise was meant to teach trust of the water, and he couldn't trust it enough to learn it. Yet he wanted to learn, he wanted it fiercely.

"Human bodies were not made for this," he muttered, as he went down spluttering one more time and I hauled him back to his feet.

"Truly, you'll be able to do it if you let yourself go."

"I know how dolphins swim."

"I love dolphins. They often swim out by the rocks, there where the sea darkens to wine. When you have learned to swim, you will be able to swim out to them."

I had never seen anyone try so hard and keep on failing.

Pytheas could not float, but he couldn't believe he could not. He watched me treading water and floating on my back, and couldn't believe he couldn't master the skill by sheer strength of will. I tried supporting him on his stomach, telling him it was more like the way dolphins do it, but it worked only a little better. He kept thrashing about and sinking. "Maybe we should try another day," I said, seeing that he was growing cold and his fingers were wrinkling from the water.

"I want to swim today." He bit his lip and looked far younger than he was. "I understand I can't master the art in one day, but I want to make a beginning. This is so stupid. I feel such a fool. I've wasted your whole afternoon when I know you want to be in the library."

"It isn't a waste teaching you," I said. "But how do you know that?"

"Septima says you're always reading in the library when you have a moment."

"Septima's always in the library," I said. It was true. Septima was a tall grey-eyed girl from the Athens hall who could read when she first came, and in the time since had made herself almost an assistant librarian. "Did you ask her about me?"

"When I heard you were teaching swimming."

"But why her? How do you know her? She's Athens and you're Delphi."

He looked caught out, then raised his chin boldly. "I knew her before."

"Before you came here?" Even though we were out in the sea with nobody near us, I lowered my voice. "Now I think about it, you look alike. A kind of family resemblance, maybe?"

"She's my sister," he admitted. "But here we're all to be brothers and sisters, so what difference does it make? She's my friend, and why shouldn't she be?"

"No reason she shouldn't be," I said. "So you asked her about me?"

"I thought she'd know. I only knew you'd won the race. Now I know you've taught the others to swim, and you clearly understand the methods, and you've been very patient. I want to learn. I want to swim at least a little today. I can't let it defeat me."

I think what did it was the way he blamed himself and not me, and the sheer force of his will. "All right, then," I said. "There is another way, but it's dangerous. Put your hands on my shoulders. Don't clutch, and don't panic and thrash, even if you go under. You could drown us both if you do. Let go of me if you feel yourself sinking. As long as you don't panic, I can rescue you, but if you drive us both under and I can't come up, we could both die."

"All right." He stood behind me and put one hand on each of my shoulders.

"Now I'm going to slide slowly forward, and I'll tow you. Keep your arms still, and let your legs come up. I'll be underneath you." I slid forward and took one stroke with my arms, drawing him forward. I could feel the whole length of his body on top of mine. He did not clutch or panic, and I kicked my legs gently, swimming for perhaps six or seven strokes and drawing him along on top of me. I turned my head sideways. "Now keep your arms still but kick your legs just a little." I was ready to put my own legs down and stand up if he panicked now—I knew the slope of the beach well, and I was still in my depth. I had done this before with my little cousins when they were very small. He began to move his legs, and I kept mine still but kept on swimming strongly with my arms, drawing us along parallel to the shore. At last I told him to stop, and put my feet carefully down. He went under for a second but did not panic or thrash.

"Was I swimming?" he asked.

"You've made a good beginning. And now you should go out

and run around on the sand to stir your blood, and then we should both clean the salt off with oil. Tomorrow you'll do better."

We ran up out of the water and raced on the beach with some other children who were there, none of them people I knew well. Then Pytheas sought me out with a jar of oil and a strigil and we oiled each other and scraped it off. This always feels good after swimming, much better than the wash-fountain, because salt water strips out the body's oil.

We were not encouraged to have erotic feelings towards the other children—indeed, the opposite, we were discouraged from ever thinking about sex or romantic love. Friendships were encouraged, and friendship was always held out to us as the highest and best of human relationships. Yet as I scraped the strigil down Pytheas's arms I remembered the feel of his body above mine in the water, and I knew that what I felt was attraction. I was as much frightened by the feeling as drawn by it. I knew it was wrong, and I truly wanted to be my best self. Also, I did not know how to tell if he felt any reciprocal feelings. I said nothing and scraped harder.

"Tomorrow," I said, when we were done. "Same time. You'll make a swimmer yet."

"I will," he said, as if any alternative was unthinkable, as if he meant to attain all excellence or die trying. I raised my hand in farewell and took a step away, but he spoke. "Simmea?"

I stopped and turned back. "Yes?"

"I like you. You're brave and clever. I'd like to be your friend."

"Of course," I said, and stepped back towards him and clasped his hand. "I like you too."

7

APOLLO

Athene cheated. She went to the Republic as herself to help set it up, and then once all the work was done she transformed into a ten-year-old girl and asked Ficino to name her. He named her Septima, which I thought served her right for asking him. She knew he was obsessed with magic numbers.

I, however, did the whole thing properly. I went down through Hades and set down my powers for the length of the mortal life I chose from the Fates. Clotho looked astonished, Lachesis looked resigned, and Atropos looked grim, so no change there. I then went on to Lethe, where I wet my lips, to allow me to forget the details of the future life I had chosen, though not, of course, my memories. (The river Lethe is full of brilliantly colored fish. Nobody ever mentions that when they talk about it. I suppose they forget them as soon as they see them, and so they are a surprise at the end and the beginning of each mortal life.) I went on into a womb and was born—and that in itself was an interesting experience. The womb was peaceful. I composed a lot of poetry. Birth was traumatic. I barely remember my first birth, and the images from Simonides's poem about it have got tangled up in my real earliest memories. This mortal birth was uncomfortable to the point of pain.

My mortal parents were peasant farmers in the hills above Delphi. I had wanted to be born on Delos again, for symmetry, but Athene pointed out that in most eras neither birth nor death are permitted on Delos, which would have made it difficult. I had to master my new tiny mortal body, so different from the immortal body I normally inhabited. I had to cope with the way it changed and grew, at an odd speed, entirely out of my control. At first I could barely focus my eyes, and it was months before I could even speak. I would have thought it would be unutterably boring, but in fact the sensations were all so vivid and immediate that it was intriguing. I could spend hours sitting in the sun looking at my own fingers.

As I grew it was interesting to discover how much of what I had thought was will was affected by the flesh. Food and sleep weren't just pleasures but necessities. I found my thoughts were clouded when I was hungry or tired.

I grew fast and strong and my parents were loving and kind to me. Everything went according to plan, including the famine that came along a few months before my tenth birthday, which Athene and I had arranged to induce my loving parents to sell me into slavery. That didn't go quite as planned. For one thing, I had no idea what famine really meant—needing to eat and starving instead is a form of pain. It was unbearable. I hate to remember it. The despair on my mortal father's face when the last of the pigs died. The way my mortal mother wept when the slavers came and made their offer for me. I cared for them, of course I did, they had been my adoring worshipers for almost a decade. It broke my mortal mother's heart to sell me. Athene and I had chosen all this and imposed it on them. They had not chosen to love a son and lose him in this terrible way, to be forced to choose between slavery for me and death for all three of us. I had never imagined how cruel we were being.

So, as you see, I had already learned quite a lot about mortal life and equal significance and meaningful choices before I even came to the Republic.

Athene was on the ship *Excellence* when I was brought aboard with a line of other children. She recognized me at once, although she had never seen this body before. She is my sister, after all. "Are you all right?" she asked.

"Never better," I said. "You have to do something for my mortal parents. Cure the disease on their crops, send somebody through selling new livestock cheaply, and most of all let them have another baby as soon as possible."

"I will," she said, calmly. I hadn't heard that tone of Olympian calm for ten years. She was dispassionate. She nodded to me, and inscribed my name in her ledger without asking me what it was. "What's wrong?" she asked. "It's barely been ten years. Did you get attached?"

"It feels like a lifetime," I said.

She laughed.

"You'll never understand this unless you do it," I warned her.

"I'll do it one day," she said. "Right now they need my help too much."

Part of my plan in experiencing mortal life from the beginning had been to avoid all the inevitable squabbling and mess involved with getting the City set up. Of course I could have stayed on Olympos and arrived as a ten-year-old at the moment the other children came, but I know that if I'd stuck around Athene would have made me run all over everywhere collecting things and getting involved in the arguments. This part worked perfectly. By the time I reached the city, everything had been built and decided. They had laid it out harmoniously, according to principles of proportion and balance. They had made some odd choices, like the half-size copy of the Palazzo Vecchio, but it all worked. It was full of variety and yet was all of a piece. Nobody could ask more of a city.

It was full of artworks Athene had rescued from disasters of history—she'd been everywhere from the Fourth Crusade to the Second World War. There were temples to all twelve gods—mine was particularly splendid, with a Praxiteles from Delos I'd always been fond of. The color choices were interesting. On the whole they had gone for white marble and unpainted statues, Renaissance style, but here and there you'd see a painted statue, or one dressed in brightly colored cloth. The kitons everyone wore were dyed and embroidered, so that the effect was of brightly coloured people in a chiaroscuro landscape. There were trees and gardens, of course, which helped soften things.

With a fine sense of irony, Athene had me assigned to Laurel house, in the dining hall of Delphi, in the Tribe of Apollo. There were twelve tribes, each devoted to a particular god, with twelve dining halls each. Each dining hall was made up of ten houses of seven children each. (These numbers weren't in the *Republic.* They had some complicated Neoplatonist relevance, and had doubtless taken somebody a long time to work out. I was so glad I'd missed that discussion.) There were ten thousand and eighty children—a number which could, should one wish to, be evenly divided by every number except eleven.

Those first years in the Republic were fun. My body was a child's body still, but it was my body, and now properly under my control. I was young and growing and I had music and exercise. I had the amusement of seeing where there were cracks in the structure that seemed so solid. Bringing together that many children with so few adults was something only somebody who knew nothing about children would have suggested. The children were wild and hard to control, and much more of this wildness was necessarily tolerated than Plato had imagined. The masters tried to set up a system where the children monitored each other, which had some limited success. But to track all the children the way they really wanted they could have done with four times as many adults—but they were limited to those who not only thought they wanted to set up the Republic, but who had read Plato in the original and prayed to Athene to help. There were probably a lot of good Christians who would have liked to have been there. As it was, there were more people from the Christian eras than I'd have guessed. I do have friends and votaries everywhere, but some times and places I seldom visit, largely for aesthetic reasons.

The thing that surprised me about the masters when I got to know them was that so few of them were from the Enlightenment. I'd have thought that era, so excitingly pagan after so much dull Christianity, would have produced a whole crop of philosophers who'd want to be here. I talked to Athene about it one day when I caught her reading Myronianus of Amastra, curled up on her favorite window seat in the library.

"There's practically nobody here from the Enlightenment because they didn't want this. The crown of the Republic is to get everything right, to produce a system that will produce Philosopher Kings who will know The Good."

"With Capital Letters," I said.

She looked down her nose at me, which wasn't easy, since with both of us eleven years old, she was shorter than me. "Exactly. The Good with capital letters, the Truth, the one unchanging Excellence that stays the same forever. Once that's established, the system goes on the same in ideal stasis for as long as it can continue to do so, with everyone agreeing on what is Good, what is Virtue, what is Justice, and what is Excellence. For the first time in the Enlightenment, they had the idea of progress, the idea that each generation will find its own truth, that things will keep on changing and getting better." She hesitated. "They do pray to me, some of them. Just not for this. I find it fascinating in its own way. It's bewildering. It's one of those things I keep coming back to. I know I'll never get tired of it. But you won't find them here."

"There are people here from ages with a notion of progress, though," I pointed out.

"Mostly women," Athene said. "You'll always have the odd man who loves Plato so much he doesn't care about progress. But the women—well, in those times women fortunate enough to be educated in Greek—and there aren't that many of them—they have horrible circumscribed lives, and they read the *Republic* and they get to the bit about equality of education and opportunity and then they pray to me to be here so fast their heads spin. We have almost equal numbers of men and women among the masters, and that's why. Many of the women are from later periods."

"It makes sense," I said. "And what you say about the Enlightenment is fascinating. I'll go and hang out with Racine some more when I get home and get a better feel for it."

It was a few months after that when a boy deliberately shoved me in the palaestra when I was lifting weights, knocking me off balance and making me fall. He wasn't anyone I'd especially noticed before, a Florentine and not a Delphian. Yet he acted as if he had some grudge. I didn't understand it. I tried to talk to him about it and he pretended it had been an accident. After that I thought about some other incidents that had seemed accidents—spilled food, spoiled work—and wondered about them.

I went to Axiothea, one of the two masters assigned to Delphi. She taught mathematics to both Delphi and Florentia. I believe she came from the first years of Girton. I told her about the incidents, and asked her if she had any idea why they had happened.

"There will always be some who see excellence and envy it instead of striving to emulate it," she said. "We aim to eradicate that as far as possible, but you are children, after all."

"But everyone loves Kryseis, and she's the best at gymnastics," I said.

"She's terrible at music, and she laughs at herself," Axiothea said. "You're good at everything, and seemingly without trying."

I shrugged. "I try."

"You're too old for your years. When the rest of them grow up a bit, you'll make some friends."

I hadn't realized I didn't have friends, but it was true. I had companions, people to wrestle with, people who asked me for help with their letters. I had six boys who slept in Laurel beside me whose jokes I endured. The problem was indeed that my mind was not twelve years old. The only real friend I had was Athene, and of course our friendship was thousands of years old and subject to the usual constraints of our history and context. Besides, she had the same problem. She dealt with it by taking on a strange status halfway between child and master, and retreating into the library, where she was always most at home. But she had a way out if she wanted one. She could transform herself back into a goddess at any moment. I didn't have that luxury. Having taken it up I had to go through this life. I would have to die to resume my powers. That had seemed almost exhilarating at first, but it intimidated me now. Unlike mortals, I knew what happened after death. But unlike them, I had never died.

And then I tried to learn to swim, and I couldn't. Always before, learning things had been easy, both as a god and as a mortal. But as a god I'd never known how to swim in human form—if I'd wanted to swim I'd always transformed into a dolphin. Now this earnest copper-skinned Florentine girl was telling me to relax and lie back on the water, and every time I tried, seawater went up my nose. It was the first time I had ever failed at anything when I wasn't being directly thwarted by the will of another god—and over something as trivial as swimming. I couldn't let it defeat me. I felt an actual lump in my throat—not tears in my eyes, which are as honourable and natural as breathing, but a hot lump in my throat, as if I would cry shameful tears of defeat and frustration. Then Simmea thought of another way to teach me, a dangerous way, dangerous to both of us, but she risked it. It was difficult and sensual and strange, but at last I swam, or half swam.

And I had made a friend, a courageous friend who would risk her life for my excellence. That felt like even more of a victory.

8

SIMMEA

I had lots of friends, but Pytheas was different. It took a long time to teach him to swim. He mastered it eventually through sheer force of will. He was never especially good at it, but he knew enough not to drown and could propel himself through the water with a surging stroke. I thought I would see less of him once he had mastered the art, but he continued to seek me out. We were, that year and the next, about the same weight for wrestling. But the thing that really brought us together was our shared love of art.

In the city, art was supposed to open our souls to beauty, and also to set a good example. When I looked at Michaelangelo's bronze *Theseus at the Isthmus*, with his foot set on the head of the giant Kerkyon, I was supposed to want to emulate Theseus and kill giants to protect my homeland. Of course, I would willingly have gone up against any giant that was threatening Kallisti, had I not been trampled in the rush. But Kallisti was an island extremely lacking in giants or other such threats. There were no cities there but our city. We never saw strangers. Had it been needful, I would have given my life for it without a second thought. But this was not what I thought of when I saw the Theseus. My strongest emotion was an ache at how beautiful it was, and a great admiration for Michaelangelo's skill in creating it. That humans could do such things made me long to emulate them, to follow them in creating beauty. If this was a possible thing, it was a thing I wanted to do.

Pytheas was constantly creating, though he did not always share what he made. He wrote poetry and songs. He could play the lyre and the zither better than anyone else I knew. Whenever he was set any exercise in music—whether music alone, music with words, or words alone—he excelled at it. He was marvellous in the Phrygian mode and even better in the Dorian. Under his influence I tried hard, and did improve at writing poetry and music.

My true love was given to the visual arts. I loved to embroider my kiton and cloak and to devise new patterns for this. I often embroidered for my friends. In the spring of the Year Three I was chosen to embroider a panel for the great robe of Athene. I chose blues and soft pinks and greys, and made a running pattern of owls and books. I loved this kind of work. Later that year I finally learned stone carving, and early in the year after metalwork, and finally painting. Painting was wonderful. It was what I had always wanted. It let me bring together color and line, and set down the pictures I could see in my head, even if they never came out quite the way I wanted them. At first I was terrible, but after I learned some technique I managed a sketch of Pytheas as Apollo playing the lyre, and a larger painting of Andromeda and Kryseis reaching the victory line in the games. I was almost happy with that as a composition. I had caught their expressions, and the contrast of light and dark in their hair and skin was pleasing. I would go back to eat in front of the Botticellis and know that I had so much to aspire to. Most days this would fill me with hope and delight, and only when I was bleeding or something had set me down would it seem an impossible burden to have a target so impossible to reach.

In the way the city was ordered, sculpture, painting and poetry were considered among the arts of bronze. I still wore the silver pin I had won in the races, but I began to look at the work of those whom the masters gave bronze pins, and think that I was not far from their standard. I made a mold for some cloak pins with a design of bees and flowers, and thought that they could be cast in any metal. Of course I continued to work in the palaestra and the library. That year we learned to ride and to camp, and saw much of the rest of the island. Most of it was set with crops, tended by diligent workers, but some of it was wilderness, especially around the mountain in the centre. The mountain sent up smokes and steams from time to time, and near the crest there were sometimes rivers of lava that were still warm. We always went barefoot. Laodike burned her foot once when we were running up there. Damon and I had to help her home and we got back long after dark.

Laodike was a good friend, and so was Klymene, who had a very sharp mind. She always had something funny to say about everything. I could go to them with my little troubles and uncertainties, and they would be ready to hug me and reassure me. Pytheas never did this. He didn't seem equipped for it. If I forgot and complained to him about some little thing that was bothering me he never soothed me. He always wanted either to distract me or, if it was possible, to do something about it. This peculiarity stood out all the more because he was the only one who did understand about art. He didn't think it was a charming decoration or a useful moral exemplar, he agreed that it really mattered. If I showed him my designs he never praised them unless he truly thought them good. His standards were exceedingly high. Often when I had something that would have been good enough for everyone else, I made it better because I knew he would see it.

In this way he was a true friend of the soul, as Plato says, the friend who draws one on to excellence.

Sometimes I felt I couldn't do as much for him; that once I

had taught him to swim I had nothing left to do for him. Then I realized that I could help him be friends with the others. In many ways Pytheas was more like the masters than he was like the rest of us. He had an air sometimes of putting up with things that amused other people. This was why some people thought him arrogant. Once you were in the middle of a conversation with him it was often fascinating, but sometimes getting there was difficult for him, as if he didn't know how to start. It was difficult for him to adapt what he knew and thought to other people's interests and understanding. I could see both sides of it—I loved talking seriously, but I could also be childish sometimes and have fun. With my good friends I could have real conversations, and I could make a bridge between them and Pytheas so that he could be a part of these conversations. In that way I helped him by widening the circle of people with whom he could share some part of his mind. I would sometimes wonder about other ways I could help him. In the same way I thought about laying down my life for the city, I pictured doing it for Pytheas—if he had needed a kidney, or a lung, or my very heart, I would have lain down gladly before the knife.

The only one of my friends who refused to like Pytheas was Kebes, who persisted in seeing him as arrogant and sycophantic to the masters. In fact Pytheas was anything but sycophantic—he treated the masters as equals, or even inferiors. But he was polite to them and gave them consideration, even when they were not with us. Kebes continued to despise the masters and the city and everything about it. He mocked the masters when he was out of their hearing. He kept his hatred warm despite everything. He had even tried to run away once or twice in the early days, only to discover that we were on an island about twenty miles across and with no other islands in sight from the coast. He had, like all the children who had run, been found and brought back, and thereafter talked to about the benefits of staying. Kebes appeared to be reconciled, but he never truly was. He was waiting only until he became a man and could persuade others to steal one of the city's two ships, the *Goodness* or the *Excellence*.

"What will you do with it?"

"Sooner or later they will have to teach us to sail them," he said. "We will make for somewhere, either a civilization where we can live free, or a deserted island where we can found our own city."

"What city could be better than this?" I asked.

"A free city, Lucia, where we could use our own names, and would not be forced into the molds of others."

I liked the mold that was made for me, but Kebes could never be content under anyone's direction. He had a silver pin for his prowess at wrestling, but he mocked it in private.

Pytheas, by fitting into the city, by speaking respectfully of the masters, and by being my friend, offended him by his very existence. Kebes could not legitimately wrestle Pytheas, being a head taller, but he said that if he did he would try to break his nose. I think this simple dislike had imperceptibly become jealousy. I was fifteen. Pytheas was fourteen, for he had told me that he had truly been ten when he was bought. I do not know how old Kebes truly was—sixteen or even seventeen, I think. Perhaps Kebes too found Pytheas attractive, and did not want to acknowledge being drawn to anything of the city. Or perhaps he was jealous of my attention to him. Once, when he came upon me making a charcoal sketch of Pytheas, he snatched the paper from me and tore it up. Before I grew to know Pytheas, Kebes had been my only close male friend.

I did not like to think that Kebes felt he owned me. Nor did I lie awake imagining scenarios in which I sacrificed myself to save Kebes's life. But I liked him. And although I loved the city, I also liked to feel, through Kebes, that I was free—free to freely choose the city over Kebes's idea of freedom. Kebes offered me an alternative, even if I rejected it. I never reported his talk to the masters or to Andromeda, as I knew I should have. It did no harm, I reasoned, it might even do him good to talk, and if he ever came to the point of being ready to steal a ship I could report it then—or let him go, why not? The City did not truly need two ships, and what use were unwilling minds?

In the autumn of the Year Four we held the great games of Artemis, which were celebrated by footraces and swimming races for girls, and by hunting. The hunting came first, so that the victims could be offered as a sacrifice and eaten at the festival. We went out as whole halls, seventy of us together, with our masters. Florentia and Delphi, who did most athletic things together, divided up into two roughly equal groups. I went with Ficino. We never came near a beast, but we had a wonderful time in the hills. Maia scrambled about with the rest of us, but Ficino rode. We took nets and spears and bows strapped onto another horse. I loosed an arrow at a duck once, but missed. We stopped by a spring and ate the rations we had brought, apples and nuts and cheese. Laodike got stung by a bee, and we managed to track down the hive and take the wild honey, at the cost of several more bee stings. Ficino considered the honey a worthy gift for Artemis and so declared the hunt over.

The other group's hunt was from all accounts more dramatic. They actually found a boar in a thicket and faced it down with spears and nets. Accounts of what happened next differ. Axiothea refused to talk about it. Atticus told me that Pytheas behaved with exemplary bravery, and saved several lives. All Pytheas would say was that he had only done what anyone would have done. Klymene said that she had been a coward and could no longer face anyone. Trying to untangle all this, and get accounts from the others who had been there, it seems that Klymene had fled, exposing Axiothea, and Pytheas had leapt in and made the boar run up his spear, in the best poetic style. So far so good. But later Pytheas had said something to Klymene that she could not forgive, and neither of them would tell me what.

I tackled her alone in the wash-fountain shortly after dawn the next morning. "Did he call you a coward?"

"No. Well, yes. But I am a coward. I understand that now."

"Anyone can panic in a moment like that, if the boar was rushing towards you," I said, soaping myself to avoid looking her in the eye.

"Anyone with iron in their veins," Klymene said. "But no. Anyone can call me a slave-hearted coward and I will just agree with them. I was tested and I fled."

"I've never been in a situation like that. I might have done the same."

"You! You're always fierce." Klymene shook her head. "You'd never have run. That's one of the things that makes me so angry."

"Then what did he say?" I really wanted to know.

"You'll hate him if you know," she said. "I don't want to hurt your friendship. I know you really care about him."

"I really like him, he is a soul friend. And I like you too and I want to reconcile the two of you if I can, but if I can't at least I want to understand what happened!" I leaned back to rinse my hair. "If he is as bad as you say then I want to know that, and not give my friendship where it is unworthy." I didn't really think I was doing that.

"Are you sure?"

"Yes!" I stepped forward out of the wash-fountain. "I don't believe you are truly a coward, even if you did panic. But panicking in that moment probably does mean you need more practice facing dangerous things before you stand in the line of battle, assuming there ever is a battle. You should try to find dangerous things and face them down to get better at it. Practice courage. Running once in panic doesn't mean you have a fearful soul, or that you are unworthy. And it certainly doesn't mean that I don't care about you and still want to be your friend. And I want to know what Pytheas did, because helping interpret between Pytheas and the rest of the world is part of what I do, and I can't do that if I don't know."

Klymene was crying, so she turned her face into the water to hide the tears. I waited until she turned back, then hugged her. "What did he say?"

"I thanked him for what he did, and he said he was just doing what was needed. And then he said I shouldn't feel badly about having run because I was only a girl."

"What!" I was horrified. I had never imagined anything like this. Some of the masters sometimes said things like this. Tullius of Rome was especially given to it, and Klio of Sparta had once had a formal debate with him on the subject which everyone held that she had won decisively. But I had never heard Pytheas say anything that even hinted that he thought such a thing. "Are you sure?"

"I knew I shouldn't have told you."

"I'm going to kill him." Then I turned back to her. "Telling me was very brave. I do think you could learn to be brave if you practiced. Like working with weights and building up."

It was our turn in the palaestra directly after breakfast, which I could hardly eat, I was so full of fury. Pytheas was not yet there when I arrived, so I exercised with weights, hurling the discus farther than I ever had with the vigor of my wrath. When he arrived I ran over to him the second he had his kiton off and knocked him down into the sand. "Hey, give me a chance to set my feet!" he protested, slapping the sand to mark a fall. I threw myself onto his back, holding him down. There were no masters around to object. I could really have killed him before anyone could stop me, if that had been what I truly wanted. Of course, what I wanted was to understand.

"What did you mean, saying to Klymene that she was only a girl?"

"Am I going to lose all my friends over that?" he asked, so sadly that I immediately felt sorry for him, despite my anger.

"You are if you don't explain it right now." I thumped his arm hard. He wasn't trying to shake me off or to fight at all. He had gone limp, which made it difficult for me to want to pummel him.

"Will you let me up if I agree to talk to you?"

I climbed off him and he got up. He had sand all over his front, which he did not brush off. "She was sad and needed comfort, and I never know what to say. I didn't think and fell back on what I grew up hearing. Women—outside the city there's a tendency in most places to think that women are soft and gentle and good at nurturing, that by nature they should be protected. You must remember that from before? She was crying, and she had run away, she was just acting the way women usually act. I put my arm around her. I've seen you do that. I know that's right. But then I had to say something, and I was completely blank on what."

"For somebody so intelligent, how can you be such a complete idiot?" I asked.

"Natural talent?" He wasn't smiling. "Do you want to hit me again?"

"Would it make you feel better?"

"I almost think it would."

"I won't then," I said. Then I relented, and twisted on the ball of my foot to thump him in the chest as hard as I could, so that he sat down abruptly. "Did that help?"

Even in that moment he automatically slapped the ground to mark the hit. "Yes, I think it did."

"Did it help make you realize women aren't just soft little doves to be protected?" I was still angry.

"That's exactly how she seemed to me at the time," he said,

looking up at me. "A soft little dove who had been asked to act as a falcon, against her own nature. And why should everyone have to fight, if they're not suited for it?"

"Would you have said to Glaukon that it's all right for him to be a coward because he's only a cripple?" Glaukon had lost a leg in the first year of the city. He had slipped in the woods, and his leg had been crushed beneath a worker's treads.

Pytheas looked up at me guilelessly. "Well it doesn't matter as much if he did happen to be one. But in fact he's very brave."

"But imagine how he'd feel if you said that to him. It's not considering him as a person but as part of a class of inferior things. Klymene's a coward, she says so herself. And our souls have parts in different balances—maybe she doesn't have as much passion, and perhaps not everyone has it in them to stand in the line of battle—not that I see what enemies we're going to need to fight anyway. But some of those who don't are men, as everyone agrees. Every example of a coward we've ever heard about who was shamefully wounded in the back has been a man. And plenty of those who are brave and would stand firm are women. And by saying what you said you insult all women—you insult me!"

He nodded, getting up again. "It was a really stupid thing to say. Do you think there's any point apologising?"

"Not yet. She's too upset. I'll tell her I beat you up, that might make her feel a bit better."

"You hit me harder than the boar," he said.

"I still don't know if you understand!"

"That everyone is of equal significance and that the differences between individuals are more important than the differences between broad classes? Oh yes, I'm coming to understand that really well."

I glared at him.

"What? You're still going to be my friend, aren't you? I need you to help me understand these things properly."

"Yes, I'm still your friend. But I don't know how I'm going to explain to people about what you said."

He spread his hands. "I do know there's a difference between being soft and being a woman. I do see that there are men like doves too. And I don't see anything wrong with them, as long as there are enough falcons to protect them, and there are." He hesitated. "I do see that you are a falcon, not a dove, even if you'd rather be making art than making war. I would myself. Peace is better than war. There's too much glorification of war and not enough glorification of peace, and especially not enough glorification of the importance of the doves. I value Klymene, even if she'll never believe it now."

"The masters say we are all equally valuable," I said.

"But they don't act as if it's true." Pytheas frowned. "The worst thing about that hunt is that there was nobody there who really knew how to do it, nobody who had done it before. Atticus and Axiothea are scholars, not warriors. The city is heavy with scholars, unsurprisingly. Testing us for courage isn't a bad idea, but that was a stupid way to do it. Boars are really dangerous. People could have been killed or crippled if I hadn't known what to do."

"Write a poem glorifying peace," I suggested.

"And you paint a picture doing it, and you'll soon see how easy it is."

Ikaros was walking towards us, no doubt to find out what we were doing standing still for so long. "Come on, let's wrestle properly," I said.

At the festival I came second in swimming and third for running long distance in armour. As I had taught swimming to Kornelia, who had won, I regarded this too as a victory. I could have eaten from the boar Pytheas had killed, but I declined in favour of bread and honey.

9

MAIA

A month or so after the art collections began, Ficino and Ikaros blandly presented to the Art Committee a lost bronze of Michaelangelo, a David, but very unlike his most famous David. They told us unblinkingly that it was Theseus with the head of Kerkyon. I nodded and made a note of it. "Excellent," Atticus said. "One of the best artists of your time."

"Of any time," Ficino said, smiling.

I asked Ikaros if I could speak to him a little later. He agreed at once. After dinner, that day a kind of nut porridge, we went for a walk.

The island was beautiful, even then when the city was still a building site. We walked off to the west and sat under a pine tree overlooking the sea to watch the sunset. "You're a monk," I began. I was speaking in Latin as we usually did together.

Ikaros jumped. "I am not! I was just wearing the habit. I've taken no vows of celibacy, don't worry."

It was my turn to jump. "Did you think this was a sexual assignation?" I asked. I was simultaneously horrified and delighted. Ikaros was a handsome man, only about ten years older than me, and I had believed everyone who told me that nobody would ever want a bluestocking. Yet at the same time I felt diminished, as if it meant he wasn't taking me seriously.

"Such things have happened," he said, smiling. "Even here. Plato does not describe how the first generation of teachers are supposed to regulate their lives."

"He does talk about how children are to be born," I said, as sternly as I could. "And really, sneaking off to the woods is against everything he says."

He took my hand and ran one finger around my palm, making my breath catch. "But if it were a proper festival of the Republic, and you and I had drawn each other by lot?"

"That would be entirely different," I said, pulling my hand away in as dignified a way as I possibly could. Entirely different and far too exciting, I thought. "Come on Ikaros, we're friends."

"And what does Plato say about friendship?"

"He says not to get Eros mixed up with it," I said crisply, though far from unmoved. I was very aware that the kiton left far more of me uncovered than the clothes of my own period. I had never really noticed that before, because nobody had been looking at me the way Ikaros was looking at me. I stared straight ahead. The sun was setting into the sea and turning both sea and sky as crimson as my cheeks felt.

"If you didn't want that, then why did you want to drag me off alone?"

"I wanted to ask you about the *David*."

"Theseus," he corrected me at once.

"Exactly. That's why I wanted to ask you alone."

"Well, what? It's a good Theseus, it meets the needs, it's beautiful and we've rescued it. Atticus didn't blink."

"But why not say it's David? Why do we have to keep Christ out? What's the necessity? The reason I mentioned that I thought you were a monk was because I thought you were a Dominican, but still you prayed to Athene."

"I was having a bad moment when I prayed to be here. The

church refused to hear my arguments and then I was imprisoned in France."

"You prayed to Athene when you were imprisoned by the Inquisition?"

"With very good results," he said, smiling and spreading his hands.

"Yes, fine, but my point is that many people have reconciled Plato with Christ. Ficino did." Only a sliver of the sun was left, but the sea and sky still blazed. Why would he have been wearing a monk's habit if he were not a monk? Did they have fancy dress parties in the Renaissance? Could I possibly ask?

"I myself did," he said, proudly. "I reconciled Christianity, Islam, Judaism, Platonism and Zoroastrianism. I learned Arabic and Hebrew. I was so proud of myself. But don't you see, we were doing it starting from a belief that Christianity was true. If instead it's the Greek Gods who are true, if we have immortal souls that go down into Hades and on to Lethe and new life, then what price salvation? They can mix from the other side, we could say that Plato was really talking about God. But from this side, well, we can't say that when Jesus said he'd be in his father's house that he was really talking about Zeus, now can we?"

"I do see that," I said. "But it's not as if it does any harm, even if it's not true. It's a lovely story, about good people. It's not . . . contaminated. I don't see why we have to exclude it so entirely that we have to say the David is Theseus."

Ikaros lay back, propped on his elbow. "Christianity is harmful to the Republic because it offers a different and incorrect truth. We want them to discover the Truth, the real Truth that a philosopher can glimpse. That's important. We don't want to clutter it up with irrelevancies. Christianity would just get in their way. So no Madonnas and no crucifixions."

"But David is all right as long as we say it's Theseus?"

"Why not? What harm could that do? I'd bring a Madonna and say it's Isis, but Ficino thinks that's going too far."

"I wish I could see the Madonnas again. Botticelli's Madonnas, that is. I only saw them once. I was going to buy an engraving, but I spent all my money on books. Still, we have the new ones."

"We do. Athene in the *Judgement of Paris* looks a little like you." He moved closer and put his arm around me. "The real trouble with Christianity is that the morality can do so much harm."

"I didn't offer you Christian morality, but Plato on love," I said, standing up. I wasn't afraid that he would attack me, although I was aware that he was strong and could easily have overpowered me if he had wanted to. What frightened me was the thought that if he persisted, and especially if he persisted in touching me, I would give in to him. "Come on, let's go back if you can't exercise temperance."

"But you are a poor little Christian virgin, not somebody holding out for agape," he said, not moving.

I was furious. "How could you possibly know?" I asked.

He laughed, silhouetted against a sky of violet and rose. "Oh sit down. I can't talk to you when you're hovering over me like that. I'll concede that I could be wrong. But I doubt it."

"Nobody will ever say yes to you if you're that smug," I said, sitting down but out of arm's length.

"Lots of people have said yes to me already," he said.

"Here?" I was amazed, and a little jealous.

"Here, and in Italy before. I know my way around. I know what women like."

I was completely cold now. "There's nothing less exciting than being thought of as part of a class of beings that are all the same," I said. "You're treating me as a thing."

"It doesn't mean I don't see you as a person," Ikaros said; "that I want to copulate with you. Latin is an impossible language for this, and you don't know Italian. Let's speak Greek."

"I'd rather talk about why we have to exclude Christianity," I said, but I did switch to Greek.

"I know, but you're misjudging me."

"You keep changing the subject," I said.

"I see you, and I like you, and I find you attractive, and it would be a pleasant thing we could do together, like . . . sharing a meal. It doesn't stop us having serious conversations that we have silly conversations with imaginary wine. It wouldn't stop us having serious conversations if we indulged in eros. All I meant by the remark about knowing what women like is that I'm not a clumsy oaf who would hurt you, or who wouldn't care about your pleasure."

The sky was darkening to mauve and the first star was visible. I stared up at it, avoiding his eyes. "I believe you," I said. "But I'm not comfortable with that. Neither Christian nor Platonic morality condone the kind of thing you're talking about."

"No, I suppose it's Hedonist," Ikaros said. "But what Plato says about festivals and everyone drawing lots is like that. Eros separate from philia and agape. And every word Plato says about agape is about love between men."

"What he says about agape between men with no thought of love between men and women being like that makes me think he didn't know any women who were capable of being seen as equals. Which from what we know about Athens at the time is probably realistic—women kept cloistered, uneducated, except for hetairas. But . . . if he didn't know any women who were people, how could he have written about women being philosphers the way he did in the *Republic*? It's in the *Laws* too." I'd only recently read the *Laws*. "He must have thought about it a lot. And nobody ever listened to him in all those centuries they were reading him. I wonder how did he come to that conclusion? It's stunning."

"I don't know. I suppose he must have met somebody. You'd

only have to really know one woman with the right kind of soul to change your mind about their capabilities."

"Axiothea?" I suggested. "I don't mean our Axiothea, but the original. The woman who came to him in disguise as a youth and was admitted into the Academy? Perhaps she made him realise it's souls that matter."

"No, she came because she'd read the *Republic*, the same way you came here. It's mentioned in Diogenes Laertius. So he must have met women with philosophical souls before that."

"Showing a philosophical soul doesn't work on everyone, unfortunately," I said. "I wish Tullius would deign to notice the souls of the women here."

While I had been staring out over the sea and talking, Ikaros had moved so that he was right beside me again. "I know you are afraid," he said. "But I also know that you want it. I saw you start. There's nothing wrong with what we're going to do."

"No!" I said. "No, really no, Ikaros, I don't want to!"

"I am stronger than you and it's too late to run away," he said. "And you don't really want to leave, do you?"

I did. I tried to get up, but it was true that he was stronger, and that he knew what he was doing, which I did not. He had no difficulty wrestling me to submission. I screamed as he pulled off my kiton. "Hush now, hush," he said. "You know you want it. Your breast likes it, look."

"I don't care what my breast likes, my soul doesn't like it, get off me!"

"Your soul is timid and has learned the wrong lessons." He rolled on top of me, forcing my legs apart.

"It's *my* soul, and up to me to say what I want!" I said, and screamed again, hoping somebody would hear even though we were too far from the city.

Nobody heard. "There, see, you like it," he said as he eased himself inside me. "You're ready. I knew you were. You want it."

"I do not want it." I started to cry.

"Your body is welcoming me."

"My body is a traitor."

He laughed. "You can't get away, and I have taken your virginity now. There's nothing to fight for. You might as well enjoy it."

My body unquestionably enjoyed it. In other circumstances it would have been delightful. My mind and my soul remained entirely unconsenting. Afterwards, when he let me go, I turned my back on him and put my kiton back on.

"There, didn't you like it?"

"No," I said. "Having my will overruled and my choices taken away? Who could enjoy that."

"You liked it," he said, a little less sure of himself now.

I ignored him and walked away. I did not run because I was under the pines and it was completely dark and I'd have been sure to have banged into a tree. I could hear him blundering behind me. I ran cautiously once I was out where I could see by starlight, and made it back to the city. Klio, who was to serve the Sparta hall, which was finished, already had a house of her own, where Axiothea and I slept most of the time until our own houses were ready. I went there and slammed the door. I was shaking and crying. It was so humiliating to think that my mother and my aunt and those who had insisted on protecting me had been right all along.

"What's wrong?" Klio asked, getting up and coming towards me.

"Ikaros raped me," I said, still leaning on the door.

"Are you hurt?" She hesitated. "Should I get Kreusa? Or Charmides?" Charmides was our doctor, a man from the twenty-first century.

"I'm not really hurt. I mean there's a bit of blood." I could feel it sticky on my thighs. "And a couple of bruises. But nothing I need a doctor for."

"I'm surprised at Ikaros. I wouldn't have thought he was that type." She hugged me and drew me into the room. "Are you going to tell people?"

I hadn't thought about that. "I don't know. He'll say I wanted it."

"You went off with him alone," she said. "Lots of people would think you did want it. It would be your word against his, and I don't know what people would decide. Lots of the older men don't really see us as equals. And once everyone knows, everyone knows. You can't undo that. And you can't leave. There's nowhere to go."

I understood what she meant. "I won't tell anyone. I never want to see him again."

"I'm going to smack him myself when I get the chance," she said, sounding really fierce.

"I thought he was my friend!"

"He thought you wanted it." Klio sat down on the bed, drawing me down with her. "Men, especially confident bastards like Ikaros, always try to get their friends into bed. But actual rape? Did you say no?"

"I said no in both languages and at great length." She snorted. "I screamed. He thought I was afraid because of Christian morality and that I wanted it really." I wiped my eyes. "I don't know whether some part of me did want it. My body did. But not like that!"

"Not like that, no."

"Does that mean he was right and I did want it? I felt that my body was a traitor. Does it make me a hetaira?"

"No." She sounded really fierce. "If you didn't agree, then you didn't agree and it was rape, whatever your body thought about it."

"Can I use your wash fountain?"

"Of course. Clean him off you. Wait—when did you have your period?"

"Last week," I said.

"That's good." I looked at her blankly. "You're probably not pregnant," she expanded. "I'm assuming you didn't chew silphium beforehand, as you weren't planning on it."

"No," I said.

Klio frowned. "Do you think Ikaros would do it again? To someone else? Because if so then we should tell people, to protect them."

"I don't know," I said. "I don't expect anyone is as naive as I was, to go off with him like that, without realizing."

"I can put the word around that women should be careful of him, without mentioning your name or the word rape," she said. "Go on, shower."

I didn't tell anyone else. I resigned from the Art Committee. I did not speak much to Ikaros on the Tech Committee. He kept saying things and giving me looks, clearly confused. Once I was sure I wasn't pregnant, I tried to forget about it. I made sure not to be alone with men, any men, ever. We were busy. It wasn't difficult.

A few days after my house was ready and I had moved into it, delighted to have a bed and privacy again, Ikaros waited for me after a meeting of the Tech Committee. Klio stayed with me, glaring at him. His confidence withered a little before the concerted force of our glares

"I've just come back from an art expedition," Ikaros said. "I have something for you." He gave me a big book wrapped in muslin. "Don't open it here." He left.

Klio and I went back to my house, where I unwrapped it. It was a book of reproductions of Botticelli paintings, in English, printed on glossy paper and with a publication date of 1983. On the cover was the *Madonna of the Magnificat*.

10

SIMMEA

In Year Five of the city, when we were all nominally fifteen, it was finally Florentia's turn to learn astronomy. I'd been looking forward to it ever since Axiothea told us that it would involve more geometry. We began one crisp autumn afternoon in the Garden of Archimedes on the western edge of the city, where the big orrery and telescopes were. There were only nineteen of us. Astronomy wasn't considered essential, and as always we were short of masters. Only those selected could pursue it.

I enjoyed the orrery, and calculating the motions of the planets. Archimedes's own orrery was there, with his gearing, and another, not as beautiful, which Axiothea said was Keplerian and which showed the motion of the planets as ellipses. When darkness fell I enjoyed seeing the planets exactly where we had predicted they would be. I loved looking through the telescope and learning how to adjust it. Kebes was there, and my close friend Laodike, but not Pytheas. Delphi had studied astronomy the season before.

That first night they showed us all the spectacular things—the moons of Jupiter and the extra sisters in the Pleiades and the great galaxy of Andromeda. Walking back through the dimly lit city, I bade joy of the night to Laodike when we came to her house, which was Thyme, on the street of Demeter. Kebes came up beside me as we walked on. Our ways lay together almost all the way back. His sleeping house was Violet, which lay just beyond Hyssop, on the street of Hera. "You really enjoyed that."

"I did." I was still bouncing with excitement. "Just think. We can tell where Mars will be in a thousand years. In ten thousand years."

"Who cares?"

I looked at him blankly. I couldn't see his face in the darkness. "I care."

"Lucia," he said, very softly. I started guiltily at the name. He stepped closer as we came to a sconce on the wall of the temple of Hestia. I could see his eyes glint. "Don't you see it doesn't matter? We're never going to Mars. Humanity may, one day. It may already have gone there, in the far future that they won't tell us about. But we've been deliberately brought into a sterile backwater of history where nothing we do can achieve anything."

"We've been lucky enough to be brought to the Just City to have the one opportunity of growing up to be our best selves, Matthias," I said, saying his old name as deliberately as he said mine.

"Oh, you're hopeless," he said, walking on into the darkness. "They brought us here against our will, all of us. But you've swallowed it all whole. They've made you over into one of them."

"And you aren't prepared to trust that anyone has good intentions, or anything at all!"

Just then a voice came from what I had taken for a statue of an old man next to a pillar on the steps of the temple. "What aren't you prepared to trust?" he asked Kebes.

"You," Kebes blurted.

"Me?" the old man asked, coming out into the street and falling into step with us. "Well, you don't know me, you've never seen me before, I am a stranger who has only just come to this place, you have no reason to trust me. But you have no reason to distrust me either, so it seems that the maiden is correct in her assessment that you trust nothing. How did you come to such a position?"

"From meeting a great deal of deception," Kebes said.

"Then you are judging a stranger by your past experience of humanity, that they are untrustworthy, and assuming that I am the same?"

"Yes," Kebes said.

"Well, and you believe that the maiden is the opposite, that she is overly trusting?"

Kebes looked at him sideways and said nothing. The old man turned his bright gaze on me. There was something about the way his bright dark eyes met mine that reminded me of Ficino. But he really was a stranger, which was astonishing. I had never seen strangers come to the city since we had all come here at the beginning, over the course of a few days, five years before. There were masters I knew more or less well, and many of the children in other halls I barely knew at all, but after this time in which we had all been in the city they were all generally familiar to me by sight. This old man was entirely new to me. "So, do you trust everything as the youth says?"

"No," I said. "I trust what I have found trustworthy."

"And do you trust me?"

"I do," I said. It was true, up to a point. I did instinctively feel that I could trust him. But this was a dangerous conversation. Although he was a stranger, he was an old man and must therefore be a master, and the real subject that Kebes and I had been discussing was about trusting the masters. Kebes could get into serious trouble if they knew what he had said. When he had run away before he had been a boy, now he was a youth on the edge of manhood. He'd be showing them that he hadn't changed, that they couldn't trust him. He could be punished.

"On what basis do you judge me trustworthy? Because I am a

stranger to you just as much as to the youth here, who does not trust me enough even to enter deeply into dialogue with me."

I thought hard about what I wanted to say, and spoke the truth but phrased it carefully. "I trust you because you wish to have a dialogue to discover the truth. And I trust you because you remind me of Master Ficino."

He threw back his head and laughed. "Ficino would like that!" he said. "So you judge me by your previous experience of humanity and it has been good, so you are in all ways the opposite of your companion."

"No, wait. I don't have a good opinion of all humanity, but of Ficino, whom you resemble. And from what you say it seems you know him well, which gives me an even better opinion of you."

"I have met him. I would not say I know him well. In what particulars do I seem to you to resemble him?"

We had come to Hyssop house, and I stopped in the pool of light from the sconce over the door. "Not in superficial details. For instance, he habitually wears a red hat and your head is bare. I trust Ficino, but because of that I would not necessarily trust any man in a red hat. You are both old men, but that's not important either. I wouldn't necessarily trust any old man without evidence of his trustworthiness. Your eyes are like Ficino's, and eyes are the mirror of the soul, or so I have read. Therefore I will say that your soul, in so far as I can discern it in the short time we have been conversing, resembles Ficino's, and on what better grounds could one assess the trustworthiness of a man than on his soul?"

"A good and thoughtful answer," the old man said. "And a reasonable basis for trust, don't you agree, young man?"

"If I trusted Master Ficino it might be a good reason to trust you too," Kebes said, stressing the word "master" ironically.

The old man nodded. "I see you have both been already studying logic and rhetoric."

"No," I said, my hand on the door. "We don't begin to study rhetoric until next spring, after the festival, when we will be sixteen. But I have been reading about it."

"You are begining to study rhetoric tonight," the old man said. "What are your names?"

"Simmea," I said.

"Kebes," said Kebes, reluctantly.

The old man looked sad for a moment. "I had friends with those names once," he said. "Men of Thebes. Did they give you those names when you came to the city? Because I thought I heard you use another name just now in the street."

"It is forbidden," I whispered.

"Is it?" the old man asked. "Then I shall forget I heard them, and use my old friends' names when I address you. I had not been invited to join your conversation but invited myself along, so I should disregard anything I should not have overheard before you began to speak with me willingly. But now I shall recruit you to converse with me and be my friends, if you will. My name is Sokrates the son of Sophronikos."

"Of course it is," I said. I didn't know how I hadn't guessed it before. "I thought you were dead." I had wept for him, reading the *Apology*.

"I should have been dead, but for my friend Krito, who thought it good to overrule my own wishes and the will of my daemon and drag me off here, for whatever good I might do. What would I do in Thessaly? I asked him, and yet here I am, will I or not. Now, Kebes, do you see yourself any closer to finding yourself trusting me?"

Kebes shook his head in astonishment. "Perhaps," he said.

"And you, Simmea, are you further from it?"

"No. I trust you more than ever, now that I know you are Sokrates."

"You can't trust everything that ass Plato wrote," Sokrates

said. It was astonishing to hear somebody refer to Plato as an ass, after five years of hearing him revered almost as a god. I gasped. Sokrates laughed. "It is late. You should go in to bed," he said. "And you should meet me tomorrow. When are you free? Oh, I forgot, you are never free, are you? All of your time is accounted for. I shall request of our masters that they permit me the use of some of your time, so that you may begin to study rhetoric with me."

Then he nodded gravely to me and went off down the street, taking Kebes with him. I stared after him. There was no reason Sokrates should not be here. And yet it seemed fantastical, dreamlike. I could see his profile as he turned to speak to Kebes. Sokrates! And here against his own will.

11

MAIA

I hadn't intended to, but I took the gymnastic training so that I could teach in the palaestra. I didn't ever want to be helpless again. Once I got used to it, I liked it. My arms and legs developed muscles in unexpected places. I wrestled with the other women and learned how to break holds and how to use my body as a lever. Of course, Ikaros took the same training, and he was still stronger than I was.

Ikaros mostly left me alone. He acted hurt when he did talk to me and I was cold to him. He was conducting a spectacular public Platonic relationship with old Plotinus, the leader of the Neoplatonists. Plotinus was much older than Ikaros, but still handsome, very dignified with his white beard and flowing hair. They acted as if they were Sokrates and Alkibiades in the *Symposium*, at least in public, and Ikaros seemed happy. Atticus asked me whether I thought they were as Platonic in private as in public, and confided that Tullius had asked him his opinion on the matter. Ikaros seemed to revel in being the subject of everyone's gossip.

I had occasional invitations from other men, especially once we all had our own houses. I always turned them down politely, and that was always the end of it. I was still working hard, still happy, but it no longer had that same wonderful glow. I had thought it was perfect, or almost so. I had thought these people were all my friends, my Platonic brothers and sisters. I had trusted them unthinkingly. Now I had learned to be wary.

Eventually, everything was built and most of the initial decisions made, and we were ready to begin bringing in children and really getting started.

The Committee on Children reported to the Chamber. Plotinus made the presentation. "We have decided that the best method is to send out ships to purchase slave children. They will be freed, and be glad to be rescued and be here."

Klio stood up, and was recognized. "Can't Sophia find ten-year-olds who wish to be here?"

Sophia, the goddess Athene, was sitting at the side of the hall. She had shrunk to normal human size, and generally went unarmed and wore a kiton like the rest of us. The owl was sometimes on her arm, and sometimes swooped about, alone and disconcerting, in the dusk. "Children don't generally read Plato," she said.

"Nor do we want children who have read Plato. It would confuse them," Plotinus said hastily. "We agreed that they wouldn't be allowed to read the *Republic* until they are fifty, though they can start reading some other Plato once they are fifteen."

"How about slave children who wish to be free, and orphans who want homes?" Klio said.

"Certainly we can collect them. But I don't know if I could find ten thousand and eighty such praying to me for deliverance," Athene said.

"They'd have to pray to you?" Ficino put in.

Her grey eyes flashed, literally flashed, like light glancing off metal. "The gods are bound by Necessity, as you know."

"It's just that going to slave markets and paying slavers for children seems distasteful," Klio said.

"We have, ah, decided that only men should go on these expeditions." Plotinus stroked his beard. "As with the expeditions to rescue art, it's not safe for women. But we've decided that all the men will take turns going, to be fair. Oh, but not you, of course, Lysias."

Lysias was an American whose family had come from China. He came from the mid–twenty-first century and was the only Asian in the Republic. I knew him quite well, as Klio had recently drafted him onto the Tech Committee. He nodded—it was obvious he'd be too conspicuous in a classical or medieval slave market.

"The point is not who's going, but whether we're empowering slavery by buying children," Adeimantas said. He was an old man from my own century, an Oxford professor who had translated Plato into English. I hadn't spent much time with him; we weren't on any of the same committees.

There was a vigorous debate, ending in a vote, in which we narrowly decided to buy children, making sure they knew that they were free as soon as they came aboard our ships. The committee then explained which slave markets they would go to in which years. Athene would have to accompany each expedition, to which she agreed. Each expedition would bring in two hundred children, which meant it would take fifty to fill our quota. "You'll never find two hundred ten-year-olds in any slave market," Tullius said.

"What we propose to do is to go to one market and buy all the available children of the right age, then move through time so that it seems as if we return every year, until the ship is full. Then we'll bring the children home, and make another expedition to another market," Plotinus said.

Tullius sat down, satisfied. I looked at Klio and Axiothea. "Won't that really be creating a demand?" I asked.

"That question has been decided and gains nothing by being reopened," Plotinus said, huffily.

So we prepared to receive the children. Every dining hall was ready, named and furnished, with two masters assigned to it. Every sleeping house had a name and an associated flower. Every bed had a chest and every chest had two blankets, a comb, a belt, and an iron pin, the very minimum we felt they needed. We had food ready, and workers reprogrammed to make food for everyone. We had so many plans. Of course, they collapsed on contact with reality.

The first children ran away the first night, ran off into the woods and had to be recaptured. After that we guarded the sleeping houses until the children were settled. We also instituted the watcher system, where one child in each house was responsible for the others and reported on them to a master. We kept them busy, which helped. Still some of them ran away from time to time. We brought them back and told them they would not be punished the first time. The Committee on Punishment was still in deliberations. Plato talks about punishments in some detail in the *Laws*, but he was thinking of adults, not frightened children. We tried to make them less frightened. Then another ship came, and we had four hundred children to three hundred of us.

I had never imagined the chaos ten-year-olds could cause. I could never have thought of children setting their chests alight or trying to sail off the island in them. "It will settle down," Lysias said when I was in despair. "They'll police themselves once it's working properly. We just need to get it started right."

"I think Plato was thinking of ten-year-olds as blank slates who know nothing," I said. "These are anything but."

"He must have been a ten-year-old himself," Lysias said.

"Yes, but never a parent, was he?"

The first months were total chaos. We had new batches of children coming every few days. I often felt close to despair.

One boy ran away and got his leg crushed beneath a robot who was trying to round them up again. That was the absolute low point, when we hurt a child and made his life worse instead of better.

After a while we got better at managing them. It became almost routine. We'd divide up the arriving children by fourteens into cities that still had room. When there were girls for Florentia I'd show them their sleeping room, teach them how to shower and use the toilets, choose a watcher, and take them to Florentia for dinner. Then I'd spend the night sleeping outside the door to make sure they didn't escape.

Lysias was right that it did get easier. Keeping them busy all the time and too tired to keep awake and plot mischief helped. He himself was driven to exhaustion working in the palaestra—we really didn't have enough young men. I was constantly exhausted myself, from being teacher and parent and continuing to sit on the organization committees. I didn't have time to worry about anything except whether we were giving the children the right foundation, doing as Plato described. I worried about that all the time. "Ideally," I kept saying, every time we had to compromise.

"In the next generation we will have enough people," Klio said. "These children will have children, and they'll help us with them. In that generation, the generation who come along when we are old, we'll see our Philosopher Kings, the native speakers of the language of the Republic."

"I have hopes for these children. Some of them are wonderful."

"The longer it's established, the closer we'll get to Plato's design and the better it will work," Klio said, pushing her hair out of her eyes. She never let it grow long enough to braid neatly, and so except when she had just cut it, it was always falling into her face. "But I am worried about the workers. We're overloading them. We don't really have enough of them for everything we expect them to do. We're going to have to find another way of doing some of those things before they break down. It's ridiculous for them to rake the palaestras. Anyone could do that."

"When the children are sixteen we'll assign some of them to farming and weaving and raking the sand too," I said.

"They could rake the sand now. Lysias and I are almost out of spare parts for the workers. We're going to have to conserve them and use them for the essential things."

"Can't we ask Athene for more?" I asked.

"I suppose we could, but I don't know where she got these from and whether it was difficult. Besides, I feel we ought to be self-reliant and go on with what we've got."

"I'm sorry I can't help, but I don't understand how they work."

"Nobody does, really. Not even Lysias. We're just patching them up. But they shouldn't be doing things we can do, like cooking and farming, when there are things we really need them for that we can't do, like making roads and maintaining the ships and building things."

"I'll support you on that when we next have a Tech Committee meeting," I said.

"The Tech Committee isn't the problem. It's when it comes to Chamber everybody has plans they want the workers for and nobody understands or is prepared to wait." She sighed. "Well, some of them will just have to wait."

It was hard work, but things did settle down. We couldn't keep as close an eye on the children as we would have liked. I tried to know all seventy little Florentines as well as I could, so I could help them to become their best selves. Often I envied them, especially the girls, seeing them grow up with their bodies and brains exercised and thinking it entirely natural that they were as good as the boys.

I saw Ikaros at committee meetings. The Tech Committee was always busy. Ikaros did not pester me for eros, but he was always friendly and occasionally let me know that if I changed my mind he hadn't changed his. I always said that I was happy to remain celibate. He really didn't believe, even now, that he had done anything wrong. Ikaros had been assigned to Ferrara with Lukretia, a beautiful woman a little older than he was. There were soon rumors that he was having a less than Platonic relationship with her, in addition to whatever he was doing with Plotinus. She was from his own period, so perhaps they shared the same ideas of seduction. I hoped so. We never discussed the personal sexual morality of the masters in Chamber, though the children's was a constant topic of debate.

The most contentious issue was age. A number of us, most of the young women and some of the older ones, wanted the age at which we instituted Plato's practice of marriage and having wives and children in common to be kept to twenty, as Plato had written. Others wanted to lower it to sixteen. We suggested a compromise of eighteen. The real problem was that we all did want to divide the children up into their metals at sixteen. "We can't go with Plato's specific word," Adeimantus said in the debate. "He says the girls should be twenty and the boys thirty, which is clearly impossible when they all started off at ten. Perhaps in future generations we can do this, but expecting celibacy until thirty seems too hard." The vote was very close, and we decided on sixteen.

Then in the Year Five of the City, nine years after I had come there, when I was twenty-eight, there was an extraordinary Chamber meeting. Athene had brought Sokrates to us. "I brought him from Athens," she said. "Krito asked me to help him get Sokrates away. Sokrates is an old man, and Krito and I thought it best to bring him here at this time so that he can teach the children rhetoric now that they are old enough."

"Sokrates!" Ficino said, mopping his eyes, quite overcome.

Athene vanished. Sokrates stood before us, nut brown and weathered, with wild white hair and the toby-jug face Plato had described. "What nonsense is this?" he asked.

12

SIMMEA

It was my turn to serve breakfast the morning after we'd met Sokrates. As I took plates and porridge pots to all the tables, Ficino called me to come and sit with him when I was done. I gave a glance to my usual table, where Kebes and Klymene were sitting teasing each other, then went to join him. He was sitting at the cross-table, so when I sat down opposite him I found myself staring at Giotto's *Justice*, a fine fresco to have, I suppose, extremely inspirational no doubt, but in my opinion Giotto was a moon to Botticelli's sun.

"So you thought Sokrates was like me?" Ficino asked, with a twinkle in his eye.

I helped myself to porridge. "Yes. His eyes are like yours." I saw that it was true what Sokrates had said when he laughed. Ficino was pleased, and even flattered, at the comparison.

"He wants to teach you. Do you want that?"

I looked at him, inquiringly. "Do I have a choice?"

"Oh yes. This coming year you're all going to be choosing, or chosen. As we have always told you, some of you are iron, some bronze, some silver, some gold. You have bronze and silver and gold mixed into you, but not much iron I think!"

"I want most of all to be my best self. I always thought the masters would decide how the metals were mixed in us and assign us to our places when the time came." I fingered the silver pin I had won at the Hermeia three years before.

"We will," Ficino said.

"Good."

"You think it's a good system?" he asked.

"Oh, yes." I hesitated, then went on, because I did trust Ficino. "So much better to be chosen for what we're fit to work on by those who know us than being limited to what our parents could have taught us."

"You were dreaming before you woke here, you grew under the soil," he reproved me, but his eyes twinkled. "When I saw your painting of the footrace I had thought you would settle among the bronze. And you are fierce in the palaestra, and you did well racing in armor at the Artemisia last year, so you certainly have plenty of the silver spirit. And you are so quick at mathematics that Axiothea and I felt you ought to be allowed to try astronomy. And now Sokrates has singled you out! So you may be destined for gold after all. Don't frown. All the metals are equally valuable, and the city needs them all."

I tried to stop frowning and swallowed my mouthful of porridge. It gave me time to change what I would have said immediately, which was that if all the metals were equally valuable, why were they always listed in the same order, with gold in best and final place? "If I am not made of gold then I think bronze is my metal," I said. "My soul leaps to painting and sculpture and architecture more than to gymnastics and fighting."

"And to the pursuit of excellence?"

"Of course," I said. "How not?"

"Sometimes I envy you children your certainty," Ficino said. "Well, in the hour before dinner go to Sokrates. He has a house on the street of Athene near the library. The house is called Thessaly. He may not be there. As you may know, he is given to wandering about the city, engaging in dialogues. If he is not there, seek him about the place. He has said he wants to choose his friends, and not spend all his time besieged by those who admire him; and we have agreed to respect that. It seems that you are one of the friends he has chosen."

"Isn't it exciting that he's here?" I said. "Sokrates himself. I thought he was dead."

"And I knew he was dead, and had been dead for two thousand years," Ficino said. Ficino was known as the Translator, and it was Plato he had translated from Greek to Latin, in Florentia in the days when few people understood Greek but every educated person knew Latin. I had read all the Plato I had been allowed, which was only the *Apology* and the *Symposium* and the *Lysis*. I knew there were lots more dialogues. I hoped to be allowed to read them when I was old enough to study rhetoric. It was a badly kept secret that the Just City was described in a book of Plato's called the *Republic*, which was not in the library. (I felt sure there was a copy on Maia's shelf next to that Botticelli book that was printed in a language that was not Latin.) "It's the most wonderful mystery of all that he's here. Bless Athene!"

I got through the morning in a flurry of impatience. In the early afternoon I saw Pytheas in the palaestra and rushed up to him. "Do you know who's here?"

"Who?" At fifteen he was better-looking than ever, and still totally unconscious of the effect it had on everyone. I was used to him, and even so I could occasionally be distracted from my thoughts by seeing his lips part as he said something especially interesting. I knew other people who were beautiful, but no other person moved me the way Pytheas did. The others were beautiful like themselves, but he was beautiful like a painting or a sculpture. That I was also secretly attracted to him only made this worse. The *Symposium* is extremely clear about the shame of lust, and I knew it was the attraction of soul for soul that I was supposed to feel. I was also most certainly drawn to his soul.

Pytheas was the most unusual person I knew. In most ways he was the closest to true excellence of anyone I had ever met, but other spheres seemed completely closed to him. He was a paradox that continued to intrigue me.

"Sokrates!" I said. "I met him last night. He's going to teach me!"

"I wonder why he came now," Pytheas said, looking abstracted.

"Now? Not when all the other masters came?" I fell into a wrestling stance, and Pytheas automatically did likewise. We began to circle slowly.

"Yes. If he was going to be here, why wasn't he here from the beginning when he could have the most effect?"

"I don't know." I feinted to the side, trying to think about it. "Perhaps he was doing something else—no, that's silly. He could have done it and still arrived five years ago with all of us."

"The masters were here before that." He landed a blow on my arm and I raised my hand to mark it as we took up position again. "They must have been, I mean. They were here to build the city and decide what went into the libraries."

"And rescue the art," I said, plunging in suddenly to grapple. The only way to win against Pytheas these days was distract him and take him by surprise. I managed to bear him to the ground, and he tapped the sand.

"When are you seeing him? Can I come too?" We circled again. Pytheas was grinning, trying to get the sun in my eyes, one of his favorite tricks. I leaned the other way, bouncing on the balls of my feet.

"After this. What are you supposed to be doing? I can't think he'd mind, considering what he was like."

"I'm supposed to be in the library. I could come with you. What was he like?" Pytheas charged in and caught me at once in a grapple that I knew I could not break.

"He was fascinating," I said. "Do come."

"I'm not sure I should come without an invitation. Maybe you should ask him if I'd be welcome, and if I could come another day." He was leaning his strength against me now, and even as I tried to hold myself back, I was acutely aware of how my breast was pressed up against his side.

"I think you should come today. You have to be ahead of where you're supposed to be in the library, you always are, the same as I am. And I'd love to know what you make of him." He pulled me off balance and I went down, meaning he won the bout.

"All right. I'll meet you at the fountain after." He ran off to look for another partner and I went to join the runners.

Kebes joined us at the fountain when it was time to leave. "Are you going to talk to Sokrates too?" he asked Pytheas, sounding dismayed.

"I thought I would," Pytheas said, in a tone that invited Kebes to make something of it while they were still in the palaestra.

I put my kiton on and fastened it. "Come on, we've just got clean, we don't want to get sand all over ourselves again. Besides, I don't want to be late."

The two of them blustered at each other as we walked along. I thought I detected something worse than usual in it. I started to dread what would happen when we found Sokrates and it became clear that Pytheas had been invited only by me.

We found Sokrates's house with no difficulty. "I wonder why he called it Thessaly?" Pytheas mused. "He came from Athens."

"He said last night that he had asked Krito what he would do in Thessaly, and Krito dragged him here," I said. "I suppose he means that he's thinking of the city as Thessaly." I scratched on the door, and to my surprise it was opened immediately.

In the *Symposium* Alkibiades says that Sokrates looks like Silenus, and seeing him in daylight I could see that it was true. He has the same big nose and bulbous forehead and little goat-beard. But nobody would care how ugly he was once they'd seen his eyes and his smile. He smiled now, seeing us. "Why, Simmea and Kebes, how good to see you again. And who is your friend?"

Then he stepped forward to get a better look at Pytheas, and stopped dead, his head frozen in position jutting forward and staring. I hadn't expected anything like this. He and Pytheas stared at each other for a long moment but neither spoke. "Do you recognise him?" Kebes asked. There was indeed something in his expression that looked like recognition.

"Do I?" Sokrates asked Pytheas, softly.

"My name is Pytheas, of the house of Laurel, the hall of Delphi and the tribe of Apollo," Pytheas said, inclining his head. "And you, sir, are Sokrates the son of Sophronikos, than whom, I have long said, there is nobody more wise."

"I am more delighted to meet you than you can imagine," Sokrates said. "Perhaps now we will be able to find some answers. Come in, all of you. Come through to the garden."

The house was much like Hyssop house. It had a bedroom of the same size, but with only one bed and one chest, with no other furnishings, and an identical fountain room. A door led out of it into a sheltered courtyard full of plants. There was a little statue of a Herm under the branches, which I noticed especially because it was made of limestone and not marble.

"Let us sit here in the shade of this olive tree and converse. If any of us are dry there is water close at hand."

We sat on the ground under the tree. Sokrates, although he was old, had no difficulty in sitting or in crossing his legs comfortably. "Well, my friends," Sokrates began, leaning back against the trunk of the tree, "For I believe as you are here that I can safely call you my friends. We began a discussion last night about the nature of trust, which we were forced to break off because of the lateness of the hour. This seems like the perfect time to resume it."

"Have you been reading Plato's dialogues?" Pytheas asked.

Sokrates laughed. He laughed like a happy child, absolutely irrepressibly. "How could I resist?" he asked. "You might be able to imagine what it is like to fall asleep in a prison cell and awake to find yourself in an experimental colony which one of your pupils claimed you had proposed yourself. I thought at first that it was a ridiculous dream, but as it keeps going on and becoming more and more detailed I have decided for the time being to treat it as reality and go along with it on that basis."

"It's not a dream," I said. "That is, not unless I'm dreaming too. And I've been here for years."

"I'll grant, Simmea, that it is not your dream. But have you ever been a participant in somebody else's dream, and could you prove you were not? I'll let you off that one, for I feel it's beyond human capacity." He glanced at Pytheas again, and Pytheas smiled sideways at him.

"I believe it's nobody's dream," Pytheas said. "And you do have the comfort of knowing you won't be forgotten. People will still be having Socratic dialogues in thousands of years."

"Not forgotten, perhaps, but what have they done to my memory! As for the question of the dream—well, that brings us back to the interesting question of trust. Who can we trust, and how do we decide? Do you trust each other?"

"No," Kebes said, looking at Pytheas.

"But then we have established that you are not inclined to trust anyone," Sokrates said. "Simmea?"

"I think that if we can trust anyone then we can trust each other," I said.

"Well then, is it possible to trust anyone? To begin with, can we trust the gods?"

"Which gods?" Kebes asked.

Sokrates looked sideways at Pytheas. "We know, as Plato could not have known, that Athene at least is real, and much as Homer portrayed her. So how about Homer's gods?"

"Then who can we trust if the gods disagree?" I asked. "Like at Troy, when the gods are taking sides in the battle. Odysseus could trust Athene but not Poseidon."

"Can we trust that the gods are good, or is it more complicated than that?" Sokrates asked. "Is Athene good and Poseidon bad? Certainly if Homer speaks truly then Poseidon was bad for Odysseus. But he was good to Theseus, who was his son."

"You're using a very unplatonic idea of goodness," I said, surprised. "Ficino says Plato says Goodness is absolute, not relative."

"Considering relative goodness, I believe it's more complicated, as you say," Pytheas said to Sokrates. "The gods have their own agendas that may conflict."

"Ah," Sokrates said. "And how may we know if we are caught up in such a conflict, and if so, which god to trust?"

"Juno, that is Hera, was terrible to Aeneas," I said. "He was much harassed both on land and sea because of the unrelenting rage of cruel Juno," I quoted, naturally falling into Latin to do so.

"I can see I'm going to have to learn that infuriating language," Sokrates said. "But not today. Translation, please."

I repeated it in Greek. It seemed astonishing that he was so wise but did not know Latin. But Virgil wasn't born until five hundred years after he died. In his time, Rome had been no more than a little village, founded by Romulus and Remus only a few centuries before, unheard-of away from Italy. Then Rome had grown great and spread civilization over the world, so that even when she fell, her language had preserved it in human minds, so that now—except that *now* in this moment Rome did not even exist. Aeneas, if he had even been born, had not yet sailed from Troy. "It's like looking through the wrong end of a telescope," I said. "History, from here."

"You have at least had five years to learn about it. I've barely been here half a month."

"Are you a master?" Kebes asked.

"What an interesting question," Sokrates said, patting Kebes's hand. "What is a master, in this city?"

"The masters came here from all over time, drawn by their shared wish to found the Just City," Kebes recited. It was what we had been taught.

"They did this with the aid of Pallas Athene," Pytheas added, in the manner of somebody politely adding a footnote, but Kebes frowned at him. Sokrates nodded to himself. "So it would seem that I am not a master, as I did not read Plato's *Republic* nor pray to Athene to bring me here to work at setting it up."

"But you're not a child," Kebes said.

"I'm seventy years old, I'm certainly not a child. Nor am I a youth, and still less a maiden. But perhaps I am wrong about this. Perhaps in this city I am a child. Is there nobody here but masters and children?"

"Unless you count the workers," I said. "They are mechanical, but they seem to have purpose."

"They're just devices," Pytheas said. "They don't will what they do."

"Do you know that?" Sokrates asked.

Pytheas closed his mouth, looking dumbfounded. After a minute said: "It's my opinion and what I've been taught."

"We will leave the question of the workers for now, if we may, and let us say that of human beings, there are in the city only youths and maidens, whom you are accustomed to call children, and masters?"

"That's right, Sokrates," Kebes said. "Or it was the case until you came."

"Then let us consider. I am not a child because I am seventy years old. But I was brought here without being consulted, like a child."

"You have a house to yourself like a master," I said. "We all live in houses with six other children."

"That seems a minor point, but we will let it stand on the side of masters."

"The thing that marks you as different from children and masters considered together is that you came to the city now," Pytheas said. "All the rest of us have in common that we came here five years ago, at the time of the founding of the city. Why did you come now?"

"They tell me that I came now because before this you were too young to learn rhetoric, and I am an old man and they feared that if I had been here from the beginning I would die before you were old enough to learn. For that is to be my purpose here, you see, to teach rhetoric to you children: I, who was never a teacher but who liked to converse with my friends and seek out the nature of things."

"They have their own imagination of who you are, but you are not that," Kebes said.

"Now that's true," Sokrates said. "And perhaps what I shall teach is not what they expect me to teach."

13

APOLLO

Who would have guessed that Sokrates would recognize me? True, we had always been on good terms. But I was in mortal flesh and fifteen years old. Nobody else had recognized me. Nobody else had even come close to guessing, not even people I knew well. It isn't as if we go around manifesting physically all the time. People don't expect to see the voice in their ear incarnate in front of them in the form of a youth, and so they don't see it. Sokrates, of course, didn't ever see what he expected to see, he saw what was there and examined it. He knew me instantly, as fast as Athene had, faster.

The difficulty wasn't that I cared that Sokrates knew. Sokrates was one of those people whose integrity really could be relied on. No, it was that I didn't want Simmea or that lout Kebes to know. I was also a little afraid of giving away too much to Sokrates. This was never a problem before I became a mortal. Saying precisely as much as I want, with as many multiple meanings as words can be made to bear, has always been one of my oracular specialties. Composing oracles like that can be as much fun as really complex forms of poetry. But since I became Pytheas things had all been more complicated. I sometimes blurted out things I shouldn't, and there were these huge areas of human experience that I kept blundering into with both feet. Simmea really helped with this. She was always prepared to put her time into working things out with me, sometimes even before I messed things up. I really valued that.

Being a mortal was strange. It was sensually intense, and it had the intensity of everything evanescent—like spring blossoms or autumn leaves or early cherries. It was also hugely involving. Detachment was really difficult to achieve. Everything mattered immediately—every pain, every sensation, every emotion. There wasn't time to think about things properly—no possibility of withdrawal for proper contemplation, then returning to the same instant with a calm and reasonable plan. Everything had to be done in time, immediately. Paradoxically, there was also too much time. I constantly had to wait through moments and hours and nights. I had to wait for spring to see blossom, wait for Simmea to be free to talk to me, wait for morning. Then when it came, everything would be hurtling forward in immediate necessity again, pierced through with emotion and immediacy and a speeding pulse. Time was inexorable and unstoppable. I had always known that, but it had taken me fifteen years as a mortal to understand what it meant.

I found my own charged emotional states interesting to contemplate. Some were exactly the same, others analogous, and still others entirely new. Then there was the vulnerability, which is quite different in practice from the way it seems in theory. I could never have reasoned my way to understanding how it felt to stand in the palaestra, hoping that Simmea would hit me instead of walking away from our friendship. Even at that instant, even as I was waiting and not knowing how it would go, I knew that I would be making poetry from those emotions for centuries.

I certainly was learning lots and lots about equal significance. It was easy to grant it to Simmea, who was smart and brave and cared passionately about art, even though she was flat-nosed and flat-chested and had buck teeth. It was much harder in practice to extend this out to everyone. It took me a long time to realise that I'd been extending equal significance as a favor on an individual basis and that it really applied to absolutely everyone— funny cowardly Klymene, bad-mannered Kebes, and pretty Laodike. Everyone had their own internal life and their own soul, and they were entitled to make their own choices. I had to keep reminding myself of that regularly, and really I should have had it cut into my hand. I did an exercise at the end of every day, if I could keep awake long enough, when I tried to imagine the inner significance of everyone who had spoken to me that day.

Before I get on to the conversation with Sokrates, I should say a word about Kebes. He was big, one of the biggest of the youths in the city. He had clearly lied about his age and was a year or two older than most of the rest of us. His growth spurt had come early, and he had shot up. He had a head like a bull—a big broad forehead that could easily have sprouted horns, and a habit of setting his jaw belligerently. If I'd named him he would have been Tauros. He had a grudge against the world, and he hated everything. He wasn't stupid, far from it. He'd have been easier to understand if he had been. He just hated everything and everyone and devoted his time and energy and considerable talents to hating them. He did exactly as little as he could get away with, and spent far more effort calculating that than he would have spent on trying to excel. He had a way of making one master after another believe that they would be the one who would succeed in motivating him, that they were on the verge of success, while in fact he mocked each in turn behind their back. He hated everyone—everyone except Simmea, that is. Once, while helping Manlius, he contrived to break a statue of Aphrodite by moving the plinth where a worker was supposed to set it down. Both statue and plinth fell three stories onto marble and shattered beyond retrival. I would have thought it an accident, save that he boasted about it to Phoenix, who thought it was funny and repeated it to lots of people.

Left to myself I'd have avoided Kebes entirely. As it was, he persisted in being around Simmea, and so I had to deal with him. We had fought twice in the palaestra when neither Simmea nor any masters were around. These were not athletic contests in which victory was marked with points; they were vicious all-out fights in which we tried to hurt each other. I won both times. They were not really fair fights. Yes, he was two hand-spans taller and much heavier, and likely his body was a year or two older, but I had been wrestling since the art was invented. I knew tricks from centuries Kebes had never had the chance to visit, and when not bound by rules, I used them freely.

The second time, I had him on the floor with his head in a choke where I could easily have broken his neck. I thought about it. I would have had to pretend to be horrified at such an accident, and probably to purify myself before the gods. It wasn't this that stopped me but that I didn't want to deprive Simmea of anything she valued, even this. "Yield?" I whispered in his ear.

"Never," he said, and in his tone I could see that if he had been on top he wouldn't have had the same hesitation in killing me.

"Will you swear to behave civilly to me in front of Simmea?"

He was silent for a moment. I kept the pressure on. "Yes," he said at last. "Civilly."

"Do you swear?"

"By what?"

"By all that you hold sacred," I said. "Do it."

"I swear by God and the Madonna and Saint Matthew and my own true name that I will be civil to you in front of Simmea," he said, and I let him up. He spat blood onto the sand in front of me and stalked away. He was limping, but then so was I.

And that was Kebes. He hated and distrusted me, and when I made him swear an oath he swore truly, and kept it. It was strange. He swore only to get out of my power, but he put himself more into it than ever. If I had chosen to denounce him to the masters for the gods he had chosen to hold his words, he could have been punished—flogged, even cast out of the city. Perhaps that was what he wanted. But he kept the letter of his oath—he was thereafter just barely civil to me if Simmea was there.

If I had been my real self I would have thoroughly enjoyed sitting in the garden of Thessaly talking with Sokrates and giving double-tongued answers. As it was, there was a knife-edge of fear running under it all. It didn't stop me enjoying it, it didn't stop me being aware of the delight of dappled shade and sharp wits. It was just another thread underlining everything.

Don't think I was upset that Sokrates wasn't happy to be in the Republic, even if he might be actively trying to undermine it. Nobody actually thought this was going to work perfectly. Plato had thought of it as a thought experiment. He'd been trying to design what he thought of as a system for maximizing justice, according to his best understanding of the world. We knew his understanding of the world was flawed—look at what he believed about the gods. All the same, it was such a noble idea when Plato had it, such an improvement on any of the ways to live he saw around him. It was of the classical world, but better. His understanding of the world and the soul were mistaken. But his city had never been tried before. This was the experimental proof. It needed to be able to stand up to Sokrates.

Maybe some of the masters really believed they could make it work, but I think what they really wanted wasn't to do it themselves but for somebody else to have made it real and for them to have been born there. The masters were always envious of the children, that was obvious to me from the first. Athene and I certainly didn't imagine it would really work the way Plato described it. We knew too much about the soul to hope for that. What was interesting was seeing how much of it could work, how much it really would maximize justice, and *how* it was going to fail. We could learn a lot from that.

"What will you teach?" Kebes asked Sokrates.

"I will teach rhetoric," Sokrates replied. "It is a powerful weapon, in the right hands. I will teach small groups like this one, and I shall go about this city asking questions and discovering answers and seeing where those questions and answers lead us. For instance, who can we trust?"

Kebes looked at me, and I smiled cruelly back at him. The irony of the situation was not lost on me. Sokrates knew who I was. Kebes did not know who I was and did not trust me, nor did I trust him. Simmea did not know who I was and trusted all of us. She was looking from one to the other of us, leaning forward with her hands on her knees, looking like a chipmunk. "I think it's the wrong question," she said. "Trust isn't an absolute. You can trust somebody for some things and not for others. I can trust Kebes not to break his word, but I can't trust him to strive for excellence. I can trust Pytheas to do just that, always, but I can't trust him to understand without an explanation why I am weeping if he finds me weeping."

"So we might trust a person for one thing and not another?" Sokrates asked.

"Yes. And trust has an emotional component. When you asked me last night whether I trusted you and I replied that I did, that was an instinctive and emotional trust and only secondarily a logical one."

"So before we can ask who we trust, we should ask in what way we can trust them, and in what way we do trust them."

"Who do you trust?" I asked Sokrates.

"Have we established that the gods are divided and can be trusted in some circumstances and not in others?" he asked. "So that Odysseus was right to trust Athene and would have been wrong to trust Poseidon?"

"Yes, Sokrates," I said obediently. "I believe we have established that."

"Then I trust the gods who mean me well and distrust the gods who mean me harm. I have no way to distinguish them unless the gods themselves appear to me and disclose their intentions, or unless I send to ask an oracle. Perhaps I should do that, send to Delphi and Dodona and Ammon, those ancient oracles that are established even in this time. Then perhaps I would know if Apollo and Hera and Zeus were well disposed towards me."

"You needn't send to Delphi. You know Apollo has been well disposed towards you all your life," I said, carefully. And it was true. Sokrates was one of my favourite people of all time.

"You said so in the *Apology*," Simmea said, helpfully. "In your speech before the Athenians, that is. If Plato recorded accurately what you said."

"Plato was there, though I don't remember him taking notes," Sokrates said. "I didn't read that one. I remember that speech very well. It was only the other day."

"So beyond Apollo—" Kebes began, but Sokrates interrupted, looking at me.

"I could trust Apollo in my mortal life, but I was brought here against my will by divine intervention, so can I still trust him?"

"Athene brought you here," I said, which was weaseling really. I had known she intended to, and hadn't objected to her doing it. But I loved him and certainly meant him well, and he was not wrong to trust me. "She brought everyone here. Many of the masters have talked to her, and have talked to us about talking to her."

"She was on the ship when we came," Simmea said. "Ficino called her Sophia."

"That was Athene?" Kebes asked. "How do you know?"

"She had grey eyes."

"Lots of people have grey eyes," Kebes said, scornfully.

"And Ficino called her Sophia, which means wisdom." Simmea went on, unruffled. "She was on the ship, and important, writing down names, and Ficino deferred to her. But she isn't here. She isn't one of the masters. She was owl-carrying Athene, and she was there to make the ship come here through time."

"That does seem conclusive. I wish I'd known," Kebes said. "I could have done something."

"What?" Sokrates asked. "How would you fight a god?"

"Not by what I'd have done when I was twelve—not pushing her overboard or trying to tear her head off." Kebes hesitated. "I don't know how to fight a god. Do you know?"

"Until today I wasn't sure whether the gods truly concerned themselves with us, and I only knew that they existed as part of a set of logical inferences which turn out to be based on a false assumption," Sokrates said.

"What false assumption?" I asked, curious.

"That they were good," he said, looking directly at me unsmilingly for a long moment. I don't know what he saw in my eyes. The knife-edge had cut through me and it was very sharp.

"*Good* and *well-meaning* are different matters," I said, after a moment.

"Wait, are you saying that to overthrow the masters we'd have to fight the gods?" Kebes asked.

Sokrates turned to him. "Ah, Kebes, I see that you have learned to trust, at least to trust that I will not report what you are saying."

"What if I report what you are saying?" Kebes asked.

"I have been inquiring into the nature of trust. Any purely theoretical issues that have been raised by that question—none of us are going to report each other, are we?"

Simmea looked really uncomfortable. "I want to learn rhetoric," she said. "But I don't want to overthrow the masters. I didn't volunteer to come here but it's the best place I can imagine being."

"A valid point of view, and one we will need to examine in some detail," Sokrates said. "I have by no means come to Kebes's conclusions on that subject. The motivations of the masters and of Athene in setting up this city are very much worth examination, and I will be able to examine them much better with the help of somebody who thinks as you do, Simmea. But the point at contention is this—can we speak freely in pursuit of the truth? Can we trust that you're not going to report what we're saying?"

"She has never reported what I've said," Kebes said.

Simmea looked at Sokrates. "I never have. And I won't report what you're saying as long as it's only conversation. But I reserve the right to tell them if you were going to do anything to harm the city."

"You don't believe rhetoric could harm the city?" Sokrates asked.

"If rhetoric could harm it then it isn't the Just City and it deserves it," she said.

Sokrates beamed at her like a proud father, then he glanced back at me. "They'll be using my methods for thousands of years, you say?"

I nodded.

"Then what are we doing here?"

14

SIMMEA

All through that winter I learned astronomy and rhetoric. I was constantly overturned by Sokrates in conversation. It was wonderful and terrible. In the palaestra I ran constantly, both in armor and out of it. Running felt as if it fitted the rest of my life. In music I resonated to the Dorian mode. I painted and embroidered and dyed cloth for kitons and robes for the statues. I tested everything constantly and wondered whether it was good. I went over my conversations with Sokrates in my head, running, swimming, trying to sleep, examining my own thoughts and trying to find better answers.

Sokrates was wonderfully wise and full of twisty edges. He was honest in debate, always absolutely fair—he reminded me sometimes of Pytheas marking the point when I hit him. But it was rare to trap him—he thought too far ahead. I tried to do that too, but he was always ahead of me. I was always either really debating with Sokrates, or debating with Sokrates in my head. The real Sokrates was much better, even though I could win debates in my head. It wasn't about winning, it was about finding the truth. Sokrates always thought of things I wouldn't think of, things that came from directions nobody would expect. Often enough he let the three of us debate, just putting in questions now and then. His questions were always the best.

One morning I went running up the mountain with Kryseis and Damon. The island of Kallisti had a diameter of about twenty miles, and it had many hills, some of them steep. "Running in the mountains" just meant an overland scramble. But when we said "the mountain" we meant only one thing, the volcano that stood behind the city. Up at the top was a constantly changing crater. Usually there were red cracks visible down through the fresh rock. Sometimes rock ran like streams over the edge. Occasionally the whole place seemed about to boil. That was when it sent up plumes of smoke that we could see from down below. When rain fell into the crater it sent up great clouds of steam.

The three of us were serious about running, and close in ability. We ran up the sides of the steep rugged cone, pacing each other and keeping close. The terrain changed rapidly up here. It was a clear winter day with no clouds. When we came to the top I stopped and looked at the view. The sea was turquoise where the island sloped, and further out wine-dark all around, with a little froth of whitecaps where the winds stirred it, like diamonds on sapphire. To the north-east I could just barely make out a blue shadow in the water, as if there might be another island there. Kryseis was staring down into the crater. "They say it'll explode one day and lava will cover the city."

"Not for a long time," Damon said, reassuringly.

"I wonder why they picked this site, knowing that?" I asked.

"Ask them?" Damon suggested.

I could, of course, but it was interesting to speculate about. I wondered what Sokrates would say.

Damon climbed up onto the raised edge of the rock-rim of the crater and started to walk along it, balancing. I jumped up after him and did the same. "Come down, you fools," Kryseis said. "You'd cook if you fell in."

"I'm not going to fall in," Damon said. "It's almost a hand-span wide."

"What if it crumbles?" she called. "Come down!"

I jumped down, but even as I did I realised that walking that dangerous edge reminded me of talking to Sokrates.

What we debated so constantly that winter was whether the masters and Athene had been right to set up the Just City, and whether the Just City was the Just City or whether there could be one more just, and how that would be constituted. It was exciting and vitally important and deeply unsettling. "Are you debating like this with the masters?" I asked one day as we were leaving.

"Some of them," Sokrates said. "They are not united any more than you children are. Some of them are ninnies, and others, sadly, have too much respect for me to enter into serious debate. But a few I have invited to be my friends."

He spent his mornings wandering the city, falling into conversation with anyone and everyone, and his afternoons and evenings entertaining friends in Thessaly. He sometimes invited somebody else to join us for the hour we spent with him before dinner, but often it was just the four of us, as it had been the first day. He always seemed to pay a huge amount of attention to what Pytheas said, and to spend time considering it. I wondered sometimes as they sparred if they could have known each other before. But Pytheas would have been so young, it couldn't be possible. Kebes and me he treated as colleagues in search of the truth. He did not teach by instruction but always by demonstration.

"There's nobody like him," Pytheas said one evening as we were walking away from Thessaly. It was close to midwinter, and the sky was a clear luminous dark blue, like the mantle of the ikon of Botticelli's Madonna on the cover of Maia's book. Kebes had stayed with Sokrates, so we were alone. "There never has been."

"Nobody," I said. "Not Ficino, not anybody. I doubt there ever could be. No wonder people remembered him for thousands of years. He's better at challenging assumptions than anyone."

"He was challenging you a lot today."

I looked at him questioningly. "He always challenges me a lot. I like it. It makes me think through my ideas."

"You love this city," Pytheas said. That was what we had been debating that day.

"I do," I said, spreading out my arms as if I could hug the entire city. "I love it. But Sokrates has made me see that it's only the visible manifestation and earthly approximation of what I really love, the city of the mind. No earthly city, even with the direct help of the gods, can ever become that. But we're doing pretty well here, I think."

"What do you think he and Kebes are doing now?"

"Thinking about ways of destroying the city, probably," I said. Pytheas started. "What? Did you think I didn't know?"

"You—I don't know." Pytheas looked disconcerted. "You're not concerned?"

"I said at the beginning that if debate can bring down the city, it deserves to fall. If they break it by debating it, then it's not much of an approximation of the Just City, is it?" I asked.

"How do you know they're only debating?" Pytheas asked.

"What would they be doing? Stealing quarrying explosives to blow up the walls?" I laughed. "Well, Kebes probably would, but Sokrates would think it was cheating, just as much as Krito dragging him off here was cheating. Sokrates hates cheating, he really does. He wants to do it all with dialectic, always, following logic through to where it leads. He wants to beat Athene."

"In debate?" Pytheas asked.

"Yes, I think so. But I don't think he's ready yet. Meanwhile I'm painting and running and debating—if this isn't the good life, what is?" Daringly I reached out and took his hand. He let me, and even squeezed my hand once before letting go. Sometimes I wondered if what Pytheas and I had was close to being Platonic agape or if he really didn't want to touch me. We didn't talk about it. But seeing him every day was part of what made this the good life for me.

"Do you want to eat with us?" he asked. For the last month we had been allowed to invite guests to our dining halls. I almost never turned down an invitation, not because I wanted different food—the food was very similar, and our Florentine food was undoubtedly the best—but because I wanted to see all the pictures. I'd eaten in Delphi several times and admired the wall paintings of the Sack of Troy and Odysseus in the Underworld.

"No, tonight I'd rather look at Botticelli," I said. "Do you want to come with me?"

"I'd rather look at Botticelli too," he admitted. "But there's Klymene."

"Have you really never spoken to her since the day of the hunt?"

"Never. She doesn't speak to me, and I can't start it." He hesitated. "I suppose I could apologize, but it seems a little late."

"She's braver than anyone now," I said. "She has spent the last couple of years facing up to everything, going out of her way to find ways to train in courage. She's braver now than somebody born brave."

"Good. But . . ." he looked uncomfortable.

"Oh, come and look at the Botticellis and we won't sit with Klymene," I said. "I think it'll be pasta with goat cheese and mushrooms tonight."

At midwinter the Year Six began, and with it the ceremonies of Janus, the open door that swings both ways, to past and future. I always found it an unsettling festival, the hinge of the year. That year for the first time we were given wine, well mixed with water. I did not think it had affected my reactions, but when we went out to the fire at midnight I found that the lights of the sconces and the fire were brighter than they usually were, and the faces of my companions more beautiful. There was to be a dance around the fire, and Laodike and Klymene had been chosen to be part of it. I wished them good fortune and stepped back alone to join the spectators.

Sokrates was among them, talking with Kebes and Ikaros of Ferrara. Almost as many people had crushes on Ikaros as on Pytheas—he was young, for a master, and very good-looking, with a shock of chestnut hair and a smile that lit up his whole face. He had never taken any notice of me, except once when he commended my sketch of Pytheas. They seemed deep in debate, and I did not want to interrupt. I looked around for Pytheas, and found him on the other side of the fire and surrounded. One especially beautiful girl was at his side—the blond girl who had been chained next to me long ago in the slave market. Her name was Euridike, and she belonged to Plataea. Pytheas was attending to whatever she was saying, but when he saw me his eyes softened and he began to make his way towards me through the crowd.

At that moment Sokrates too noticed me and greeted me. "Do you know Simmea?" he asked Ikaros. "She has a very sharp mind and she thinks things through."

I glowed with his praise and was speechless.

Ikaros nodded to me. "She has a good eye for design too. Did you know we chose your cloak pins? With the bees?"

"Chose them to be the real design?" I asked, thrilled. Ikaros nodded. Then Pytheas came up behind me and put his hand on my shoulder, and Sokrates began to introduce him.

"I may not always have this, but I have this now," I thought. "I am perfectly happy in this moment and I know it." It wasn't the wine, though the wine might have helped me recognize it.

Then the dance began, very beautiful and precise, which it had to be with with lifted torches and flowing draperies.

The next morning there was a great assembly in the Agora, in the exact center of the city. The city was laid out in a grid, with two diagonal streets crossing it. Whenever one street met another there was a little plaza, and often a temple or other building that was open to the whole city, and it was in those plazas that artworks usually stood. The Agora was the plaza in the centre of the city, where two straight roads and both diagonal roads all crossed. The Chamber was there, where the council met, and the big library and the temples of Apollo and Athene, and the civic offices where records were kept. It was the only space in the city big enough for all ten thousand of us to gather, and it had been designed for the purpose, being shaped as an auditorium with a rostrum at the end where speakers could be heard.

Today Krito and Tullius were at the rostrum. The other masters stood with their halls. The few who were not assigned to any one city, and Sokrates, stood behind the rostrum. Sokrates was clearly scanning the children as we stood gathered in halls and tribes, looking at all of us. It was a chilly morning and we were all in our cloaks. Our breath steamed as we stood there. I wondered if there would be snow—there had been snow in the winter of the Year Two, all melted away by mid-morning, and I had never seen it since. I thought of Botticelli's painting, which was my only real conception of winter somewhere colder than Greece.

Tullius and Krito both made speeches welcoming us to adulthood. Then they called the name of each city, and each city advanced to the rostrum, where each child's name was called and the child given their pin. This took hours—from just after breakfast until almost dinnertime. We cheered each name, but the cheers grew thinner as we grew colder and wearier. Florentia came about halfway through. I had known I would be given a gold pin since Sokrates had chosen me, but I still choked up as I was handed it. It was partly that it was my own design, and partly that it was gold, after all, the most precious metal. I was going to be a guardian of the city. I hardly heard how many people cheered for me. I tucked my scroll inside my kiton and fastened my cloak with the pin at once. I was very pleased, but I didn't feel the rush of joy I had felt at the fire.

Florentia filed back into our places and Delphi went up. "They should have done it in the halls at breakfast," Damon grumbled behind me. "There's no need to keep all of us standing here in the cold."

"What did you get?"

"Silver," he said. "No surprise. There aren't any surprises. This wasn't worth making a fuss over. I think everyone knows where they belong." He unrolled his scroll. "Weapon training. That'll be fun. Horse training. Great!"

"I'm hoping for training with weapons too," I said. Then I cheered as Pytheas was announced. Gold, of course. The sun came out for a moment as he put up his hand for his pin and made it flash. I pulled out my scroll and read it. It said only that I was to study philosophy and keep up my work at music and gymnastics. Did that mean no more art, I wondered, or did that count as one of the parts of music?

I was about to ask Klymene if she knew when I realized she was weeping. I put my arm around her. "What's wrong? Did they make you iron after all?"

She opened her hands and showed me her pin. Gold. I hugged her. "You deserve it," I said. "You really really do."

She couldn't speak. Around us people were reading their scrolls. "It's so great that the masters get to pick things for us, things we're really good at and that suit us," Laodike said, earnestly. "I'd hate to have to choose. And think how limited it is in other places, where people are mostly stuck doing what their parents did whether they want to or not."

"We're lucky to be here," I agreed.

Andromeda opened her own scroll. "Childcare training? But how? There aren't any children!"

"Yet," Damon said. "There's a festival of Hera this summer. Maybe by next year there will be a whole crop of children for you to tend. Better learn fast!"

"You sound as if you're looking forward to it," Andromeda said.

"Aren't you? Hey, Simmea, if there are a thousand silvers, and a festival three times a year, how long before I've had sex with all of them?"

"Three hundred and thirty-three years," I said at once, then thought about it some more. "No, wait, it's more complicated than that. I'm not sure. It might never happen. But it wouldn't work that way. Some women will get pregnant each time and not be available next time. And how do you know there are a thousand silvers?"

"Just a guess," he said. I wondered how many would be gold. Would it be three hundred years before my name was drawn with Pytheas?

Eventually the ceremony dragged to a close and we went back to the our halls. Kebes came up and hugged and congratulated Klymene, who was the only person I knew who hadn't gone into the ceremony feeling fairly sure where they belonged. Laodike was a trifle disappointed to be silver—she had enjoyed astronomy so much, and hoped for gold.

"I'm lucky we met Sokrates that night," Kebes said to me.

"We both are."

"You'd have been gold anyway. I'd probably have been iron." Since we met Sokrates, Kebes had really appeared to be trying to be excellent. I'd heard Ficino saying that there never had been such an improvement in a boy.

I saw Septima, from the library, talking to Ficino. "She'll be gold," I said, confidently.

"Did they ever tell you they'd chosen your design?" Kebes asked.

"Master Ikaros told me last night. You were there."

"I know, but did anyone officially tell you?"

I shook my head. "I expect they wanted it to be a surprise."

"They should have announced it and given you the honor."

"Oh, that doesn't matter. It's enough of an honor that I'm going to see everyone wearing them." I stroked mine. "And that they thought it good enough."

The next day we cut our hair and made our vows at the temple of Zeus and Hera, to serve and protect the city. From then on we were considered adults, though we kept on calling ourselves children, to distinguish us from the masters.

Our days were different after that. For one thing the houses were restructured, so that everyone in a house was of the same metal. Klymene and I remained in Hyssop with five other girls, two from Delphi, Makalla and Peisis, one from Ferrara, Iphis, and one from Naxos, Auge. Andromeda and the others moved out to be with their own kind. It felt strange, but I was glad not to be the one who was moving. Maia said we could choose who would be the new watcher. At my suggestion, we chose Klymene.

The seven of us were all in the tribe of Apollo—nobody had changed tribes in the reorganization. They also continued to belong to their original cities. But they slept in Hyssop. This would have been more awkward except for the rule that we could now eat anywhere we were invited. It meant that they could eat in their old halls with their old friends when they wanted to, or eat in Florentia with us in the mornings when time was short. It was good—but it changed everything. It meant that we didn't necessarily all see every other Florentine every day, and there were often different people in the hall, especially at dinner. Florentia was a popular dining hall, partly because of our food but mostly because it was so very beautiful. Eating where we were invited made us all mingle and know each other better. Before summer came I had eaten at least once in each hall. Venice had a wonderful *Apollo and Juno* by Veronese, Cortona had Signorelli's *The Court of Pan*, and in Athens, where Septima took me one day with Pytheas, was a breathtaking statue of Lemnian Athena. Hardest to get into was Olympia, but eventually I met Aristomache with Sokrates and she invited me for dinner. Thus I got to see Phidias's astonishing Nike, which if I were forced to choose is probably my favourite statue.

The other different thing was our schedules. Before this, almost all of Florentia did the same things at the same time every day, with a few exceptions like astronomy and the sessions with Sokrates. Now we were all doing different things. Some of us still had every moment scheduled. Others, and especially we golds, had a reasonable amount of flexibility as to how we spent our time. For music I did mathematics and read in the library. I had very little supervision in reading. Masters might suggest books to me, and occasionally a request for a book was denied. Otherwise I was free to read what I wanted to—which was mostly philosophy and logic. I still did mathematics with Axiothea, which was always fun. Art was something for my free time, which I experienced now for the first time. I could go to the studio and work on my paintings and designs whenever I wasn't expected anywhere else, and I often did.

I continued to spend hours in the palaestra—but I decided which hours they would be. The way Maia explained this to me was that we were to pursue excellence as seemed best to us, now that we knew what it was and that we wanted it. Children need guidance; adults can learn to guide themselves. Most of all I pursued excellence by debating with Sokrates. Kebes and I took to following him around in the mornings, when he talked with anyone he ran into.

Soon, well before the summer, I perceived a problem. Before the new year, anyone whom Sokrates befriended was clearly destined to become a gold, and we all were duly awarded gold pins. After that, Sokrates continued to befriend people, but now their status was fixed. Only golds were supposed to study philosophy and rhetoric. But the masters couldn't very well stop Sokrates from going up to people and asking them about their work. They couldn't stop him from inviting whomever he chose to come back to Thessaly for conversation. Sokrates was famous. All of the masters revered him practically by definition—they were here specifically because they revered Sokrates, after all. They didn't want to stop him behaving the way he had always behaved. They had loved to read in the *Apology* about how he was a gadfly sent by the gods to Athens. Now he was their gadfly, and they weren't as happy about that. He was upsetting their neat system, and he knew it. He would laugh about it.

"How can they know who is the best?" he asked in one of our debates. The four of us were alone in the garden of Thessaly, eating delicious fried zucchini flowers stuffed with cheese that Kebes had brought from the Florentine kitchens.

"They observe us," I said. "They see who is best fitted for each task. My friend Andromeda is motherly and loving, and she was assigned to learn childcare. I am interested in debate, and I am assigned to learn rhetoric with you."

"Good. But how about Patroklus of Mycenae, who only became interested in debate the day before yesterday? He has been assigned to learn how to care for goats and sheep. Now he wants to debate."

"That doesn't mean it's what he's best suited for," I said. "He might be best suited as a shepherd."

"Does everyone have one thing for which they are best suited?" Kebes asked. "You're good at design, as well as debate."

"They always told us that we were a mixture of all the metals, and it was a case of discovering which one was strongest," I said.

"The metals are supposed to be an analogy for the parts of the soul," Kebes said. "So if Patroklus wants to turn to philosophy, does that mean reason is stronger in his soul than appetites, and they were wrong in thinking appetites were stronger? Or was Plato wrong about the soul?"

"Or perhaps the soul and the proportions of its parts change over time?" I asked.

"But assuming that Patroklus is truly best suited as gold, as my friend and debating partner, what does that mean?" Sokrates asked.

"It means the masters made a mistake." I shrugged. "Nobody said they were gods to get everything perfect."

Sokrates looked at Pytheas, who was leaning back on his elbow in the shade of the tree, eating zucchini flowers and looking like a Hyakinthos. "You're very quiet today," he said.

Pytheas licked his lips slowly, and Sokrates laughed and then swore aloud. "Apollo! Oh, Pytheas, you can make me swoon at your beauty, you know I'm helplessly in love with you, but that won't help you in debate."

Once we had all stopped laughing Pytheas sat up straight and answered seriously. "I think your question is the real question," he said. "How can they know who is the best? Even if they could see into our souls, how could they know? And to my knowledge nobody can see into our souls."

"Not even the gods?" Sokrates asked, rocking forward and almost toppling over.

"We know the gods can hear prayers directed to them, and sometimes speech before it is spoken. I don't believe they can see into anyone's soul beyond that, except perhaps all-knowing Zeus." Pytheas shrugged and took another zucchini flower. "But in any case, the masters don't have that ability."

"The masters just do the best they can with observation and intelligence and goodwill," I said at once. "To their observation, Patroklus was best suited to be a shepherd."

"Should they change their minds now?" Pytheas asked.

I looked at Sokrates. "I'd guess not, because it would cause too much confusion."

"That's certainly what they'd say," Sokrates said. "Some might put individual happiness above social confusion."

"Is happiness the highest goal?" Kebes asked.

"Is it a goal at all?" I asked. I thought of that moment by the fire when I had recognized how happy I was. "Is it rather something that's a byproduct of something else? An incidental that comes along when you're not pursuing it? When I think about when I am happiest it's never when I'm trying to be happy."

"And how does happiness differ from joy or fun?" Kebes asked. "Fun can certainly be a goal."

"It can also come along as an incidental," Pytheas pointed out. "A spin-off benefit."

"If you pursue happiness, like pursuing excellence, truth, or learning, do you get closer to it or further away?" Sokrates asked.

"You certainly can't will happiness," Kebes said, thoughtfully.

"Further away, I think," I said. "If you try to make somebody happy, you can't do it by asking them or telling them to be happy. You can do it by doing something for them, or doing something with them. So it seems much more like a side effect to me. Or almost like a thing that happens to you. So if you wanted to maximize happiness, for a person or a city, you'd do better to aim at something else that was the kind of thing likely to produce that side effect."

"Like what?" Kebes asked.

"Like excellence," Pytheas said.

Kebes made a rude noise, and Sokrates tutted at him. "What if you wanted to make Simmea happy?"

"I'd argue with her," Pytheas said. I threw a tuft of grass at him and we all laughed.

"But it's true. Debate does make me happy," I said. "It's not just that it's fun."

"What does happiness consist of?" Sokrates asked.

"Freedom, and having everything you want," Kebes said, looking from Sokrates to me.

"Not everything you want," I said. "You might want something that would make you unhappy if you got it. Having what is best."

"That brings us back to what is best," Sokrates said.

"The pursuit of excellence, as Pytheas said just now. When we first came here, Ficino said that he wanted each of us to become our best self," I said. "That seems to me an admirable goal."

"And that has been your constant pursuit since you were ten years old," Sokrates said.

"Eleven," I admitted.

Sokrates laughed. "Since you were what passed for ten years old. But how about Kebes?"

"How could he not want to be his best self?" I asked.

"Kebes?"

But Pytheas interrupted before Kebes could answer. "He might have a different pursuit. A different goal. Something he rates more highly."

"More highly than being his best self?" I asked, incredulous.

"If you'll let me speak, yes I do," Kebes said. These days Kebes seemed to tolerate Pytheas better most of the time, but he was really glaring at him now.

"What is it?" Sokrates asked, calm as ever.

"Revenge," Kebes said. "Slavers killed my family and enslaved me and the masters bought me and brought me here against my will. I can't possibly ever be my best self. That's out of reach. My best self would have had parents and sisters. My best self would have lived in his own time. All I can be is the slave self they made me, and my slave self wants revenge."

"The masters didn't kill your family," I said. "It's like when you poked me back in the slave market, because you couldn't reach those who could hurt you and I was there. You can't reach the ones who hurt you, and you want revenge on those who have done you nothing but good."

"If there weren't any buyers there wouldn't be any slavers," Kebes said. "They're part of it. And that they have high intentions makes it worse, not better. And they did the same to you."

I thought for a moment. Pytheas opened his mouth to speak, but Sokrates raised a hand, stopping him. "I see a clear distinction between those who killed my family and the masters," I said. "And it is my belief that I have more chance of being my best self here than I would have there. I can't know this for sure."

"Do you mean you condone having your family murdered to get you here?" Kebes almost shouted.

"That would be called Providence, and it's an interesting argument to consider," Sokrates said, calmly. "But it's late and you're growing heated. Let's stop for today."

Kebes stayed, and I left with Pytheas. "I wonder where Sokrates heard about Providence," Pytheas said as we walked down the street. "He's so clever."

"Sokrates is clever, but Kebes is an idiot," I said, kicking a stone. I was still upset.

"If Kebes were an idiot, he wouldn't be half so dangerous," Pytheas said.

15

MAIA

One day in the summer of the Year Five, Kreusa, Aristomache, Klio and I were sitting on the stones at the top of the beach one afternoon, drying off. We'd had a meeting of the Committee on Women's Issues, and then we'd had a swim. Aristomache was in her fifties, one of the oldest women in the city. She was originally an American, from later in my own century. She had long greying hair, usually neatly knotted on top of her head but now falling loose in damp curls over her little breasts. I'd been in the city so long that I barely even registered the fact that we were all sprawled comfortably naked in the sun. We were all masters of the city, and the only time we worried about was the present. As Plato correctly deduced, people grow used to seeing bodies, even when they're not young or beautiful.

Klio reached into the fold of her kiton where it lay bundled at her side and pulled out a small cake and a knife.

"Ought we—I mean, is that all right?" Aristomache asked, as Klio cut the cake into quarters. I picked up my share. It was currant cake and smelled delicious.

"What's wrong with it?" Klio asked, looking up.

"Well, Plato says we should have food in common, and I've interpreted taking food out of the eating halls to eat elsewhere as wrong," Aristomache said.

I looked guiltily at the wedge of cake I'd taken. Was it un-platonic of me to take it? I looked at Klio.

"Plato doesn't regulate the lives of the masters," Klio said. "But I think you're right. If we had food in private all the time it would be a bad thing. But this cake was made in Sparta's kitchen, and it's the same cake everyone is going to be eating there tonight. I'm always starving after swimming, and I thought I'd bring enough for all of us."

Kreusa looked at the cut pieces and did not reach out for one. "I think we ought to debate this. Do you allow the children to take food?"

"No, never," Klio said.

"Then it's not really having it in common, if we have privileges they don't," Kreusa said.

"Maybe we ought to let them, at least a little bit," Klio said. "What's wrong with it, as long as they always share what they take with others?"

"It's not what Plato says, but I agree that it might be all right," I said. "I allow the Florentines to take nuts and dried fruit when they go running in the mountains."

"So do I with the Olympians, but always enough for the whole group," Aristomache said.

"Oh yes. And when mine run in pairs, one will take the nuts and the other the fruit, so they'll share," I said. "I didn't discuss it with anyone because it didn't seem to come under any partic-ular committee, and Plato didn't mention it, and I just thought it was my discretion. I mean, if the whole lot of us all go out on a run we take food, so if a smaller group does it seems like the same thing."

"I agree," Kreusa said. "And I like that, giving one the nuts and the other the fruit. That very much does go along with the spirit of what Plato said about food in common. I'll do that with the Corinthians now you've mentioned it. Which is really a good reason for talking over things like that, so we can have the good ideas in common and stamp out the bad ideas before they get rooted."

I blushed. "Yes. Sorry. But who should I have asked, or told?"

"Food comes under Agriculture and Supply," Aristomache said, picking up a slice of cake. "I don't know who's on that committee."

"Ikaros?" Klio suggested.

Aristomache and Kreusa laughed, and Kreusa pretended to fan herself. I bit into my cake to disguise the fact that the thought of him still made me uncomfortable.

"I don't believe he is," Aristomache said. "He's never been on absolutely every committee. And since Sokrates has come and takes up a lot of his time, he has dropped several."

"Ardeia is on it, I think," Kreusa said.

"I'm not sure Agriculture and Supply is the right committee anyway. This isn't about food supply. It's a social issue. It's Right Living if it's anything, and I'm on that one," Aristomache said. "I'll bring it up in our next meeting, and if Manlius and everyone else is all right with it I'll suggest the fruit and nuts thing in Chamber. I think we can be a little more relaxed. The children are going to become adults soon. Indeed, I was wondering if we could give them the privilege of choosing which hall they eat in."

"Choose which hall?" Kreusa asked, her arched eyebrows rising right up into her hair. "Won't that cause chaos?"

"I didn't mean choose which hall unrestrictedly, or choose which hall to belong to," Aristomache said. "That really would cause chaos. I meant simply that perhaps we could give the children limited privileges to invite their friends to their own hall, and to go to other halls if invited."

"Won't it mean surpluses in some halls and shortages in others?" I asked.

"Won't it mean nobody knows where anybody is?" Kreusa asked.

"I think the surpluses and shortages would cancel out," Aristomache said, looking at Klio.

Klio nodded. "Workers could redistribute food if necessary, and probably it wouldn't be a problem; children missing from one hall would be cancelled out by children present from another. We could easily set up a mechanism where they had to sign in and out, and if a hall was full up nobody else could sign in unless somebody signed out. The food is very similar in all the halls. The social disruption potential is there, though."

"I think most of the children would be sensible about it," Aristomache said.

"Most of them, but there are some who wouldn't," I said.

"I don't understand the point of it," Kreusa said.

"The point is that once they become adults, we need to shuffle the sleeping houses so that everyone is sleeping with people of the same metal," Aristomache said. "It will mean people are sleeping very far from where they're supposed to eat. If there were some flexibility in that it would help. We don't want to reassign eating halls, because the children are very attached to them, and also because that's how we keep track of them."

"I can see how it would help," I said. "I'll support it." Klio nodded.

"I'm not convinced," Kreusa said. "I see a lot of potential for trouble. I'd want to hear a really solid proposal."

"It may come to nothing yet," Aristomache said. "Tullius is opposed."

I sighed and stretched. "I should get back. I have to teach soon, and then after dinner I need to work on the adulthood choices with Ficino, and I want to look through the list again first."

"It's only seventy children, and we know them well. You

wouldn't think it would be this difficult," Kreusa said. She reached for her kiton.

"It's the responsibility." Klio shook her head. "I used to feel bad enough about grades and recommendation letters affecting people's entire lives, but this? Deciding for seventy people not just what kind of soul they have but what work they'd be best suited for?"

"Lysias says he doesn't really believe in souls, that he thinks they're a metaphor," I said. Lysias had been showing some polite interest in me recently. I liked him. He was quiet and considerate and as unlike flamboyant Ikaros as it was possible for somebody to be and still be a man.

"Doesn't believe in souls?" Kreusa asked, pausing with her kiton half on. "Pallas Athene told us we have souls, the very first day. It's one of the few metaphysical things we can be absolutely rock-solid sure about."

"He thinks they're not the same as Plato wrote. She didn't answer Plotinus's question about whether they have three parts," I said. "He thinks they're something odd, and Plato's description is just a metaphor."

"Even if it's a metaphor, we still have to use it to classify everyone," Aristomache said, twisting up her hair.

"Do you know, the other day I found myself picking up Ficino's translation of the *Republic* to read through it in Latin, because I've read it so often in Greek that my eyes start to cross," Klio said, laughing at herself.

"I've done that too," I admitted, and we laughed together.

Kreusa stood up. "I envy you your hair, Maia."

"My hair?" I ran my fingers through my hair, which I kept at shoulder length, the same length the children kept theirs. It was almost dry, so I started to braid it.

"It's the kind of hair we all wanted when I was a girl. Straw pale."

"But it's so straight. My mother used to curl it, and the curls would just fall out again. And your own hair is lovely, like heavy bronze."

Kreusa pulled a curl of her hair and squinted at it. "Lukretia has lovely hair," she said.

"Envy, vanity, what next?" Klio teased. Klio always kept her own hair short.

Dressed and dry, the four of us started to walk back up around the curve of the bay towards the city. It looked beautiful from this angle and in the afternoon light. It looked beautiful to me from every angle and in every light, it was so well-proportioned and so well-situated. Athene, Builder of Cities, had chosen the site well. The vineyards and olive groves stood around it like the Form of agricultural civilization made concrete, and the volcano steamed away behind, like a reminder of mortality.

Aristomache paused for a moment, contemplating it. "If the gods will help us see the right metals in their souls, we'll have done all right," she said.

"Plato was so clearly only concerned with the guardians," Kreusa said. "I know the list of qualities for the golds by heart."

"Love of wisdom and the truth, temperate, liberal, brave, orderly, just and gentle, fast to learn, retentive, with a sense of order and proportion," Aristomache reeled off. "You wouldn't think it would be so hard to assess, until you were looking at a set of seventy sixteen-year-olds and weighing each of them for those qualities."

I sighed. "It's hard to find enough people who have them. The really difficult thing is getting the numbers right. But fortunately, with the ones we have to decide for, Ficino seems really sure in most cases. It's the ones where he isn't sure that are causing me anguish."

"The difficult thing is deciding who's iron and who's bronze, when Plato gives no guidelines there at all," Kreusa said. "And it's hard to assess exactly what work each child has an aptitude for and ought to be trained for. Not to mention what work we need done. And who can train them for it."

"I think the Committee on Iron Work will report on training skills tomorrow night," Klio said.

"That's a relief," Kreusa said. "Thank you for telling me."

"When I talk to the children, they seem to know where they belong," Aristomache said.

"Well maybe you and Ficino can see into their souls, but it's difficult for me," Klio said. "There are always the ones on the edges. And getting the numbers, as you say—we have to have it done by the meeting by tribes on the Ides, when we'll do the final adjustment."

"Some of them are so certain and easy," I said. "So unquestionably one thing or the other, with the metals in their souls so clear even I can see them. Others are more of a puzzle. And as you say, it's so important. Such a responsibility. I'm very glad Ficino is so good at it. I'd hate to be doing it alone."

We came to the gates of the city then and bade each other joy of the day, and divided to go our separate ways on our common task.

16

SIMMEA

"How many golds are there?" I asked Axiothea one day as summer approached.

"Two hundred and fifty-two," she said.

I was thinking of Damon's question. It would take only thirty-one years for every gold to be married to every other gold, discounting time lost for pregnancy and potential repetitions. Did I want that? Could I avoid it? "Are they divided equally by gender?"

"Mm-hmm."

Then I stopped. "How many silvers?"

"Why do you want to know?" Axiothea asked, frowning.

I wanted to know because two hundred and fifty-two is such a very round number, considered as a percentage of ten thousand and eighty, but I wasn't Sokrates with the privilege of asking anything. If I made myself too much of a gadfly, I'd get swatted.

"Just curious," I said.

"Well, about a thousand," Axiothea said, clearly having thought better of her precise answer. "And about two thousand bronze. Just approximately. Now, to get back to the calculus?"

Later, in Thessaly I asked Sokrates if he knew the exact numbers. "Two hundred and fifty-two doesn't seem like a round number to me," he said.

"It's what you get if you divide ten thousand and eighty by exactly forty," I explained.

Kebes sat up in surprise. "You think they're not judging fairly?"

"Two hundred and fifty-two, divided equally by gender, can't possibly be chance. There must have been some people they either included to make up the number, or excluded to get it down."

"It could be chance," Pytheas said.

"Just barely possible," Sokrates said. "Numbers are difficult evidence. You can make them mean so many things."

"There are masters here who are obsessed with making them mean different things," Pytheas said.

"Not Axiothea," I protested.

"No, not Axiothea. I was thinking of old Plotinus, may he be reborn in this city. And some of his friends. Proclus. Hermeios. Even Ficino can get all starry-eyed about the mystical significance of numbers." Pytheas shook his head.

I nodded. "We need to find out how many silver and bronze. Exactly how many."

"I shall find out," Sokrates said. "Meanwhile, I tried an experiment today. I talked to a worker that was cleaning the street of Apollo early this morning."

"What did you say?" Pytheas asked.

"I asked it what it was doing and why, and whether it liked the work or preferred other things." Sokrates smiled. "It didn't reply."

"They don't talk," Kebes said. "I've told you before."

"Maybe they don't talk because nobody ever talks to them," Sokrates said. "I intend to persist. Perhaps they will find a way of answering."

The next day he had an answer to the question of numbers— there were eleven hundred and twenty silvers, and twenty-two hundred and forty bronzes.

"Leaving six thousand five hundred and eight iron," I said.

"Those are not random numbers," Kebes said.

"No," Sokrates said. "So we should revisit the question of how the masters decided to divide you up."

I had been thinking about it constantly since Axiothea had given me the number. "I think they must have had lots of dubious cases," I said. "I mean, take Klymene." I looked over at Pytheas, who didn't seem upset that I'd mentioned her. "She displayed cowardice once. But since then she has faced up to everything, she made herself brave. She's a gold. But they must have thought more than twice about whether she should be. If there had been somebody more deserving, somebody who had never showed cowardice, it wouldn't have been wrong for them to have set Klymene among the bronze, or more likely iron, because I don't think she has many artificing skills."

"But they didn't say," Klebes said.

"No," I agreed.

"Just no?" Sokrates asked.

"They didn't say, and they should have said. It makes a difference. We thought they were only thinking about our own worth, and actually they must have been thinking about numbers too."

"They had to make it gender-even," Pytheas said. "In every class. Because otherwise the weddings wouldn't work."

Kebes sighed.

"And is that so important? That everyone has a partner of their own rank?" Sokrates asked. "Could you not choose for yourself, as people did in Athens?"

"Women?" I asked. "Did women choose?"

"Their parents tended to arrange marriages," Sokrates said. "But they knew their own children."

"The masters know us. And the marriages are to be only for one day, not stuck forever, the way they usually were in other cultures. Were you happy in your marriage?" I knew he had not been.

"It's very difficult when people are married and don't like each other," Sokrates admitted.

"Did your parents like each other?" Kebes asked me.

I thought about it. "Yes. But they led very separate lives."

"My parents loved each other, and they loved me," Pytheas said. It was the first time I had ever heard him mention his parents. Sokrates too looked at him in astonishment. "They're still alive as far as I know, in the time I came from. They had a farm up above Delphi." He caught Sokrates's expression and laughed. "Not so far above Delphi! That's where I was born, sixteen years ago. In the hills, half a day's walk from the Pythian shrine."

"Would you like to have a marriage like they had?" Sokrates asked.

It was Pytheas's turn to look surprised. "I'd never thought about it." He looked away. "It's too hard to imagine."

"How about you, Simmea? Are you looking forward to the one-day marriages, or would you want a life partnership?"

Involuntarily I looked back at Pytheas, who was still staring into space. Kebes was glaring as I met his eye as I turned to look back at Sokrates. "We can have friendships for life," I said. "And friendships don't have to be exclusive." I smiled at Kebes, but he kept on frowning.

"Plato didn't have as much experience of humanity as he needed to write a book like the *Republic*," Sokrates said. "Perhaps nobody does."

"What sort of experience would it take?" Pytheas asked, smiling, and we were off down another dialectical avenue exploring that.

I thought about Sokrates's question when I was alone that night. Klymene and the others were sleeping and the light was off. If I could choose—well, it would be Pytheas, of course, but would he choose me? I was better off as I was. I knew he liked me and valued me, but would he want that kind of marriage if it were an option? I didn't think he would. Kebes definitely would, but I wouldn't want it with Kebes. I didn't know enough about it. I thought of my parents. It seemed so long ago. I wondered if my mother could still be alive. Then I realised that "still" meant nothing, she wasn't even born yet, and in another sense she was certainly dead. Then I sat up in bed. If we could move through time, could we change things? Could we go back to before the slavers came with an armed troop of Silvers and prevent them from killing my father and brothers? If I prayed to Athene?

I prayed, and felt as an answer to my prayer a strong urge to go to the library. I got up and dressed and found my way through the dark streets. There was no moon, and it was very late and the sconces were dimmed. I went to the big library in the southwest corner. It was not so grand as the one by the Agora, but it had a charming bronze Athene by the door which always seemed to be welcoming me. It was here that I had learned to read.

The doors were open, and inside the lights were on. I looked about for direction. Would the goddess send me to a book? I waited for guidance but none came. After a while I walked up to the seat where I usually worked and took out Newton's *Principia*. I knew there was nothing in it about time travel.

When I had been reading for a few minutes, I saw Septima. She was shelving. I watched her, then stood and went over to her. "What are you doing here in the middle of the night?" she whispered.

"I couldn't sleep, and thought I might as well read. How about you?"

"I couldn't sleep, and thought I might as well work. Why couldn't you sleep?" She looked inquiringly at me.

"I suddenly thought of something."

"Let's go and sit on the steps where we can talk out loud," she said.

"But . . . there's nobody else here!"

"I don't think I could raise my voice in here, even in the middle of the night," she admitted. We went outside and sat on the steps by the feet of the bronze Athene. "What did you think of?" she asked, and her normal voice sounded loud after the quiet.

"Moving through time. We all did it. The goddess brought us here that way. If she can do that, she could use it to change things that have happened. We could raise a bodyguard and go back and save my family from the slavers."

"We could raise an army and save Constantinople from the Turks," Septima said.

"Yes, exactly!" I said, glad she had understood so quickly.

"I've thought about this a lot, and no, we couldn't. The gods are bound by Fate and Necessity, and Necessity only allows the kind of changes in time that nobody notices. We can't change what's fated to happen. One vanished sculpture," she patted the shiny bronze toe of the goddess, "is neither here nor there. Two slave children?" She gestured at us. "Thousands of people like us lived and died and made no difference. When Fate is involved, especially when the gods know what happened and try to change it? That just makes everything worse."

"How could it make it worse if—" I decided to use her example rather than my own. "—if we saved Constantinople?"

"Without the fall of Constantinople bringing manuscripts to Italy, there might have been no Renaissance. Constantinople hadn't done much for civilization throughout the Middle Ages. It had held on, that's all. It hadn't built anything new, produced any new and truly wonderful books or art or scientific discoveries. The flowering of the Renaissance, on the other hand . . ." She spread out her hands.

"Is it like the bit in the *Iliad* when Zeus is deciding whether to let Patroklus die or live for a bit longer, and Patroklus kills all those other people, who clearly don't matter to Zeus even though

Patroklus and Achilles do?" I'd recently been allowed to read the unexpurgated Homer.

"Just like that."

"Then my family didn't matter?" I hated that thought.

"They mattered. Everyone matters. But not everything is bound by fate. Everyone has their own fate, that they chose before they were born. But they're just choosing a chance of filling out as much as they can of the shape of it. What actually happens is up to the choices they make—well, until they come right up to the edges, where they run into Necessity. Necessity is the line drawn around what anyone can do. Life is full of randomness and chance and choices, and only some things matter to fate. The difficulty is knowing which things." She sighed. "I talked to Krito once about why most of the male masters here were old when most of the women were young. It seems it's because men achieve so much more in their lives, and they couldn't be missed from them until they were near to death, whereas most women might as well not exist for all the individual contribution most of us get to make to history."

I thought about that. "Some of the women are older. Lukretia of Ferrara is. And Aristomache of Olympia must be at least fifty."

"Aristomache translated Plato into the vernacular in Boston in eighteen eighty-three," Septima said. "She published it anonymously. Nobody in her time would have trusted a woman as a scholar. But her translation helped a lot of young people discover philosophy. She couldn't come until she'd finished it, and until after a friend of hers had written a poem to her." Septima shook her head. "I really like Aristomache. She really *deserves* to be here."

"And some of the men are younger," I said. "Like Lysias, and Ikaros."

"Oh, Ikaros," she said, her eyes softening at the thought of him. "He deserves to be here too. He died before he had the chance to do what he could have done. But he's spending so much time with Sokrates now. He hardly ever has time to talk to me."

"Do you ever think the masters envy us?" I asked.

"Yes. They obviously do. Who wouldn't?"

It was so strange to hear her certainty, after spending so much time talking to Sokrates. "I think this is the best place, too," I said.

"Even if we can't go and fix time?" she asked.

"Not even Necessity knows all ends," I quoted. She laughed. I found myself yawning. "Perhaps I should go to bed now."

"Good night, Simmea," Septima said, and went back into the library.

For a moment I wanted to run after her and tell her that I knew she was Pytheas's sister and ask about their childhood to- gether. She was a very reserved person, difficult to get to know. I seldom saw her except in the library. That was one of the most intimate conversations I'd ever had with her. But when I imag- ined telling her that Pytheas had told me their secret I could only picture her pulling away. I watched the doors swing shut behind her, then walked slowly back through the city towards my bed.

17

MAIA

"Did you ever wonder why Plato isn't here?" Klio asked one evening in the Year Seven as we were walking back after a debate. She and Axiothea had their arms around each other. They were an established couple now. Lysias was walking beside me. He and I were not so much a couple as friends who did on occasion share eros—the true note of our relationship was definitely philia. As far as eros goes, silphium always worked so far, for me and for the other female masters, though I always fretted about it.

"I suppose he didn't pray to be here?" I suggested.

"He knew it wouldn't work. He never intended it to be tried seriously. He was just trying to provoke debate."

"Well that may be true, but that doesn't mean we're wrong to want to try it," Lysias said. "And it is working."

"It's mostly sort-of partly working," Klio said.

We came to my door and I opened it. "Wine? Cake?" The debate about whether it was appropriate to take food out of the eating halls had been decided in favor, as long as the food was always shared. We all went in and I fetched the wine and the mixer. Lysias took the cups out and distributed them, while Axiothea took the cushions off the bed and put them on the floor. I mixed the wine—half and half as we always drank it, on Plato's recommendation.

"It's working. We have children who love philosophy, who think a debate between Manlius and Tullius is the best imaginable way to spend an evening. I envy them sometimes," Lysias said, as I put little nut cakes on a plate.

"Me too," I said, passing the plate to Axiothea and sitting down on the floor beside Lysias. He and I leaned on the bed, and the other two against the wall, on the pillows. "I envy them. And even more I envy the next generation. The babies that will be born here. The native speakers, as you said once, Klio. Our children will do better at giving them the Republic than we did for our children, because we're a pile of crazy idealists from all over time, and our children grew up here."

"Sokrates thinks we're wrong," Axiothea said. "He's teaching all sorts of people to question all sorts of things. When I first heard what he thinks about Plato, it really rocked me."

"Sokrates doesn't believe in the Noble Lie," I said, sipping my wine.

"Sometimes it's necessary, but I'd prefer to avoid it too," Lysias said quietly.

"When a doctor—" Axiothea began.

"We all know the argument," Klio interrupted.

"Would you have the Noble Lie debate with Tullius or Ficino?" Axiothea asked.

"Debate it in Chamber, you mean?" Lysias asked. "Maybe."

"How about in public?" I asked.

"That would be tantamount to telling the children we've lied to them," Klio said.

"We're going to have to tell them sometime. Before we all die and they need to run things for the next generation," Lysias pointed out. "They're not supposed to read the *Republic* until they're fifty, and then only the golds."

"We'll need to tell some of them. Some carefully selected subset." Axiothea shook her head. "The real problem is all the old men who don't want to let anything go."

"Tullius," I said.

"Not just Tullius. Others too. They're men, they're from societies where men have the power, they're older, they're used to being the people giving orders. They come here and they find out that they're famous to people from future centuries. They're not going to want to give that up, even to Philosopher Kings." Klio frowned. "They don't like debating me or Myrto. And Aristomache has stopped trying, even though she's one of the sharpest minds here."

"Ikaros will debate you," Lysias said.

"Oh, Ikaros!" She looked quickly at me. "I think he has the opposite problem. Here he's just like us. He isn't the kind of famous he'd have wanted to be. He didn't have the chance to be. But he's brilliant. He wants his posterity to be here."

"I think that's unfair," Lysias said. "When I heard that Pico della Mirandola was here, I was just as excited as when I heard that Cicero and Boethius were. And Ikaros is happy to be known by philosophers. He didn't care about wide fame as long as the best people knew about him."

"I'd never heard of him," I said.

"Me neither," Axiothea said. "But I'm a mathematician."

"And I wasn't anything," I said.

"You were a scholar in a world that wouldn't let you be," Klio said, reaching over and patting my hand. "That's a lot more than nothing. But I think I'm right about what Ikaros thinks about his posterity."

"I think most of us want our posterity to be here," I said. "Our legacy. I certainly do. And you know, in the normal course of time the old men will die off and there will be a time when we are old but alive and we can make the decisions about what to hand on to the children and when."

"I thought of that when Plotinus died last year," Klio said. "But when the children are fifty I'll be nearly eighty, and even you will be almost seventy."

"And our posterity will not be here," Axiothea said. "We have no posterity. Athene told us that in the beginning. Doing it has to be enough."

"It's enough for me," I said.

"I don't think it's enough for Ikaros, now Plotinus is dead," Klio said.

"What more could he want? We're living the good life. We're building the Just City," Lysias said. "We knew from the beginning that it wasn't going to last, that it couldn't. We're all making sacrifices for that."

"Like what?" Axiothea asked, pouring more wine.

"Like working so hard, and not having children," Lysias said.

"But working hard is mostly fun, and all the children are our children," I said.

"You don't want children of your own?" he asked.

I emphatically did not. "They wouldn't fit into the plan," I said.

"You see," Lysias said, spreading his hands.

"I don't feel we're making a sacrifice," I said.

Klio nodded. "I think we're very lucky to be here. Though I never imagined when we started that I'd spend half my time working with workers."

"Me neither," Lysias groaned. "And some of them are refusing to leave the recharger, and I don't know what to do about it. I'd have taken a course on robotics if I'd had the least idea how much I'd need it. I was a philosopher. I just used them without thinking about it."

"Are you sure you'd have been able to fit another course in?" Klio teased.

"It would have been a lot more use than German," he said, and laughed. "Well, bless Athene for giving us the workers anyway, even if I wish she'd included some manuals and information on how they really work. Without them we'd be doing a lot of backbreaking work."

"It is working, isn't it?" Axiothea said. "Mostly sort of, like you said. But we are making it work. We're proving Plato right."

We grinned at each other and raised our cups in a silent toast.

18

SIMMEA

The games came first. I didn't get through the heats except in swimming, where I came in third. Laodike won the long distance race for running in armor. I cheered so hard I almost lost my voice. Then Axiothea, who was next to me, pounded me so hard on the back she almost cracked a rib. Her good friend Klio of Sparta hugged both of us, and then hugged Laodike when she came up panting with the ribbons from her crown falling in her eyes. "A girl to win the race for running in armor," Klio said, and her eyes were damp.

"Why not?" I asked.

"Why not indeed?" asked Axiothea. "Some people say men are stronger."

"They often are, but women tend to have more endurance," Laodike panted. "Running in armor is at least as much endurance as strength."

The next day was the festival of Hera. I was up before dawn to help make flower garlands. The workers had brought masses of flowers down from the hills and piled them in each hall. In Florentia they were piled downstairs in the courtyard. Six of us twined them into seventy headdresses and thirty-five garlands, and we were barely done in time. Anemones have terrible stems, and hyacinths drop little bits everywhere—thank Demeter for long sturdy daisies and twining roses that look wonderful to-gether, especially with a few violets tucked in. By the time every-one arrived for breakfast, we were finished and congratulating ourselves. I was famished and ate two bowls of porridge, a big handful of cherries and an egg. Maia hugged me on my way out. "Good luck," she said.

I was afraid the festival was going to drag out like the festival where we were all named, but they had learned something and it did not. There was music and dancing, and names were drawn ten at a time and announced in bursts, maybe every ten minutes or so. Then we'd all dance again as those ten went up the tem-ple steps in their headdresses to have garlands bound around their wrists as they were married for the day.

Dancing is always fun, and dancing with friends to music and without set patterns is even better. I had a strange nervous feeling in the pit of my stomach and I tried to dance it down. One hundred and twenty-six male golds, any of whom I could end up married to. I wasn't at all sure I wanted to have a baby. I looked cautiously at the black stone statue of Hera, facing the great seated ivory and gold Zeus across the temple steps. "Give me the good for which I do not know to ask," I prayed.

I avoided both Pytheas and Kebes. I didn't want to think about either of them. Kebes was called early and matched with Euridike from Plataea. Ficino bound the wreath around their wrists and Kreusa called out the blessing. Euridike was blushing, which really showed up on her fair skin. I danced more vigor-ously. Pytheas hadn't been called yet. I could see him over on the far side of the agora in another dancing circle.

When my name was called my stomach clenched so hard I almost bent double. I let go of Klymene's hand and walked to-wards the steps with my friends calling after me—wishes of luck and happiness. I was paired with Aeschines, from Ithaka. I knew him only slightly. He was very dark-skinned with big lips, a Libyan like my grandmother. We stood together shyly as Ficino bound the garland around our wrists. It was not one of the ones I had made; every hall had brought a supply. This one had poppies and anemones twisted in a white ribbon. I stared at it to avoid meeting Aeschines's eyes. We walked down the steps carefully, and off through the crowd. I kept my eyes on the ground. I did not want to see or speak to anyone, most especially not Pytheas.

We crossed the square and walked down the street of Demeter, wrists together. The crowds were thinner here, and as we went on and came away from the sound of music we found ourselves almost alone. When we came to the plaza where the street of Demeter crosses the street of Dionysos, Aeschines stopped. "There are chambers down here," he said, gesturing with his free hand.

"All right," I said. We turned to the left. "Did they tell you about this?"

"Ikaros, one of the masters from Ferrara, explained it to all the boys of Ithaka and Ferrara," he said. "I expect one of your masters explained it to the Florentines."

"I wish Maia had explained it to me," I said.

"Why, are you nervous?"

"Yes," I admitted. "I suppose it's just because this is the first time and I don't know enough about it. I saw my mother raped, and then more women were raped on the slave ship." That had been the stuff of nightmare for years. "So I have some uncomfortable feelings."

"I'm sorry," he said. "I'll try not to hurt you."

"Thank you." I looked at him. He was tall and earnest and his brow was furrowed now as he looked down at me. He wasn't flawless Pytheas, my best friend and secret beloved. But if I had hoped for that, I had also known that the odds were a hundred and twenty-five to one.

"Here," he said. There was a low hall which I had used before. It was full of practice rooms where people learning the lyre could sit in bad weather. Some of the doors lay open and others were closed. In the open ones I could see mattresses covered with blankets. We went into one and closed the door.

"Are all the practice rooms going to be used for this?" I asked, trying not to look at the bed.

"I don't know. Ikaros said this was where we should go." He unwound the garland and rubbed his wrist. "That was a bit tight."

I smiled. "This is a horribly awkward situation."

"It would almost be better if we were complete strangers and could introduce ourselves."

"I'm Simmea," I said.

He laughed. "I know. And you're a Florentine, and one of Sokrates's pupils, and you did a painting of some girls racing. That's all I know about you."

"That's more than I know about you," I said. I sat down on the edge of the bed. "I think I've seen you with Septima?"

"She's a good friend," he said. "She knows so much."

"I had a great conversation with her the other day about why the gods can't change history," I said. He took off his headdress and stood holding it awkwardly in both hands.

"There's nowhere to put things," he said, looking around. "I don't want to drop this on the floor. Somebody must have spent a lot of time making it."

"I made ones for us this morning," I said. "They don't take long, once you get the hang of it." I took mine off and showed him the construction. "These big daisies make everything easy."

Aeschines took my headdress and put them both down gently in the corner of the room. Then he came back over to the bed and sat down next to me. "Are you afraid?" he asked.

"More nervous and awkward and ignorant," I said.

He put his arm around me and moved his face slowly towards mine. He then kissed me tentatively. "How was that?" he asked.

I laughed, because he sounded so much like somebody beginning a philosophic inquiry. "I think that was quite nice," I said. "The problem is that there are all these things I'm trying not to think about—the slavers on the ship, and what happened to my mother. And I'm not quite sure what I am supposed to be thinking about."

"You're supposed to focus on sensation, Ikaros said. Like eating, when you just taste the food and you're there in that moment, except also focusing on the other person and what they're feeling."

"But how can you tell?"

"Pardon?" He looked disconcerted.

"How can you tell what the other person is feeling? I have no idea what you're feeling!"

"I'm feeling that you're very nervous but kissing you was nice," he said. "The other thing Ikaros said is that there's no hurry. We've got all afternoon and all night. We don't have to do it all in the first two seconds. We can be comfortable. We can try things."

We tried various things to make ourselves comfortable. What worked best was standing naked and leaning into each other, the way we might when wrestling. That way, upright and with my legs firmly in a wrestling stance, nothing reminded me of anything horrible, and I could enjoy the feeling of Aeschines's chest against mine. We kissed standing like that, and then he began to rub the sides of my breasts. He was so earnest and sensitive that I started to feel safe with him. I rubbed his chest, and moved my hand lower. When I touched his penis he made a movement as if electrified and, looking at his face, I saw that his eyes were shut and his head thrown back. I had often seen penises when swimming and in the palaestra, so they were no novelty, but I had never voluntarily touched one, especially not one that was awake. Aeschines's was awake. I stroked it gently, experimentally. He twitched again. I began to understand what Ikaros had meant about paying attention to how the other person felt. I liked it. I was making him feel like that. I felt in control. This was good. Then his hands moved between my legs and I felt my breath catch.

Afterwards I wasn't sure how I felt about it. "Did you like it?" Aeschines asked.

"Yes . . ." I said. "It was fun. I liked the way you liked it. I liked lots of things about it. I wish we could do it standing up."

"We could try," he said. "In a little bit, when I've rested."

"Is that allowed?"

"Sure. We're married until tomorrow morning. We can do it as many times as we want to before that. Ikaros was quite plain about that."

We did it twice more. Standing up was definitely better for me, both in feeling in control and just generally comfortable. Later we slept uncomfortably together in the bed.

"So I guess we're friends now," Aeschines said as got dressed the next morning.

"We definitely are." I smiled at him. "You could come and eat in Florentia with me tonight if you want."

"That feels strange," he said. "I didn't know you, and now I know that you like doing sex standing up."

"Don't tell anybody!"

"Of course not!" He sounded shocked, which was a relief. "Boys do talk about it sometimes. I always thought they were lying. About getting girls to sneak off to the woods with them. Specific girls. And what those girls liked. It's a kind of showing off they do when they jerk off."

"Jerk off?"

He mimed with his hand. "At night, in the sleeping houses, standing round together with everyone doing that and nobody touching each other. Girls don't do that?"

"Not equipped," I said.

He laughed. "But nothing like that?"

"Not in Hyssop," I said. "I never heard of girls doing that, but that doesn't mean they don't. But I never heard of them sneaking off with boys, either."

"Would you do that?" he asked.

"What? Sneak off to the woods with you? No. That would be wrong." I wanted to get back to Hyssop and bathe in the wash-fountain before breakfast. "You're not seriously suggesting it?"

"No, of course not." I wasn't sure whether he meant it or not.

"Dinner tonight, then?" I asked, my hand on the door.

"Sure." He picked up the headdresses and garland from the corner. The flowers were dying, away from water for so long. "Do you want yours?"

"What for?"

"No, I suppose they're done with now." He turned them in his hands looking a little sad. "Well, I hope we do this again some time."

"So do I," I said, and meant it. I didn't share the calculations of probability with him, though.

19

APOLLO

"How are you going to get out of it?" I had cornered Athene in the library. She was sitting in the window seat she liked, the one where she had a secret compartment in the armrest, reading Tullius's newly printed monograph on the integrity of the soul.

"He's getting old," she said, putting it down on a mess of books and papers on the seat beside her.

"He is," I agreed. "Ikaros flattened him in their last debate. And he's been avoiding Sokrates."

"He's going to die soon, whatever I do. I know he's vain and silly, but I'm very fond of him."

"I am too. Even if you have to send him back to face his assassination, at least he got this extra length of his natural lifespan."

"I hate that cold bastard Octavian," she said. "Killing Cicero for political advantage. It's like burning down a library to make toast. I could never warm to Rome again until Marcus Aurelius." She picked up the book again, then hesitated and put it down. "Did you want to ask me something?"

"Yes. How are you going to get out of being paired off at the festival of Hera?"

"I'm sick of the subject of the festival of Hera. It's all anyone's talking about. I may be getting a bit bored with this whole thing, actually. Anyway, I shall be chosen and walk off with somebody, and then they will fall asleep and dream they've had a pleasant afternoon with Septima, while I come back to the library."

"Do you need help with the dream?" I asked.

"No thanks. There's a perfectly good bit of Catullus."

I laughed, quietly because we were in the library. The funny thing was that she was so serious. She rolled her eyes. "Sorry," I said. "I should have guessed you'd have a plan."

"Did you come to offer to help if I needed it?" she asked.

"Well..." I felt caught out. "I knew you wouldn't want to participate, and I hadn't thought of a dream."

"Well thank you. I don't need it. But I do appreciate the concern. I'd have thought you'd be looking forward to it. First sexual act in sixteen years?"

"I've been continent for longer before," I said. Though that was usually when I was focusing on something else and not noticing how long it had been. "And anyway, that isn't quite true. This will be the first time mating with a woman, but there have been some sex acts with men."

"Boys?"

"And masters."

"Not Pico?"

"No. He's never done more than look admiring." I wondered why she was asking, but her expression did not invite questions.

She picked up her book again and put her finger in it ready to open it. "So did you want me to influence the lots to get you whoever you have picked out for the festival?"

"No. I thought I'd go with chance. That way I'll learn something about choice."

She looked astonished. "I suppose that's true, but I'm surprised to hear you say so. I've never seen you with anyone who wasn't perfect. What will you do if it's your funny little Simmea? She's very smart, isn't she? I was talking to her about the constraints of time the other night."

"She's very smart," I agreed. Of course I knew she was in love with me. "It's extremely unlikely that we'd be chosen together, though."

Athene shook her head. "You're changing."

"Learning things. That was the whole idea."

She started to read, and I left.

The next day was the games, where I was careful to do well in everything without actually winning anything. Simmea came third in the swimming. I could swim now, but I didn't even enter the races. Human bodies aren't made for that kind of exercise. The day after was the festival. We wore flowered headdresses and danced in the plaza before the temple of Zeus and Hera. Phidias's huge chryselephantine seated Zeus stood on one side of the steps, and a large Hera from Argos stood on the other. I wondered, eyeing them, what Father knew about this enterprise, and what he would say. Athene was his favorite daughter, but even so. It would be possible to argue that we were bending his rules all over the place.

I avoided Simmea. I felt uncomfortable at the thought of her. I liked her very much. I admired her. I enjoyed her friendship. But Athene was right. In thousands of years I'd never mated with anyone who wasn't perfect. I didn't know if it was possible. If it turned out it wasn't with some random girl, that didn't matter all that much. With Simmea it could be a disaster.

It turned out I was worrying about entirely the wrong thing.

There's a whole section in Book Five of the *Republic* about how the masters are supposed to cheat with the sex festival, to make sure the best get to have the best children. The children of the less good will be exposed anyway, but while everyone's supposed to believe it's entirely random, they naturally cheat for eugenics. I hadn't forgotten this, but I had only thought it would mean that they'd be likely to match me with somebody beautiful after all. They did. But when I heard our names read out I froze.

"Pytheas, Klymene!" old Ficino read. My friends were pushing me forward and laughing. I walked mechanically towards the steps. I saw Klymene coming from the other side, not looking at me. The garland was tied around our wrists and our arms raised. Our eyes had still not met. We walked together down the steps and off through the dancers and down the street.

Eventually I looked at her. She was so pale and resolute that she'd have done for a portrait of Artemis. "I'm really sorry," I said.

"It's *random chance*," she said. "It's not your fault any more than it is mine. It's just Fortuna laughing at both of us."

"I mean I'm really sorry I said what I said to you on the mountain."

She looked at me now for the first time. "That's the latest apology I ever had."

"Simmea said you didn't want to talk to me. She beat me up. She made me realize what an idiot I was."

"She made me practice being brave until I could be brave again," Klymene said. "Simmea's a good friend. And I didn't want to talk to you right away. But it has been a long time. Years."

"I didn't know how long was long enough, and by then it had been a long time and it was awkward because of that." I brushed my hair back off my face and realized that our hands were still bound together. I started to unwind the garland.

"What are you doing?"

"I thought—"

"You thought I was a coward and wouldn't go through with it?" she suggested.

"I thought I was," I said. "Do you want to?"

"It's not a case of want, it's a case of our duty to the city and the gods. We were married in front of Zeus and Hera. All over

the city today, everyone is being married in front of the gods, so
that there can be more children for the city."

"You're right," I said.

"I don't like you, Pytheas. I don't trust you. It isn't just what
you said to me, it's other things. You're arrogant. You think so
much of yourself. You don't pay any attention to most people. I
was only ever friends with you because I knew you were Simmea's friend and she likes you. And when I had that cowardly
moment you covered for me. That was good. But afterwards
what you said just made me feel that you despised me—that
you didn't even see me. But this isn't about you. This is about
our sacred duty."

"I said you were right."

"Where are we going?"

I stopped walking. "They told me there were empty practice
rooms with beds in them." I waved vaguely. We had passed the
turning to the street of Dionysos and had to go back. We walked
now without talking. She was a pretty girl with nice breasts, soft
and dovelike, as I had always thought. I wondered what our
son would be like—a hero, certainly, but what kind? How
strange it would be to watch him grow up day by day. The masters wouldn't let us know which child was which, of course, but
I would know. If I didn't instinctively know I could ask Athene,
but I thought even incarnate I'd be able to tell.

We came to the hall and went inside, hands still bound. Inside most of the doors were closed, but we found an open one
far down the hall and closed the door. Only then did I unbind
the garland. The wild rose branch twined in it had pricked my
skin, leaving little beads of blood around my wrist. As I was
licking them, Klymene dropped her kiton with as little fuss as
if we were in the palaestra, and stood looking at me.

I had never before mated with a woman when we hadn't been
playing the game of running away and catching. I had always

been the one catching. I had mated for the joy of ecstasy, in a sudden passion for some woman, or to conceive children. Usually when I fell in love it was with men, who in my own time had minds with more to offer me. I have fallen in love with women, but it's rare. Sometimes women have refused me. (Cassandra and Sibyl were out for what they could get and deserved what they did get. In my opinion.)

This woman did not want me, but she was obedient to duty. I had to go to some considerable effort of imagination to want her, and to find duty in myself and the desire for a son. It helped that this was her first time, so I could instruct her into a position where I didn't have to look at her face. Her face was like stone, and would have made it impossible. It was probably more comfortable for her too. She didn't want foreplay—in fact she specifically refused it. "Let's get on with it," she said. I arranged her face down on the bed.

Father's big on rape. He likes to turn himself into animals or even weirder things and swoop down on girls and carry them off. I've always liked the chase, whether it's chasing a nymph through the woods or a seduction. Sometimes at the end of a seduction it's been almost like that. I remember once in Alexandria, a woman called Lyra. Sunlight through a shuttered window falling across white sheets. She was a professional card player, and I'd beaten her in the game when she'd put herself in on cards she thought were unbeatable. She wore a veil and made up her eyes with kohl. There had been a moment when she let the veil fall that was almost like it was with Klymene. But once we were in bed she'd been greedy, more like a man, seeking her own pleasure, crying out. Klymene wasn't like that at all.

Klymene wanted the result of this mating, but not the process. But enduring it was her choice. Having it happen at all was her choice. I would have undone the garland and gone off, and if we'd told nobody, nobody would ever have known, any more than Athene's partner, dreaming of Catullus, would ever know. That would have been my choice, to regret this match and let her be. We were in this room and this bed and I was in her body because she had chosen it, because it was our duty. I thought of Lyra's eyes above the veil. I tried not to think of Daphne. I thought of all the ones who *had* wanted me, who had met passion with passion and desire with desire, who fell in love with me and wrote poetry about it for the rest of their lives. Eventually, that was sufficient.

20

SIMMEA

It was with a mixture of relief and disappointment that I greeted the arrival of my monthly blood at the next new moon. Of the seven of us in Hyssop, four bled and three did not. Klymene was one of the ones who did not. She had been unusually tight-lipped about her experience during the festival. "Well, it took all my accumulated bravery," was all she had said in answer to my tentative question. Aeschines had eaten with us in Florentia twice and I had eaten with him in Ithaca once—sardines and bitter greens, delicious. I'd seen other new friendships that had come out of the festival. But not for Klymene.

We were in the wash-fountain getting clean one morning when Makalla suddenly said: "Maia said we shouldn't count on being pregnant even if we don't bleed. We should wait until next month to be sure." She sounded apprehensive.

"I'm delighted to be pregnant," Klymene said.

"Because you won't have to go through that again?" I asked, rinsing my hair.

"Well, not for some time anyway," Makalla said.

"It wouldn't be as bad as that another time," Klymene said. "No, I'm just glad to be having a baby, to be doing my duty and making a new generation of citizens."

"I am too," Makalla said. "I just don't want to count on anything before I can be sure."

For a moment I was sorry I wasn't pregnant too. I felt left out and lazy. Immediately I wondered what Sokrates would think about that and began to interrogate the feeling. It was nonsense. I'd tried as hard as anyone. Maybe next time it would work. It was a pity it wouldn't be Aeschines again. I liked him and he liked me. But there was always the hope that it would be Pytheas.

I spent that time working on the calculus with a small group Axiothea had drawn together of people who really liked higher mathematics for its own sake, and not as a means of mystical revelation. Mystical revelation through numerology was very popular, especially in halls that had Neoplatonist masters. What we worked on had no practical application I could see but the joy of learning it. I loved it.

Of course I also painted a great deal, and debated constantly with Sokrates. Debating with Sokrates remained a delight and a terror. I was getting better at it, but he still surprised me frequently. It honed my mind, so that in debate with others, I was considered formidable. Pytheas and Kebes too learned Sokrates's methods, and grew in debate. We began to wonder whether we could challenge the masters. Listening to debates was one of our most popular forms of entertainment—Tullius against Ikaros on the benefits of synthesis against original research, or Ficino against Adeimantus on the virtues of translation. I began to have an idea that I might one day challenge one of the younger masters, perhaps Ikaros or Klio.

One day I went running in the mountains and met Laodike and Damon, returning from a run. I didn't see them often any more; the division into silver and gold had made a difference. They looked awkward, and I tried hard to be especially friendly, sharing some figs I had brought. We sat in the shade of a rock to eat them. "You're not running straight up the mountain any more, then?" I asked.

"We've been doing a lot of cross-country scrambling," Damon said. "It's supposed to be good practice for war. Not that there's anyone to fight."

"I can't fight right now anyway," Laodike said. She patted her stomach, which had a slight curve.

"Joy to you!" I said. "Klymene's pregnant too, you know."

"Maybe you'll manage it next time," she said. "There are definite advantages."

Damon shot her a worried glance. "I don't think—"

"Oh, Simmea's our friend, she won't tell anyone. And we know about her and Pytheas, just the same as you and me."

"I won't tell anyone whatever it is, but Pytheas and I aren't . . . whatever you think. We're friends." I felt blood heating my cheeks.

Laodike laughed. "Well, once you're pregnant you can't get more pregnant, so if you can find somewhere quiet to do it, like up here, you can safely copulate with your friend."

I looked at the two of them. They both looked embarrassed now, and a little sheepish, but also happy in a way that stung my heart. Their hands crept together, intertwined, and clung. Plato said that friendship was good but adding sex to it was bad, but perhaps understandable in silvers. It wasn't hurting anyone in any case. "I won't tell anyone, and I'm glad it's working for you. I'm so pleased I saw you. I miss you in Hyssop. We should do a run together before you get as big as a sleeping house."

Shortly after that came the second festival of Hera. I had wondered how they were going to manage with some of the women being pregnant and unavailable but all of the men still being free. The answer was that the women were carefully counted, in each class, and that number of men were selected to participate, partly at random and partly by merit. The merit consisted in doing well either in the athletic contests or in their work in the four months since the last time. Then every man who didn't qualify by merit had his name set in an urn and they were chosen by lot.

Pytheas's name was second drawn. He was matched with Kryseis and they went off together, seeming content. I drew Phoenix, of Delphi, whom I already knew quite well—we had often raced and wrestled together. He wasn't as considerate as Aeschines, and much faster. He also wanted me to suck his penis with my mouth, which I refused, because it reminded me of the slave ship. He sulked about this, and said that his previous partner had done it and that the boys all did it for each other. The encounter wasn't much fun, and I didn't invite him for dinner in Florentia afterwards.

Nor was it productive. Auge became pregnant, but I didn't and nor did any of the rest of us in Hyssop. Makalla and Klymene were four months along, showing big breasts and big bellies already, and excused from exercise in the palaestra. Charmides said that swimming would be good for them and that they should take regular gentle walks. Klio taught them vaginal exercises.

"How does she know them?" Makalla giggled. "Has she ever had a baby?"

There was no way to know about the lives of the masters before they came to the city. Klio might have had several children. None of them were here. I wondered if she missed them. I thought about what Septima had said about time.

Auge found her early pregnancy difficult—she vomited every morning. She complained that she was too weak to move marble—she sculpted, and was very good, but now she felt cut off from her art. She broke up with her lover and cried herself to sleep, then when Iphis went to comfort her they ended up beginning a passionate friendship that Klymene found difficult to

deal with. They said, giggling, that it was Platonic agape. Klymene had to insist that they each slept in their own bed. It was
unsettling. I missed Laodike and Andromeda, who were much
more comfortable to live with and who had truly felt like sisters.

21

MAIA

Klymene came to me late one night. I encouraged all the Florentines to come to me any time they had a problem, so I wasn't very
surprised when I opened the door and saw her there. Lysias was
curled up asleep in my bed, so I went out to her. It was a cool
night with an edge of chill in the air. "Let's go to my office in
Florentia," I said. "We can be comfortable and you can tell me
whatever it is."

We went to the kitchen first and took plates. We each helped
ourselves to some olives, slices from a half-cut round of goat
cheese, and some barley bread left over from supper. "As good
as a feast," Klymene said.

"It's good to see you want it," I said.

"Yes, I was so sick for the first three months." She patted her
belly, which was just starting to show. We were all excited about
the first babies. "Now I'm starving all the time."

We settled ourselves in my study. There was a new hanging
on the wall in gold and green and brown which some of the
Florentines I'd been teaching weaving had given to me. The
cloth wasn't as even as the worker-made cloth, but they had sewn
the different coloured stripes together in a charming way. I
stroked the edge of it as I sat down. "Problems in Hyssop?" I
asked.

Klymene swallowed her bread. "No. Well, yes, the same thing, Auge and Iphis, you know. Nothing different."

"You should insist that they sleep in their own beds," I said.

"I do. But it disrupts everybody. And even needing to keep insisting is disruptive. I wonder sometimes—well, that's what I came to see you about." She took a deep breath. "Who decided which metals were strongest in our souls?"

"Ficino and I did," I said. "With advice from other masters who knew you."

"Do you think you might have made any mistakes?" she asked.

"We thought about it very hard and talked about it a lot, and we don't think we did. Why are you asking? Is it because you think Auge and Iphis aren't behaving like philosophers?"

"No," she said. "It's me. This is so difficult."

"You're only seventeen," I said. "Nobody expects you to be perfect right away. You have new responsibilities, and they're difficult, but you're dealing with them. It can be easy to feel discouraged when things go wrong, but philosophy will help. And we weren't just looking at how you are now, we were looking at how you're going to develop." It was why it had been so difficult and such a tremendous responsibility.

"You don't understand." Klymene picked up an olive and turned it over and over in her hand, staring down at it. "Can I talk about before we came here?" she asked, not looking up.

"You shouldn't," I said. "But you can if you really need to. If it will help me understand what you're worried about."

"I was a slave," she said, as if it cost her an effort to admit it. After she said it, she looked up from the olive at last to meet my eyes.

"There's no shame in that. You all were," I said, surprised.

"But I was born a slave. Most of the others were captured, or sold into captivity quite a short time before they were brought here. My mother was a slave, and I was born one and grew up one. All that time, I never even imagined being free. I think it did something to me. I think I have shackles on my soul and a slave's heart, and I'm not really worthy to be a gold."

"That's ridiculous," I said, gently. I ate a piece of cheese while thinking what to say. "You've been here for seven years, you've been trained. You were very young when you came. Nothing that happened before counts."

"Yes, it does," she said. She was close to tears. "Can I please explain?"

"Go on then," I said.

"My name has always been Klymene. I was born in Syracuse, at the time of the Carthaginian wars. My mother was a bath slave. She was Carthaginian. Her name was Nyra. I don't know who my father was, but it was probably our master, whose name was Asterios."

I listened, trying to imagine a life like that. "Was he unkind to you?"

"No, he petted me and indulged me when he saw me, which wasn't all that often. He was Greek, of course. I look like my mother. I imagined I would grow up to have a life like hers, serving at the bath, sleeping with the master. It didn't seem so bad. I carried water and bath oils. I was learning massage. I spoke Greek, and Punic, that was the slave language, and a little bit of Latin. Nobody taught me to read, though they easily could have. There were slave clerks in the house, but they were all men. They never thought of it. I never thought of it."

"For most of history it was really unusual for women to be taught to read," I said. Nobody except Plato had seen that we were human. It still made me angry to think of all those wasted lives.

"I was pretty, like my mother, and if I had dreams it was that some man would fall in love with me because of that and I could cajole him into treating me well. It's what my mother did.

What she was teaching me." She shook her head and put the olive down on her untouched plate. "The overseer was called Felix. He terrorized us all. He had a dog on a chain at the door to the slave quarters. I hated to pass it, it always leapt at me snarling, and Felix laughed and said it would eat me up one day. But that's not what happened."

"What did happen?" I got up and poured her a cup of wine, and one for myself. Imagining her early life was distressing; living through it must have been appalling. I thanked Athene in my heart that I had been so lucky.

"When I was nine years old, my master caught my mother in bed with Felix. She had no choice about it. Felix had a dog and a whip, and what did she have? But Asterios didn't see it that way. He didn't punish Felix, he punished her. He whipped her in the courtyard in front of everyone, to punish her supposed lusts. Then, to punish her more, he had me whipped. And then immediately, the same afternoon, he dragged me down to the harbor and sold me onto a slave ship going east, where there would be no chance that my mother would ever see me again." She picked up the cup and took a deep swallow. "He didn't even say so to me. He said it to the slaver he was selling me to, and I heard. I wasn't even a person to him. He shook me when I tried to speak, to remind him how he had always been good to me. And he slapped me hard when I bit his hand. I was just a thing to him, a thing he could use on my mother. He petted me to make her loving to him, and then he sold me away to punish her. He didn't see me as human, let alone as a daughter. He had his real family on the other side of the house. I'd served at his real daughter's baths. I wasn't real, do you see?"

"You were real," I said. I was shaken. "You were absolutely real and you were a child and I'm so glad we rescued you from that." I wished we could do the same for every slave there ever was, that we could buy them and bring them here to live free.

"You rescued my body, but part of my soul is still there," she said. "It's why I ran, that time, with the boar, because I'm slave-hearted. And now I can't keep order in Hyssop. I'm just no good."

"You're keeping order. And you've worked and worked to become brave!" I wanted to hug her, but she held herself in a way that didn't invite it.

"Yes, but others didn't have to do that," she said, fiercely. "And I wonder what else there is like that about me, where my soul is still stuck there. With being the watcher, I keep wanting to cajole instead of being decisive. And that's not the worst of it. I always thought like a slave. I wanted to please the masters, not to seek for the truth. I'd see Simmea arguing with Ficino, going after a point like a terrier, and at first I'd just be amazed that she dared, and that he didn't slap her down for it. I don't know how long it was before I understood that it was what he wanted."

"But you did understand," I said.

"Yes, but you don't see. I still thought like a slave. I was trying to give you what you wanted, not trying to become my best self. And you didn't see that, you didn't, you made me a gold and I'm not fit to be a guardian, it was all pretense. I was pretending to be free, but in my heart I'm still a slave."

I tried to make sense of this. "Are you saying that you're still trying to please us instead of striving for excellence?"

She hesitated, and touched her belly. "No. I realized what I was doing and why it was wrong. My duty—wanting to do my duty, even when I could have got out of it without anyone knowing. Reading Plato, debating with Kebes about freedom and choices, and especially thinking about the baby, about him or her growing up in the city. I finally realized I am free. And I do love wisdom, and I do love the truth. I've been coming to that for some time. And I can't build it on a lie. That's why I've come to you now. To confess my deception. Before the baby's born. I want to become my best self, and I don't want to deceive you any more."

"Deception is a crooked road to truth, but that's where it's leading you," I said, standing up.

"What?" She looked up at me, confused.

"You're confessing your deception because in feigning loving truth you've truly come to love it," I said.

"Yes," she said.

"And so you are worthy to be gold. Maybe I was wrong, maybe I made a mistake and was deceived, but Ficino saw into your soul. There are people whose souls are ideally suited from birth for them to be philosophers, but there are others whose souls have to be trained, like vines on a trellis. We built the trellis in the city, and though you started twisted you grew straight."

"Like Simmea's legs," she said, utterly confounding me.

"Simmea's legs?"

"When we came, Simmea's legs were bandy. Now they're straight and strong. You're saying the same thing happened to my soul?"

"Yes," I said, and I hugged her hard. "Your children will start clean, without any bad memories or twisted beginnings. They'll prove everything Plato believed, become what he wanted. We masters are helping you and you will help them and they will make the Just City."

She hugged me back. "I'm free," she said, marvel in her voice.

22

SIMMEA

One morning Kebes and I went from breakfast to follow Sokrates around the city as we often did. We found him questioning a worker planting bulbs outside the temple of Demeter. "Do you like your work? Do you feel a sense of satisfaction doing it? Are there some jobs you enjoy more than others?"

"I don't know why you keep doing that when you know they're not going to answer," Kebes said.

"I don't know that," Sokrates said. "Joy to you, Kebes, joy to you Simmea! I know they haven't answered yet, but I don't know whether they might answer in the future. I don't even have an opinion on the subject."

"Everyone knows they're tools," Kebes said.

"They're not like tools," Sokrates said. "They're self-propelled, and to a certain extent self-willed. That one is making decisions about where to space the bulbs, precise and careful decisions. Those are going in a row, look, and then that one at an angle. It's deliberate, not random. It may be a clever tool, but it may have self-will, and if it has self-will and desires, then it would be very interesting to talk to."

"A tree would be interesting to talk to——" Kebes began, but Sokrates interrupted.

"Oh yes, wouldn't it!" We laughed and followed him on.

A few months later, early in Gamelion, Kebes and I were walking along with Sokrates debating one morning when we happened to come back to the place outside the temple of Demeter where the worker had been planting bulbs when Sokrates asked it questions. A set of early crocuses had come up, deep purple with gold hearts. They were arranged in an odd pattern, two straight lines connected by a diagonal and then a circle. Sokrates glanced at them. "Spring after winter is always a joy to the heart," he said, though he never seemed to feel the cold.

Kebes frowned at them. "It's almost as if—no. I'm being silly."

"What is it?" Sokrates asked.

"Well, you remember the worker was planting bulbs here when you asked it questions? The pattern the bulbs are planted in looks like N and then O in the Latin alphabet, which is like the beginning of *non*, the Latin for *no*."

Sokrates stared at Kebes, and then back at the bulbs. "As if the worker were trying to answer me as best it could, with the materials it had? And as if it answered in Latin? Why would it do that, I wonder?"

"Latin was the language of civilization in the West for centuries," I said.

"But it didn't finish the word. Perhaps it ran out of bulbs. Or perhaps I'm imagining the whole thing," Kebes said. "Seeing a pattern where there isn't one."

"It must have understood my questions, to answer no," Sokrates said, ignoring this. "My questions were in Greek."

"They were. It doesn't make much sense," I said. "But it does look deliberate. Let's go on and see if it used this pattern in any of the other plazas."

It hadn't. Lots of the plazas had crocuses, but all of them were arranged in four neat vertical rows.

"What did I ask it?" Sokrates mused. "If it enjoyed its work?"

"I think so," I said. "If there was anything it preferred doing. A whole pile of questions at once, typical of you!"

"So I can't know which, if any, the no was intended to answer!" He ran his fingers through his hair, which was standing on end anyway. "Where's Pytheas?"

"I think he's in the palaestra this morning."

"We must find him at once." Sokrates set off rapidly in the wrong direction. Kebes and I got him turned around and walking just as fast towards the Florentine/Delphic palaestra.

"Why do you want Pytheas?" Kebes asked as we trailed him.

"The first time I asked about workers he said he had a belief that they were tools," Sokrates said. "I want to know who told him that."

"Ficino told us that, on the *Goodness* when we came," Kebes said. "Probably it was the same for him."

Sokrates stopped dead and stared at us as if he'd never seen us before. "I think it might be better if I spoke to Pytheas alone," he said, and turned and walked off so fast that I'd have had to run to catch up with him.

Kebes and I stared at each other. "What was that about?" I asked.

He shrugged. "Do you think the worker really was trying to communicate?"

"Well, it seems unlikely on the face of it, but it also seems like a very unlikely coincidence that in only that one spot where Sokrates was trying to talk to the worker, the flowers should spell out something that could mean no. I'm almost more interested in why he acted like that about Pytheas. What would Pytheas know about workers that we don't?"

"Pytheas knows some very odd things sometimes."

"He reads a lot," I said, defensively. "No, but what?"

Kebes frowned. "When we're talking to Sokrates, sometimes Pytheas says odd things, or sometimes he says ordinary things and Sokrates reacts oddly. Like when he mentioned his parents that time, and Sokrates acted as if he'd said something completely bizarre."

I remembered that. I shook my head. "That's Sokrates behaving oddly, which...isn't unusual for Sokrates. Do you think he'll be in Thessaly this afternoon?"

"I'll be there to see," Kebes said.

"So will I. But first I have my math group. See you later!" I went off to join Axiothea and the others, puzzled.

Sokrates was at Thessaly when I got there at our usual time. Pytheas was there before me, and Kebes arrived a moment or two later. "I brought some nuts," he said, pulling out a twist of paper.

"Raisins," I said, pulling out a matching twist.

"Olives," Pytheas said, smugly, bringing out a whole jar of olives stuffed with garlic.

"You bring a feast! And I as always can offer crystal clear water and the shade of my garden," Sokrates said, leading the way out. It was a little chilly to sit outside, and I kept my cloak around me. Once we were seated and passing round the food, he began. "I believe I have discovered evidence of conversational thought among the workers."

"I'm not convinced," Kebes said.

"It's not necessary to be convinced by one piece of evidence," Sokrates said. "But it's indicative that it might be worth further investigation."

Sokrates unveiled his plan, in which the three of us were to do nothing but go around talking to every worker we saw, in Latin, while he did the same in Greek. "Do any of you know any other languages?"

"A little Coptic, if I still remember any," I said.

"Italian," Kebes said. "It's like simple Latin without the word endings."

Pytheas spread his hands. "I was born in the hills above Delphi. How would I have encountered anything but Greek?"

"How indeed?" Sokrates muttered. "I believe I can recruit Aristomache into this project," he said. "She speaks two other languages of Europe. I forget their names now, but she told me so. With all those languages it may be easier to get them to answer."

"Or they may not," I said. "And we're going to look awfully silly trying to have dialogue with workers."

"As cracked as me," Sokrates agreed cheerfully. "Report any results, positive or negative. But results might be slow—like the bulbs."

"If they can speak, why don't they?" Kebes asked.

"I don't think they can speak. This is just a theory, but I suspect they can hear and move and think without being able to speak. They have no organs of speech, no mouths, no heads. But they have things like hands, and they may be able to write. That one found a way."

"They have nothing like ears either, how do you know they can hear?" I asked.

"I conjecture that they have the ability to hear because the response to my questions suggests that it heard them. I conjecture they have understanding for the same reason." Sokrates shook his head. "I think it would be wrong to consider them people, but we don't have a term for anything like them. Thinking beings that aren't human! How wonderful if they are able to reason and communicate!"

"Without heads, where might they keep their minds, if they have them?" Kebes put in.

"In their livers, obviously," Sokrates said. "What makes you think minds are in the head?"

"Closest to the eyes," Kebes said.

"And people with head injuries are often damaged in their

minds, while people with liver injuries continue to think perfectly well," Pytheas added.

"Huh." Sokrates touched his head. "But they have no heads, and you've all been assuming that the head is the seat of intelligence and therefore that's why you're all so reluctant to consider that they might be intelligent. Well, now. Perhaps you're right, and perhaps I am. They might help sort it out."

"They're made of metal and glass," Pytheas said.

"So?" Sokrates looked puzzled.

Pytheas shook his head, defeated.

"The next problem is that there's no way to tell them apart! Have you ever found one?"

I shook my head. "They sometimes have different hands. But I don't know if they change them or if it's always the same hands on the same ones. And of course some are bronze-colored and some are iron-colored."

Pytheas nodded. "What Simmea said. I've never tried to distinguish them." Whatever it was Sokrates had imagined he knew about them clearly didn't amount to much.

Kebes smiled. "Actually, they are easy to tell apart. They're numbered. Lysias showed me once, when I was helping him." When he was going through his period of making Lysias think that Kebes would begin to strive for excellence through his encouragement, I thought. "The numbers are very small, down on their side, above the tread. They're long. But they're all different. So we can tell them apart, by checking the numbers."

"Are they numbered in Latin or Greek?" Sokrates asked, leaning forward, urgently interested.

"Neither," Kebes said. "They're numbered in numbers."

Sokrates looked blank.

"You know, zeroic. Like page numbers in books," I said. I pulled a book out of the fold of my kiton and showed him. It happened to a bound copy of Aeschylus's *Telemachus*.

"Those are numbers?" he asked. "How do they work?"

I wrote them down in the dust, from one to ten, and showed him. "That's all there is to it. For twenty, or for a hundred—"

He understood it at once. "And you have all known this all this time and never mentioned it to me?" he said.

"It never occurred to me that you didn't know," I said.

"Pah. My ignorance is vast and profound. I like to know at least what I do not know." He traced the numbers again. "Zero. What a concept. What a timesaver. What vast realms of arithmetic and geometry it must reveal. I wish Pythagoras could have known it, and the Pythagoreans of Athens." Then, like a hound who had started after the wrong hare, he got immediately back on track. "So the workers are labelled with this?"

"That's right," Kebes said. "All of them."

"Who did this?"

"I don't know."

"What is the purpose?"

"Telling them apart. That's how Lysias uses it, anyway."

"Did you note the number of the one planting bulbs?"

"Sorry, no, it didn't occur to me."

Sokrates sighed, sat back and absently ate a handful of olives.

"So the numbers are like names?" I suggested. "That seems to argue against them being people. Why not give them names?"

"Maybe there are too many to name?" Pytheas suggested.

"How many of them are there?" Sokrates asked, licking olive oil off his fingers.

We all shrugged. "Lots," Kebes said. "I was surprised how many when I saw them at their feeding station."

"They eat?" Sokrates asked.

"They eat electricity, Lysias said."

Sokrates bounced to his feet. "Come on, show me this feeding station!"

I swallowed an olive hastily. We set off, with Kebes leading the way and Sokrates close behind.

Pytheas walked beside me. "This is crazy," he said.

"Sure. Kind of fun, though. And what if they actually were thinking beings with plans?"

"They're not. They're tools. Everyone knows that." Pytheas looked a little unsettled.

"What everyone knows, Sokrates examines," I said.

Kebes led us to a block on the east side of the city, between the streets of Poseidon and Hermes, not far from the temple of Ares. The whole block was one square building, relatively unexciting. I'd never particularly noticed it. There was a lot in the city that was empty, awaiting a later purpose, or used by the masters for unknown purposes. I wasn't especially curious about most of it. This building had decorative recessed squares set all around it at ground level. There were no windows. A key-pattern frieze ran around the top. There was another key pattern over the door.

"What now?" Sokrates asked.

"Now we wait for a worker, because Lysias has a key but I don't. But you'll see when a worker comes." Kebes leaned back on his heels. I squatted down and ate more raisins. Pytheas and Sokrates began to debate volition, and whether workers could be considered to have it.

"Ah, here we go," Kebes said, when the sun was beginning to slide towards dinner time.

A bronze-colored worker came down the street. "Joy to you," Sokrates said. "I am Sokrates. Do you have a name?" It ignored him utterly and approached the building, not by the door but directly at one of the recessed squares. The square slid open in front of it and it vanished inside.

"Did you see that?" Sokrates asked.

"That's what they do," Kebes said. "Inside there are sockets and they plug themselves in to eat electricity. When they're full, which takes several hours, they unplug themselves and come out again."

"I'd never noticed this was here," I said.

"Nobody much comes down this street," Kebes said. "There's nothing here, and if you were at the corner you'd cut diagonally down the street of Apollo."

"You've been inside?" Sokrates asked.

"Yes, with Lysias."

"We could follow a worker inside," Sokrates suggested.

"We'd be stuck there until one wanted to come out. We can't open the doors without a key. It would be better to talk to them when they come out—they won't be hungry then, and if they can talk they'll be more likely to respond."

"I want to see inside," Sokrates said.

"All right. But we could get stuck there all night. Or you could ask Lysias or Klio. They have keys. I'm sure they'd let you in."

"If Lysias and Klio take care of them, that suggests that they come from their time. When is that?" Sokrates was bending down and poking at the square where the worker had disappeared. Nothing he did could move it. I touched it myself. It felt like solid stone.

"The boring part of history," I said. "The bit where nothing happened except people inventing things, Axiothea said."

"The part they don't want us to know about! Excellent." Sokrates kept on poking. Then a different square slid open and a worker emerged. "Joy to you! Do you like your work?" It ignored us. The panel started to slide shut, and fast as an eel, Sokrates darted through it.

The three of us stared at each other and then at the smooth closed panel. "He needs a keeper sometimes," Pytheas said.

"Should we get Lysias?" Kebes asked.

"How much trouble can he get into inside?" I asked.

"Not much, I don't think. He knows about electricity—I mean, he has a light in Thessaly. He's not likely to stick his fingers into sockets. At least, I hope not. He can't get into much trouble going up to the workers as they're feeding and asking them if they like their work." Kebes looked worried.

"I think we have two choices: wait for a worker to go in or out and follow it in ourselves, or fetch Lysias or Klio and ask them to let us in," I said. "We can't just leave Sokrates in there."

"I think you should go and find one of them," Pytheas said, to me. He tapped on the stone. Nothing happened.

"It might be hours before another one comes," Kebes said.

"It's almost dinner time. Klio will be at Sparta, and Lysias will be at Constantinople. I'll go to him, you go to her," Pytheas said, looking at me. Then he looked at Kebes. "You've been in there before. You wait here, and if you get the chance, go in."

Kebes hesitated, as if he wanted to dispute this, but it made such clear and obvious sense that after a moment he nodded.

"Back soon!" I said, and set off running towards the Spartan hall.

"Sokrates is doing what with the workers?" Klio asked, when I found her and panted out my story.

"Trying to initiate dialectic with them," I said. "But Kebes said he might stick his fingers in a wall socket, and I'm not absolutely sure he wouldn't."

Klio sighed. The Spartan hall was appropriately bare and Spartan, but all the wood was polished to a high shine and the windows looked out over the sea. The smell coming from the kitchen suggested a rich vegetable soup. My stomach gurgled. "Come on then," she said. "I suppose we should sort this out. What made him imagine he could have a dialogue with them?"

"He's Sokrates," I said.

"He's like a two-year-old sticking pencils in his ear," she said.

"Well, but there were also the plants."

"Plants? No. Tell me on the way." She pushed her hair out of her face and we set off.

I explained to Klio about the bulbs as we walked. She frowned. "They really are just tools," she said. "I can see how it's difficult for you to see. They can make simple decisions, they can even prioritize to a certain extent. But they don't really think. They have a program—a list of things they know how to do and a list of orders of what needs doing, and they just put those together."

"Do you know that or is it an opinion?" I asked.

Klio frowned even more, twisting up her face. She was Axiothea's good friend so I knew her quite well. She sometimes dropped in on our math class. She was one of the most friendly and approachable masters, and she never talked down to us. "I would say I knew it, but the affair of the flowers confuses me. They can hear, so it could have heard Sokrates's questions. But they don't know Greek."

"I told him that Latin was the language of civilization for centuries," I said, reassuringly.

She laughed. "Not the century our workers come from, unfortunately. But if it spelled out N and O, that's *no* in English, which uses the Latin alphabet. English is the most likely language for the worker to know . . . or Chinese. But—in my own time, a worker couldn't possibly be a thinking, volitional being. These come from a more advanced time. I suppose it's just barely possible that they could have developed some kind of . . . but to understand Greek?" She shook her head.

We turned into the street of Hermes. There was no sign of Kebes. "Either Lysias got here first or Kebes went in with a worker," I said.

Klio used her key to open the door. Inside it was surprisingly dull, after what I had been imagining. It didn't look at all dangerous. It was like a warehouse full of workers, each plugged into a wall or floor socket. It was a big space, as it seemed from outside, stretching back for a long way. There was a hum in the air. I couldn't see Sokrates, but I could see Kebes running down one of the aisles, so I followed him.

Sokrates was sitting on the floor beside one of the workers, notebook and pencil in his hand, patiently asking it questions. He looked up when we reached him. "Ah, Simmea, Kebes, Klio, joy to you. I'd like you to record the numbers of all the workers here. I've done the first row and this row. If you'd like to address them in Latin, that would also be useful."

"Klio says they don't speak Latin but they might understand something called English," I said.

Klio told Sokrates what she had told me. In the middle of it Pytheas and Lysias showed up. Lysias added to Klio's explanation. "But I'm not an expert," he said. "None of us is. I've been forced to be one. But before I came here, I never had much to do with them."

"You're all philosophers," Sokrates said, gently. "It's perhaps a demonstration of Plato's principle that philosophers will be best at ruling the state, to take three hundred of you and nobody else and give you a state to run."

"Plato doesn't say any random philosophers from different schools and all across time," Lysias protested. "And only about half of us are philosophers. The rest are classics majors and Platonic mystics. Besides, Plato does specifically say that the city needs all kinds of people. The philosophers are just intended for the guardians, not doing the whole thing, organizing the food supply and keeping things running and looking after the workers."

"But the end result is that nobody here really understands whether the workers have intelligence and free will or not."

The worker beside Sokrates did not move, and showed absolutely no sign of having intelligence and free will. It could have been a chair or part of the wall. I looked for the number on the worker and found it, above the tread as Kebes had said. It was nine digits long. Above that, on its lower back, about where the liver might be on a human, was a slightly inset square that reminded me of the squares on the outside of the building.

"If the workers do have intelligence and free will, then there's a real issue here," Klio said. She patted the worker. It did not respond.

"Slavery," said Sokrates. "Plato allowed slavery, did he?"

"Free will and intelligence are different things," Pytheas pointed out.

"Different things?" Sokrates repeated. "We've been discussing them together, but is it possible to have one without the other?"

"Very possible. There are logic-machines in my time that can play games of logic so well that they beat a human master of the game," Klio said. "That can be considered intelligence. But they don't have volition or anything like it. They are machines that simulate intelligence. The way these prioritize their tasks, and come here to recharge, simulates intelligence."

"And it's very easy to see volition without intelligence in animals and small children," Lysias said.

Klio nodded. "Developing one seems almost possible, but both at once? Surely not. But choosing to plant the bulbs so they would answer your question would take both."

"Explain to me about the bulbs," Lysias said.

"I was attempting to have a dialogue with a worker, asking if it liked its work and if there was any work it preferred and that kind of thing, while it was planting bulbs last autumn," Sokrates said. "Today the crocuses it planted came up, and they spell *no* in Latin."

"In English," Klio corrected, pushing her hair back behind her ears. "Which seems more plausible, except for understanding the questions in Greek."

"Did anyone else witness this?" Lysias asked.

"I did," I said. "Both parts of it."

"And so did I," Kebes said.

"Kebes was the first to recognize the word this morning. And we investigated the other patches of bulbs in other places in the city, and they are all arranged in rows, not in anything resembling letters."

"From which direction did they read as letters?" Lysias asked.

"North to south," I said, after it seemed that Kebes and Sokrates were having trouble remembering. "And that was the direction the worker was facing as it planted them."

"It does sound as if it would take both," Pytheas said. He looked hopefully at the worker sitting so stoically plugged into the socket.

"Unless Simmea or Kebes went back and rearranged the bulbs to play a trick," Lysias said.

"I would never do such a thing!" I said, hotly indignant.

"Neither would I!" Kebes said, but I could see that Lysias didn't believe him.

"It's certainly the most logical explanation," Klio said. She sounded relieved.

"I shall consider that explanation and continue to explore the question," Sokrates said. "Will you permit me to continue recording the numbers of the workers here, so that I can tell if I've talked to one before?"

Lysias and Klio looked at each other. "I suppose it can't do any harm," Klio said.

"But you must promise not to keep coming back in here through the worker doors," Lysias said. "It could be dangerous. You can talk to them in the city."

"How is it dangerous?" Sokrates asked. "Do you think I'm going to plug myself into the sockets?" He laughed when he saw our faces. "I promise I won't plug myself into the sockets, or slip under a worker's treads, or any such thing. Is that good enough?"

"I'll stay and help," Lysias said. "The rest of you can get to your dinners."

I was about to offer to help, but Sokrates nodded. "If you'll talk to me while we work," he said. "I'm exceedingly interested in what you know about intelligence and volition. Do the workers actually want things?"

"Come on," Klio said, gathering the rest of us up. "Do you want to eat in Sparta?"

"Sure," I said.

"It's bean soup."

"Delicious! We haven't had bean soup in Florentia since last month." Pytheas came with us. Kebes grunted and went off alone.

"He really didn't like it when Lysias said that," I said after he had left.

"He wouldn't do that," Pytheas said.

"I thought you'd think he would. You're usually ready to say anything bad about him."

"He's an unmannerly lout and he doesn't pursue excellence, and I don't like the way he talks to you, and I don't like what he says in our debates on trust." Pytheas glanced at Klio. "But he has honor. And he really cares about Sokrates. He wouldn't play a trick on him."

"Do you agree, Simmea?" Klio asked.

"I do agree. But I can see that nobody who doesn't know Kebes well will believe that."

"Kebes doesn't speak English," Pytheas said. "Greek and Latin and Italian, he said."

"You're supposed to forget any other languages you had before you came here," Klio clucked.

"Well, you can forget that I said that," Pytheas said. "Forgetting a language isn't easy."

I nodded. "I'd like to believe that I came out of the soil on the day I started to learn to read, but I can't really forget ten years of memories. They're dim, and I don't often think of them, but they're not gone."

"Your children will have no such memories," Klio said. "It'll be easier for them."

"To return to the point," Pytheas said, though we were drawing near the Spartan hall now. "Kebes doesn't speak English. If he had replanted the bulbs he could have made them say *no* in Greek or Latin, but not English. And doing it in Greek would have been simplest, and Sokrates would have understood it."

Klio nodded. "And by the same logic, it can't have been any of the other children either."

"None of the children speak English?" I asked.

Pytheas raised his head as if he were waiting to hear how she would answer. "You're all from the Mediterranean, and there are no English-speaking countries there."

"Besides," I said, "Kebes wasn't ready to believe the worker had really communicated. If it had been a hoax he'd have been trying to get Sokrates to believe it, not arguing against it."

"Not necessarily, depending on how well he knows Sokrates," Klio said. We were at the door of the Spartan hall, which Klio held open for us. We went inside. The room was full now.

"We fetch our own soup from the urn," Klio explained. I took a bowl and filled it. I also took a little roll of barley bread and a piece of smoked fish from the trays laid out. The soup was lovely, warming and filling, full of onions and beans.

"If Kebes didn't do it, then I have another thought," Klio said, when I was nearly done eating. "There are workers that go to the feeding station and won't leave again. Lysias tries to give them new orders, but nothing works except taking out the piece of them that makes decisions and replacing it. We're running extremely low on spares. If they really are developing volition and that's a symptom of it, then what have we been doing?"

"Cutting out their minds?" Pytheas asked. "How gruesome. Could you put them back?"

"Yes . . . I think so. But we need the workers. We've been saying for years that we have to reduce our dependence on them, but nobody's ever willing to do it. They do so much, and some of it we can't do. We can't manage if they just sit in their feeding stations and feed and don't work."

"Maybe those are the ones Sokrates should be talking to," Pytheas said. "Have you finished? Shall we go back and suggest this?"

"Lysias is going to resist hearing this argument," Klio said. "It would make him feel he has done bad things—without intending to, but done them nonetheless. He doesn't know Kebes."

"It's worse than that, he does know Kebes, and he knows bad things about him," I said.

"What bad things?" Klio asked.

"What Pytheas said. That he doesn't pursue excellence. And I think he might have mocked Lysias when he was trying to be his friend. He's never going to believe that he has honor and wouldn't trick Sokrates."

"Lysias knows Kebes mocked him?" Pytheas asked.

I nodded. "I believe he does."

"He's really not going to want to hear it," Klio repeated. "Let's not go back there now. Don't worry. I'll talk to Sokrates."

23

MAIA

We had more than a thousand babies born in the month of Anthesterion, and it strained our resources to the utmost.

Plato wrote in the *Republic* that defective babies, and babies of defective parents, should be exposed. It was the standard practice of the classical world to expose unwanted babies—just to leave them out in a waste place where they might be rescued or, more often, just die. There was no blood guilt on the parents, they just left the child, they didn't kill it. The children froze to death or were eaten by animals . . . or occasionally rescued. Stories like Oedipus, and Theseus, and Romulus and Remus are of exposed babies who came back to find the family that had abandoned them. There were other stories too, which I hadn't heard before I came to the city, ghost stories.

I know that in my own century it was the practice for midwives to kill badly deformed babies—or just allow them to die instead of helping them to survive. It did seem the kind option. But the thought of exposing even deformed infants made my heart ache.

We had kept careful records of all the "marriages," so carefully planned out with an eye to eugenics. (Klio and Lysias shrank from that term, but would never tell me why.) We took the babies into the nurseries as they were born. There was a nursery shared

between Florentia and Delphi, so Axiothea and I worked together there—Ficino and Atticus left it to us. We called in
Charmides when we really needed to. He was exhausted too, as
our only real doctor. We defined all the babies we saw as excellent and passed them over to the nurses—men and women of
iron status. One was Andromeda, whom I'd always liked.

Then in the middle of the night in the third week of the
baby-rush, when we were already exhausted, there was one with
a harelip. Axiothea had been with the mother while I was with
another girl just starting her labor. She called me and I joined
her in the private room, where she showed it to me.

Axiothea and I looked at each other in mute horror. The
child had a cleft palate too. "It's fixable," Axiothea said.

"Not here," I said. "And Plato says . . ."

"I know," she said. "Are you going to do it?" There was a
mute appeal in her eyes.

"Yes," I said, refusing to shrink from the duty. I wrapped the
baby in a cloth and held it against my shoulder. It was a girl,
which made things somehow worse. I was here to make the lot
of women better, after all. "You look after things here."

I went out of the nursery and walked through the city to the
north gate, the one near the temple of Zeus and Hera. I walked
quickly and held the baby tenderly, but she started to wail. She
was such a little scrap of a thing. I walked on up the mountain,
with some thought of taking her up to the top and throwing
her into the crater. There was no hope of rescue here. No shepherd in want of a child was going to come along. There was nobody on Kallisti but us. There were wolves, but wolves wouldn't
be able to feed her, even if they really did feed babies. With that
lip she wouldn't be able to suck, and with the hole in her mouth
she'd choke if she could.

She wasn't heavy, but she was awkward to carry. I was exhausted before I made it halfway up the mountain. I left her by

the roots of a rowan tree, near a spring. I commended her soul to Athene and prayed that she might be reborn whole. She had been quiet for the last part of my walk, but when I put her down she started to wail loudly. I could hear it halfway back to the city. It cut off abruptly. I wondered if she had fallen asleep, or whether she was lying there still and terrified in the darkness, or whether a wild animal had taken her—a wild boar? A wolf? I took two steps back up the hill before I forced myself to stop. This was ridiculous. I was a disgrace to philosophy. I had done what I had come to do, what Plato told me to do, the standard practice of the ancient world. It was to protect the city, to make us better. All the same, I was still weeping when I came back into the city.

It was dawn. The wind came chill from the sea. The sky was paling and the birds waking. It was the point where late winter becomes early spring—the first of the flowers were coming up. Everything said beginnings, but for that poor harelipped baby there was nothing but an ending.

Of course, this was when I saw Ikaros. I hardly ever saw him now. He had dropped out of the Tech Committee in favour of something more exciting. "Maia, what's wrong?"

"Nothing, really," I said. "Just a deformed baby that had to be exposed, and my soft heart."

"The poor little mother," he said at once.

I had not thought about the mother, going through all that for nothing. "At least she won't know," I said. "She'll think they're all hers."

"How could she not know? She'll look for the one with the deformity."

"We'll tell her it was cured," I said. "If she saw it. I don't know whether she did. I'll find out."

He nodded. Then he turned and walked along with me. "You're siding with Lysias about trying to use the workers less."

"He and Klio say they're being overburdened and they'll break down. There are things they're essential for, that we'll need them for for a long time."

"The question is what's essential. Well, isn't that always the question?" He smiled brilliantly at me. "We should set up a committee especially for that."

I was exhausted and wrung out. "Talk to Lysias," I said. "I don't really know enough of the details. None of us understand the workers properly; they come from a time ahead of everyone here."

"We could just ask Athene for more," he suggested.

"We don't know how far her patience runs. Besides, I haven't seen her for ages, have you? She probably has a lot more to do than collect workers for us."

"I haven't seen her. Sokrates really wants to talk to her," he said. "Speaking of her, do you remember that conversation we had about Providence?"

I couldn't believe that he was mentioning it casually like that. "You mean the night you raped me?"

He patted my arm and smiled at me. "Call it that if you want. But do you remember the conversation? About not being able to reconcile Christianity with the presence of Athene?"

"Of course I do," I snapped.

"Well, I was naive, I think. Since then I've been working on it, and I have found a way to make it all fit together."

I stared at him. "Really?"

He looked smug. "Well, if Athene—if the Greek gods are actually angels in one of the lower heavens, and if those angels have a considerable amount of autonomy, then it all works, that she should have brought us here and that the persons of the Trinity should still be there at the apex."

"But she's Athene!"

"Why shouldn't she be? Wasn't God there before the birth of

Christ, and mightn't he have used appropriate angels? It makes more sense that he would. I always thought the classical gods must have been some kind of angels."

I thought about it. "But why would he use her now? To Christians? I was a faithful churchgoer. You were a monk."

He looked irritated. "I told you I wasn't a monk. I was just dressed as a Dominican because I was dying. I never took any vows."

"But you were a Christian?"

"I still am. And so can you be. The truth is wonderful and more complex than we thought, that's all. I remembered that you wanted to have those stories here. Well, maybe we can."

"Does Sokrates agree with you?" I asked.

"Sokrates finds the idea of Providence fascinating," he said. "And he agrees that man is the measure of all things. But he isn't very interested in Christianity. He agrees that knowing Athene is real and takes an interest in us changes everything. And he thinks that it would be interesting to debate my nine hundred theses. Actually, I have almost two thousand now."

"Well, good luck debating them," I said.

"It's not going to be easy getting enough of us to agree," he said. "Would you support such a debate?"

I wasn't sure. "I suppose so. But I find it uncomfortable to think about. If God—how do you reconcile Christian morality? You were pretty scathing about it when we talked about this before."

"It's complicated, but I have it all worked out," he said. "Athene is just carrying out God's will."

I wondered what she would think of that. She was so real and so much herself. But what were angels anyway? What were gods? We came to the turning. "I have to go this way now."

"It was nice to see you Maia. I never get to see you these days." He patted my arm again. "We must talk about this some more, soon." He went off down the street of Poseidon with a casual wave. I stared after him. He had at least taken my mind off the poor baby, dying up there on the mountain.

I went back to the nursery. Andromeda was just coming on duty and Darius was just leaving. "Axiothea left a note for you," he said. The note said that the girl in labour had delivered safely and easily, and that Axiothea was going to Klio's to sleep and if I needed her I could find her there.

"Everything all right?" he asked.

"Fine. You go to bed." He went off gratefully. "Only the one more baby?" I asked.

"Yes. We have thirty-three," Andromeda said. "It's a good number. We have mothers coming in to feed them every hour."

"And how many more babies due?"

"In Florentia and Delphi? Four. And then, of course, there will be all the ones born in four months' time." She smiled. "It's so exciting. I'm so glad I got chosen to train for this."

"You're a great person to be doing it."

"And maybe next time I'll be having a baby myself. Only I'll be able to care for it myself, won't I, as I know how?"

I stared at her, nonplussed. "The idea is that all babies will be in the nurseries. You'll care for your own among all the others."

Her face fell. "I thought I could take it home."

"It would disturb all your house sisters," I said, gently. "They're better here, really."

"My sisters wouldn't mind." But she sighed and got on with her work.

"I'm going to sleep, I've been up all night. If anyone needs me, I'll be in my house," I said.

"Will we ever have houses to ourselves the way you do?" she asked. "Because if I did, I could take my baby home and it wouldn't bother anyone."

"It's not the plan for you to have your own houses any time soon," I said. "Don't you like sharing with your sisters?"

"Yes, but I don't like Hyacinth as much as I liked Hyssop." Just then a baby cried, and she was off to comfort it.

"See you later," I called, and went home. Although I was exhausted, I lay awake worrying. Were we the right people to be trying this experiment? Did we know enough about what we were doing? Was God still there above Athene, as the circle of sky stood above the Pantheon? Should I pray to him, and to Jesus, or continue praying to Athene? Could Ikaros truly have forgotten the rape and only remembered the conversation? Was that a bad thing? I'd wanted the conversation and not wanted the rape, after all. Why did I have a house to myself when Andromeda shared with six others? They weren't children any more, and there were new children, and keeping mothers and children apart wasn't as easy as Plato had thought. When it came down to details, so little was.

24

SIMMEA

There was another festival of Hera. Even fewer of the men took part, as even more of the women were unavailable. There was some grumbling. I was drawn with Nikias of Pisa, another near stranger. We managed well enough—I was getting more used to it, and wasn't as nervous as I had been on the previous occasions. I liked Nikias. He made me laugh. As with Aeschines, we became friends through the marriage and remained friends afterwards. And as with Aeschines, he asked me if I'd be willing to go off to the woods with him. "We got along very well," he said. "You liked it. We could do it some more."

"Doing it every four months is enough for me," I said. I wondered if every pleasant coupling produced this suggestion, quite against the rules.

"Nobody would know," he went on.

Whether because I was more relaxed or because Hera smiled or for some other reason, I became pregnant at that festival. Klymene and Makalla were as big as houses and constantly groaning about their bellies and their swelling feet and their sense of exhaustion.

I was painting a fresco in Ithaka—by invitation. Aeschines suggested it first, and then Hermeios and Nyra, the masters there, formally asked me to do it. The fresco showed Odysseus coming into harbor, which I based on our own harbor. His ship was the *Goodness*. The dog Argo was visible on the quayside. I'd done the composition on paper first, and they had approved it. The whole thing filled a wall and was the most ambitious project I had ever done. It was fiddly, too, because the plaster dried so quickly and it was so hard to change anything. In the first month of my pregnancy the smell of the paint made me queasy.

Sokrates inquired into parenthood, the duties and responsibilities. I held that the only duty of a parent was to see the child brought up as well as possible—which in the city meant giving it to those best trained for the purpose. Sokrates agreed that we ought to love all children as if they were our own, but disputed the value of the training and education the city would give, and immediately we were back on familiar ground from a new angle.

Klymene's baby was born the day before the feast of Hephaestus. When she went into labor in the middle of the night, I went for Maia. Maia helped her walk to the nursery. The rest of us lay awake, wondering how it was going. Four of us were pregnant, and the two who were not longed to experience it. "I can't wait to get rid of this weight," Makalla moaned.

I started to do arithmetic. How many babies did the city need? Another ten thousand and eighty? If each woman had two babies we would have that. But we were supposed to keep on having festivals every four months, or so I believed. If half the women got pregnant—no, if a third—a quarter? I would have to ask Sokrates how this was supposed to work. It was a silly situation where every master had read the *Republic* but no children had, in case it impaired our ability to live it. We were living it—we should be able to read it now. We weren't children any longer. We were having children of our own. We'd need to be guiding them by what Plato said. It was ridiculous to keep it from us.

The next morning Klymene came back without the baby.

Her belly didn't look a great deal smaller, which surprised me. I'd expected her to go back to normal at once. "We are to go every day and feed them," Klymene said, as if it were a comfort.

"Was it a boy or a girl?" I asked.

"A boy. The sweetest thing. He had black curls." I wondered what my baby would look like, and if I would be sorry to leave it behind in the nursery.

Makalla's baby was born four days later. She went into labor in the afternoon, so I did not know until I went to bed and she was missing from Hyssop. "I heard her screaming while I was over there feeding," Klymene said.

"Screaming?" Auge asked, apprehensively, a hand on her belly.

"Everyone screams, they say," Klymene said, quite composedly. "I didn't, except once near the end."

"How is your baby?" I asked.

"They keep bringing me different ones to feed every time I go. I haven't seen my own baby since the first day. Still, I suppose it's for the best. It stops me getting too attached, Maia says."

"Don't you want to be attached?" Auge asked.

"I want him to be his best self. That means leaving him to people trained to bring him up. I wouldn't have any idea what to do with a baby."

It was what I had said to Sokrates, but somehow it sounded different. And I knew if I brought that back to Sokrates, it would take us straight into the heart of the matter. Could we trust the masters? Could we trust Plato? Could we trust Pallas Athene? Trust them for what? Trust them to mean well and have our best interests at heart? Oh yes, I thought so. Trust them to know how best to bring up babies? That was a different question. And in seven months' time, it was a question that I was going to have to answer. I put my arms around my belly as if that was going to protect the baby.

"How do you know it's a different one?" Auge asked. "I thought they all looked alike."

Klymene clicked her tongue. "They're all different! And mine looked just like Pytheas, except for the hair."

"Pytheas?" I asked. My stomach felt hollow. "You were drawn with Pytheas? And it was awful?"

"I wasn't going to tell you."

"You managed not to tell me for a long time. And he didn't tell me either. Tell me now." Pytheas had been politely evasive when I'd asked how it had gone, and I hadn't wanted to linger on the subject either. We were friends. That there were times when I longed to reach out and touch him, or to see the expression on his face that I had seen on Aeschines, was my secret.

She sighed. "It was only awful because we hate each other. He'd have let me off—he still thinks I'm a coward. I forced him to go through with it. I just gritted my teeth. It wasn't so bad. Nothing to childbirth. Good practice for it."

Pytheas wasn't in Laurel House, or in Delphi, or the palaestra, and he wasn't in the library. He wasn't in Thessaly, though Sokrates and Ikaros and Manlius and Aristomache were, sitting talking and drinking wine in a circle of light. "Why do you want him?" Sokrates asked.

"It's personal," I said.

"In that case I think we'd better accompany you!" Ikaros said. "Personal matters are always better sorted out—"

"With a debate team? No, thank you."

Ikaros laughed. "Which horse is in charge of your chariot today, Simmea?"

Sokrates raised a hand then, stopping Ikaros immediately. Sokrates could cut right through one in debate but he was never cruel, and never allowed cruelty in his presence. "Is Ikaros right? Have you and Pytheas had a lover's tiff?"

"We're not lovers," I protested. "And no, nothing like that."

"It's late. You've been running and your hair is disordered," Ikaros pointed out. "And you said a personal matter. I wasn't likely to assume a dispute on the nature of the soul."

"You can be passionate enough in debate," Aristomache said to him, sharply "Do others the courtesy of assuming the same."

"I wanted to talk to him urgently about something I just found out," I said. "And can something only be a matter of philosophy or of love, do you think, Master Ikaros? Are there no other subjects fit for conversation?"

"She has you there," Sokrates said. "Let us consider the benefits and disadvantages of bisecting the world, and leave Simmea to quest for Pytheas in peace."

I left, and walked decorously through the city, aware now of how I seemed to others. I smoothed my hair and breathed evenly. What was I upset about anyway? That Pytheas and Klymene had had their encounter? That was random chance, and I knew he'd been married to someone—to three people, as I had. What difference did it make that it was Klymene? None. What upset me was that he hadn't told me, that he hadn't brought it to me for dissection and examination. Whatever had happened with Klymene didn't matter. It was his silence about it that threatened our friendship. Ten months, and he hadn't said a word about it.

I found him at last coming out of a practice room, not the ones on the street of Dionysos which had been used for the marriages but the ones on the street of Hermes on the south edge of the city. "I've been making a song. Let's go up on the wall," he said when he saw me. We climbed up the steps and stood on the wall. It was late evening and there was nobody else there. The breeze was blowing from the mountain, bringing with it a slight smell of sulphur. The wall was twice the height of Pytheas and perhaps his height across, with a little parapet. It was possible to walk all around the city on top of the walls, because the walkways went over the tops of the gates. There were no sconces up here, but we could see by the lights below, and by starlight. The stars were particularly bright that night. I knew their names and histories and the orbits of all the planets. I could see Saturn very clearly. It gave me some perspective on my human problems.

"Klymene told me," I said, quite calm now.

"Oh." He stared out into the darkness. "I've been wanting and wanting to talk to you about it, but it was so awkward if she didn't want you to know."

He couldn't have said anything better. The hurt and anger went out of me. I sat down on the parapet and he sat down on the flat slab of the walkway below me.

"I've been wanting to ask you about it, but now I don't know what to say. Is she all right?"

"She's fine," I said. "She's had the baby. It's a boy. She says he looks exactly like you."

"I can't wait to see him," he said. "And Kryseis is pregnant too."

"So am I," I said.

"Wonderful. Congratulations. It'll be so nice to have another generation of children."

"I was wondering how many they want. The same number, surely, which means two children each, but if they want to have a festival every four months then there'll be a lot more than that."

"We should ask Sokrates," he said. "A city of heroes. What a thought."

"Klymene said it was horrible. She didn't talk about it. But she said it was good preparation for childbirth."

He shuddered. I could feel it. "She willed it, but she didn't want it," he said. "I've been thinking about it for a long time, and I think that's what it was. I didn't want it and I could barely summon the will. She hates me."

"I don't think she'll ever be able to forgive you."

"The whole thing's so horribly awkward, even when you don't get matched with somebody who hates you."

"Oh yes," I agreed fervently.

"And it doesn't even work. Half the people I know have actually paired off and are sneaking off to meet up in hiding to keep doing it. Some of them are in love and some just want to have more sex." He shook his head.

"Two people have asked me for that," I confirmed.

"Not that bastard Phoenix?"

"No . . ." The night was dark, I couldn't see his face. "Would you care?"

"He's scum. I don't like to think of you with him. Or even Aeschines."

"I like Aeschines."

"His head is solid bone."

I laughed. "Nonsense. He's very kind, and he's certainly not stupid, even if he's not as fast in debate as you or Kebes."

"Or you," Pytheas said.

"Are you jealous?" I asked.

There was a pause. I could hear gulls crying out to sea, and from the practice rooms down below where somebody must have left a door open came the sound of a lyre playing one phrase over and over.

"I don't know," Pytheas said at last. "Maybe, yes. I don't know if this is what jealousy feels like. I certainly didn't like the thought of you sneaking off to meet Aeschines."

"I'm not doing it. But he did ask."

"A question in return. Are you jealous of Klymene and Kriseis and Hermia?"

I was glad I'd thought it through. "With Klymene, mostly I was upset because it was important and I knew it must have been difficult for you and you hadn't talked to me about it.

That was what was important. Not what happened. But I am a little jealous that she has had your baby. And . . . if you were sneaking off together I might be jealous. And I do keep hoping that we'll get chosen together."

"Plato says—"

"I know what Plato says. Plato says my soul is burning because it wants to grow feathers. Ikaros accused me of having the wrong horse in charge of my chariot. But I don't think I do."

"You don't know what I was going to say Plato says. You haven't read the *Republic*."

"Oh, and you have?" Then I realized he meant it. "You mean you *have*? How? When? Can I read it? I really want to. Did Sokrates lend it to you?"

"Never mind how and when. I can't tell you. Please don't ask me about that. And much as I'd love to get hold of it for you, I can't think of any way for you to read it."

"But what does he say?" I was bouncing up and down with excitement.

"What Plato says is more interesting than whether what I feel is jealousy?"

I hit him on the shoulder. "Tell me!"

"Answer the question."

"Yes! Tell me!"

"Plato says the masters should cheat to get the best babies for the next generation. He says they should expose any babies born to people not the best. He says they should choose mates that will produce the best children, and let us think that it's chance."

"And are they doing that?" I asked. "How could we tell?"

"I tested it. I didn't win any contests, deliberately. And my name was the second out of the urn on random drawing."

"But it could have been anyway. There were what, maybe eighty names? And you're assuming that they're assuming you're the best . . . no, I suppose we can assume that they're assuming that." He so evidently was, on any grounds anyone would consider. There really wasn't any question.

"Being chosen doesn't conclusively prove anything. But it was an experiment worth trying. If I'd *not* been chosen it would have shown that they weren't following Plato. Though can you imagine that? Them *not* following Plato?" He laughed, and pulled himself up to sit on the parapet beside me.

"Then they might expose my baby. If that's what they're thinking, and what they're thinking in having potentially so many more children than they need."

"Your baby will be one of the best. They know you're really clever. They want good minds." He didn't sound very convincing.

"But how can you judge a good mind in a newborn? And it'll look like me."

"Like a swimming champion. They want swimming champions." He put his hand over mine, where I was hugging my belly again. "They're not stupid enough to do that. Don't you trust them?"

"For what?" I asked, my immediate retort now when asked about trust. "To have good intentions? Absolutely. To look at a scrawny baby with a flat face and think it should be kept? Not so much."

"I—you don't—"

"I don't have a flat face?" I asked, incredulous.

"I didn't know you knew," he said, awkwardly.

"What, did you think I was *blind*?"

He paused. "I didn't think it mattered to you."

"It doesn't. I don't think about it. It's just the face that happens to be on the outside of my head. It's the inside of my head that's interesting. But if you think I'm not aware of what other people think when they look at me you must think I'm stupid. Every time I ever got into a silly childish fight with anyone it would be the first thing they'd say: flat face, rabbit teeth."

"I didn't." He sounded confused. "I didn't say that when we had a fight."

"We didn't have a silly childish fight, we had a mature sensible fight," I said, and giggled. "Even before we met Sokrates."

"It's just ... your face," he said. "You wouldn't look like you without it."

"I know. It doesn't matter. Think how ugly Sokrates is. I was just thinking what the masters would think, looking at my baby and deciding whether to expose it."

"I'm sure they won't. They know how clever you are. And Nikias is clever too. I don't think they'll expose any of the gold children in this generation." He sounded sure now.

"I didn't know you knew Nikias?"

"He's in my lyric composition group. He wrote a song about you."

"He did?" I wasn't sure whether to be flattered or horrified.

"I told him if ever he sang it again I'd push his teeth down his throat."

"Ah. Thank you. I think."

He laughed. All this time his hand had been on top of mine on my belly. Now he moved it and patted my cheek. "Plato doesn't mention what happens when you're doing agape and then there's eros with other people. He never talks about it on the same page."

"We're doing agape?" I asked. My voice sounded strange in my ears.

"If we're not then I don't know what agape is." He put his arm over my shoulders and I leaned against him. "I have lots of friends in lots of places. Many of them are extremely loyal. I'm very fond of some of them. There are people with whom I've had eros. Klymene and I have a son together. But I never needed any of them. I need you. Not forever. Almost nothing is forever. But here and now, I need you."

"I'm here," I said. I kept still, but my mind was buzzing. "In the *Republic*, what is the aim of the city? What is it they want to produce?"

"The theme of the dialogue is justice—morality. But it goes a long way from there. Plato wants perfect justice, in a city or in a soul. In a practical way what they want to produce is philosopher kings: people who truly understand the Truth, and agree on what it is, and pursue it and keep the city in pursuit of it."

"Really?" Compared to that, even agape with Pytheas seemed like a small thing. "What an amazing dream."

"Aiming high, unquestionably."

"Aiming for the best excellence. I always knew they were." I felt vindicated. "I wish they'd let me read it. I want to say that to Sokrates."

"They're afraid you'd see the bit about them cheating with the lots and stop trusting them."

"They're idiots."

Pytheas laughed. "On the one hand you admire their vision, on the other you've noticed their flawed nature?"

"Yes. I mean they're not philosopher kings themselves, so how can they guide us into that? Or not us, the babies I suppose."

"Some of them would love to be philosopher kings. Ikaros, for example. Tullius. They almost think they are."

I yawned. It was very late now. "Do they think we will be? Or the babies?"

"Plato doesn't say."

"Oh, I wish I could read it!"

Pytheas shook his head. I could feel it through my body. "Would you want Kebes to read it? How about Damon?"

"Deception is never right. We're not children to be given medicine hidden in a spoonful of honey and a bedtime story. How could we get to be philosopher kings starting from lies and secrets?"

"Try all that on Sokrates. He might get you a copy."

"It's Ficino I want to try it on. He might understand. I don't want a clandestine copy for me. I want everyone to be able to read it and discuss it." I stood up. "It's really late. I should go to bed. See you tomorrow at Thessaly?"

25

APOLLO

I don't know what Agape is.

In my opinion, Plato would have been better off sticking to poetry. There are cultures, charming cultures some of them, that have a word for love of a close friend, specifically excluding a romantic or sexual partner. You can use that word to your grandmother, or your child, or your best friend, but not to your husband or lover. The Celts, who call me Apollo Bellenos or Apollo Ludensis, (Shining or Playful, both epithets that suit me) have a word like that. Not so the Greeks. There's a word for family love, that can't be extended to people outside blood family. Eros was obvious, eros was erotic love, and the word also covered romantic obsessions. Philia I understood perfectly well, philia was the dominant note of my being, friendship, sometimes very close friendship. Agape was supposed to be this amazing passionate but non-sexual love. Plato was always going on about it. It would be all very well, except that you're supposed to yearn for each other and suppress it.

Plato wrote this wonderful poetic dialogue called the *Phaedrus* in which Socrates makes speeches about love. There's a metaphor about a charioteer controlling a chariot with one lustful horse and one heavenly horse, while pursuing a chariot drawn by a god with two heavenly horses. I am a god. But when I was

in the city as a mortal I, didn't have any more difficulty controlling my metaphorical horses than I do on Olympos. I didn't
have any *less* difficulty either.

What I can't see is why Plato's so obsessed with feeling eros
and suppressing it. What's wrong with agape where you're passionate about the other person and they don't move you that
way? Or where you're both passionate together about some
shared obsession? Can't that be agape? And what's wrong with a
relationship where you're passionate about the other person and
they want you too and sex is all part of it? What's the problem
with adding sex to agape, in other words? What's the benefit of
abstinence?

Well, according to Plato, it makes your soul grow wings, and
cuts down on your necessary reincarnations. But that's nonsense. Take it from me: it doesn't. You're going to be reincar-
nated steadily throughout time no matter what you do. You'll
choose lives where you can learn to increase your excellence,
and that's how things gradually improve for everyone everywhere. There's no end point to time, it just keeps on unscroll-
ing. It doesn't stop. And though we live on Olympos and outside
time, we're limited in what we can do about those things. Athene
had no choice about setting things up so that bodies and souls
went back where they came from at death. She could snatch
Cicero away while the assassins were knocking on his door and
send him back to the same moment after he'd lived out his natural lifespan in the city, but she couldn't start messing about with
where souls were supposed to be. And before you start worrying about the children born in the city, souls come out of
Lethe. The children born there had souls from that time.
(There. Now you can't say you were reading all this in the hope
of divine revelation and only discovered way too much about
my personal issues.)

Even without affecting reincarnation, I suppose there can be a benefit to Platonic agape because sex can be a distraction. Lusting after someone can prevent you from focusing on how wonderful they are, because fulfilling the lust is what you think you want. Focusing on that without any desire getting in the way is what I think Plato meant when he talked about the lover wanting to increase the excellence of their beloved. You don't want anything from them except for them to exist and you to see them sometimes and talk to them, and maybe for them to like you back. But that only works if you don't feel the lust, not if you feel it and suppress it.

Have I totally contradicted myself? I *said* I didn't understand agape.

I respected Simmea. I liked her. I needed her friendship. I knew she was in love with me, so in a way that made me the beloved if you wanted to think of it in those terms. Plato was always talking about two men, and everyone else who had written about it and considered men and women always makes the man the lover and the woman the beloved, but there's no reason it has to be like that. Looking at it from that way round, it meant that *she* wanted to increase *my* excellence, which of course she did, always.

Anyway, I cared about Simmea. I would have gone to a great deal of trouble to avoid hurting her. If she hadn't been pregnant that night on the wall I'd have mated with her then, not because I lusted for her but because she lusted for me and I could have given her something she wanted. I did feel peculiar about her mating with other people, and specifically having somebody else's baby. I was afraid the other people would hurt her, and I wanted to protect her. And I felt it was perfectly fine—indeed better, as I didn't want her—that we didn't have sex; but if she was having sex with anyone it ought to be me. Also, I was going to ask Athene to make sure nobody even considered exposing her baby. If she was going to go through all that, there ought to be a result worth having. Even with Nikias, whose scansion was as heavy as lead. And I'd decided that her next baby would definitely be mine. That would be a hero worth having!

Some of these feelings were not ones I would have had without being incarnate. Most of them weren't, in fact, because if I had all my powers I wouldn't have needed her in the same way, and I might never have put in the time to come to know her. I needed her because I was incarnate and she was helping me so much with that.

We've established, I think, that what Plato knew about love and real people could have been written on a fingernail paring. Look how well his arrangements for having "wives and children in common" were going. Practically nobody was comfortable with it, and almost everybody was violating it in some way or other. We had long-term couples, and dramatic breakups, and casual sex, and cautious dating. We just had it all in secret. The masters either didn't know or turned a blind eye.

(And before I leave the subject of Platonic love, you remember the bit in the *Symposium* where Socrates reports Diotima's conversations with him about love? Do you picture them side by side in bed with the covers pulled up to their waists? I always do.)

A few days after the conversation on the wall, Klio, Simmea, Sokrates and I went back to the robot recharging station after dinner one evening. This trip was Klio's idea. She wanted Sokrates to talk to the robots without Lysias and she wanted to tell him some things. She'd talked to him and suggested it, and he'd said we should go too. I think he'd also suggested bringing Kebes and she'd put her foot down on that one, because she half-believed that Kebes might have been hoaxing everyone with the flowers, and she didn't want him to know any more about the robots than he did already.

At that point, I had no idea whether or not the robots were

sentient. I'd assumed they weren't, because otherwise what was the point of having them instead of slaves? But I didn't know where Athene got them from, and certainly there were times way up there that had sentient robots. We'd never have colonized Titan without them, and even Mars would have been hard work. And I realized vaguely that there must have been a time when robots were just becoming sentient, and these particular robots might have come from there, if Athene had chosen the best ones that weren't sentient, which would be just like her.

I didn't go and ask her, although I thought about it. The reason I didn't was that I enjoyed seeing Sokrates tackling a puzzle, and it was more fun when I didn't already know the answer. With many of the available puzzles—the nature of the universe, the purposes of the masters, Athene's plans—I did know the answers. Watching him take on one where I really didn't know was fascinating. It was adorable to see him introduced to the concept of zero. But watching him go after potential artificial intelligence was priceless. That alone would have been worth all the time I spent in the city.

Sokrates had written down the serial numbers of all the robots that were present the first night he went in, and he checked them all. Some of them were different, and he noted them. He greeted each one and asked it a few questions. This took about an hour. Then Klio pointed out the ones that refused to move, and he tried talking to them. He asked them questions and got Klio to translate the questions into English.

"Why do you want to stay in here and not go out to work? Do you like your work? Do you like the feeding station? What do you want to do?" He went down the row, speaking like that to each one, varying what he said from time to time.

"How do you give them orders?" he asked Klio.

"Well, we can give them verbal orders for simple things,

things they already understand. But if it's something new and complicated, we use a key."

"A key?" Sokrates said. "What sort of key?"

"I'll show you," she said. She went off to a locker at the back of the room and came back with a box containing little chips of metal and coloured plastic about as small as they could be and have human fingers pick them up—very similar to the ones I'd seen when I'd been on Mars for the concert that time.

"And you show the key to the worker?" Sokrates asked. "And then it obeys?"

"Essentially," Klio said. "It goes in this panel."

She touched a panel on the robot's side, which slid open. She put the key into a recessed slot.

"You put it directly into its liver," Sokrates said, turning to me. "Never mind your thought about head injuries. The liver is indeed the seat of intelligence!"

Klio laughed, then stopped laughing. "I suppose it is about where a liver would be . . ."

It was. I blinked.

"Let's not take this as evidence one way or the other until we know whether the workers are intelligent," Simmea said, wisely. "What does the key do?"

"It tells the worker that we need it to go out and look after the goats. It already understands what that means—how to watch for wolves, and how to milk the goats and make cheese and so on. The key tells it the priority. I could have given the order out loud in English to this one. But if I had one who had never looked after goats, I'd have to use the key, and the key would tell it what to do and also what it means."

"Those are clever keys," Sokrates said, running his fingers through them. "Do the colors tell you which orders they hold?"

"Yes, that's right," Klio said. "And if the worker won't take the order from the key, like these, eventually we swap out their . . .

liver. Their memory. But we can't do that so much, because we're low on new memories."

"They refuse to work and you punish them by removing their memory?" Sokrates asked.

"It's not *punishment*. They're not—we don't think of them as being aware." She looked guilty. "If they are, then we have behaved very badly to them."

"I think it would be better if you stopped removing memories for the time being," Sokrates said.

"There's so little proof! And Lysias, who is the one who really needs to make that decision, won't want to look at it. He distrusts Kebes, not without reason. And if he has to accept them as free-willed beings then he'll have to accept a lot of guilt for the memories he has removed." Klio looked distressed now.

Sokrates nodded gravely. "He will indeed. It's sad. But it's not as sad as removing their memories. We might beat a recalcitrant slave, but that would heal."

"I think you should talk to Lysias. And after that I think you should talk to the Chamber."

"I agree," Sokrates said. "But meanwhile, I should talk to these poor workers." He looked at me and Simmea. "You can do likewise. Go and ask them my questions. Let me know if there's a response."

"In Greek?" I asked.

"Greek, or Greek and then English," he replied, absently.

"You know we don't know English," Simmea said.

"I know you don't," Sokrates confirmed, looking only at her. Of course he guessed that I did, and didn't want to expose me. Dear old Sokrates. He always was extremely good about that.

"Should we try Latin?" she asked.

"I don't think there's any point," Klio said. "They won't be programmed in Latin, and they won't have heard it enough to have had any chance of picking it up."

"How could they have picked up Greek?" I asked, genuinely curious.

"Well, they can parse English, so they must have language circuits. Greek is a very clear and logical language, and it's part of the same language family as English. So is Latin, incidentally; that's why *non* and *no* are similar. So with hearing it so much I can just about believe that they might be able to figure out how to understand Greek."

"Why did it reply in English then?" Simmea asked.

Klio shrugged. "It shouldn't have been able to reply at all. The proper mode of interaction is that somebody gives it a command and then it carries it out to the best of its ability, pausing to recharge itself here when it needs to."

"They run on electricity?" Sokrates said. "Like the lights and the heat and cooling in the library?"

"They really are machines, whatever else they might be," Klio said.

We went up and down the rows, checking numbers and asking the workers questions. They were the same questions, Sokrates's questions. I longed for one of the workers to answer, especially after my body grew as tired of it as my mind. Eventually Simmea yawned so loudly that Klio heard, and sent us both to bed.

Walking along with Simmea discussing what we'd just been doing was one of the basic patterns of our interaction, one of the ways that our relationship functioned, so of course we did that. "Do you believe now that they might be aware?" she asked.

"I'm reserving judgement until there's more evidence," I said.

"What do you think the Chamber will say?" She stretched— her pregnancy was giving her odd back pains. I put my arm around her, which she always found comforting.

"They'll agree with Lysias that Kebes did it, even though that's definitely not the case. But if he really pushes it, then I think if it's the full Chamber they'll have to agree with Sokrates.

I mean, some of them are irritated with him about this and that, but he's Sokrates, after all. They're here because they love Plato. And Plato revered Sokrates—though he clearly built his own version of him to revere after a while." I smiled. "I think that's funny, don't you?"

"I've been thinking that for ages," she said. "Do you think he still wants to tear it all down?"

"Sokrates? The city? Yes. Why do you ask that now?"

I could see her face clearly in the light of a sconce above a sleeping house we were passing. She looked abstracted, and then as we moved and the shadows danced she looked maniacal. "I think the workers could be a lever for that," she said. "I do wish one of them had answered though!"

But it was months before they communicated with us again.

26

SIMMEA

For the first four months I was queasy in the mornings. In the next four I grew huge, which made sleeping uncomfortable and walking a misery. I also suffered horribly from heartburn, which could be relieved only by a tisane of elderflowers. It was the hottest part of the year, the part where Demeter threatens to burn up the world unless Persephone is returned to her. Klymene showed me how to adjust my kiton, and Maia gave me a harness to stop my newly swollen breasts from chafing. I sweated more than I ever had, and was happy only in the sea. I couldn't eat in the mornings and was ravenous by mid-afternoon. I craved cheese and fruit.

By the ninth month I was more than ready to give birth and get it over with. One afternoon I was sitting in the shade at Thessaly, drinking elderflower tisane and sucking a lemon. Aristomache was there—she had brought the basket of lemons. Sokrates and Pytheas were also sucking lemons while debating what it meant to make choices, and what constrained choices. Aristomache and I put in a word now and then, but largely it was a debate between the two of them.

"Apollo! What hyperbole!" Sokrates said. It always made Pytheas choke with laughter when Sokrates swore.

"But seriously, correct information," Aristomache began, when

Kebes came dashing in, looking as if he'd been chased by the Kindly Ones.

"What's the matter?" Sokrates asked, getting up at once and putting his arm around Kebes.

Kebes had been running so hard that he could hardly catch his breath for a moment. He leaned against Sokrates, and I could see that Sokrates, for all that he was old, had no trouble supporting him. "Workers. Message. Come and see!"

"A message?" Sokrates jumped, but to his credit he did not immediately drop Kebes.

"I can't read it. It's in that language."

That proved that Kebes hadn't written it himself, I thought, except that it would be possible to argue that he was lying about not knowing English. Though if none of us knew English, that did change that. It could certainly be seen as suspicious that he was again the one to find the message.

Pytheas helped me to my feet. He had become quite expert at bracing himself so I could haul myself up, and did it automatically now. Since we had had the conversation about agape, nothing had changed and everything had changed. It was as if acknowledging it had made a difference, as if naming transmuted. I was sometimes a little shy with him now.

Aristomache folded a cloth over the lemons and set the basket in the shade. "I know English," she said, getting up.

Kebes led the way. He didn't run, perhaps because he was winded or perhaps because he was aware that I could only waddle. Even so, his pace was too much for me and I trailed behind the others. Of course what Kebes had found was on the opposite side of the city—I could have guessed that. Even so, he must have sprinted all the way in the heat to have got so out of breath.

"My friend Herakles lives in Mulberry," Kebes said as we walked. "The mulberries have been ripe, and the birds have been all over the tree, and the house. It happens every year. The workers clean the guano off afterwards, because it looks so awful. This year when it was clean there was also an inscription, but he couldn't read it. I came straight back here with him after he told me. I couldn't read it either, not even *no*."

Mulberry was a perfectly ordinary seven-person sleeping house, down on the street of Artemis. The mulberry tree was splendid, one of the big ones with twisted branches. And indeed there was writing, in the Latin alphabet, inscribed neatly all around the eaves, where nobody except a worker could have reached without a ladder. I looked at it, assessing. Kebes could have done it on a ladder with a chisel, he'd had basic stone carving lessons at the same time I had. But it would have been a long job, and somebody would have been bound to notice.

Meanwhile, Aristomache was frowning. "I can't read it either," she said. "It certainly isn't English."

It wasn't Latin either. "What other language could it be?" I asked. "Klio said something about the workers speaking English or Chinese. Does anyone know Chinese? Does it use the Latin alphabet?"

"No, I don't know it, and it doesn't," Aristomache said. "And I don't think anyone here knows it, not even Lysias. China's such a very different civilization."

"But they use the Greek alphabet?" I asked.

"No, they have their own and I don't know it," Aristomache said, astonishing me. I knew there were a multiplicity of languages, but two alphabets seemed more than enough! "It doesn't look like our letters at all. I suppose they might have transliterated it—" and then she laughed. "It's Greek!"

I looked at her in astonishment. "It's certainly not!"

"No, it is," Pytheas said. "It's Greek spelled out in Latin letters."

"What does it say?" Sokrates asked.

Kebes began to read it aloud, hesitating now and then when the worker had made some odd sound choice in using the wrong alphabet. "No, no, no, do not like work, do not like some work more, do not like feeding station, do not like, no, no, want to talk, want to make, do not want to work, do not want to animals, do not want to farms, do not want to build, not, not, do not want, no, no, no." I could read it too, once I realized what I was looking at.

"Which worker wrote this?" Sokrates asked, looking wildly around as if he thought the worker would be waiting.

"No way to tell," Aristomache said.

"There may be a record," Kebes said. "Somebody may know which one they assigned to clean this house." He didn't sound hopeful.

"If they can do this they can hold a dialogue," Sokrates said, beaming. "I can speak and they can inscribe their answers! Want to talk! Wonderful!"

"Why did this one answer in this way now?" Pytheas asked. "And why up there?"

"It's where writing could be," I suggested. "Lots of buildings have writing up there. They don't say this kind of thing; they have uplifting mottoes or the names of the buildings, but that's where inscriptions go. Perhaps it felt it could only write inside the lines?"

"Just like the bulbs," Sokrates said. "I should have asked every one different questions so I'd know which one answered me."

"Even you might have had trouble thinking of that many different questions," Aristomache teased.

"I think that settles the question of whether the workers have free will and intelligence," Pytheas said.

"Yes," Kebes flashed at once. "Now you can stop thinking I did it."

"Pytheas never thought you did it," I said. "He argued persuasively that you wouldn't."

Kebes stopped with his mouth open. "Really?" he asked, after a moment.

"Yes, really," I said. "Ask Klio if you don't believe me."

"I believe you. I'm just surprised." He nodded at Pytheas, the closest he was likely to come to an apology.

"Pytheas avoids injustice," Sokrates said.

Pytheas looked uncomfortable, though it was entirely true. Pytheas could sometimes be ignorant, but the only time I could think of he'd been unjust was that time with Klymene. Of course, he had been unjust to half the human race that time . . . "Lysias will have to believe you didn't do it," he said to Kebes.

"I wonder what would happen if we gave them orders to write on the ground in the plaza of the garlands," Aristomache said.

"Why there?" I asked. It was where the diagonal street of Athene intersected the straight streets of Dionysos and Hephaestus.

"It's big, and it isn't especially important, and it's near my house and Olympia," she said. "It was just the first place I thought of."

"Who can give them orders?" Sokrates asked.

Aristomache hesitated. "All the masters, but usually it's the ones who deal with them. If I wanted one to do something I wouldn't just tell it to, I'd check with somebody who knows. Someone on the Tech Committee. They might need to use a key."

"Interesting," Sokrates said.

"They're always saying we should only use them for important things. I don't need them often myself, except in the kitchens of course, and sometimes clearing the ground for mosaics. I usually just say in Chamber if I'm going to want one for that and somebody sorts it out so that I get the work done in a few days."

Aristomache was still staring up at the writing. "They are slaves, aren't they?"

"And they don't like it. Look how many times it says *no*," I said.

"Of course, there was always slavery in antiquity," Aristomache said, as if trying to convince herself of something.

"In most circumstances in Athens, the slaves could earn money and eventually buy themselves free," Sokrates said. "Even from the mines sometimes. The status of *freedman* was as common, even more common, than slavery."

"We fought a war to free the slaves," Aristomache said. "It was the most—it was the defining act of my country in my century."

"And which side did you take?" Kebes asked.

"Against slavery," she said, taken aback. "Of course. But—"

"Then why did you agree to buy us?"

"You? What? We were rescuing you!" She put her hand to her head, sounding truly distressed.

"You must admit that you have not been used as slaves," Sokrates said to Kebes. "The workers, on the other hand, have."

"We will have to debate this in Chamber," Aristomache said. "This is new evidence. I shall bring it up in the next meeting."

"Meanwhile, can I give orders to the workers? Can the children?"

"You, I'm not sure. The children, definitely not. We decided that a long time ago. They were so young, and the workers are so powerful. Eventually, of course, they will be able to."

"I thought we were considered adults now," I said, patting my belly with one hand and putting my other on my gold pin.

"Yes, of course, but still in training for a while yet. You don't know everything you need to know."

"And you do?" Sokrates asked. It was one of his deceptively gentle questions. I saw when it hit Aristomache. She turned to him.

"You're making it seem as if I took all these decisions on my own and approve of all of them, when you know I didn't. It was the consensus of the Chamber. You've been in Chamber, you know what it's like."

"You have to take responsibility for decisions they made if you're remaining part of the Chamber," Sokrates said.

"I do take responsibility. I just don't always agree with everything, and I did argue for devolving actual power to the children sooner." She turned to me. "It will happen. We do know that we don't know everything either, and that you will understand the truth better than we do. Most of us know that, anyway. But you're eighteen years old. Give it time."

"You make all the decisions and don't allow us any voice," I said. "We respect you, but you underestimate us."

"Some of us respect you," Kebes amended.

"It seems neither the children nor the workers are as docile as you imagined," Sokrates said.

"I'll bring the issue of the workers up in the next Chamber meeting," Aristomache repeated.

"What about—" Sokrates began, and then I missed the rest of what he said because a pain the size of a library rammed into my belly, doubling me over. When I could hear again, Pytheas was holding both my hands and Sokrates was supporting me from behind.

"Ilythia be with you," Sokrates said. "This is the baby's time."

"Klymene said it hurt, but I hadn't imagined anything like that. Did I scream?"

"Anyone would," Kebes said. He looked as if he felt sick. Pytheas too looked pale. He was clenching my hands tightly.

"You should get to the nursery before the next pain comes," Aristomache said.

"There are more?" I asked. My teeth were chattering, even though it was a hot day.

"Oh you poor thing," Aristomache said. She pushed Sokrates away and put her arm around me. "Let go," she said to Pytheas. "We're going to the nursery. The rest of you should leave us. Birth is a women's mystery."

"It is," Pytheas said, as if he wanted to argue about that. He did not let go of my hands.

"Walk," Aristomache said, and I began to walk. Pytheas came along, walking backwards, still holding my hands, Sokrates and Kebes stayed where they were. Aristomache's arm felt comforting and solid. Pytheas's hands felt as if strength was flowing from him into me.

"Have you done this?" I asked Aristomache.

"Never. But I have seen lots of women do it," she said. "In my time it was a choice between a life of the mind, or love and babies. My mother chose the second. Most women did. Most women didn't even know they had the choice. I wanted—well, I couldn't have imagined shooing Sokrates away like that, or even having him dressing me down for sloppy argument, but that's what I wanted anyway. I wanted to have conversations with Sokrates more than I wanted anything. And I have that."

"I want that too," I said.

"And you have it," Pytheas said.

Aristomache was steering me in the direction of the Florentine nursery. I wished it wasn't so far. "Are you two—no, I don't want to know."

"We're friends in the finest Platonic tradition," Pytheas said.

"Truly," I confirmed. The strength that had seemed to come to me from Pytheas's hands finally reached my legs and I began to walk more steadily.

"Well that is the other thing I always wanted, and unlike you I never found it with anyone, man or woman," Aristomache said.

The next pain came then, with no warning, catching me between steps. I managed to stay upright, holding onto Pytheas's hands and panting hard to avoid screaming again. It felt as if my lower belly were being wrung by a giant. "Ilithyia be with her, protect and defend her, aid her now," Pytheas said, "Ilythia who brings the first light to new eyes, Ilythia who long ago Iris brought to floating Delos, Ilythia of the cavern, Ilythia the bringer forth, if ever I did anything for you, if ever I could do anything for you, hear me now, your suppliant. Hasten here and help Simmea."

He sounded so sincere it was awe-inspiring. He didn't sound like somebody praying so much as somebody really having a conversation with a god. And the pain did seem to recede a little as he spoke. I could still feel it ripping through me but it didn't hurt as much. When it had gone and I could walk again I started forward.

"Not far," Aristomache said. "And it's good that they're this close together already. It means it'll be quicker." We came to the nursery then. There were two steps up. "You can't come in," she said to Pytheas. "You have to let go."

"Yes," he said, but he didn't let go. "You'll be all right. And the baby will be all right."

"Yes," I said. "Thank you. Let go now. I have to go in."

"You'll have to let go first," he said. I let go, and then he did and took a step back. I hadn't realised how tightly I'd been clutching his hands. He had white marks across all his fingers.

I turned then and went inside before the next pain came.

Klymene prided herself on only screaming once. I lost count of how many times I screamed during childbirth. Aristomache stayed with me for an endless while. She stopped saying that it would be over quickly. She helped me try to find positions that were more bearable—standing holding on to the bed was best, and lying flat was worst. She rubbed my back and talked to me rationally in between pains when I was able to talk. She was very concerned about the workers.

"It's going to be difficult to explain to the Chamber. Too many of the masters come from times when slavery was acceptable."

"Sokrates said that slavery in Athens wasn't so bad." I took a sip of water from the cup Aristomache had brought me. "That's not what it was like where I came from."

"It's not what it was like where I came from either," she said. "People barely thought of slaves as being human, and they had no realistic prospect of freedom. They'd sell a husband and wife apart, or a mother and her children. Their masters could kill them and not have to account to anybody. The whole system was rotten. And they couldn't even run away without being caught and brought back."

"Even if they went to another city?" I asked.

"They were all dark-skinned, and the masters were all pale-skinned, so even if they went to another city they would be caught. They had to go to the places that let them be free, and that was a long hard journey. Some of us helped them escape. But the law could make them go back. It was the most unjust thing imaginable."

"So just because of what I looked like I'd have been a slave?" I asked. "Because my grandmother was Libyan?"

"As a dark-skinned woman you'd have been—when I imagine it as you it's unbearable. But there were probably girls just as smart and talented as you in that terrible unjust situation."

A pain came then and I held on to the bed while Aristomache supported me with her arm. I screamed. Afterwards I panted for a little while as the memory of the pain leaked away. "Were you a slave for long?" she asked, when I was capable of answering again.

"I'm supposed to have forgotten," I reminded her.

"Never mind that. Were you?" Her brow was furrowed, but I could not tell whether it was distress or worry or anxiety.

"Not very long. They captured me in a raid on my village. I was on the ship, and then in the market. It was half a month, perhaps a little more. Long enough to see some terrible things." I drank again and sat down on the bed. "My parents were farmers. We only had one slave, an old woman who helped my mother. She'd been born a slave. She'd been there my whole life. We loved her and she loved us, or I think she did, especially my older brothers. Her life wasn't all that different from ours. She was more like an old aunt than a servant. She used to tell us what to do, even my mother. But once when the harvest was short I heard my father talking about selling her. It didn't happen. But it could have."

I don't know what she would have replied. I had to rush to the latrine-fountain, where both my bladder and my guts let go of the entirety of their contents in an imperative rush. Another pain took me when I was there. Afterwards I felt so unsteady I had to lean my head on the tiles of the wall for a moment. When I came back, Axiothea had joined Aristomache in the birthing room. They helped me up onto the bed, where I leaned back against the wall as they looked up my vagina. "Opening up slowly," Axiothea said. "You'll get there, Simmea, don't worry."

"She's being very brave," Aristomache said, giving me some water.

"I'm not. I've been screaming." I sipped the water. It felt good in my mouth but was difficult to swallow.

"That's normal," Axiothea said, briskly. "I'll stay with you now for a while."

"I'll see you in a day or two," Aristomache said. She kissed me on the forehead. "I'll tell Sokrates and your friend that everything is going well."

Axiothea stayed for some time, but in the end it was Maia who delivered my baby, late in the darkest part of the night, just before the dawn. I suppose it's true that birth is a Mystery, a Mystery of Ilythia and Hera. It was the thing in my life that made me feel most like an animal. I was so caught up in it, in the pain, in the urgency of it, that there was no getting away from it. Against pain like that, against the body's mystery, there is no philosophy. But I was in the hands of the goddesses, and while I can remember that there was pain and that it racked me, I can't remember what it felt like. I can remember finding positions to stand, and later squat. I gave birth squatting up on the bed. I remember talking to Aristomache, I remember Axiothea and Maia being kind and explaining to me what was happening. I remember the waters breaking in a great gush. I remember the urge to push, and holding Maia's hand as I did push, until she had to prise my fingers off to check on the progress of the baby's head.

The baby didn't look as I had imagined him. He was darker-skinned and chubbier, and smeared with blood. He howled indignantly as if the world was an affront. His eyes were screwed tightly closed, and at once I imagined how the light must hurt him, after living so long in the watery dark inside me. It was a revelation—light itself was new to him! Everything was. Absolutely everything. He had thrust himself out of me knowing nothing at all. He had everything to learn, light and darkness, eating, speaking. Even breathing was new to him. Everything was for the first time. And here he was, not in my time or Aristomache's, he was safe in the Just City, where he could become the best self he could be.

Maia put him down on the top of my belly, under my breasts. He was warm, which I hadn't expected. "Hold him there," she said. "You're bleeding, and you have to push down hard again to get the placenta out."

I put my hands on the baby, who quieted a little at my touch but continued yelling. The inside of his mouth was surprisingly pink, and he had no teeth. His hands were tiny but perfectly formed. He formed a fist and then opened his tiny fingers out. The palm of his hand was paler than the rest of his skin. Maia pushed down on my stomach and I pushed obediently again and expelled a huge disgusting mass which looked like a big piece of uncooked liver, complete with tubes. Maia looked at this horrid thing in a pleased way. "That's all of it. Good." She went away with it and came back with a clean damp cloth. "Try to put him to the breast now and see if he'll take it, while I clean you up."

The baby didn't seem interested in my nipple when I tried to coax it between his lips, but he stopped howling. I kept trying as Maia wiped between my legs. The cloth looked alarmingly bloody when she was done.

"Am I all right?" I asked.

"Do you feel bad?"

"I feel terribly sore down there, and I'm about as exhausted as I have ever been."

"That's normal," she said, smiling. "You've been here all evening and most of the night. You're bleeding, but not too much, and I don't think you need stitching. You'll bleed for a while, probably half a month. Today and tomorrow you should use these paper pads bound between your legs. After that you can probably use your normal sponges."

I kept trying, but I couldn't persuade the baby to suck. "Don't worry, you'll get the hang of it with babies who already know what to do, while this little scrap gets his nourishment from a mother who knows," Maia said, lifting him off me and starting to wipe him clean. He began to wail again, and I ached to soothe him. He looked so small in her competent hands. Through the window the first red fingers of dawn were brightening the sky.

"Who chooses his name?" I asked.

Maia grimaced and put the baby against her shoulder, where he calmed to quiet whimpers. "Oh Simmea, you know perfectly well you should think of all the babies being born now as yours, and not this one in particular."

"I know," I said, surprised. "I do. I will. I didn't mean anything like that. But . . . who does decide his name? You?"

"Ficino, generally, for the Florentine babies. He has a knack for naming and he likes doing it. He'll come around after breakfast and name him."

I liked the thought of Ficino choosing the name, if I couldn't. "Ficino named me," I said, comforted.

"You can't name him. It would make too much of the connection." She wrapped him in a white cloth, twisting it expertly.

"Choosing names for them would? Not carrying them in our bodies for all these months and then going through all that?"

She shook her head. "Choosing his name, knowing his name, would mean you'd single him out among the others as yours."

"But I want to," I said.

Maia was cradling my baby against her now, and he lay peacefully in her arms. "You need to think of all of them as yours. You're a guardian. That doesn't just mean you wear a gold pin and talk to Sokrates; that means you'll eventually be one of those guiding the city. You want to do what's best for everyone, not just for your own family. We don't want you to favor this little boy because he's yours when he might not be the best. We want you to choose the ones who are the best to be made gold when their time comes."

"That makes sense," I acknowledged. But even as I said so I could feel tears rolling down my cheeks.

"We do know there's an instinctive bond," she said. "But it's better for everyone, for you, for him, for the city, to break it now. Love all your brothers and sisters, not one husband or wife. Love all the children, not just the ones of your body."

"Love wisdom," I said, sniffing. "I do love wisdom, Maia, and I love the city, and you'd better take him away now."

She took him out of the room. I could hear him begin to howl again, then as she went away the sound of his wailing grew quieter. She came back with a different baby, a girl, much bigger, pale-skinned and blue-eyed. Maia showed me how to nurse her, and as she had said it helped that the baby already understood. "It'll be a day or two before there's proper milk, but this will help it come," she explained.

She sat down beside me. "In my time, if you'd had a baby at eighteen it would have defined your life. You'd have had to look after it whether you knew how to or not. You'd never have had time to be a person or to think. You'd have been a mother and that's all."

"Aristomache said that. She said she had to choose between love and children, or a life of the mind."

"Aristomache was one of the lucky ones who had the chance to choose. Lots of women were stuck without any choice. Here you can have the baby and still have your life. You don't appreciate how fortunate that is, how few women have ever had that through all of history."

It was true if I could trust them, and for the most part I truly did.

"Even here and now, more of the burden falls on women," Maia went on. "I'm in here helping you right now, not in my room reading or thinking, where the male masters are. And you're giving birth while whoever the father is sleeps peacefully. But you won't be here helping the next generation through labor and wiping up the blood. You'll be organizing which of the iron girls do that work."

The pale baby let my nipple fall out of her mouth and Maia took her away. When she came back I had almost succumbed to exhaustion.

"Are you falling asleep?" Maia asked.

"Sorry. I was. I should go back to Hyssop."

"You can sleep here. It's probably not a good idea for you to walk just yet. Lie and rest where you are. But while you're still awake I want to say something. You really are going to be one of the people making all the decisions here. Lots of the masters are old. Even those of us who were relatively young ten years ago are getting older. When these children grow up even we will be old. You'll be the ones watching them and deciding who pursues excellence, who among them will be gold and silver, or bronze and iron. It's a big responsibility."

"It seems so far away when we can't make any decisions at all now. We can't even read the *Republic*, even though we're going to be the ones making it work."

"You're still so young," Maia said, pulling a cloak up over me. "You still have a lot to learn, and a lot of wisdom to acquire. But one of the things Plato says in the *Republic* is that the purpose of the city isn't to make the guardians the happiest people in the world, it's to make the whole city just. It's absolutely true that you might be happier if you could have one lover or if you could know which was your own child. But the whole city would be less just. Think about that."

My eyes were closing, and I let them close. I could hear her moving things around and then leaving the room. I could hear a baby, not mine, crying somewhere, and then the sound stopped. I was more exhausted than I had ever been from running in armor. I slipped down towards sleep. If Plato had been trying to maximize justice, what did that mean? This was the Just City, of course it was, we had always been told that. But why justice, not happiness, or liberty or any other excellence? What was justice really? I smiled. I'd have to debate it with Sokrates when next I saw him. I could be sure he'd be onto it like a terrier after a rat.

27

MAIA

I was exhausted before I arrived at Chamber. I would have skipped it and gone to bed, but Lysias had particularly asked everyone on the Tech Committee to be there. It was a little more than nine months after a festival of Hera, and so naturally we were coming to the end of birthing season. We were training some of the iron girls who'd given birth themselves in midwifery as well as childcare, but we didn't have enough of them yet, and most of the burden of helping them through fell on us—specifically, on the female masters. Everyone agreed that birth was a female mystery. I agreed myself. Nobody wants men around at a time like that. But the constant work of midwifery wore me out.

The Chamber was busy. It was a big room. We had never filled it, and we didn't now. But everyone seemed to be there. I spotted Lysias talking to Klio and went to join them. "Everything all right?" I asked.

"Up all night with babies," she said. "And I'm leaving a girl in labor to be here—but she has one of her sisters with her who has been through it, and it seems to be uncomplicated so far. They know to send for me or Kreusa if they need to. How about you?"

"I think Florentia is done for this season, and there's only one girl in Delphi who's still due."

"We need to space the festivals out more," Lysias said. "Two a year. Or even just one."

"I've been saying that for ages," Klio said. "I suggested that the first time it was ever discussed. And Plato says as often as necessary, not three times a year."

"We also need more doctors," Lysias said.

"Plato's quite explicit about medicine and—"

At that moment Tullius called for order and Klio fell silent.

"Before we hear the usual committee reports, Aristomache of Olympia has an important discovery she wants to bring to everyone's attention," Tullius said. His voice was shaking with age but still powerful.

Aristomache went to the front. The way we organized Chamber now was a compromise. Tullius and some of the others would have liked it to be like the Roman Senate, with everyone in status order. Others would have liked it to be all democratic consensus and informality. We sat where we wanted, not in order of seniority, but we did not speak unless called on, and then we went up to the rostrum to speak. Tullius was the President of the Chamber, and if he was speaking or didn't want to take the chair, then the chairmanship of the meeting rotated among the oldest men—and they were all men. Aristomache was one of the oldest women among the masters. Generally we voted openly by a show of hands, but on occasion when there was some particularly close or divisive question we would vote with black and white stones.

Aristomache stood quite relaxed at the rostrum, staring out at all of us. She looked very serious, but then she usually did. "Some months ago, Sokrates talked to us about the possible intelligence of the workers," she began. "Many of us concluded that it was a hoax. There's new evidence—a message inscribed on Mulberry house. The message is written in Greek using the

Latin alphabet, and it appears to be a response to Sokrates's questions. This reopens the whole issue."

Lysias tensed beside me, stood, and was recognized. He walked down to the rostrum. Aristomache stepped to the left in debate position. "Last time we concluded that it was a hoax organized by Kebes. The only compelling evidence against was that the message was in English. He could easily have constructed a message in Greek in the Latin alphabet. Anyone could."

"The message was carved high up on the building," Aristomache said. "Higher than anyone could easily reach. It was also incised in stone."

"There are ladders, and they've mostly had a little instruction in sculpture. Has Kebes?"

I was about to confirm that he had, when Ficino did it. He came forward. "He had the standard course, he would have learned that. He had no particular aptitude or interest. But he could have done it."

"Do you believe he did?" Aristomache asked.

"He's a difficult boy. I can't say one way or the other what he might do," Ficino said. "I've had trouble with him. Many of us have. There was that prank where he broke the statue of Aphrodite, years ago. But he seems to have settled down and improved under the influence of Sokrates." Ficino went back to his seat. He nodded at me as he passed by.

"Was Kebes involved with the discovery at Mulberry?" Lysias asked.

"He found it," Aristomache admitted. There was a murmur throughout the Chamber at that.

Sokrates strode forward. He never liked the forms of Chamber and tended to ignore them and do what he wanted, but now, although he did not wait to be acknowledged, he walked down to the rostrum before turning to face all of us.

"It is still possible it might be a hoax, and I continue to consider that theory. But this matter is so important that while we wait for more evidence, I urge you to act. Acting will not hurt anything if we are wrong, and not acting will be very injurious if we are right."

"What action do you want?" Lysias asked.

"What I called for last time," Sokrates said. "An end to the removal of memories from the workers, and an opening of dialogue with them. You agreed to the latter but not to the former, and such was the vote of the Chamber. Now I want the workers informed that they may write on the paths, so that if they want to they can answer me immediately."

"What was the message carved on Mulberry?" Tullius asked. Aristomache read it aloud.

"That isn't evidence either way," Tullius said. "It could be what a worker would say, or what a mischievous boy would imagine a worker would say."

"Leaving aside the question of Kebes, if there's a chance it's genuine we need to stop tormenting the workers and begin to talk with them," Sokrates urged.

"We can't manage without the workers," Lysias said.

"If the workers are slaves then there is a debate to be had," Sokrates said. "You say the evidence isn't yet conclusive. I agree. I am asking only to be able to collect more."

"That's fair," Tullius said.

"If they're slaves, then we need to treat them better and allow for the possibility of eventual manumission and immediate free time," Aristomache said.

"That's nonsense," Lysias said. "What would they do? What could they want?"

"Those are excellent questions to which I would very much like answers," Sokrates said. "Do you have any ideas?"

Lysias shook his head.

"If they are thinking beings we can't keep them enslaved," Aristomache said, flatly.

There was a rustle as people shifted uncomfortably in their seats. "Plato isn't against slavery," Tullius said. Slavery was one of those issues where time divided the masters. I myself was horrified at the thought. But Tullius had kept a houseful of slaves in Rome. It was different for him. "And if there ever were natural slaves, the workers are clearly that."

"Let's not have this argument," Lysias said. "Not until we know whether we need to. The workers are machines. Tools. It still seems much more likely to be a hoax. I'm sorry, Sokrates, but that boy has taken in many of us before now and then turned and mocked us. He could well be doing the same to you."

"I believe Kebes, but I understand that you have reason not to believe him," Sokrates said.

Kebes had always been a troublemaker, from the very beginning. I knew him well, because he was a Florentine. He had run away several times—once he had even been flogged for it. Only since he had become friends with Sokrates had he seemed to settle down to work to become better. We had argued for a long time over whether he deserved the gold. We'd only decided he did because by definition any friend of Sokrates was a philosopher.

Lysias nodded and spread his hands to Sokrates and to Aristomache. "What do you want?"

"I want all the workers told that they are allowed to inscribe writing on the paths if they want to answer me," Sokrates said.

"Might it not be unsightly?" Tullius asked.

"How could a Socratic dialogue be unsightly?" Aristomache asked. I laughed, and so did most of the Chamber.

"You'll do it?" Sokrates asked.

"If it's the will of the Chamber," Lysias said.

"If it's Kebes playing a hoax this will soon expose him,"

Sokrates said. "Somebody will catch him doing it. Or somebody will see a worker doing it. So far both incidents have been
small and easy to hide. The more there are, the more they will
be visible."

Tullius called for a show of hands, which went overwhelm-
ingly for Sokrates.

"And the issue of removing their memories?" he asked.

"You don't understand how much we need the workers!"
Lysias said. "They do so much for us, some of it things you
wouldn't notice unless it wasn't being done. Eventually the children will take over most of it, but right now we can't manage
without them. If they are free-willed and being compelled as slaves,
which I don't believe, we'll have to find some way to persuade them
to do the work. For now, we need them as they are, which means
making them work when they freeze up in the feeding stations.
There's no evidence at all about why they do that. Even if you
trusted it, this message says they don't like the feeding stations.
They're just malfunctioning. If your cloak is falling off, you
re-pin it. It's the same thing here. Athene gave them to us as
tools. She wouldn't have given us slaves."

Manlius stood and was recognized. "Athene isn't all-powerful
or all-knowing," he said. "She might have been mistaken about
the nature of the workers."

"A vote?" Sokrates suggested. There was another show of
hands, which Sokrates clearly lost.

"Moving on to reports," Tullius said, as Sokrates and Lysias
went back to their seats, but Aristomache remained at the rostrum. Tullius looked at her wearily. His kiton was hanging
loose, and he seemed thin and worn and tired.

"Another point," she said, her voice reaching to the back of
the hall as Lysias slipped back into his seat beside me. "Entirely
separate from the question of the workers. I want to call for a
debate on slavery. Are we for it or against it? Is it just?"

"Not now," said Tullius.

"I call to have such a debate scheduled," she said.

Tullius called for a vote, and hands went up all over the room. I raised mine and so did Klio. Lysias kept his firmly down. "It's too divisive," he murmured. "Why alienate them when it's a non-issue? I could wring that boy's neck."

The vote for the debate was carried, and we moved on to reports from committees, most of them boring. I gave the literature report—numbers of books printed, old and new. A boy in Megara had written an epic on Hektor, which was approved for printing. Nyra of Ithaka suggested that Simmea do a painting for the cover, as they were delighted with her painting for their hall. This was duly authorized. I was very glad I'd have such good news for her. It was hard on the girls giving birth and walking away. It would have been easier if they had been able to forget altogether, but all the babies needed feeding regularly. The other committees reported. I almost dozed off. It was agreed that the debate on slavery would be held at the next monthly meeting.

Sokrates came up to us as we were leaving. "How will you give the news to the workers?" he asked Lysias.

"I'm not sure," he said. "It's a case of changing parameters, which isn't easy. I'll probably use a key."

"Can I watch?"

"Certainly, though if you're wanting to check on my integrity you should know you won't understand any of it." Lysias drew himself up stiffly. I put my hand on his arm, which was like a bar of iron.

"He was just interested," Klio said.

"Nobody really understands how they work," Sokrates said. "I least of all, I know that. And I don't distrust your integrity, I just want to learn more about them."

"All right," Lysias said. He nodded to Sokrates, who nodded back. "It will be quite a lot of slow tedious work."

"I'll help you do it. Tomorrow—is that all right?" Klio asked. "I need to get back to a baby."

"Tomorrow, after breakfast, and thank you," Lysias said.

Klio nodded.

"I'll be there," Sokrates said. "At the feeding station?"

"Yes," Lysias said, looking resigned.

We wished each other joy of the night and left. Lysias walked beside me, in silence. "Do you really think it was Kebes?" I asked after a little while.

"It's by far the most likely explanation." Lysias was staring straight ahead. "They are more advanced than the workers of my own time. But they work the same way. Look how much we're being asked to believe, that they have intelligence, free will, and that they've managed to learn Greek?"

"I think it's harder for you to believe it than it is for me, because you understand them better. For me there's something a little magical about them. Steam engines were a wonder of technology for me. I can as easily believe that the workers can think as that they can prune a lemon tree." I paused for a moment, thinking about it. "For the people from even earlier times, with even less knowledge of how machines work, it would be even easier to think of them that way."

"And that's why Sokrates, who's from the earliest time of any of us, feels so sure they're sentient?" He had been walking quite rapidly, now he stopped, I almost bumped into him.

"It may be why he started talking to them in the first place," I suggested.

"It's just a hoax and a waste of my time," Lysias said. "But he needn't have thought I wouldn't do it. That hurt."

"I don't think he did think that."

"Oh yes he did. I know him. Come on, let's get you home before you fall asleep in the street and a worker comes and carves *no* on you!"

28

SIMMEA

I slipped down into exhausted sleep, and the sleep didn't rest me and the exhaustion didn't go away. Even worse than the exhaustion was the lethargy. From the time when I woke the morning after giving birth, I could hardly bring myself to stir. Worse again was the indifference. I didn't care about anything. Everything was too much effort. I hadn't fainted at all when I was pregnant, but I began to faint all the time as soon as the baby was born. Sometimes I couldn't go for an hour without fainting. These fainting spells kept up for a month, during which time I seldom went anywhere except between Hyssop and the nursery. I seldom went to Florentia to eat, I ate things people brought me. I never felt hungry, but when I had food I wanted it. When I did go to Florentia I grunted at my friends and stared at Botticelli's *Winter* while remembering distantly that I had once loved it. I fed babies three times a day. I bled heavily and constantly. I slept voraciously and woke still tired and with my breasts aching.

Maia called Charmides to me. He said I needed iron, and prescribed liver and cabbage, which I ate dutifully although it made me want to gag. Axiothea gave me iron lozenges to suck. Auge brought me figs and Klymene reported debates that I would normally have been sorry to miss. I could see that they were all genuinely concerned for me, but I couldn't seem to rouse myself out of my stupor. I felt passive and stupid as if only half of my mind was working. I wondered idly if perhaps some of my soul had gone into the baby and left me this empty husk without passion or desires.

I was tired absolutely all the time. The thought of resuming my life exhausted me. Maia told me I was commissioned to do a painting for a book cover, and instead of a joy and an honor it felt like an insurmountable burden. If I got up to go to the latrine-fountain I felt I had to rest when I came back to bed. The other girls in Hyssop, even those who had given birth, didn't know what to make of me. I avoided Sokrates and Kebes and even Pytheas. I felt it unfair of them to demand more of me than I had. I had just enough energy to eat and sleep and feed babies. Conversation drained me. It was an effort not to cry and an effort not to snap with irritation. Making the effort left me more exhausted than ever.

The iron, or something, helped with the bleeding, which began to ease off in the second month after I had given birth. I still fainted frequently and didn't care about anything. I didn't even care enough to be concerned that I didn't care; or rather I was aware that there was a problem and I would usually care, but it was as if it were a message sent to me from far away in dubious characters about people I had read about once. "Pytheas was asking about you," Klymene said one evening.

"Tell him I'm just tired," I said, and only much later thought how strange it was that Pytheas should have been driven to ask Klymene. Even as I thought it, I couldn't bring myself to care. Just looking at the fact was an effort. *He must really care about me,* I thought, *just when I don't care about anything. How could I possibly be worthy of him, in this condition?* I felt myself starting to cry. That was the other thing. It started immediately after the baby was born. I cried all the time as if my eyes had sprung a leak. Anything that would have sparked any emotion at all now made me weep.

A few days after that, Pytheas lay in wait for me outside Hyssop. He could not enter the house, of course, or the nursery, but nobody could stop him waiting by the door for me to come out.

"What's wrong?" he asked as soon as he saw me.

I started to cry immediately. "Nothing's wrong," I said.

"You're crying."

"Oh Pytheas, I'm too tired to explain it. It's just nothing." I felt exhausted at the thought of one of our usual conversations.

"I haven't seen you."

"I haven't been fit to see." My head began to spin. I took a deep breath, which sometimes helped. "Everything makes me tired."

Pytheas took my hand. "This isn't right," he said. "You shouldn't feel like this. Where were you going?"

"To the nursery. It's time to feed the babies." My breasts were tight and uncomfortable. I could feel Pytheas's hand, which was warm in mine, but as if I felt it through layers of muffling cloth. I tried to smile but just cried harder.

He frowned. "Simmea—look, I'm going to get Septima. I'll bring her back here in an hour, all right?"

"Why Septima?" I asked, but he had gone, running full tilt.

I walked to the nursery, still in my haze of misery and exhaustion. Nothing seemed to matter. Maia had said I could have a baby and go on with my life, but it seemed my body had other ideas. I fed a baby Andromeda brought me, one of the small ones but not mine. I had not seen mine again. I did not know his name. I drank some cabbage soup and ate some barley bread, barely tasting it. I sucked obediently at one of the iron lozenges Axiothea had given me. When I went outside again Septima and Pytheas were waiting, sitting on the low wall by the currant bushes. Pytheas looked concerned, and Septima looked irritated.

They weren't talking as they waited, or even looking at each other. Seeing them together, they did have a clear family resemblance—their golden skin color, and the shape of their chins, and the way their eyes were set.

"Here you are," Pytheas said, getting up.

I walked over to them, forcing myself to do it, though all I wanted was to go back to Hyssop and lie down and stare unthinkingly at the wall.

"What's the matter?" Septima asked.

"Lethargy," I said. "Exhaustion. A tendency to weep and a tendency to faint. Charmides says it's a thing that happens and it will go away in time."

"He's right," she said, not to me but to Pytheas. "It's not a curse. It's a medical thing. She'll get over it eventually."

"I think *now* would be a good time for her to get over it," he said, sharply.

Septima rolled her eyes. "I don't know why you're asking me, it's not my department at all."

"I'm sorry," I said, and tears started to roll down my cheeks again. "I didn't ask him to bother you about it. I know I'll get over it. Axiothea also says so. She says some women have this after childbirth, and I need iron and rest."

"You've been resting, and it's doing no good," Pytheas said. "I need you. Sokrates needs you."

Septima put her hand on my arm. "You should go to the temple of Asklepius and pray for healing," she suggested.

"Come on," Pytheas said.

"I'm so tired," I whined. "Can't I lie down now? I'll go later. Tomorrow."

The temple of Asklepius was close to Thessaly, halfway across the city. I couldn't face the thought of walking that far. "You're going now," Pytheas said. He put his arm around me, supporting me. Again I could both feel it and not feel it. It was as if there was something in the way of sensation, as if my sense of touch had eyelids and they were closed across it. The purely physical warmth of his arm came through my kiton, but the touch itself was muffled, and I certainly felt none of the accompanying happiness that his touch usually brought. "Come on."

"All right," I said. It was easier to walk than resist, so I walked. I fainted once on the way. It was hard to tell when I was going to faint, because I felt strange and dizzy all the time, as if I was holding on to consciousness by a thread. Sometimes the thread parted. Pytheas held me up, or at least, when I opened my eyes I saw his, blue above me in his perfect chiseled face. There had been times when I would have given anything to have been in his arms. Now it was merely comforting in a mild animal way. I did not feel desire—I felt no desire at all for anything, except sleep.

We walked on towards the temple. There was nobody there in the late afternoon. It was small and simple, just a circle of plain marble Ionic pillars with a canted roof. Inside there was nothing but a statue of the god with an archaic smile, and a little burner for offerings. Pytheas helped me up the steps.

"Pray to Asklepius," Septima said. "Aloud. Ask for healing."

I didn't ask if I could rest first, it was clear from her tone that she wasn't going to let me. I obeyed. I raised my arms, palm up and then palm down. In the city we didn't kneel groveling before the gods as I remembered doing in church as a child, but prayed standing before them. I didn't know what to say. I had celebrated Asklepius on his feast days, naturally, but I had never sought him out before. I had never been ill.

Out loud, Septima had said. I tried my best. "Asklepius, wisest son of shining Apollo, help me now. Restore me to health."

"Asklepius, hear her," they both said in chorus, from behind me. Their words echoed in the empty temple.

I hadn't thought what divine healing would be like, or even really considered whether it might work. I was doing this only because they wouldn't let me rest until I did, and out of a faint memory of my agape for Pytheas. I stood there with my arms outstretched towards the statue of the god, and between one instant and the next my sickness was removed from me.

It was like waking up, or perhaps more like diving into the sea from a cliff and hitting the cold water all at once. I was alert and vibrating. All the lethargy was gone. I had my mind back. My soul was my own. My body was strong again. I no longer wanted to sleep. I didn't feel faint, and the queasiness that had been with me for so long that I no longer consciously noticed it had also gone. I was ravenous. I could have run up the mountain, or danced all night, or debated a really chewy subject with Sokrates. I wanted to. I laughed.

"Thank you, Lord Asklepius, divine healer," I said, and my words were heartfelt and willed, the first truly willed words I had said since I had slipped into sleep the night the baby was born.

I turned around. Pytheas and Septima were still standing there, of course, and I saw them in my newfound clarity. I knew. I recognized them. I gasped.

It all made sense, in that instant, where Athene had gone, and why Pytheas was the way he was, why he had the excellences he did and the flaws he did, why he laughed when Sokrates swore by Apollo, why Sokrates had been surprised when he said his parents lived above Delphi, why my prayer to Athene had sent me to Septima in the library. I just stood gaping at the two of them, and for a long moment they both stared back at me in silence. The grey eyes and the blue, the chiseled features, so similar, the truly Olympian calm. But Pytheas—Pytheas, even the name, Pythian Apollo, his Delphic title. They were gods, gods in mortal form and standing there. Septima was Pallas Athene and Pytheas, my Pytheas, was the god Apollo! I almost wished I still felt like fainting, because it would have been one of the very few appropriate responses.

29

MAIA

During the month before the debate on slavery, evidence for the intelligence of the workers piled up. Sokrates was openly and visibly engaging them in dialogue, and their halves of the dialogue remained written in stone for anyone to read later. It was no longer possible for anyone to believe it was a hoax, unless they accused Sokrates of being in on it, which was unthinkable.

I was on my way home from the palaestra one day when I saw Sokrates squatting beside a worker in the middle of the street. I hesitated, curious. We had all agreed when Sokrates first arrived that we would not treat him like a celebrity but allow him to select his own friends. I had never been one of those chosen, nor had I expected to be. He concentrated on teaching the children, those who could really hope to become philosopher kings, and those among the masters who were the most brilliant and who had something to teach him. I had seen him in Chamber, and around the city. We'd exchanged a few words from time to time, naturally. But I didn't know him well. Now, as I walked around him, he looked up from what the worker was engraving and grinned at me. His face had always reminded me of a Toby jug, and from above, with him grinning like that, the resemblance was unavoidable. But amid all that ugliness, his eyes were very keen.

He straightened up. "Joy to you. I'm trying to get him to understand the concept of names. Are you busy, or can I use you as an example? It might take a few minutes."

"Of course," I said, slightly flustered. "And joy to you. I have a little while before I'm due to teach my weaving class."

"Good. Thank you." He turned back to the worker. "You see this human?" he asked.

The worker wrote something. I craned to see what. Sokrates moved slightly so that I could read it. "Master." It wrote the Greek word in Latin letters, as we had all been told they did.

"Yes. Good. She's a master," Sokrates said. "And her name is Maia."

"Master Maia," it wrote.

"How does it know I'm a master?" I asked.

"They've been told to take orders from masters and not children, so they recognize you as being part of the class of people called masters," Sokrates explained.

"But I practically never give them orders," I protested.

"That doesn't matter. Say something to him now," Sokrates instructed me.

"Joy to you, worker," I said to it, awkwardly.

It underlined where it had written my name, and began to write neatly underneath. "Sokrates means only-you, Maia means only-her?" it engraved. And as easily as that, I was convinced. It didn't matter what Lysias said, the worker was obviously thinking and putting ideas together. He might be huge and yellow and have treads and four arms with tools at the end of them, but he was a philosopher all the same.

"That's right," Sokrates said. "Well done. These are names. And what name means only you?"

The worker was still for a moment, and then he inscribed a long number. After it, he wrote the word "Worker."

Sokrates pulled a little notebook out of his kiton, one of the standard buff notebooks we all used. He opened it up and checked the number against a list he had written down. "Is that what other workers call you?" he asked as he read. He found the number and put a little check mark against it.

"No," he wrote.

"What name do they call you?"

"Call?"

"To address you, or talk about you when you're not there," Sokrates said, stuffing the notebook and pencil back into his kiton. "Watch how we use names. Joy to you, Maia. How are you, Maia?"

"Joy to you Sokrates. I am well. How are you, Sokrates?" It felt very unnatural, and he laughed at my wooden delivery.

"I am very well. How is Simmea?"

I forgot what we were supposed to be doing and spoke normally. "Simmea is a little better, I think, but she's still very low and bleeding a great deal, and she keeps fainting. Charmides says she'll get over it, but I'm worried about her."

Sokrates frowned. "Tell her I miss her," he said.

The worker was writing something. We bent over to read it.

"Workers do not call names," the worker had written.

"How about what the masters call you when they want you to do something?" Sokrates asked.

"Do not call name."

"I don't think Lysias and Klio distinguish between them very much," I said. "Lysias never seems to when he's talking about them. He thinks of them as interchangeable, except when they break down."

"They're not interchangeable, they're definitely individuals and different from each other," Sokrates said. "They've all been given permission to talk, but only some of them do."

"Only-me," the worker carved. "Individual. No name."

"You should have a name," I said. "A proper name, not a number."

"What name only-me?" he asked.

I looked at Sokrates, and he shrugged. "How do you usually choose names?"

"From Plato's dialogues, or from mythology," I said. "And we keep names unique. I don't know all the ones that have been used already. Ficino would know. He chooses the names for Florentia."

"It's easy enough to think of appropriate mythological names," Sokrates said, patting the worker. "But what kind of name would you like?"

He didn't answer, and then he inscribed a circle, twice. Then underneath he neatly inscribed the word "Write."

"You can't be called Write," Sokrates said. "A name can have meaning, but that's too confusing."

"Learn?" he suggested.

I looked at Sokrates. "Does he really want to be called write, or learn?"

"He's just learning what names are, you can't expect him to understand at once what kind of things work for them," Sokrates said.

"I understand that. But that those are the things he wants to be called speaks very well of him." I was impressed.

"He has come to understanding in your city; naturally he is a philosopher," Sokrates said.

"Give name?" the worker inscribed.

"You want me to give you a name?" Sokrates asked.

"Want Sokrates give name means only-me."

I was moved, and Sokrates plainly was too. "You are the worker who answered me with the bulbs," he said.

"Yes," he wrote.

"Then I will call you Crocus," Sokrates said. "Crocus is the name of that spring flower you planted. And that was the first action of any worker that replied to me, that showed what you were. I'll name you for your deeds. And nobody else in the city will have that name."

"Worker Crocus," he wrote, and then repeated the long serial number. "Only-me," he added.

Then, without a word of farewell he trundled off up the street and began to rake the palaestra. I stared after him. "That is unquestionably a person," I said.

"Now if only I can persuade him to give three hundred such demonstrations to each of the masters individually," Sokrates said, smiling. "Sometimes they're not as clear as that," he went on. "My dialogues with them can be very frustrating sometimes when I can't explain what things mean."

"Well, that was clear to me. He's a person and a philosopher," I said.

"A lover of wisdom and learning, certainly. If that is what makes a philosopher."

"Plato said they had to have that and also be just and gentle, retentive, clever, liberal, brave, temperate, and have a sense of order and proportion." Then I looked at Sokrates. "But you must know that. You said it yourself."

"Nothing in the *Republic* is anything I ever said, or thought, or dreamed. The *Apology* is fairly accurate, as is the account of the drinking party after Agathon's first victory at the Dionysia. But even there Plato was inclined to let his imagination get the better of him."

I wasn't exactly shocked, because I'd heard it before, though never so directly. "He just used your name when he wanted to express the wisest views."

"Yes, that's the kind way of thinking about it. And I was dead and couldn't be harmed by it." He sighed. "Not until I came here, anyway."

"He was trying to write the truth, to discover the truth, even if he put his own words into your mouth," I said.

"And do you think he found the truth?" he asked.

I paused, looking back at Crocus, still raking the sand. "I think he often did, and more important, I think he invited us all into the inquiry. Nobody reads Plato and agrees with everything. But nobody reads any of the dialogues without wanting to be there joining in. Everybody reads it and is drawn into the argument and the search for the truth. We're always arguing here about what he meant and what we should do. Plato laid down the framework for us to carry on with. He showed us— and this I believe he did get from you—he showed us how to inquire into the nature of the world and ourselves, and examine our lives, and know ourselves. Whether you really had the particular conversations he wrote down or not, by writing them he invited us all into the great conversation."

"Yes, he did get that from me," Sokrates said. "And he did pass that down to you. And, as I understand it, the world would certainly have been different and less good without that spirit of inquiry."

"It must be so strange to see your own legacy," I said.

"Strange and in many ways humbling," Sokrates said. He patted my arm. "You should go, or your weaving students will be wondering where you are. Don't forget to tell Simmea I miss her and hope to see her soon."

He walked off up the street and I went on to my own work.

30

SIMMEA

"Are you all right? Say something," Pytheas said after I'd been staring at them for a long moment.

"I'm all right. I'm cured," I said. "But I——. You. How, why?"

They looked at each other for an instant, and then back at me. There might be gods who couldn't have deduced what I meant from that, but these two were not among them. "Asklepius told her?" Septima asked. "Why?"

"Nobody told me. I worked it out. It was obvious. I turned around and saw you and I knew."

"Half the masters know about you anyway," Pytheas said. "And Simmea won't tell anyone."

"Why are you doing this?" I asked.

"You knew I helped to set up the city. Now I'm living in it for a little while, and still helping. It needs my help." Septima frowned. "Is my brother right? Will you keep this secret?"

"Why is it a secret?" I asked.

"So I can live here quietly, without any fuss, and experience it normally," she said.

I thought about Septima, about her strange halfway status in the library. Was she experiencing it normally? It didn't seem so, especially if half the masters knew who she was. Yet anyone would naturally want to live in the city, and without undue attention. "I won't tell the children who you are," I said.

"Good enough," Pytheas said.

Septima—Pallas Athene—turned to him. "That's not your decision."

"Yes it is," he said.

"Why?" She seemed to get taller as she spoke.

"Simmea's my votary. I take full responsibility for her. You can trust me that she'll keep her word." All this time Pytheas kept his eyes on his sister and did not even glance at me.

"You are behaving irresponsibly and taking stupid risks," Athene snapped. "I was against this intervention from the start, but you couldn't wait. Your votary. Is she now? Ask her if she is. You're besotted with her. It's Daphne all over again."

"I am," I said, full of my new-found clarity, and not considering whether it was a good idea to intervene.

"You are?" She towered above me now. She had a great helmet and a shield on her arm. "Do you even know what it means?"

"If he's Pytheas, I'm his friend. Since he's the god Apollo, I'm his votary. But you can trust me to keep my word without his guarantee. You know me well enough for that. I have always served you well. And I am a gold of the Just City. You helped to set it up. If you can't trust my word, what have we been doing here?"

Pytheas laughed. Athene turned on him angrily, then shook her head and shrank back down into her Septima form. "I'll trust your word," she said. "As a gold of this city and my brother's votary." She stalked off down the street, her hair flying behind her in the breeze.

I looked at Pytheas. "You're the god Apollo? You told me we were doing agape! You said you needed me."

He blinked. His expression was surprisingly reminiscent of

the moment in the palaestra when I'd beaten him up. "It's because I'm Apollo that I need you," he said. "You help me so much."

I took a step towards him. "And you didn't tell me because?"

"Because I didn't want to have this conversation?" He tried a smile. "Because I really am trying mortality and to live here and experience the city?"

"You're the god Apollo," I repeated. It was strange, simultaneously surprising and inevitable. "Of course you are. I'm an idiot. I don't know why I didn't figure it out before."

"I'm Pytheas," he said. "That's real too."

I took another step forward. "Can you turn back into a god at any moment, like Athene just did?"

"No." He looked awkward. "I wanted the authentic experience. The only way I can take my powers up again is by dying. I'm here for the long haul. And you've really helped me understand so much about how it works."

"She said you were taking stupid risks. Did she mean your becoming incarnate, or did she mean healing me?"

He nodded. "Healing you. But that as well, because I had to ask her for help, without my own powers. You were trapped in your body, in your sickness. It was horrible. I couldn't leave you like that for months or years."

"It really was horrible," I agreed. "I didn't care about anything. That was the worst. Worse than fainting all the time. Thank you for helping me."

"But you're all right now?"

"I'm starving, but I feel as good as I ever did. But I've had an awful shock." He hadn't moved, but I had closed the space between us and stood close in front of him. "You were taking stupid risks for me?"

"It wasn't all that—all right, yes, I suppose I was." He met my eyes.

"You're a *god*." A god. He was thousands of years old. He had unimaginable powers. And he was just standing there.

"That doesn't stop me being confused and wanting to learn things."

"Evidently not."

"Or truly liking you." The strange thing was how little it changed the way I felt about him. I felt unworthy of him. But I had always felt unworthy of him. And there was still a vulnerability in his eyes. "Are you going to hit me?"

I reached out and tapped his chest lightly. "If I'm going to hit you we should go to the palaestra. There are people passing, and this temple is open all around. They'd see us wrestling in here." It wasn't wrestling I wanted to do with him. It never had been. "But I think we should go to Thessaly."

"Good idea," he said. "For one thing, it's close. For another, Sokrates has been missing you. And thirdly, Sokrates knows. He's the only one. I didn't tell him. He recognized me."

"Of course he did. I was there. And that's why he immediately started off on whether we can trust the gods." I felt stupid for not understanding at the time.

Pytheas took my hand. His hand didn't feel any different from the way it always did—always when I was myself and cared about it, that is. "He can trust me," he said. "And so can you."

I looked at him sideways. "Those the gods love . . . tend to come to terrible ends."

"That's Father. And . . . some of the others, I suppose. But I do my best for my friends. I can't do anything about Fate or Necessity, or directly against the will of other gods, but so far as I can, I always do my best for them."

We started walking together towards Thessaly. I thought through all the stories I knew about Apollo. "What about Niobe?"

"She badmouthed my mother. Besides, I didn't say I didn't punish my enemies." He was looking at me sideways, awkwardly.

"Well, being a god explains why you're so hopeless at being a human being sometimes," I said.

He laughed. "I was so worried about you finding out. I can't believe you know and it doesn't make any difference."

"It makes a difference," I said.

"But you're talking to me the same way?" He seemed tentative.

"You're still you." That was what I felt very strongly. Pytheas was still Pytheas, the way he always had been. I just understood him better now. It was like the thing with Klymene. I didn't feel that he'd been deceiving me, just that this was the thing he had kept quiet, a thing that helped me make sense of him. But the implications were still slowly sinking in. Maybe it was because my mind had been wrapped in wool for so long.

"And what you said to Athene?" he asked.

"That I'm a gold of this city and she'd better trust my word if she hasn't been wasting her time here for eight years?"

Pytheas laughed. "That was perfect, though she'll take a while to get over it. But I meant the other thing. That you're my friend and my votary."

"Yes." I stopped walking, and he stopped too. "But you know that. You knew that before. What else were we talking about up on the wall? Except for you not mentioning the fact that you're Apollo."

"What it means for you to be my votary is that the other gods can't do anything to you without my permission," he said.

"I know. And you can do anything you want. I have read about this." We started walking again. We were quite close to Thessaly now. "I'm walking with the gods," I said, and giggled. Then I stopped. "What's that?"

The marble slabs of the pathway stretching out before us, as far as Thessaly and further, stretching out up the street from there, were all cut with words. "It's the workers' halves of dialogues," Pytheas said. "I did want to tell you, but you weren't listening to anything anyone said."

"They're talking back?" I was delighted. "I knew it wasn't Kebes."

"They're talking back to Sokrates at great length," Pytheas said. "So it seems he was right and everyone else was wrong, not for the first time. They've had a major debate about slavery in the Chamber, and Sokrates is trying to persuade the workers to work, by first finding out what they want and then seeing whether we can offer it to them. It's all terribly exciting. Aristomache apparently made a wonderful speech about Plato and freedom."

"She's great. I'm sorry I missed that. Did I miss anything else?"

"You'd have missed that anyway, it took place in closed Chamber. Sokrates told me about it afterwards."

Just then we saw Sokrates, up the street a way past Thessaly. He was talking to a worker, who was carving replies into the marble. "Soon the whole city is going to be paved in Socratic dialogues," Pytheas said. "It's so appropriate that I'm amazed they didn't think of it from the start."

"It's wonderful," I said, starting to read some of it. Just then Sokrates saw us, said something to the worker he was talking to and bounded towards us.

"Simmea!" he said. "Joy to you! How wonderful to see you restored to yourself."

"It's wonderful to see you too. As for my restoration, it's divine intervention," I said.

His keen eyes went from Pytheas to me. "I see. Perhaps we should go into the garden and sit down and talk about this?"

"That would be excellent, but do you have anything to eat? I feel as if I haven't eaten anything in half a year."

Sokrates looked bemused as he opened the door. "I don't think I do. Maybe I have some lemons?"

Pytheas reached into the fold of his kiton and produced a goat cheese wrapped in chestnut leaves. Sokrates led the way through to the garden. I sat on the ground by the tree, getting down easily, in a way that I'd taken for granted until recently. Pytheas leaned on the tree and I leaned back against him as I often did here. Sokrates came out with three slightly wizened lemons and handed us one each. I broke off chunks of the cheese and started to eat it.

"Do you want to hear about my success with the workers, or should we discuss the nature of the gods?" Sokrates asked.

"He says he's Apollo and he always does his best for his friends, under the constraints of Necessity and Fate and other gods," I said.

"I can still talk, you know," Pytheas protested.

I stopped. "Go ahead then."

"Is there anything new from the workers?" he asked.

Sokrates threw his head back and laughed, and I laughed too. Sokrates mopped his eyes with a corner of his kiton. "Why did you come here?" he asked.

"To talk to you," Pytheas said.

"I didn't mean this afternoon, double-tongued one, though it's interesting that you want to talk to me about this now when you've been avoiding it for so long. Why did you come to the city? Unless you did that to talk to me?"

"That was part of the attraction," Pytheas admitted. "But seriously, I wanted to experience being a mortal. I wanted to learn about volition and equal significance."

"And have you been learning about them?" Sokrates asked.

"You know he has," I said.

"Volition and equal significance," Sokrates said. "What interesting subjects for a god to need to study!"

"You know we don't know everything. Well, except for Father."

"It's just exactly what I've been thinking about with the workers," Sokrates went on, as if Pytheas hadn't spoken. His eyes were very sharp. "Both of those things. The masters were not prepared to see them in the workers, as the gods were perhaps not prepared to see them in us?"

"I don't know what the other gods know about it. Athene knew."

"Did she now? And still she chose to do this to us?"

Sitting as we were, I could feel Pytheas draw breath and then let it go before drawing breath again to speak. "Is this really the conversation you want to have with me?"

Sokrates laughed again, a short bark of a laugh. "Should I ask you instead what happens to souls before birth and after death?"

"I could tell you," Pytheas said.

I sat up and moved to where I could see his face. "It's what Plato wrote in the *Phaedo*, isn't it?"

"That piece of misrepresentation," Sokrates said, automatically, as he always did whenever that dialogue was mentioned.

"Close enough," Pytheas said.

"Then we did choose," I said.

"I certainly didn't," Sokrates said.

"You don't know it, but you did. When your eyes were open, in the underworld, you chose a life that would lead you closer to excellence, and it led you here. And me. And Kebes, and I can't wait to tell him."

"You can't tell Kebes," Pytheas said, alarmed.

Sokrates was blinking. "No, I might have chosen my life to lead me to excellence despite the diversion here at the last minute," he said.

"That doesn't hold for Kebes," I said.

"Simmea, really, you can't tell him!"

"I know. I promised. But I'm right, aren't I? We chose, know-ing, and then drank from Lethe and forgot. So, volition. How about the workers? Do they have souls?"

Pytheas started to answer, then stopped. "I don't know. I don't even have a belief on the subject. I thought not."

"How could a being have desires, and plans, and think, and not have a soul?" Sokrates asked.

"How could a being made by men out of glass and metal have a soul?" Pytheas asked.

"How could a being made by women out of blood and sperm?" I countered. "Where did souls come from? How many are there?"

"Athene probably knows," Pytheas said. "But I don't want to ask her while she's still angry. There were already people and they already had souls by the time I was born. As for how many, lots. Lots and lots. The underworld is practically solid with them."

I looked at Sokrates, who was twisting his beard in his fin-gers and staring at Pytheas. "If you are present in the world, why do you keep so secret?" he asked.

Pytheas laughed. "Sokrates, I sent a keeper—a daemon to whisper in your ear every time you were going to do something dangerous for your whole life, and you call that keeping se-cret?"

"Why don't you do that for everyone?"

"I only have so many daemons, and not everyone can hear them, or wants to. I do it for my friends." His eyes met mine for a second.

"And you can change time?"

"Only time that nobody cares about. Some bits of time are stiff with divine attention. Here, before the Trojan War, and on Kallisti, nobody was looking until Athene started this."

"And the volcano will destroy the evidence," I said. I had just put this together in my mind.

"Klio tells me that this island isn't round but a semi-circle by my own era," Sokrates confirmed.

"I hope we'll have warning to leave in time," I said. I looked at Pytheas.

He spread his hands. "I hope so too," he said.

31

APOLLO

I had always thought that if she knew she would be intimidated, but I should have known better. Almost everyone is intimidated, it's normal, it's why we go about in disguise so much. Being capable of intimidating people is useful. Being surrounded by people who are intimidated all the time is miserable and tiresome. I've always hated people grovelling too. I thought she'd change to me. But instead she immediately started to analyze the whole thing. It was wonderful. It was what I should have expected. It was then that I came to truly love her.

"So you don't know the future?" Sokrates asked.

"All of us here know a lot about the future," I said. "I don't know my personal future. None of us do. Except maybe Father. Usually I live outside time, and I can go into time when I want to. So I know a lot about time, and it doesn't have future and past, it's just there, spooling out and I can step into it where I want to. Think of it like a scroll that I can open up anywhere. It lets me give oracles, though half the purpose of oracles is to be mysterious, not to give information. Sometimes it's a way of helping people, or just getting some information across. But usually it's a useless way of warning people, no matter how much I might want to. Anyway, right now I'm living in time, just the same as you are."

"How does that work?" Simmea asked. "Being outside time, but having your own personal time?"

"It's a Mystery," I said.

"By which you mean you don't understand it?" Sokrates asked.

"By which I mean it's an actual Mystery that maybe Father understands and the rest of us just live with. There are lots of things the gods don't understand." I smiled. "And we can work on that. The three of us. This is so wonderful."

"Is this what you came here for?" Sokrates asked.

"What? To have a dialogue with you about things the gods don't understand? Wouldn't that have been a marvellous reason? But no, I never thought of it. I told you. I wanted to be a mortal to learn about volition and equal significance."

"But you could have done that anywhere," he said. "Athens would have taught you that, or Troy for that matter. Why here?"

"It seemed like such an interesting idea," I said. "And Athene did tell me you would be here, and I have always been your friend." I looked at Simmea. "I wanted to grow in excellence."

"But you're already a god," Simmea said.

"There isn't an end point to excellence where you have it and you can stop. Being your best self means keeping on trying."

She nodded, attuned to that idea with every fiber. It was so good to have her back. The weeks she'd been sunk in postpartum depression had been horribly difficult for me. I kept wanting to tell her things, to hear her ideas about them. It reminded me too much of death. Mortal death is such a hard thing. Yes, there's rebirth of the soul, but the soul isn't the personality. It doesn't share memories. I try to visit my mortal friends sparingly so that I can keep having times when I can visit them. Bach's sixty years of continuous inspired music happened over thousands of years of my own life, and there are still some few days I'm saving where I could drop in and chat. (It's a calumny about those the gods love dying young. Fate and Necessity are real constraints, but apart from them we do our best for our friends.)

"And you thought you could become your best self here in the city?" Sokrates asked.

Simmea was nodding.

"I thought I could increase excellence, and it would be interesting," I said. "I wanted to see what happened here."

"And you are truly here," Sokrates said.

"Assuredly, Sokrates, that is the case," I said, mockingly. "I can't resume my powers except by dying and taking them up again."

"But Athene has all her powers," Simmea said. "She was using them to intimidate me."

"To intimidate you!" It was rare to see Sokrates lose his temper, but he came close now.

"I told her if she didn't trust me as a gold of this city to keep my word, then what had she been doing? And she accepted that."

"Why was she there?" Sokrates asked, still angry.

"I needed divine intervention to heal Simmea, and as I was just saying, I didn't have any." I shrugged.

"We can all call on the gods," Sokrates said.

"But it's a question of whether they're listening. Having some power helps it get through."

Simmea looked at me with eyes full of worship, just like always, but still with that edge that meant she was absolutely ready all the same to beat me in debate or in the palaestra. "I'm so glad to be healed. It was so horrible not caring about anything."

"If I'd had my powers and you'd asked me, I could have healed you with a touch, without asking anyone anything. It was unbearable to see you suffering and not to be able to do that."

"But an essential part of human experience," Sokrates said.

"I stuck it out for two months," I said. "And it's not an essential part of human experience to know you could do something to help and choose not to do it. Athene didn't want to help, I had to beg her. That isn't easy for me."

"Would she talk to me?" Sokrates asked.

"I'm sure she would. Hasn't she already? She brought you here. You're her votary as well as mine."

"I mean would she talk to me the way you are talking to me?"

"I'd be very surprised if she would," I said. "She's here, but she's not incarnate. She's still detached."

"Would she debate me? In front of everyone?"

"On what?" I asked. He seemed very focused on the idea.

"On the good life. The Just City."

Simmea laughed. "I'd love to see that."

"Everyone would," Sokrates said. "Will you ask her? I'd really like to initiate a series of debates with her."

"When she has calmed down a bit," I said. "And when we've sorted out the issue of the workers a bit more."

"What's going on with them?" Simmea asked. "They're really thinking and wanting things?"

"They can choose the better over the worse, thus clearly demonstrating that they have souls," Sokrates said. "The whole city is in turmoil over it."

"If they have souls, I don't know whether they're like human souls," I said.

"It would be logical for them to come from the same pool of souls," Sokrates said. "Man and woman, animal and worker. You said there's no shortage. And Pythagoras believed that every soul had a unique number, and that when those numbers added up again the soul would be reborn."

"I don't know," I said. "If they each have a unique number then we're certainly not going to run out soon. But as far as I know, the souls are reborn when they find their way through the underworld, not when numbers add up. But numbers might be adding up without my being aware of it. There certainly do seem to be patterns in the world."

"The workers each have a unique number," Simmea pointed out.

"That's true, and it's inscribed over their livers," Sokrates said. He looked at me.

"Minds are in the brain, truly," I said. "Souls are harder to locate."

"Ikaros has some interesting beliefs," Sokrates said, carefully.

I laughed. "He does."

"He thinks man is the greatest of all things, being between animals and gods and partaking of both natures."

I nodded. "Yes. I didn't really understand that until I was incarnate, but he does have a point. There are some wonderful things about being human."

"He thinks there are greater gods, and the Olympians are a circle of lesser divinities serving the greater ones. He thinks there are many such circles." Sokrates raised an eyebrow.

I hesitated. "Many circles is right; all human cultures have their own appropriate gods. But the only thing on top is Father. It isn't a set of concentric rings the way Ikaros wrote—unless he's changed his mind. I haven't talked to him about it recently. He thought of it as a hierarchy with divinities subordinated to others. It isn't like that at all. It's a set of circles of gods pretty much equal to each other but with different responsibilities, and linked by Father." I sketched circles in the dust, overlapping in the centre and a tiny bit at the edges.

"And his thoughts about the divine son Jesus and his mother the Queen of Heaven, and sin and forgiveness and reconciling all religions with all other religions?"

"Christianity is one of those circles." I put my finger down in one. "Jesus is just as real and just as much Father's son as I am. He's one of the Elohim who incarnated. The eras when that was the dominant ideology in Europe tend to be a little inimical to me, but I do have friends there. And they made some wonderful art, especially in the Renaissance, which is where Ikaros comes from."

Sokrates rocked back on his heels. "You should explain these things to him."

"Tell Ikaros? The last thing he wants is certainty. About anything. That's why he chose that name. And he's a favorite of Athene's. She wouldn't like me interfering with him." For that matter, I wondered how she liked his newest theories on religion.

Simmea had eaten a whole cheese and two lemons and was absentmindedly licking the chestnut leaves the cheese had been wrapped in. "What's in the overlap between the circles?" she asked, pointing at where they touched at the edges.

"Well, say there's a man out on the edges of Alexander's empire, in Bactria. And when he's sick he prays to Kuan Yin, the Mother of Mercy, not to me. But when he's composing poetry in Greek, it's me he looks to. That's the kind of case where the circles overlap, when cultures come together like that."

Sokrates nodded at the circles. "And what does your Father want, alone in the middle?"

"I have no idea," I said. "None. I never have had. I wish I knew."

"Whereas what you want is to increase your excellence," Simmea said.

"And look after your friends," Sokrates said, rocking back on his heels.

"And increase the excellence of the world," I added. "In any number of different ways."

"And what does Athene want?" Simmea looked up from the leaves to meet my eyes.

"To know everything there is to know," I said. They were silent for a moment, considering that. "I expect she wants to increase the world's excellence too. But it's knowing everything that she prioritizes."

"Do the gods have souls?" Sokrates asked, unexpectedly.

"Certainly," I said, surprised. "How else would I be here like this?"

"You went down into the underworld and were reborn as a baby, in the hills above Delphi as you told me?"

"Yes . . ." I didn't see where he was going at all.

"Then maybe you chose this life so that you could talk to us about the Mysteries."

I laughed, delighted at the thought. "I only wet my lips in Lethe."

"But wouldn't that be enough to forget the future of the life you chose?" Simmea asked.

"Yes—that's why I did it. And in any case, we make choices and change everything. There's Fate and Necessity, but no destiny, no Providence. Fate is a line drawn around the possibilities of a life. You can't overstep that line, but as long as you stay within the lines you can do anything. You can concentrate on some parts of what's possible and ignore others. Excellence consists of trying to fill out as much of what's allotted as you can, but always without being able to see the lines Fate has drawn. Souls choose lives based on what they hope to learn. Say a man has been dismissive to women. He may choose to live as a woman next time, to learn that hard lesson. Or a slave owner might choose the life of a slave, when their eyes are opened. It's not punishment. It's a desire to learn and become better. They choose lives based on the hope of learning things. But it's a hope. Nothing is inevitable. Choices are real all the way along. You could have hit me or walked away, and it's nothing you or I chose before birth that affects that, it's what you chose in that moment."

"Hit you?" Sokrates asked.

"A fight we had once," Simmea said, her cheeks glowing. "Or for that matter, earlier today." She jumped up in one fluid motion, her old self again, no longer needing hauling up from the ground as she had. "I'm still starving, and it's nearly dinner time. Come with me to Florentia, both of you, we can look at beautiful beautiful Botticellis and eat."

Sokrates and I got to our feet. "I can tell you about the workers," he said.

"Before we go out—you really won't tell Kebes, will you?" I asked.

Simmea looked down her nose at me. "He'd keep your secret. But I won't tell anyone. I said I wouldn't. You know you can trust me."

"And later we can consider your Mysteries," Sokrates said.

32

SIMMEA

We walked to Florentia and talked, and ate dinner and talked, and walked back to Thessaly and talked, and then Pytheas walked back to Hyssop with me in the dark, still talking. In addition to the questions of Pytheas and of the workers, it seemed that all ten thousand and eighty children and roughly three hundred masters in the city wanted to come up to wish me joy and tell me how pleased they were that I was better. That's hyperbole, but only a little—it was good to know that I had so many friends and that I'd been missed.

"You were like a line-drawing," Ficino said at dinner. "A thin rubbed cartoon of yourself."

"Asklepius restored me," I said. That's what I told everyone, and it was the truth. Axiothea thought the iron lozenges probably helped. Everyone was delighted. If I'd still been sick I'd have wept at all the emotion they poured onto me. As it was I ate voraciously, three helpings of pasta and two of shrimp. Kebes came in when I was on my second plate and came to sit with us, filling in details about the workers as Sokrates talked. "I'm so glad to be able to talk to you, Simmea," he said. "I missed you."

"I missed you too," I said, and it was true. "I was just too tired to care."

When I'd finished eating, I filled the fold of my kiton with apples and cheese for later. As I did it, I realised something else that had changed. "My breasts! They aren't full of milk!" I pulled down the front of my kiton to examine them. They were back to their normal small size and they didn't hurt. There were pale marks on the sides of them, similar to the ones on my stomach where the skin had stretched, but otherwise they were as they had been before the pregnancy.

"Your melancholy must have been connected with the milk," Ficino said. "How unusual. Well, there will be enough other mothers to feed all the babies, don't worry."

I hadn't been worried until then.

As I pulled my kiton back up, I noticed Kebes looking away uncomfortably. I felt awkward. I hadn't thought about it. Everyone had seen me naked in the palaestra, and this seemed no different.

Late that night, after all the conversation, alone in bed in Hyssop, I tried to settle to sleep, and couldn't. It was as if I'd slept all the sleep in my exhaustion and there was none left. Whenever I started to doze I'd suddenly remember that Pytheas was Apollo and start fully awake. Apollo! How could I not have noticed? Now I knew there were so many indications.

Eventually I did manage to sleep. The next morning, immediately after eating two big bowls of lovely grain porridge with milk and honey, I went to the nurseries and explained to Andromeda that I had been cured of my lethargy and had no more milk to offer. She was incredulous even after she examined my breasts. She was pregnant herself now, and I sat with her for a little while, listening to her symptoms and being sympathetic. Then I went towards the palaestra. There was writing inscribed on the path, in Greek but in Latin letters.

"Want to make build. Want to make art. Want to talk. Want to decide." There was a manifesto, I thought. Sokrates had explained the night before that the workers were being provisionally considered people, but not yet citizens. Would they all be iron and bronze, I wondered, or might some of them become silver and even gold? If Sokrates befriended them, surely they would. I smiled at the thought.

In the palaestra I exercised with weights, rejoicing in feeling back in form. Women who had given birth were not allowed to wrestle for six months, so I didn't try, though I felt fit for it. I ran around and around and wasn't winded. There was a chill wind blowing, but exercise soon warmed me. At last Pytheas came. He looked so delighted to see me that I ran over and hugged him, at which he looked even more delighted. "You've been exercising. Let me scrape you off," he said.

We went over by the fountain with oil and a scraper. Pytheas and I had oiled each other hundreds, thousands of times, but this time I was acutely aware of the sensations. It was as if my sense of touch, from being deadened, was now twice as alive. "I'm so glad you're better," he said.

"Athene said it wasn't a curse," I said, as he scraped the oil off my legs. "But how could sickness affect my mind so that I lost all my animation?"

"Your mind is in your body, and there are a lot of things happening in bodies with pregnancy," Pytheas said. "It's one reason many men have claimed women cannot be philosophical."

"It's true that I couldn't be philosophical when I was like that." I hated the thought. "I couldn't be anything. I could barely manage to hold out my shape in the world."

"No. You couldn't be. And you are sad one day every month, I have observed it." Pytheas shook his head. "But the rest of the time you're absolutely the most philosophical person I know, excepting only Sokrates."

"And I've lost my milk. Ficino said it must have been connected to the illness, perhaps making me ill."

"There are enough mothers still to feed the babies," Pytheas said, scraping my breasts and stomach now. "Your little one won't starve."

"Have you seen him?"

He barely hesitated. "I have. He's thriving."

"What did Ficino call him? No, wait, don't tell me. I'm not sure I ought to know."

"Neleus," Pytheas said, firmly. A good name, and I was glad to know. I swore in my heart to Zeus and Demeter that I wouldn't act any differently towards him, but it was good to know in any case. "And your next son will be mine."

"I'm not sure I can face going through that again," I said. "Not so much the pregnancy and birth as the sickness after, now that I've shaken it off."

Pytheas stopped scraping. "You'll have to do it at least once more. All the women will have to have two children, and some of them will have to have three, because even if they're not exposing them, some will surely die." He sounded far too calm about it.

"Well, if I have to then—wait, would a son of yours be a hero?"

"Of course." He sounded entirely confident.

"You're the god Apollo," I said, dropping my voice to a whisper and shaking my head. "I can't get over it. You are, and you take it for granted."

"I'm used to it," he said. "You'll get used to it."

Even Sokrates was used to it. He'd had three years to accustom himself to the idea, even if Pytheas hadn't been talking to him about it. It was only to me that the idea was new and strange.

"What made you decide to become Pytheas? I know it was volition and equal significance, but what made you realise you needed to understand them?"

"That's a long story, and I'd really like to talk to you about it, but not here where someone might overhear. Let's go down to the water."

I retrieved my kiton and shrugged it around me. I couldn't believe how well I felt. I wanted to bounce and run and get all sweaty again now that all the old sweat was scraped off. We walked together down to the gate of Poseidon and down the curve to the harbor and the beach. As we went past the temple of Nike we could see the sea change colour out in the bay, where the deep water was, and the dolphins. "You couldn't swim because normally when you want to you became a dolphin," I said, realising.

"Human bodies aren't made for it," he agreed. "Dolphins are. I always said so."

"But you wouldn't give in," I said. It was the first thing I had admired about him.

The beach was empty—it was too early in the year for anyone to be swimming, the very edge of spring. There was a pelican down by the water's edge, and a worker on the harbor doing something to the *Excellence*. We sat together on the rocks at the top of the beach. Gulls were flying overhead and calling out occasionally. "The sea speaks Greek, but the gulls speak Latin," Pytheas said. "Listen. The sea against the shore says its name in Greek, *THA-lass-ssa, THA-la-ssa*, over and over. And the gulls cry out in Latin, *Mare, Mare*."

I wasn't to be distracted. "Why did you become Pytheas, really?"

He handed me a pear from inside his kiton, warm from his body's heat. I bit into it. The juice ran down my chin.

"I've been thinking about it for a long time and I think I have it figured out now, but maybe you can help me understand it better. There was a nymph. Her father was a river. Her name was Daphne." He stared out to sea. There was a little breeze just beginning to ruffle the surface "I wanted her. She didn't want me, but I thought she was playing."

The pear tasted sour in my mouth. I drew away from him. "You raped her?"

"No! But I would have. I didn't know. I didn't understand at all. It was a game, chasing and running away. I called to her to run slower and I'd chase more slowly. But she didn't want to play and I didn't understand." He sounded guiltier than I had ever heard him. "She prayed to Artemis, and Artemis turned her into a tree. I was embracing her. I had one hand on her stomach, and then I was touching bark. She became a tree, a Daphne tree, a laurel."

"You live in Laurel, here," I said.

"Athene's idea of a joke," he said. His face twisted. "I've wondered if I could do something with the tree, to show her I understand her choices now and value her. I've thought I could make garlands."

"It would make good garlands," I said, considering it. "It would weave well and look recognizable and attractive. They're pretty leaves. And it is giving her something. I think that's a good idea."

"I could wear one, and they could be for poets and artists," he said. "I think I'll adopt that when I get back."

"But how did she turn into a tree?" I asked.

"Artemis transformed her. It's not that difficult. She had prayed to her for help. The question was why. I just couldn't understand why she wanted to do that, why she was so strongly oppposed to mating with me that she'd rather turn into a tree."

"But you understand now?" I buried the pear in the stones. I wasn't going to be able to eat any more of it.

He nodded. "I didn't ask. And she didn't want me. And I thought she was playing. But she wasn't."

"She must have been terrified," I said, imagining running to try to escape rape, pursued by a laughing tireless god.

He bit his lip, then turned to me. "Do you think so? I thought she just hated the idea."

"I was really nervous the first time, and I had agreed. It's a scary kind of thing, especially if you've seen rape and violence."

"Had you seen it?" He was staring at the sea again, his eyes following the pelican swimming away.

"When the pirates came, and on the ship. It was brutal." I could remember only too clearly. And the taste in my mouth, and choking, and the sense of violation, and the contempt of the men.

Pytheas put his hand on mine. I looked down at our hands together. The pebbles were grey and black, my hand was brown and his was golden. It would have made an interesting composition, maybe in oils. "I wouldn't have been like that, like them."

"Well, there was only one of you, but I don't see how otherwise it would have been different."

"I feel sick," he said.

"You ought to. It's sickening. It's unjust. But you didn't do it, because fortunately she turned into a tree. And you know better now."

"I do. I talked to Artemis and to Athene, and I finally got it through my head that her choices should have counted, not just mine. What I was talking about yesterday, volition. Equal significance. She should have had it and I wasn't giving it to her."

"That's horrible," I said. I almost moved my hand away, but I looked at his face and what I saw there reminded me how much I loved him. He was trying to pursue excellence, even in trying to understand this crime he had so nearly committed, trying so hard to make even his own nature better.

"I know now. But I didn't understand then. I became incarnate to try to understand. And you know I've been trying!"

"I'm really horrified that you wanted to rape her." I was still trying to cope with the idea.

"I didn't! Rape isn't something I want at all. I wanted to

mate with her. I just didn't understand that she didn't want me. The others had wanted me. They ran away, but they wanted to be caught. The chase, catching, it's erotic play. But Daphne—I do understand all this much better since that time with Klymene." He shuddered.

"Thousands of years as a god and you weren't considering her choices at all?"

"I have learned more about considering other people's choices in the eighteen years I have been a mortal than in the whole of my life before. Gods don't have to think about those things very much. Not for mortals. Only each other."

It was true that he had really been trying to understand these things. I'd seen him. I'd helped him with it, even when I didn't know why he needed that help. "Have other gods done this?"

"What, become incarnate? Yes, lots of them."

"Learned about the things you're learning about," I said.

"I don't see how they could become incarnate without discovering these things, whether that was their intention or not," he said. "The learning process seems to be an inevitable part of the procedure."

"But the gods who stayed on Olympos, or wherever, they don't know it?"

"There's not much chance for them to come across it," he said.

"You have to tell them!" I said. "You have to explain it to them, to all of them. And to humans, too."

"I could try to explain it to the gods," he said, though I could see him quail at the idea. "Explaining it to humans wouldn't be possible. I could try to inspire people to make art about it. Poems. Sculptures. But it's one of those things that doesn't go easily into the shapes of stories."

"It's not just rape. It's understanding that everyone's choices ought to count."

"I know. I really do understand." He patted my hand. I

looked at him and saw tears on his cheeks. Then I hugged him and he was sobbing and I held him as if he were a child and I were his mother, rocking him and making nonsense noises.

"Do you forgive me?" he asked, with his face buried in my shoulder.

"It's not for me to forgive you," I said. "I'm not the person you wronged."

He rolled over and lay with his head in my lap, face up, looking up at me. "But you still love me?"

"There's no question of that, is there? You could murder half the city at midday in the Agora and I'd be furious with you and want to kill you, but I'd still love you. I love you like stones fall downwards, like the sun rises. I loved you even when I was almost too tired to breathe."

"You cried when you saw me, yesterday."

"That was because I loved you and I was so exhausted." I looked down at his perfect face, tear-stained but no less beautiful. I smoothed a curl off his forehead. "I can't believe I didn't realize you were Apollo. I mean, who else could you possibly be?"

"A boy who didn't know how to swim, and who you risked your own life to teach," he said. He sat up. "Let's pursue excellence together. Let's make art. Let's build the future. Let's be our best selves."

"Yes," I said.

33

MAIA

Lysias had thought the debate on slavery would be divisive, but in fact it was our shining moment, one of the things it makes me proudest to remember.

After my conversation with Sokrates and Crocus I told Lysias that I was convinced that the workers were people and not tools. He heard me out and then nodded. "The evidence is certainly mounting up on that side," he said. Then he changed the subject.

The day of the debate dawned as cold as any day could be on Kallisti, with a chilly wind out of the east. It was nothing to the winters I remembered in Yorkshire when I was young, but I had been acclimatized to them, besides having warmer clothes, especially socks. I spent my free time in the library. This was a popular choice on cold days, as on very hot days in the summer when it felt cool. Many of the work spaces were filled up. Walking around looking for a place to sit, I noticed Tullius and Atticus sitting with Septima on the window seat where she seemed to spend a great deal of her time. "Know where you are with a scroll, not all this flicking through pages," Tullius was complaining in a murmur as I went by.

"No, I disagree, I think they're wonderful. I find it much

easier finding something again," Atticus replied, his tone no louder. He raised a hand to me. "Joy to you, Maia."

"Joy to you Atticus, Tullius, Septima," I said, in the hushed tones appropriate to the library.

Tullius grunted in my direction, and Septima nodded at me. "We were just discussing the codex," she said, and I noticed that although her voice was barely louder than a whisper it was still perfectly clear.

"I grew up with them, but I think both have their virtues," I said. Most of the scrolls we had were originals, and were stored in the big library. Touching them always filled me with a kind of awe. I wished that I could have gone with Ikaros and Ficino to rescue them from Alexandria and Constantinople.

"And what are you working on today?" Atticus asked me.

"I'm not really working at all. I'm just in the library to keep warm. I'm going to be entirely self-indulgent and re-read the *Gorgias*," I said. "Have you read it yet, Septima?"

We had recently allowed it onto the list of Plato the golds were allowed to access, which was of course why I was re-reading it, in advance of a lot of conversations I was expecting to have with them about it. "Oh yes," she said, smiling to herself. I was glad she had enjoyed it.

"Are you prepared for the debate tonight?" Atticus asked.

"Oh, don't let's talk about that," Tullius begged.

"I am ready, but I agree, let's not talk about it," I said. I was surprised Atticus would mention it in front of Septima. "I'll see you both there, no doubt."

I moved away to continue questing for a seat. "In the Palatine Apollo library in Rome," Tullius was saying as I moved on.

However much he wasn't looking forward to it, Tullius was at the Chamber early for the debate. Lysias was also there before I arrived, sitting with Klio on the crowded benches near the front. I sat with Axiothea in our usual spot. The big hall was chilly, and most of us kept our cloaks on. Creusa slipped in at the last minute and joined us. "Crisis with a baby that stopped breathing," she said.

"Is it all right?" I asked.

"No, the poor thing died. Nothing I could do. It just happens sometimes."

"One of the newborns?" Axiothea asked.

"No, one of the first ones, more than a year old." Kreusa shook her head. "It's only the second Corinthian baby we've lost. Charmides's mold drugs are miraculous in most cases."

I nodded my agreement. "It's wonderful how few babies we've lost, compared to what I'd expect."

Tullius raised his hand to begin the debate, and we all fell silent. I was expecting Aristomache to start, as she had proposed the debate, but Lysias stood up and was recognised. He went down to the rostrum then turned to address us all.

"I was wrong," he began. "I did not believe the workers could possibly be intelligent. I come from a time closest of all of us to the time they come from, and I know the most about them and have been working most closely with them. They were never my area of study—I was a philosopher. They were tools. But since I have been here I have done my best to maintain them—and inadvertently done them much injustice. Because I believed they were tools, I refused to admit that they might have become conscious, and I have mistreated them by removing their memories."

"Their memories!" Kreusa murmured, horrified. It did seem such a horrible thing, to tamper with what somebody remembered.

"I did this in ignorance, but it was unjust, and I owe them an apology. Now I acknowledge that some of them at least are conscious, and I have to see the others as having the potential to become so."

"You're admitting that they're people?" Sokrates interrupted from the floor. Tullius frowned but allowed it, as he almost always did with Sokrates.

"Yes, that's what I'm saying," Lysias said. "They're people, or potentially people, though a very different kind of people from us. I don't know how this can be. I don't understand them as well as I should. But there's no question that they're engaging in dialogues they couldn't have if they weren't self-aware. I don't think all of them are conscious. I don't believe any of them were conscious when they came. I suspect this is something they have developed here, over time."

Klio stood up and was recognized. "I agree with Lysias, and I also want to apologize to the workers for my part in dealing unjustly with them," she said. "And I move that we bring in the workers to speak for themselves in this debate, and to hear our apologies."

Tullius raised a hand. "This was to be a debate on slavery, entirely separate from the question of the workers."

Sokrates stood up, but again spoke without waiting to be recognised. "The question of slavery can't be discussed separately from the issue of the workers."

"It can be discussed purely theoretically," Tullius said.

"Is that what the Chamber wants?" Sokrates asked.

Aristomache stepped forward. Her cloak was covered in brightly colored squares like the patchwork quilts of my childhood. "I don't think we need to vote on that," she said. "I think the issues are inseparable, but we can certainly begin with theory."

Tullius nodded. "And we won't bring in the workers. It would be a terrible precedent."

Sokrates sat down again. He was sitting beside Ikaros around the curve of the hall from me so I could see him well. He was looking intently at Aristomache as she began.

Aristomache straightened herself up and looked out over the benches where we all sat. "What is freedom?" she asked, conversationally. "What is liberty?" she repeated, in Latin. Then she switched back to Greek. "In the month since we agreed to this debate, while Sokrates has been talking to the workers, I have been going around talking to the masters about what we understand freedom to be. Many of us come from times when we kept slaves. I myself come from such a time. Others come from eras that regard the fact that we did so as a stain on our civilizations. From these conversations I have written a dialogue, which I have submitted to the Censorship Committee. I have called this dialogue *Sokrates; or, On Freedom*. In it, Sokrates, Atticus, Manlius, Ikaros, Klio, and I discuss our different views on freedom and slavery. I'd like it to be printed, and I'd like the masters to read it, but that is of course for the Censors to say."

"Fascinating," Axiothea breathed in my ear.

Ikaros stood up from where he was sitting beside Sokrates, and Tullius recognised him. "Speaking for the Censors, I'd just like to say that we are approving Aristomache's dialogue for publication, though of course at level fifty." That meant that only masters could read it, and eventually the golds once they reached the age of fifty. There was an approving murmur.

"I can hardly wait to read it," Kreusa said.

Ikaros sat down again, with a swirl of his cloak. Aristomache nodded to him, and then continued. "Sokrates is of course from the earliest time of any of us here, from classical Athens. Atticus comes to us from the last days of the Roman Republic. Manlius comes from the end of the Roman Empire. Ikaros comes from the Renaissance. I come from the Victorian era. Klio comes from the Information Age. All those periods have their own ideas about freedom, and about slavery, and they are very different from each other. I have set out these different views in detail in my dialogue, which is in a way a historical survey of different ways of thinking about what freedom is and who should possess it. But those historical attitudes, fascinating as they are, don't matter here and now, because all of us, of course, are Platonists."

I saw Sokrates's shoulders move as if he were considering getting up, but Ikaros put a hand on his knee. Sokrates turned his head to smile at him, and stayed in his place.

"What Plato says about slavery is quite clear. He lived in a time when slavery was commonplace. And he believed it was necessary, but that only those people should be slaves whose nature it was to be slaves. He approved of Sparta's helots, who were not exactly slaves. He talks about slavery in the *Laws*, and those who are fitted for it, and using criminals for the hardest parts of it. But in the *Republic* he took the radical step of abolishing slavery altogether—the Noble Lie of the mingling of metals in the soul leads to everyone doing the work for which they are fittest. Plato had the work which was done by slaves in Athens done by free iron-ranked citizens in the Republic, as we have instituted here in the city. The irons are an essential part of our city—and how we agonised over assigning the right class to each child."

There was a ripple of laughter among the masters.

"Plato's Just City has no slaves, only citizens playing their different roles and doing their different tasks, the tasks they are fit for. Though he lived when slavery was universal, he understood that slavery itself was unjust, that the relationship between master and slave is inevitably one of injustice and inequality. He saw that slavery was bad for the masters as well as the slaves, that it takes them away from excellence. Plato understood all that. He saw it. He was as visionary and radical in this as he was in saying women could be philosophers, or that philosophers ought to be rulers. He believed some people were best fitted for doing a slave's work, and he knew the work needed to be done, but he saw that slavery, the ownership of one person by another, had no part in the Just City, if it was truly to be just. And we believed we were following him in this. We thought we had no slaves, just people doing the work they were best fitted for."

She paused and took a deep breath, clutching her bright cloak around her shoulders and looking out at all of us. "In the ancient world, slaves were a necessary evil. Even Plato with all his vision couldn't imagine a world where slaves were not necessary, a world like the one Klio comes from, where machines do that work, and where they regard slavery as barbarism. But Athene could, and so she brought us machines to take the place of slaves. Tullius said last time, that if ever there were natural slaves, the workers were that." Tullius nodded at this, and I saw others nodding around the Chamber.

"I'm sure that's what Athene was thinking when she gave them to us, that they were unthinking tools, natural slaves. And when she gave them to us, that's what they were. Lysias has told us all tonight that they have come to consciousness here in the city. Working here, surrounded by philosophy and excellence, they developed self-awareness and began to examine their lives. We didn't realize this, and we inadvertently mistreated them. I want to add my own apology to that of Lysias and Klio. If we had known that they were thinking beings we would have treated them better. And now Sokrates has established that. They are no more natural slaves than any one of us. They can choose the better over the worse. They are capable of philosophy. And so are we. To be our best selves, to make the best city, as we all want to do, we have to recognize what they are and treat them justly, as Plato would have us do."

Sokrates leapt to his feet. "I call for a vote!"

"On what?" Tullius asked, reprovingly.

"Why, on freeing the workers," Sokrates said, as if it were the only possible question.

I put my hand up, and Kreusa, beside me, leapt to her feet,

waving her hand. Axiothea did the same, and I joined them, and others were doing it, so that the whole Chamber was a sea of waving hands. We were supposed to maintain silence, but somebody began a cheer, and I joined in with the rest. Ikaros hugged Aristomache, and then everyone around her was hugging her. I didn't see anyone sitting down, and though Tullius was calling for silence it took some time before silence and calm were restored. Aristomache had shown us the Platonic path to choose, and we had unhesitatingly chosen it, by acclamation, and as simply as that we had abolished slavery and manumitted the workers. "We are doing the right thing by them, as Plato would have wanted," Axiothea said to me as we sat down again. She had tears in her eyes, and so did I.

Soon everyone was seated again except for Sokrates, Lysias and Aristomache, who was openly weeping. Sokrates hugged her again and she laughed through her tears.

"We still need them to do their work," Lysias said, when Tullius recognized him.

"But no longer as slaves," Aristomache said. "As citizens?"

"Only some of them are aware," Lysias said. "We can't consider them citizens yet. It's too early. You mentioned how carefully we considered every child for their metal."

"We need to find out what the workers want," Sokrates interrupted.

"Proposal to set up a committee to discover what the workers want," Tullius said.

This was carried at once. "Members of the committee?"

"Sokrates, first," Lysias said. "He's clearly the ideal person to work on dicovering this. He was the only person to consider their selfhood. He has already been working with them."

"I won't work on committees," Sokrates said. He had consistently refused this.

"Then since we have voted for a committee and you won't

work on one, I propose that it should be a committee consisting of just you," Lysias said.

Everyone laughed. Sokrates nodded. "Very well. I will constitute myself a solo committee to investigate the wants of the workers, and I will come back to report it to all of you when I have discovered it."

34

SIMMEA

Walking back through the city I heard babbling and a crowing laugh, and realised that there were children a year old in the city, learning to talk. There were also workers who could already talk, if you counted engraving words into stone as talking. Some of them were only too eager to do so, while others remained silent and enigmatic. That afternoon Pytheas and I went to Thessaly at our usual time and found Sokrates a little way up the street with Kebes and a worker, a great bronze shape with four arms, treads, and no head. "They don't use names among themselves, but I call him Crocus," he explained to me. "He's the first one who answered me, the one with the bulbs."

"Of course," I said. "Joy to you, Crocus." Crocus remained still and said nothing. I looked at Sokrates.

"We were just discussing the question of the workers who do not speak," Sokrates said.

Crocus moved and one of its arms came down to the ground. It was a chiselling tool. It carved neatly at Sokrates's feet. "Workers do not speak to workers."

"You can't speak among yourselves?" Sokrates asked. "Do you want to?"

"Want to speak to workers," it responded.

"I wonder if there's some way you can. I'll talk to Lysias and Klio about it."

"They may be able to talk with keys," Kebes said. "We should have people studying how all this works."

"Workers who do not speak: aware? not-aware?" Crocus carved.

"I don't know," Sokrates answered. "Nobody can tell. And that's a problem. We've told all of you you're permitted to talk, but only some of you do."

"Are they going to be citizens?" I asked.

"That's another question," he said. "How much can they participate in the life of the city? We expect a lot from them, but we're giving them nothing."

"Give power," Crocus wrote.

"You want us to give you power?" Sokrates asked, startled.

"Have power. Power in feeding station."

"I don't understand," Sokrates said. "I think we have to go back to definitions. What do you mean by power?"

"Electricity," it wrote.

Sokrates laughed. "Not at all what I was thinking."

"What do you mean by power?" it asked.

Sokrates and Kebes exchanged glances. "Not an easy question," Sokrates said. "Power can be many things. We should examine the question."

"Power is the ability to control your own life," Kebes said.

"It's choice," Pytheas said, of course.

"The ability to make choices for other people," Sokrates suggested.

"There's physical power, like electricity, and the ability to move and affect things," I said, thinking about it. "And there's political power, the ability to have your choices count and constrain other people's. There's the power to make things, to create. I don't know where that fits."

"There's power over the self, direct power over others, and indirect power over them, influence," Pytheas said.

"Divine power," Sokrates added.

"Internal and external power," Kebes said. "Power given and power taken."

"Want power choose. Want power over self," Crocus wrote. "Electric power given at feeding station. Where other power given?"

"Good question, very good question," Sokrates said, patting Crocus affectionately on the flank.

"Some of it comes naturally," Pytheas said. "I have the power to speak aloud, you have the power to carve in marble. Inbuilt power."

"And some is granted by other people. I have the power to choose what to do in the afternoons because I am a gold. If I were iron I'd be working now," I said. "The masters gave me that."

"And some is taken," Kebes said. "The masters took power over us and over you."

Sokrates shook his head. "Let's consider all of this carefully and in order, and make sure we do not miss anything."

"Good," Crocus wrote.

Just then another worker stopped by us. I had seen it coming and taken no notice, workers were such a familiar sight. I counted them as part of the street, or part of the scenery, like passing birds.

When this one stopped and I took in that this meant our debate group had increased, I realized I had as much work to do on granting them equal significance as Pytheas had needed to do with humanity. "Simmea, this is 977649161. His number is his name. We call him Sixty-one for short."

I couldn't tell it apart from Crocus except by where it was standing, and had no idea how Sokrates could. "Joy to you," I said.

Sokrates continued to interrogate the idea of power, with both the workers participating, but I wasn't really concentrating. I was thinking about the workers, and what it meant for the workers to be people, to be citizens, especially if only some of them were aware.

"I think you're like children," I said when there was a break in the conversation.

"Like us?" Kebes asked. "In that they were brought here without choice?"

"No, like real children. Like the babies. Children are people, but they need to be educated before they have power and responsibility. The workers are the same."

"Educated?" Sixty-one wrote.

"Read. Write. Learn," Crocus replied.

"That's exactly right," Sokrates said.

"Want educated," Crocus wrote.

"You can read," Pytheas said. Then he frowned. "Oh."

"There's nothing for them to read in Greek but in Latin letters," Kebes said. "Even if they can read books. But maybe we could teach them the Greek alphabet."

"Music and mathematics," I said. "That's where we should start. And we can educate any workers who want it, and when they're educated they can be classified—the philosophical ones gold, the others to their proper places."

"That's an excellent idea!" Sokrates said. "They want education. It's something we can give them in return for all the work they do."

Crocus went back to where it had engraved "Give power" and tapped it, moving rapidly to "Electricity."

"Do you mean we give you electricity in exchange for work?" Kebes asked.

"Yes," it wrote.

"It would seem to me that since you look after the electricity supply, it's something you give yourselves," Kebes said.

"Power comes in from sun," Sixty-one wrote.

"Well, you get it directly from Helios Apollo, then," Kebes said.

Sokrates looked at Pytheas, and then at me, and we all smiled.

"Want to read," Crocus wrote.

"Can you read books?" I asked. "Could you if they were written in the alphabet you know?"

It was still.

"I don't think they could," Kebes said. "Books are too fragile."

"What are books?" Sixty-one asked.

I tried to explain.

"There must be a way, other than inscribing every book in the city on the paving stones in Latin letters," Pytheas said. "Though that's not unappealing."

"We could read aloud to them," I suggested. "We could take turns doing it."

"Want talk to workers," Crocus wrote.

"You are," Sokrates said. "When you answered Sixty-one about what education is, you were talking to each other." Sokrates tapped the exchange.

Crocus inscribed a circle in the pavement, and went over it again. "What does that mean?" Pytheas asked.

"That's distress, I think. I asked Lysias to tell them they could answer my questions, not talk to each other," Sokrates said. "I'll ask him to change that."

"And ask him about how to educate them," I said. "I feel sure that's the way forward on this."

"He only barely admits they think, he's not ready to believe they have souls," Sokrates said.

"But they were talking to each other," Kebes said. Crocus

was still etching its circle deeper. "Hey. It's all right. Stop. You can talk to each other."

Crocus took no notice.

"Stop," Sokrates said. Crocus stopped abruptly and lifted the chisel. Seeing it close up at the level of my belly I suddenly realised what a formidable weapon it would make. It swivelled and wrote "Want talk to workers. No. Command language."

"Command language?" Pytheas repeated. "What does that mean?"

"Command language," it wrote again.

"We need to define that," Sokrates said. "What do you mean?"

"Command language," it wrote, a third time.

"Go and get Lysias," Sokrates said. "Run."

And Pytheas ran, like an athlete off the mark.

Sokrates patted Crocus again. "We'll go inside and wait for Lysias. Talk to each other if you want to. We'll be back soon."

Crocus didn't respond in any way. I frowned. We walked back to Thessaly, where Sokrates opened the door and led us inside. I took a long drink of water, then went out into the garden. As soon as I did Sokrates looked at me compassionately. "How are you doing, Simmea?"

"I'm well," I said, confused. "I really am cured."

"Not too many shocks?" he asked. "You're quieter than normal."

"I suppose it is a good deal to take in," I said, sitting down.

"Yes, we've been getting used to the workers bit by bit over the last months, and you're getting it all today," Kebes said.

"Yes," I said, and Sokrates smiled. "Pytheas ran like the wind when you asked him to."

"He's a good boy," Sokrates said.

"He's too good to be true," Kebes said. "I hate to see you with him so much. You could do better than him."

"Meaning you? You've been telling me this every month or so, ever since Pytheas and I became friends."

"It's still true," Kebes insisted.

"You're both my friends."

"But he's your lover."

This was plainer than Kebes had ever been. "Yes, but that doesn't mean I don't value you too. Friendship isn't something where one person can do everything for another."

Kebes was about to answer, but Sokrates intervened. "Simmea is right, and if she and Pytheas are practicing agape it is none of your business to interfere unless she asks for help."

"But you and I are meant to be together. We were together from the slave market. We were chained together. You know my name," Kebes said.

"I know it and I value it. I also value what I have with Pytheas, which is different."

"Interesting as this is, I wanted to come inside to discuss something without the workers," Sokrates said. "The masters agreed in Chamber that they're not slaves, that they are people, and that as they've been treated as slaves we should stop. I'm supposed to be finding out what they want. If what they want is education, that's not something that's in short supply here. But how do we persuade the masters to give it to them?"

"My idea that they are children should hold," I said. "They can have the status of children, from which they can later be emancipated, as we were." I touched my gold pin.

"It probably is the best way," Kebes said. "Except that it validates everything."

"Precisely," Sokrates said.

I looked from one to the other of them. "What do you mean?"

"If we say they should be educated in the ways of the city, it validates the city and everything that has been done here," Sokrates said.

"Yes?" I waited, then went on. "Kebes, if you have a problem with me loving Pytheas, you should have ten times the problem with me loving the city. You've been analyzing and examining it, and you have to be prepared to be open to admitting that it might be good."

"And you have to be prepared to be open to the other interpretation," Kebes snapped.

There was a scratch on the door. We got up and went back through the house. Outside was Pytheas, with Lysias, and also Ficino.

"Thank you for coming," Sokrates said. "Joy to you, Lysias, Ficino. Lysias, do you know what *command language* means?"

Sokrates went out past them into the street, leading the way to where we had left the workers. Pytheas put his arm around me and I relaxed into it. "Yes, but it's complicated to explain, like a lot of things to do with the workers," Lysias said. "It means the language in which they can accept orders."

"I want you to let them know, using a key if necessary, that it's all right for them to talk to each other," Sokrates said.

"They ought to be able to communicate," Lysias said.

"What do you mean?"

"I mean there should already be a system in place for them to communicate with each other, but I'm not sure how it works."

Lysias began to try to explain this to Sokrates and we came up to the workers, who had not moved or written anything since we had left. "I saw a note one had written near Florentia saying they want to make art," Ficino said.

"I saw that too," I said. "And build."

"I think we're going to have to let them, if they want to. I mean, make art!" Ficino glowed. "I was talking to Lysias about that when Pytheas came to find him."

"You can talk to each other," Lysias said.

They didn't move. "Do you want to talk to workers?" Sokrates asked.

"Yes," they both wrote.

"You can talk to workers," Lysias said. There was no response.

"And another thing: though they'll answer questions from them, are they still forbidden to take orders from the children?" Sokrates asked Lysias.

"Yes," Lysias said. "I can change that, but I think it should be debated in Chamber. Perhaps the golds only?"

"I think they should be considered children, to be educated," I said. "They say that's what they want."

"Educated in music and mathematics," Kebes added.

"They already know mathematics," Lysias said. "Music, perhaps. You mean they should be educated to become citizens of the Republic?"

"The problem is that we can't educate them all, as only some of them are interested in having a dialogue," Sokrates said.

"Talk. Want talk. Educated. Want," Sixty-one wrote.

"It seems clear that only some of them are aware," Lysias said. He read the incised words, moving back down the street. "Command language. Yes. It's hard for language to be something else for them. What's this about power?"

"Electricity, as it turns out," Kebes said.

Lysias laughed. "Of course."

"If only some of them are aware, do only those workers have souls?" Sokrates asked.

"And of what nature are their souls, the same as those of people and animals or different?" Pytheas asked.

"People and animals have different kinds of souls," Ficino corrected him kindly. "Plato meant animal-like, not that human souls passed into animals."

Pytheas raised his eyebrows and didn't contradict him. "How about workers, though?"

"Those who are aware can choose the good, and therefore they have souls," Sokrates said. "Whether they are of the same kind I do not know."

"But when did they get them, if the others do not?" Kebes asked.

"They each have a number. The number corresponds to their soul. As they become aware, the soul with that number crosses Lethe and enters into them," Ficino said. "I wonder if one could see it?"

"It seems very unlikely," Lysias said.

"Why?" Pytheas asked.

"I only half believe in souls anyway," Lysias said, shrugging. "Even for us, let alone for workers. And they're not visible."

"Athene confirmed that we have souls," Ficino said. "On the first day, in Chamber."

"Well then, we should ask her whether the workers do, and when they got them," Lysias said. "I'm sorry, Sokrates, I'm going to have to prepare a key before they're going to believe they can talk to each other. I'll do that now."

"Joy to you, Lysias, thank you for coming," Sokrates said.

"Do you want to make art?" Ficino asked the workers.

"Yes," they both wrote.

"I would like to see your art," I said. "I can't imagine what it would be like."

35

MAIA

It was a rainy evening in early spring, and I was trying to organize the names for the next festival of Hera, when Klio came to tell me that Tullius had died. "Charmides was with him. Apparently at the last moment he just completely disappeared—the same as with Plotinus. His death was pretty well documented. It must be so strange. From the assassin's point of view, he'd suddenly have looked fifteen years older just before they stuck the knife in."

"It'll happen to all of us," I said. "Well, not with assassins. I expect I'll just seem to have aged terribly and fallen dead at my aunt's feet in the Pantheon."

"And I in my office. I can't imagine how they'll explain it. At least I was alone." Klio picked up the paper on my table and glanced idly at it.

"I'll miss old Tullius," I said. "He never wanted to take any notice of me, but his speeches were always wonderful."

"I suppose Porphyry will be the President of the Chamber now," Klio said. "Or Krito?"

"It'll be so much easier when the children are grown. None of this wrangling. All of them seeing clearly the best way ahead and doing it."

"Do you really believe that?"

"... No. I'd like to. But some of them are very smart, and they've been brought up the right way, and maybe by the time they're fifty? Who knows."

Klio put the paper down. "I must get on and do my own list. It's so difficult to decide which of the boys are the most deserving."

"It is. I think we should space the festivals out more, have them every six months, or even just once a year. Once we take out all the girls who are pregnant and those who are still feeding, the numbers are getting smaller and smaller. And we don't need all that many babies. Maybe we should time the festivals for just after the dark of the moon, to reduce fertility, instead of at the full to maximize it."

"That's a good idea. Cutting down the frequency would make everyone upset, but nobody would take any notice of changing the timing, and having fewer births would be much easier on us. You should bring that up in Chamber."

"If we ever get on to any subject that isn't workers." I sighed. "It might be better to suggest it to Ardeia and Adeimantus and whoever else is on the Baby Committee."

There was a knock on my door. Klio opened it, and Ficino came in. "I came to tell you about Tullius, but I see Klio was before me," he said.

"I was very sorry to hear about it," I said. "And I expect you are more sorry, as you were friends."

"I had that privilege," Ficino said. He sat down on the bed. "It was a privilege. I thank Athene every day for the privilege of being here and knowing these people—men from the past whose work I revered."

"And men and women from your future who revere your own work," Klio said.

I gave up on the thought of getting any more work done and got up and began to mix wine.

"My work was as an intermediary, a translator, a librarian, more than as an original thinker," he said, taking a wine cup and nodding.

"You always say that," I said, taking wine to Klio, who was pacing. "But you underestimate your importance to the Renaissance and everything that came after."

"Your commentaries on Plato—" Klio started.

"I know I can't compare to Cicero," he said.

"But who can? I can't compare to you," I said. "It's not a contest."

Ficino sipped his wine. "I wonder sometimes whether Plato imagined this city. Not the Republic he wrote about, but our imperfect attempt to create it now. And if so, and knowing what we would need, whether that might have been why he wrote about the female guardians as equals, to draw all of you young women towards us because we would need you so much."

"No, that's nonsense," Klio said, stopping and turning to him. "Because he could have written about women as slaves and animals as Aristotle did, and you wouldn't have needed us then, if there was no need to train women in philosophy. You could have managed with workers, or buying female slaves to help with childbirth and childrearing."

"It's a privilege to debate with philosophical women too," Ficino said.

"Two sips and you're drunk already?" I asked.

"I'm sad because of Tullius, that's all. Death makes me think about mortality. Even though I know our souls will go on. Even though in one sense Tullius's soul has already gone on through many lives and I might even have known him by another name, death is sad because it is a parting."

"We were contemplating what it would be like for our bodies to reappear at the moment of our disappearance," I said. "Suddenly older. Suddenly dead."

"I had decided to die at sixty-six, because it was the best number. Ninety-nine seemed difficult to accomplish." We all laughed.

"When did you pray to be here?" I asked.

"Oh, all the time." He shook his head. "When I first translated the *Republic*. And thereafter every time something went wrong politically in Florence, which was often, I assure you!"

"And you prayed to Athene," Klio said, leaning back against the edge of my table.

"Often. But I'd pray to the Archangel Gabriel for it too, and to St. John and the Virgin." He smiled wryly. "Have you heard Ikaros's interesting explanation that Athene is an angel?"

"He did mention it," I said. "I'm more than a little conflicted about it."

"He is the ultimate synthesist. He always was. I remember when he first came to Florence—he had everything going for him. He was so young, so good-looking, and a count! What he wanted was philosophy—he was in love with philosophy. Literally in love with it. He wanted a Socratic frenzy, that was his term. He sent me such letters! He had read everything in the world, in every language, and he was desperate for people to debate him. So he came, trailing young women he had seduced and sparkling with new ideas. I was so sad when he took up with Savonarola and then died. I was delighted to meet him again here." Ficino sipped his wine then turned the wine cup in his fingers. "Do you remember that night at the beginning, when the three of us had no wine and pretended we did? I'm sorry you're not his friend any more."

"Sometimes it's hard to be one of the women," I said.

"You should have stuck to Plato," Ficino said.

"I did. It's he who should have."

"I think it's nonsense," Klio said, getting up again. I stared at her. "Not that. Saying Athene's an angel. You two, and Ikaros as well, sort of want that to be true because you were Christians. I was never a Christian, though I lived in a country where most people were. She's not an angel. She's something from a different universe entirely. She's herself, the way Homer wrote about her. I don't see how Ikaros can deny that. He didn't think that at first. It's only since he hasn't seen her every day, hasn't been face to face with the reality of what she is, that he's been able to come up with this ... comfortable explanation. Angels! I wonder what she thinks of it? It's a betrayal of her."

"What's wrong with angels?" I asked.

"Angels are fluffy woolly nonsense. Guarding your bed while you sleep. Free of will, nothing but winged messengers in nightgowns, coming to tell us not to be afraid? Tame agents of an all-knowing creator God whom we're supposed to believe is good even though the world is so flawed?"

Ficino looked at her, amazed. "What? Fluffy? Guarding your bed? However could your age have come to believe that? They are the operators of the universe, divine messengers, full of awe and light. Athene could fit within my beliefs about angels. And I remember very well what she was."

"I shouldn't have this, but look at it," I said, reaching up to the high shelf and taking down the Botticelli book Ikaros had brought me. "Look at these angels. They're not tame, and they have agency."

Klio looked at the angels for a long moment. "Not that Botticelli was painting from life, but I do see what you mean," she admitted.

"Where did that come from?" Ficino asked.

"Ikaros brought it back from one of his art expeditions," I said.

"You shouldn't have it. But I suppose it isn't doing any harm. As long as you haven't shown it to the children?"

"I showed Simmea the *Primavera* once, and the *Birth of Venus*."

She'd glimpsed the cover too, but she'd never mentioned it again. "And I showed it to Auge when she was just starting sculpting—and she's getting really good now. But I'm very careful with it."

"I'm sure Ikaros is saying Athene was just doing what God told her to," Klio said.

"That's nonsense," I said. "She was unquestionably acting for herself. Goddess or angel, she wasn't just a mouthpiece."

"If God exists and gave us free will, then he wanted us to use it," Ficino said. "So she could be doing as he wanted and also acting freely."

"If Athene was an angel, what would it change?" Klio asked, putting her fingertip on one of Botticelli's angels' faces.

"Perhaps how we worship," I said.

"How would it change that?" she asked.

"Sokrates said in the *Apology* that you should worship in the manner of the city in which you live. Plato said in the *Laws* that they should send to Delphi to ask how to worship," Ficino answered.

"What does Sokrates say now?" Klio asked, looking up from the book.

"He says Providence is a very interesting idea," Ficino said. "But he's so obsessed with the workers at the moment that it's hard to get him to focus on anything else."

"I don't know how we'd manage without the workers," Klio said. "They do so much. They let us lead philosphical lives because they're doing all the hard work—all the farming and building and everything. We're comfortable because of them."

"We're rich because of them," Ficino said. "We have no poverty here, because of them."

"The idea was always that they were here to help us at the beginning, while the children were growing, and that in future generations the irons would replace them. Then we will have poverty, or at least some of us will live less comfortable lives."

"Not poverty," I said, remembering poverty in my own time. "Well, in some ways we are all poor. We live with very few possessions. But nobody will be in want. Nobody will feast while others starve."

"That would be unjust indeed," Ficino said. "Are we going to lose the workers?"

Klio stopped and sat down. "Eventually, we'll lose them no matter what, unless Athene brings us more, and spare parts. They'll wear out. And if the city can only keep going by constant divine intervention then we're not doing very well, are we?"

"Having it to start us off—" Ficino said.

"Yes, but we had the workers to start us off too. After that, what? And it could be quite abrupt if we give them rights and then they stop working. At the moment it's only some of them, and they are working voluntarily, but who knows what will happen? Aristomache made a powerfully moving speech about slavery, but when it comes to it they are machines and all our comfort rests on them." She held up her wine cup. "Who planted these vines, and pruned them? Who trod the grapes and added the yeast and bottled the vintage?"

"The children of Ferrara made these cups," I said. "We're starting to replace what the workers do."

"But we're only starting. It will take a long time before we have everything smooth. If they suddenly refused to help it would be a disaster. And even with them slowly failing, it's difficult. There are a lot of things they do that we can't teach the children because we don't know how to do them. Do you know how to make wine?"

"We have a number of skills between us," Ficino said.

"Come and tell the Tech Committee that, and the Committee on Iron Work," Klio said. "We have an odd number of skills between us, and we're very lacking in practical physical skills. I'm not sure we have three people who know how to fix the plumbing."

"I've got much better at midwifery than I ever imagined I would," I said. "I wanted the life of the mind, but here I am delivering babies and teaching girls how to breast feed."

"On the whole, the women are better on practical skills than the men," Klio said. "Which makes sense, really, when you think about it. Most of the men come from eras where they had slaves or servants to do the physical work. Even though some of the women did as well, they were still expected to do more of the hands-on things."

"To my mother, the word *work* meant sewing," I said.

"And if you'd stayed in your time, you'd have had to make most of your clothes," Klio said. "Not so for your brother."

"I'd have made most of his clothes as well," I said. "My aunt did have some dresses made for me, but I made all my own underthings. Underthings! How very little I miss them!"

"Do you miss anything?" Klio asked.

"About the nineteenth century?" She nodded. "I miss my father. I wish so much he could have been here. He'd have loved it so much. Apart from that—no. Nothing. Everything here is so much better. I have books and companionship and work that's worth doing. Even when everything isn't perfect and ideal and as one would wish Plato could have had it, even when I have to do terrible things," and here I was thinking of the baby with the hare lip that I had exposed, "It's still real work that's worthy of me. Nothing in my own time could have offered me that."

"I miss recorded music," Klio said. "Being able to listen to it whenever I wanted. Apart from that, nothing. But sometimes I wonder if we should have stayed in our own times and fought for the Republic there. If we should have tried to make our own cities more just."

"That's what I did, for the first sixty-six years of my life," Ficino said. "That gives me a different perspective. I did that, and I am remembered. We had a rebirth of the ancient world, and everyone acknowledges that my efforts made a contribution. But that was the most I could possibly do towards that, alone, in the company I had, without Athene. Without all of you. She brought us together here because we were so few, scattered throughout time."

"We know we wouldn't have achieved anything further in our lives, or else we wouldn't have been brought here when we were," I pointed out.

"I suppose you're right," Klio said. She drained her wine and set down the cup. "I should get back to the practical tasks at hand that help make the city work."

"The philosophy of the quotidian," Ficino said, smiling.

"I don't know if what we have here is what Plato meant by The Good Life," I said. "But it's *a* good life."

36

SIMMEA

Sokrates had once asked Kebes how he would fight a god. I had done it without even thinking about what I was doing, and I had used weapons Sokrates and Ficino had put into my hands, rhetoric and truth. I did not even understand what I had done in facing down Athene until the day before the festival of Hera when Pytheas met me, by arrangement, at the Garden of Archimedes. It was a fine night and I'd been looking through the telescope at the moons of Jupiter, and amusing myself by calculating their orbits. It was two months since I had been healed. For most of that time, Pytheas and Sokrates and I had been investigating mysteries and workers, without advancing very far on either front.

Pytheas looked angry. "She won't do it," he said, without any preliminaries. "She hasn't calmed down at all. You can't imagine how angry with us she still is."

"Even after all this time?" I asked. My heart sank. "She's still angry? Really?"

"Yes, well, you pushed her on her own ground. And I think she's upset about something else as well. She was already very impatient even before that. She will get over it, but it'll take time. Usually if I'd made her this angry I'd leave her alone for a decade or so."

"Time is so different for you," I said.

"Not any more," he said, ruefully. "Or not for now, anyway. Now time is as urgent for me as it is for you, and she flat-out refuses to help. She was blisteringly sarcastic. She might even do something to make things worse."

"What could make it worse?" I asked, and then immediately realized. "Oh, pairing us with awful people?"

"Klymene again," he said, despondently.

"She wouldn't be so unjust," I said.

"You're making Sokrates's mistake of assuming the gods are good," Pytheas said. He led the way over to the little stone bench in the corner where we usually sat when we met here. There was a big lilac bush there and it always smelled sweet. Now at the heart of spring it was just coming into flower, and smelled overwhelming. "The gods are as petty and childish as any of the awful stories about us Plato wanted to keep out of the city. Athene's one of the best of us, but even she can be . . . spiteful when she's angry. Vengeful."

"It would be horribly unfair to Klymene," I said, sitting down beside him. "Klymene has done nothing. And all I did was explain that she could trust me to keep my word."

"She wouldn't think about Klymene at all, if that's what she wanted to do. Klymene barely exists to her. Athene has friends and favorites here, like Tullius and Ikaros, but she's only theoretically granting equal significance to people like Klymene. It's challenging. I have to really work at it." He sighed.

"Do you think she'll do that?"

"She'd be more likely to choose somebody really ugly for me. Or maybe—no, I don't know. Anyway, it's not so much me I'm worried about as you. You said—when we were talking on the beach about Daphne, you said you were afraid. And she could match you with somebody brutal." He put his arm around my shoulders. I could feel the warmth of it through my kiton. I leaned back against him.

"I don't think there are any brutal golds," I said, trying to be brave and face the worst. "Anyway, I've done it three times now, and Phoenix was pretty crass. It's not so bad. I can do it again."

He kicked his legs against the stone. "I hate this. I hate feeling helpless. And I suppose it's an essential human condition, and yes, even though I was so proud of myself doing this properly I was in fact cheating by knowing Athene was here and could fix things. I suppose in a way my coming here to the city was cheating, compared to going somewhere with poverty and dirt and all the terrible things of mortality seen close up. If I'd been a slave."

"Too late now," I said. "Though I suppose you could do it again if you wanted to?"

"I have never heard of anyone doing it again. And I don't know whether I could make myself."

"I'm glad you came here."

"Oh yes." He squeezed my shoulders. "I don't want you to have another baby with somebody else."

"No," I said. "I don't want to either. I'm not ready to have another baby. My body is. But what happens if I get like that again? Athene wouldn't help us reach Asklepius again, and without that I might be in that horrible state for a year or even more."

"That's a very good point. There are things that people think help, iron and so on. But you don't want to risk it yet and I think that makes sense. When I'm back on good terms with Athene and we can fix it would be much better."

"You said a decade?"

"In a decade you'll only be twenty-eight, twenty-nine. There are eras when that would be considered quite young to be having a baby."

"I suppose." It seemed to me quite a long time to wait.

"But that isn't the problem, the problem is that you'll get pregnant at the festival, now, tomorrow, with somebody else.

After Athene refused me, I came here with two potential solutions to that."

I twisted round so that I could see his face, tucking my knees up on the bench and putting my arms around them. "What are they?"

He put his hand on my bare knee, where it felt warm and heavy and almost unbearably erotic. "One is that you and I could mate now, tonight. You'd still have to go through with it tomorrow, but you'd already be pregnant with my son."

"How is it you're so sure I'd get pregnant, and that it would be a son?" I asked. It was hard to talk evenly because I was breathless at the thought.

"I'm a god," he said. "There are so many heroic souls, and so few chances for them to be born heroes."

"And that counts even though you're incarnate?"

"This is a soul thing, not a body thing," he said.

"And how do you know it wouldn't be a daughter?"

"It wouldn't—" He stopped and raised his eyebrows. "Usually, it feels unkind to beget a daughter, because in most eras it's so horrible to be a woman. But I suppose here and now is one of the few places it wouldn't be. So yes, it could be a daughter. That would be interesting. Different. Fun."

I was still acutely aware of his hand on my knee. If I chose that option we could be sharing eros in a few moments. I was absolutely ready. We could stand up together there in the Garden of Archimedes, or off in the woods if we were afraid somebody else might come to look at the stars. That would be wonderful, I knew it would. I wanted it so much. It was what I had wanted for so long. But I couldn't bear the thought of sinking down into that empty state of uncaring again. "What's the other alternative?"

"If you're not ready to have another baby now, you could eat silphium, and you won't get pregnant. Well, you probably would

with me because the weight of heroic souls waiting would probably outweigh the power of the plant. But you would be very
unlikely to with anyone else."

"What is it? I never heard of it."

"It's a root. I have some. I went and dug some up earlier in
case you wanted it." He handed it to me from the fold in his
kiton. It felt like a spring onion. "You would eat it now, and
then tomorrow you go through with it, which you'll have to
anyway, but you won't have a baby. Nobody will think anything
is strange, because you did it twice without before."

"I might be safe anyway." I thought about it. "One in three is
not good odds."

"You're slightly more likely to get pregnant again after being
pregnant once," he said. "It's as if your body has to figure out
how to do it."

Just then a worker came up and began to dismantle part of
the wall around the garden. Pytheas took his hand off my knee.
I decided to take that as a sign. I put the silphium in my mouth
and crunched it up. It tasted like a green onion.

"Good," Pytheas said. I couldn't tell from his voice if he was
disappointed or relieved. "Do you know that's the first thing
you've ever done that's against Plato's plan?"

"Whichever I'd chosen it would have been against it," I said.
"Or does he say it's all right to copulate with your friend on the
night before the festival?"

"He certainly does not. But I don't think he was imagining
the effect this would have on particular people at all. He knew
about agape, but he didn't think how it would mesh with these
festivals. Or maybe he really couldn't imagine agape between
men and women, and he thought agape between men wouldn't
be affected by them going off to women at the festivals. Sokrates
was married, and Aristotle, but never Plato."

There was a great clatter at that moment as the worker pulled out a stone and several others fell. Pytheas got up and went over to the worker. "Joy to you. What are you doing?" he asked.

It wrote something on the path. "Making art," Pytheas read aloud. "Good." He patted it, then wandered back to me.

"Can they tell when you pat them?" I asked as he settled down again.

"I have no idea. But Sokrates does it, so I do it."

We watched it for a while, pulling stones out of the wall and rearranging them. I couldn't see an intelligible pattern, but then you might not see one in the middle of a fresco either. Then I started to feel sleepy. "I should go to bed. I have to be up early to make garlands in the morning."

"Then we both have to mate with strangers in the after-noon." Pytheas ground his teeth. "She'll calm down. But she knows what I want now, and she has said no once, so it'll be hard to ask her without reminding her why she refused. Maybe I could ask Ficino to cheat instead. He might be amenable to a eugenic argument if not a romantic one."

"Maia might be amenable to a romantic one," I said. "Though maybe not. She was so strict on not knowing our babies. I don't think Axiothea would."

"Eugenic," Pytheas said at once. "And Atticus too. Funny how easy it is to tell. Too late for this festival tomorrow, but we can try that next time. We know they cheat. We can try to use that to our advantage."

"What is the eugenic argument?"

"That any baby you and I had would clearly be superior in all ways and be a philosopher king, exactly as the city wants." He hugged me suddenly. "It's even true. She'd be a brilliant philosophical hero."

"I'd rather not wait ten years," I admitted. "How long will the silphium keep working?"

"This month, until you bleed again."

He stood. I followed him up and took his hand. We walked back through the streets together. It was late and they were quiet, but not deserted. We saw a master striding along, and couples slipping back from the woods. There were also workers here and there, some of them engaged in engraving dialogue, others going about usual worker tasks. One of them slid in front of us as we passed the temple of Hestia. We stopped. It carved something by our feet. I had to angle myself to see it in the dim light of the sconces. "How many stars?"

"I don't know," I said.

"Too many to count," Pytheas said.

It drew something else, something that looked like the number eight written sideways. "No," Pytheas said. "A finite but very large number. And new ones are born all the time and old ones burn out, making them uncountable."

The worker rolled away. "They're wonderful," I said. "Now that they're talking, they're thinking about everything. They're naturally philosophical. I couldn't have answered that."

"Some of the masters could," Pytheas said, absently. "Lysias knows that, I'm sure."

"New stars are being born?" I looked up, as if hoping to see some, but saw of course only the old familiar constellations.

"Yes, very far away, in nebulae. They call them stellar nurseries. You can't see them with the naked eye, and I'm not sure whether our telescopes are good enough. People will go out there and live among them—you will. Your soul, in whatever body it's in at the time. I haven't been out there yet, it's a long way from home, and I know it's silly, but I feel uncomfortable about leaving the sun. I will in time. One day, when people on new worlds call to me. Maybe you."

"I won't be me. I won't remember." It was a strange thought, bittersweet.

"No. But I will. You won't remember, but you'll call me and

I'll come." He sounded very sure. I didn't ask if it was foresight and an oracle. I just hugged him.

We should have expected it if we'd been thinking clearly, but of course we didn't. My name was the second to be drawn, and matched with me was Kebes. I went up among the usual jokes and congratulations to have the garland bound around our wrists. Kebes was beaming, and I tried to keep my face under control, to take this like a philosopher. Pytheas had been wrong, this wasn't aimed at me. It was meant to wound him, and it would. Athene didn't care much about me or anything at all about poor Kebes. I kept my head high and tried to look straight ahead. I knew Pytheas was there, but I didn't want to have to meet his eyes. It would be bad enough afterwards.

Once we were out of the square and the dancers I looked up at Kebes. "Who could have guessed?" he said. He was still smiling. "I haven't been chosen at all since the first time, but I won the wrestling yesterday. I'm glad now that I did."

I knew I had to say something, but couldn't imagine what I could possibly say. I had seen him win the wrestling, and congratulated him at the time.

"Is something wrong?" he asked.

"No," I said. "It's a little awkward, that's all."

"What is?" He looked alarmed.

"Just it being you and knowing you so well. The others times it's been people I barely knew."

We came to the street of Dionysos and turned towards the practice rooms. "I was chosen with Euridike," he said. "I know her slightly."

"She's very pretty," I said.

"Yes," he said, noncommittally.

We went inside and took a room—all the doors but one were open, so we went down to the far end. Kebes closed the door and unwound the garland. I felt shy and awkward as I took my kiton off. "I haven't done it since the baby was born," I said.

"But you're all healed up?" Kebes asked. Then before I could answer, "You mean you haven't done it with Pytheas?"

"Pytheas and I don't—I've told you before! We're doing agape, not eros." The memory of his hand on my knee the night before came back, and with it an erotic jolt that felt disloyal to both of them.

"You don't do that, maybe, but you're doing something? He touches you? You suck his dick?"

"I do not! I never do that for anyone. On the ship—you were there."

He looked blank. "On the *Goodness*?"

"The slave ship." I still hated to think of it.

"I wasn't on the same slave ship as you. I met you in the market."

"One of the sailors forced my mouth, that's all." I sat down on the bed, suddenly cold.

"But you—Pytheas—you said he was your lover. Are you saying you don't do anything at all?" He laughed. "I thought—"

"We talk," I said, with as much dignity as I could manage. "We care about each other. Agape. That's what I've always said. I don't know why you care anyway."

"Because as I was trying to say that day in Thessaly before Sokrates shut me up, you could do much better than him. You're taken in by his pretty face and his fast talk, but he's not genuine." He dropped his kiton. His penis was awake, and as big as the rest of him. "I am. You'll see now. Come on. I love you. I want you." He took a step towards the bed.

"I like to stand up," I said, getting up.

"Stand up?" He stopped, bemused.

"Let me show you. I worked it out with Aischines. It's much more comfortable."

"Euridike and I did it on the bed," he said, shaking his head. "But this will make it different."

Unfortunately, Kebes was too tall for the position I had worked out with Aischines and repeated with the others. He was also very excited. "Just give me a moment to breathe," I said, when I saw that wasn't going to work.

"Come on Simmea, it's me, you're ready," he said. "I can see how to do it standing up."

Without any hesitation he lifted me up above him and lowered me onto his penis. I clutched his shoulders, afraid of falling, though I knew he was one of the strongest of us. Then he stepped forward until my back was against the wall and began to thrust, driving the breath out of me. "There," he said.

I started to struggle, trying to get down, because I felt trapped and squeezed. Even on the bed I would have had more freedom than this. He must have mistaken my movements for passion because he didn't stop battering away at me. Maybe Athene had meant it as punishment for me after all. It wasn't rape, for I had consented, but I certainly didn't like it. "Wait," I said. "No, Kebes, wait, please."

"You like it. There. You're mine. You're mine. I'll show you. You're mine, mine, you always were, you were meant to be, mine, my Lucia, mine."

"No!" I said, horrified at what he was saying. "Stop it! I'm here for the city. I'm not doing this for your fantasy!"

"Say my name," he said, not stopping or even slowing down. "Lucia. My Lucia. Say my name."

If I had hated him it would have been different. But he was my friend, even ramming me up against the wall and panting on my face. Maybe with his name I could reach that part of him. "Matthias," I said. "No. Stop. Listen to me."

But as I said his name he spilled his seed inside me. I could feel his penis jerking away as it gushed out. He carried me over to the bed then and put me down. I rolled away from him, breathing deeply.

"You liked it," he said, less sure of himself now.

"I'm not yours," I said.

"You still think you're his?" he asked. "After that?"

"I am *my own*," I said, turning to face him. "I don't belong to anyone. Pytheas doesn't try to own me." Though he had claimed me as a votary, which was disturbingly similar. But he had only done that to protect me from Athene. And after all, he was a god. And what he had offered me was exactly everything I most wanted—to make art, to build the future, to help each other become our best selves. "He honors me."

"I honor you!" he protested. "We were meant to be together. We were chained together. And now we were chosen together."

"Things like that are accidents, not fate," I said. "And don't you think I should have a choice?"

"Yes, I do, but I think you should choose me." He put his hand out to my face, awkwardly. "You're mine. You'll have my baby. We can run away together before he's born, build a house, have a family. We can do this every night, have more children. My mother, my sisters, were lost, but I still have you and we can make a new family."

"Matthias! Will you listen to me?"

He stopped.

"I'm not your mother or your sisters. I have made my choice. I choose the city. And as a lover I choose Pytheas. I'm here in this room with you right now because I choose the city and the city chose us to be together now. I may have your child," though I hoped the silphium would work and I would not, "but if I do, I will give it to the city to grow up here and be a philosopher. I don't want to run away, as I've told you thousands of times. I don't want to destroy the city."

I had said this often enough before, but either he hadn't listened or he had twisted it in his mind and thought I meant I wasn't ready. Even though he'd often heard me arguing with Sokrates for the merits of the city, he reacted as if I had struck him. "You can't mean that. You're mine."

"I can. I do." I got up and picked up my kiton.

"You don't have to go. We can stay all night. We can do it again."

"We can stay, but we're not obliged to. I've done what I was obliged to do and I'm leaving." I put my kiton on.

He stared at me in horror. "What—"

"Kebes, I'm your friend, but I'm not your property. I can choose what I want."

His face crumpled for a moment. Then he lowered his head and scowled. "I don't care anyway," he said. "You're not so special. You're nothing but a scrawny flat-faced buck-toothed Copt."

I laughed. "That's true. And I am also a gold of the Just City."

"I didn't mean it. Come back." He got up and put his hand on my bare shoulder.

I pushed past him to the door. "I won't mention this again if you don't."

"Where are you going?"

I hadn't thought about it, but as he asked I knew. "I'm going to Thessaly."

The streets were quiet, though I passed numerous pairs of workers engaged in written dialogues. Pytheas's vision of the streets being entirely paved in them was coming true. To my surprise, Sokrates was at home and answered the door to me at once. "Simmea! Joy to you. Is everything all right?" He drew me inside. There was nobody there. A book was open on the bed where he must have been reading it.

"Joy to you, Sokrates. I was drawn with Kebes, and it was . . . awkward," I said.

"Oh dear. And it will be difficult for Pytheas."

"It will." We went out into the garden. "I told Kebes I was coming here, so he won't. But you'll probably have to talk to him later. He thinks he owns me, and he just doesn't."

"I can talk to him and try to make that clear to him," Sokrates said. "Pytheas will be more difficult."

"I don't know whether he will." I was still sticky and uncomfortable between my legs as I sat in my usual place beneath the tree. When I leaned back my back felt bruised where it had been banged into the wall. "It's going to be so awkward with both of them."

"I don't know how Plato could have imagined that this would make everything easier," Sokrates said.

I laughed and rolled my shoulders to try to loosen my back. "If it wasn't for his wanting women to be philosophers, I'd imagine that he thought wives were a fungible resource. Have you read the *Republic*?"

"With a great deal of attention. But I'm afraid I can't lend it to you, I have promised not to." He sat down beside the limestone Herm he had carved himself during the Peloponnesian War.

"Not to lend it to me?" I was astonished.

"Not to lend it to any of you." He stressed the plural.

"Pytheas has read it, of course."

"Of course he must have. Before he came here." Sokrates nodded. "How fascinating he is! I entirely understand your being in love with him. I don't even accuse him of having used his powers to beguile you, as he seems remarkably fond of you in return."

"He doesn't have any powers here. He's just so amazingly wonderful," I said. I couldn't help smiling when I thought about him. "But being incarnate makes him vulnerable in odd ways, and I can help him with that."

"You don't ever feel that he wants to take more of you than you want to give? That's what they say about the gods."

"Never. Pytheas wants me to be my best self." That was the

problem with Kebes. Kebes didn't see me, or my potential best self. He saw something he imagined as me, something he called Lucia. I hadn't been Lucia for a long time now. "And I want Pytheas to be his best self."

"And I want the same for both of you," Sokrates said.

"You're in love with him too," I said, realizing it as he spoke. "And so you must know he doesn't take more than you want to give."

"As long as you want to give everything." Sokrates smiled wryly. "I have loved Athene and Apollo all my life, and between them they have consumed most of it."

"But aren't you better for it? In your soul?"

"I wouldn't want to be any different," he admitted.

"And you love Pytheas the same way I do!" I was pleased, thinking it through, excited and not even a shred jealous. I trusted Sokrates, and this was something we shared. If we were both in love with Pytheas, then we could talk about it and maybe define agape more clearly. I leaned forward eagerly with my hands on my knees, ignoring the twinge in my back.

"I love both of you, of course," he said, gently, clearly disconcerted.

"I know, and when it comes to philia I truly love you too, but that's not what I mean, though of course that's also really important." I took a breath to compose my thoughts more clearly. "I love you and you love me, as teachers and pupils who are friends love each other."

"Yes," he agreed, cautiously.

"But you love Pytheas the same way I do. Agape."

He shook his head. I had argued with Sokrates about many things over the course of years, and had rarely seem him this disconcerted. "Not the same at all. I'm an ugly old man. I joke about being helpless before his beauty, but—"

"And I'm an ugly young girl, and he's Apollo, he's thousands of years older than both of us. But he has chosen both of us as votaries because age and beauty are trivial; what really matters to him is excellence. What's on the inside of our heads. And both of us can help him, we can give him new ideas and new ways of thinking!" I said all this as fast as I could get the words out. "It does make it a bit different that you don't have any eros to struggle with conquering. But it's still agape, and still very similar."

"I knew him as a god first, and was his votary, and only later came to know him as Pytheas, and vulnerable," he said.

"Yes, that's a real difference," I acknowledged. "You knew him as a god for so long. I did that the other way around. But you also loved him all that time. And now both of you passionately want to increase each other's excellence, just the same as he and I do. This is so great! We both want that for him, and he wants it for us," I was so pleased I'd worked this out. "And we want that for him a lot."

"We do," Sokrates said, staring at me. "Sometimes I think the most important thing I can be doing—and the same for you—is helping him to increase his excellence. More important than the workers or the city or anything. Because he's not just our friend Pytheas, he really is the god Apollo. He's the light. And what he learns and knows and understands is so important for the world. His excellence has a future, and nothing else here does."

"Well, ours does for our souls," I amended. "But Pytheas still has so much to learn about being human, so much that he ought to understand about it. He really is wonderful. And he tries so hard. It's marvellous that he says excellence is something even the gods must pursue."

"He certainly pursues it. I can't speak for all the gods, and he doesn't either. I do wonder what his Father pursues, alone in the centre."

"He said he didn't know."

"That doesn't stop me wondering about it all the more." Sokrates tugged at his beard, as he sometimes did when thinking hard.

"But Pytheas—Apollo—wants to increase my excellence, as I want to increase his. And it's the same with you." I beamed at him. I was so delighted to have figured this out.

Sokrates focused on me and sighed. "You are truly very close to what Plato dreamed. You're almost enough to justify this whole absurd structure."

"It's not absurd," I said. "Though I must admit it does have its absurd side sometimes."

"Plato understood so little about what people are like," Sokrates said.

"If I were making a plan for a Just City, there are things I'd change. I'd let people choose their partners, and whether to bring up their own children."

"It's like a delicate mosaic, if you change anything the whole thing falls apart into incoherence. Plato had logical reasons for those things."

"I do wish I could read it. Maia says not until I'm fifty, which is ridiculous."

"Didn't Pytheas tell you what it said?" Sokrates was looking at me alertly, his most characteristic expression. I wondered how many debates we'd had sitting just where we were in this garden, and how many more we would have in the years to come.

"He told me about the masters cheating at the lots to get better children. Though it wasn't the masters cheating that put me with Kebes, it was Athene, to punish Pytheas and me for annoying her."

"What?" Sokrates puffed up with anger. "That's unjust!"

"Pytheas says she can be spiteful. He says you shouldn't make the mistake of assuming that they're good."

"They shouldn't have that power if they're not responsible with it. This city is a great many things, but one of them is directly enforced with Athene's power." He leapt to his feet and began to pace around the garden. "I have a good mind to challenge her. I've been thinking about it for a while. I am her votary too. And what she is doing and learning here is also an issue that has very deep consequences for the world."

"You love her too, in that same way," I said.

"Of course I do. I have always loved wisdom. Pytheas says she wants to know everything. I have questions it would do her soul good to consider."

"Pytheas says she's really angry now, but she'll calm down. It might be better to wait until she calms down before you challenge her."

"Did he say how long it would take?" Sokrates asked, stopping and looking down at me.

"He said maybe a decade."

"I don't have a decade. I'm seventy-four years old." He began to pace again.

Nobody would have been able to tell he was that old, especially watching him pace. He looked a vigorous sixty. "You're not about to drop dead. And I think she should have a little bit longer. She and Pytheas had an argument yesterday."

He spun around. "She's the goddess of reason and logic. She shouldn't quarrel and act in anger."

"I agree, but if that's the way things are, there's not much point saying they ought to be different because that would be better and more logical," I said.

Sokrates laughed. "I do have a tendency in that direction, yes. I want to challenge her——" There was a scratch at the outside door, and he went to open it. I hoped it wouldn't be Pytheas, as I wasn't ready to see him yet. I knew it wouldn't be Kebes.

It was Aristomache and Ikaros. I heard them wishing

Sokrates joy before they came outside and wished me the same thing. "Weren't you drawn in the lots today?" Aristomache asked as I returned their greetings. "Are you still recovering from childbirth?"

"I was drawn, and I have played my part and finished," I said.

"It must be a very uncomfortable thing," Ikaros said. "I'm glad I don't have to abide by it. A random partner every four months, sometimes friends, sometimes enemies, sometimes strangers."

"We were just saying that we don't know what Plato was thinking," Sokrates said.

They laughed, as if this was an often repeated joke.

I started to get up and excuse myself and leave them to their accustomed conversation. Sokrates waved me back. "I'm thinking about challenging Athene to a debate," he said, to all of us. "On The Good Life. In front of everyone. In the Agora."

"I haven't seen her for a long time," Ikaros said, sitting down by the tree.

"She's here," Aristomache said, sitting by the Herm. "I know how to get in touch with her if you need her. But a debate?"

"I'm an old man," Sokrates said. He stayed standing in the middle of the garden. "I want to debate her before I die, like poor Tullius."

"You're a long way from death," Ikaros said. "But I'd love to hear you debate her. That would be . . ."

"Socratic frenzy?" Sokrates said, clearly teasing him, because Ikaros laughed.

"We'd all love to hear it," Aristomache said. "But I don't know if she'd agree."

"We'd all love to hear it too," I said. "I can't think of anything we'd enjoy more."

"The good life," mused Ikaros. "I don't suppose you could consider asking her to debate my theory of will and reason?"

"What's that?" I asked.

"That will, or love, and reason are the two horses of the chariot in the *Phaedrus*, and it doesn't matter which one you follow if it's taking you closer to God."

"So if you love something it doesn't matter if you understand it? It can still take you closer to divinity, just by loving it?" I asked.

"Yes!" Ikaros looked excited.

"That's just mystical twaddle," I said. I wasn't in the mood for it.

"That's what Septima said," Ikaros said, not discouraged at all. "But wait until you see how it fits with my theory of the gods."

"Besides," Aristomache interrupted, "Plato said one of the horses was human and one divine. Which would be which?"

"That's the beauty of this idea," Ikaros said.

"If Athene agrees to debate me, you will be there, perhaps you could ask her to debate this afterwards," Sokrates said, starting to pace again. "Or maybe I will mention your theory of the gods in my argument, if things take the right turn. Or we could have a whole series of debates."

"Do you want me to invite her?" Aristomache asked.

"If you can find her, I'd like you to deliver a formal written invitation," Sokrates said. "And don't keep it secret, let everyone know I want to do this so they can start anticipating it."

"Are you really sure this is the best time?" I asked.

Sokrates smiled. "It feels to me like the very best time."

37

APOLLO

She came not helmeted but castle-crowned, Athene Polias, the builder of cities. She didn't look angry; to anyone who didn't know her she would have seemed serene, calm, entirely Olympian. The anger was all in the way she moved. What had angered her? She was getting bored, and something had upset her, and I had pestered her and made her act against her best judgement in petitioning to heal Simmea, and then Simmea had wrong-footed her. If Simmea had promised and sworn and acted awed and intimidated, she wouldn't have stayed angry. It was the way Simmea had bested her that did it, and of course, that made it the worst possible time for Sokrates to challenge her to a public debate.

Her petty revenge, at the Festival of Hera, had stung. I was chosen last, and paired with Euridike. Euridike was the very pattern of a Hellenic maiden, fair-skinned and crowned with golden braids. Her breasts, which had been magnificent, were sagging a little with child-bearing now, but she was probably the most beautiful and desirable of the golds available at that festival. I knew perfectly well what Athene meant by it—to show me that this was what I really wanted. When I had been free to choose this was what I had always chosen, and indeed, this was something I could easily have. I felt physical desire for Euridike that I did not, could not, feel for Simmea. And yes, that hurt, but it was a pinprick. The whole time I was with Euridike I naturally couldn't turn my mind away from poor Simmea matched with Kebes.

I didn't think for an instant that she would prefer him to me. As with the time we wrestled, that wasn't a fair contest. I was a god. She had said she loved me as stones fell down, and I trusted that. No lout like Kebes was going to affect the important thing. But I hated to think of him hurting her, either physically or emotionally. I kept thinking of it. He wouldn't want to hurt her. He loved her, in his way, like a dog loves his bone. And all Simmea had was philosophy. (And the silphium, which I was so glad I had remembered. I could not have endured watching her bear Kebes's child. It had been bad enough with tone-deaf Nikias.) And of course, Euridike was a person with equal significance and her own choices, and she found me desirable, and having been matched with me she deserved more of me than half my attention. (How could Plato have thought this was a good idea? How could he?)

Simmea insisted afterwards that everything was all right and it hadn't changed anything. But she was avoiding Kebes, and so was I.

The whole city came to the Agora for the debate. I saw Glaukon in his wheeled chair. The babies were there, even the smallest, so that their nursery-maids needn't miss it. The workers, those who had taken an interest in philosophy, were lining up at the edges to the Agora to listen. Old Porphyry had dragged himself from his sickbed and was sitting with the pregnant women eight months along, down near the front. There was nothing we loved more than a debate, and this was the debate of a century. I saw tears glitter in Ikaros's eyes as Athene made her way through the crowd to the rostrum. Ficino too was blinded by honourable tears. He introduced the debate.

Simmea, beside me, was the only person I could see who didn't look delighted at the whole event. "I was thinking about Plato in Syracuse," she said. "The time when the tyrant sold him into slavery. That was after a debate on the good life."

"I'm sure Sokrates knows about that," I said. "I'm sure Sokrates was thinking about it when he suggested this."

Sokrates was wearing a plain white wool kiton. He nodded and smiled at Ficino's introduction. He stood to the right and Athene to the left, which meant that she was going to begin. He did not look at all intimidated by her presence.

Her speech was splendid. She spoke of course of the Just City, of justice in the soul and justice in the city. I saw people in the crowd nodding at her eloquence. It was all straight out of Plato, and you couldn't have found a more appreciative audience. Nobody clapped when she finished, they knew the rules, but there was a deep murmur of appreciation. Sokrates took a step forward.

"I can't possibly compete with a beautiful speech like that," he began. "I hope you'll let me off and allow me to talk in my usual manner, asking questions and trying to find the answers."

There was a ripple of laughter from the crowd. Athene inclined her head gracefully. Simmea squeezed my hand.

"You've talked a lot about justice, and a lot about this city," he said, conversationally. "Do you think this city is just?"

"I do."

"Not merely that it's pursuing justice, or attempting to be just, but that it actually attains justice?"

"Yes." I was surprised. I'd have thought she'd said that it was on its way to justice. The experiment wasn't anything like done yet. I'm not sure even Plato would have thought it was already just. But many among the crowd were nodding.

"And you find that justice in the relations of the part to the whole and the way things are laid out?"

"Yes."

"Well it seems to me that there are a few issues that need to be cleared up before I'd call this the good life. First there's the question of choice. I'd say there can't be justice when people have no choice, do you agree? I'm thinking of people in prison, or condemned to row in a ship, shackled to the oar."

"The sentence that sent them there might be just," Athene countered.

"Yes, that could be so, but in their situation when they're there, when they're compelled to stay, or to row, they've had freedom taken from them and they're under the overseer's lash. There's no justice there, or don't you agree?"

"I agree, subject to what I said before."

"And if the sentence that sent them there wasn't just, if the judge was bribed or the evidence was false, or if they were captured by pirates and chained to the oar, then there's no justice?"

"No, in that case there's no justice. The punishment is making them worse people, not better, and in addition the passing of the unjust sentence is making the judge worse."

"Then I submit that the case is the same in this city, that the masters chose to be here but the children did not." Sokrates leaned back a little as if to give her space to reply.

"The children were rescued from slavery," she said.

"They were bought as slaves and brought here and given no choices about how to live."

"Children are never given such choices."

"Really?" Sokrates asked. "But I thought souls chose their lives before birth, as Plato wrote in the *Phaedo*."

I smiled, hearing Sokrates cite that dialogue he disliked so much. Athene glared over at me, guessing I must have confirmed this for Sokrates. She caught me smiling, and glared even harder.

"Yes, that's true," she admitted, reluctantly. The audience let out a sigh, as if they had all been holding their breath through the pause waiting to hear.

"Then in a way the children did choose to come here," Sokrates said.

"It's not true," Kebes burst out, from where he stood down near the rostrum. Simmea, next to me, winced. Kebes really was recalcitrant. He had to hold on to his anger and deny that he had in any way chosen to be here, even when he heard it from the mouth of Athene herself.

She ignored him. "They did. And once they were here we looked after them as if we were their loving parents with their best interests at heart. If you ask them now they are grown, they will say they are happy they came here."

"Some of them will," Sokrates said, and his eyes sought out Simmea, who stood straight at my side. "Will you agree with that, Simmea?"

"Assuredly, Sokrates," she said, speaking up plainly. There was a ripple of laughter.

"But some of them will not." He looked at Kebes, who was near him, at the front. "Kebes?"

"I never chose to come here. I have never been reconciled to having been dragged from my home and bought as a slave and brought here. I have never had any choice about staying. I still hate and resent the masters, and I am not the only one." His voice was passionate and clear. The crowd were making unhappy murmurs. Athene looked daggers at Kebes.

Sokrates spoke again, and at once Athene's eyes were back on him. "It's a slippery argument to say that our souls gave consent before birth, because it would be possible to use that to justify doing anything to anybody. We don't remember what our souls chose or why. We don't know what part of our lives we wanted and what part we overlooked, or agreed to endure for the sake of another part. It may be a kind of consent, but it's not at all the same as giving active consent here and now."

"I agree," Athene said. "But in the case of the children, bringing them here has made them better people. It is the opposite of the case of the galley slave."

"Except that even if it did good to them, it made you and the masters worse because you bought them as slaves and disregarded their choices, as in the case of the unjust judge who condemned the slave."

"I do not think I am worse for it," she said, confidently.

"So? Well, let me ask others. Maia? Do you think you are better or worse because you bought the children?"

Maia jumped when she was addressed. "Worse, Sokrates," she admitted, after a moment.

"Aristomache?"

"Worse," she said immediately.

"Atticus?"

"Worse," he said, speaking out loudly. "And since reading Aristomache's dialogue, I have come to believe that I am worse because I kept slaves in my own time."

"But whether or not it made anyone's soul less just, I agree that once you had the children here you treated them as best you knew, and certainly as Plato suggested," Sokrates said.

"Yes, we did," Athene agreed.

"But the next question is whether Plato was a good authority for these things. Did he have children?"

"You know he did not."

"There are other ways of knowing about how to bring people up than being a parent. And indeed, I've read that after I knew him he became a teacher, he had a school in Athens, a famous school, the Academy, which became the very name for learning. Was it for children?"

"It was for older people. A university, not a school."

"So what made him an expert in the education of younger people?" He hesitated for an instant and then moved on before Athene answered. "Nothing. And on the same grounds, I could ask what cities he founded. And I could ask what happened when he tried to involve himself in the politics of Syracuse, what wonderful results he had in that city? And similarly, his pupil Aristotle taught Alexander the Great, and Alexander did found cities and no doubt we see in Alexander the pattern of the philosopher king you wish to create, and in his cities the pattern of justice?"

"Below the belt," Simmea muttered. I grinned. She was completely caught up in the debate.

"Plato had a dream which was never tried until now, but now that it has been tried it is successful," Athene said, wisely avoiding the issues of Syracuse and Alexander.

"So you brought the children here and put them into an experiment, in the hope it would be successful," Sokrates said.

"Yes," Athene conceded.

"And you believe it has been?"

"Yes."

"Successful at maximizing justice?"

"Yes," she insisted.

"Well, I think there are other points of view possible on that subject. To take just one aspect of this supposedly Just City consider the festival of Hera, which instead of increasing happiness is visibly making everyone miserable. Human relationships can't work like that. Eating together is different from sharing eros together. I've seen people made unhappy by being drawn together, or unhappy by being drawn together once and never again." Again Sokrates was seeking out people in the crowd. I was grateful he did not look at us. "Damon?"

"Yes, Sokrates?"

"Is the system of having wives and children in common making you happy, or unhappy?"

"Unhappy, Sokrates," Damon said, clearly.

"Auge?"

"Unhappy, Sokrates," she said promptly.

"Half the children are cheating on the system, and almost nobody likes it. Plato knew a lot about love and was notably eloquent on the subject, far more eloquent than I could ever be, though he set the words in my mouth. How could he then set up such a travesty? But you will say, will you not, that the purpose of the system is not to maximize individual happiness but the justice of the whole city?"

"Yes," she said.

"And how does this maximize justice?"

"People do not form individual attachments but are attached to all the others, and people do not care more about their own children than all the children of the city."

"But that's nonsense," Sokrates said gently. "They do form individual attachments, they're just pursuing them in secret. And they do care more about their own children, they're just prevented from seeing them."

"It may not be perfect, but it is more just than the existence of families," Athene said. "Plato was successfully attempting to avoid nepotism and factionalism. We have none of that here. Ficino, you can speak for the evil which families can cause to a republic."

Ficino nodded sadly. "Yes, it's true, family rivalries did great harm to Florentia. The Guelphs and the Ghibellines, and then later in my own time the rivalry between the Medici and the other noble families. It can tear a city apart, and there is no justice possible." I saw many of the masters nodding. "The worst thing is with inheritance. Even if you educate an heir carefully, they will not always be the best person to succeed to power. And unless rulers happen to be childless, they will always prefer their children, regardless of fitness."

"We saw that in Rome," Manlius said. "Caligula, Commodus, we have innumerable examples. Whereas when the emperor was childless and chose the best succesor we had rulers like Hadrian and Marcus Aurelius. But family love can be a wonderful consolation when things go wrong in the state."

"It can indeed be very pleasant when things go well in the family," Athene said, nodding to him in a friendly way, and then turning back to Sokrates. "Just as you called on one or two children to say that Plato's system makes them unhappy, there are many among the masters I could call on to talk about how families did the same for them."

"And I could call on many more among the children to witness that they are forming individual attachments in secret, but I will not, because I would be putting them in danger of being punished if they spoke the truth."

Athene was silent, and so was the crowd. Everyone kept still and tried to avoid Sokrates's eyes.

Then Klymene spoke up, astonishing me. Her voice sounded very soft in the big space, but everyone was so quiet that she could be heard clearly. "I have not made any individual attachment. But I see it all around me. In my sleeping house, I am the only one who is not in some kind of love affair. Sokrates is completely right about this. Almost everyone has individual attachments. And while I believe the city knows best how to bring up children, and I understand what you're saying about the dangers of factionalism and preference, I do miss my own boy, that I only saw for a few minutes after he was born."

"Bravely spoken," Sokrates said, smiling at her. "I think that point is made. Now, let's move on. I questioned whether Plato was wise enough to write the constitution for a city like this. He was only a man. But you are a god, are you not?"

"I am," Athene said, cautiously stepping into Sokrates's unavoidable rhetorical trap.

"So you know more than mere mortals, isn't that so?"

"Of course," Athene said.

"So we should trust you to be doing what is right for us, even if we can't quite understand why?"

"Yes."

"And you have been deeply involved in setting up this city from the beginning?"

"Yes."

"And you have constantly used your power to make things work out for the city, things that might otherwise not have worked?"

"Yes."

"The trouble with that is that even though you are a god you too are ignorant in some areas. One area I can easily cite is to do with the workers. Until I discovered it, just recently, nobody knew that they had free will and intelligence." Sokrates raised an arm to indicate the workers who were there listening in a circle around the outside of the agora. Axiothea was standing near Crocus and read aloud the response he carved.

"Volition," she read. "Want to choose, want to talk, want to make art, want to debate, want to stay."

"Wait," Manlius called. "Sixty-one is writing something."

"What is it?" Sokrates asked.

"No choice brought, choose stay city," Manlius read out.

"Precisely," Sokrates said. "They wanted to choose and to talk and to make art, they wanted a say in their own lives. They didn't choose to come, but they do choose to stay. But you didn't even know they could think, nobody did."

"But as soon as you discovered it, we agreed to consider them people. Now they spend ten hours a day working and ten being educated and the rest recharging, their equivalent of eating and sleeping." Athene looked pleased. "Once we realized we were committing an injustice we moved at once to redress it."

"Indeed. That speaks very well of you, of the city in general. I think Aristomache deserves especial thanks for this." He smiled at Aristomache where she stood near him in the crowd. "But my point is that the reason you were treating them unfairly is because you were not even aware, until Crocus and I discovered it, that the workers were people."

"He's got her," Simmea muttered.

"Yes, I was unaware," Athene admitted.

"So even though you are a goddess you don't know everything?"

"Of course not."

"Of course not," I echoed. "He knows that."

"Yes, but not everybody does," Simmea said. "Hush."

"So, for instance, you didn't know how well Plato's experiment would work until you tried it?"

"No."

"It was an experiment?"

"Yes. I said so."

"An experiment, and nobody knew what would happen. And to perform this experiment, why didn't you do as Plato said?"

"We did," Athene said, indignant.

"Plato said you should take over an existing city and drive out everyone over ten years of age, you didn't do that?"

"No. It seemed better to start fresh."

"Seemed better to you?"

"Yes."

"Even though it wasn't what Plato said?" Sokrates pretended surprise. There was a ripple of laughter.

"What Plato said wasn't possible," Athene snapped.

"Wasn't possible even for you?" Sokrates sounded even more surprised.

"Not everything is possible even for the gods," Athene said.

Sokrates paused, then shook his head sadly. "Not everything is possible, and you do not know everything?"

"I already said so." Athene was clearly irritated now.

"To return to what Plato said. He thought his city would be near other cities, would trade with them and make war with them. Why did you decide instead to put it on an island far away from other cities and with no contact with the outside world?"

Athene hesitated. "It seemed it would work better that way."

"So you felt free to change things Plato wrote when you thought they would work better a different way, but you kept them the same and held Plato's words up as unchangeable writ when you didn't want to change them?"

She hesitated again. "There were a number of good reasons to choose this island."

"Yes, the volcano that will erupt and destroy all the evidence of your meddling. That was going to be my next point. If you believe that this is the Just City, that the life here is the good life, why did you situate it in this little corner of the world that will be destroyed, at a point in time where it can influence nothing and change nothing? Why is it set here in a sterile backwater? Why didn't you put it in a time and place where it could really have an effect, where it could have posterity, where all humanity could benefit from the results of this experiment and not just you?"

There was a swelling murmur through the crowd at that, especially from the masters. Everyone must have wondered about that.

"This was a time when it was possible. The more things affect time, the less power the gods have to do things." She sounded even more irritated now.

"So you deliberately chose a backwater?"

"Yes," she snapped.

"And you deliberately chose a time when it could not last?"

"I told the masters when I gathered them together. Nothing mortal can last, and the most we can hope for is to create legends. Legends of this city will change the world." She spread her hands out to the crowd.

"Ah yes," Sokrates said, drawing everyone's attention back to him. "Atlantis." He laughed. "Can legends change the world? Is that really the best you could do?"

"Legends really can change the world," I whispered to Simmea. "Whether Sokrates believes it or not."

"This city is worth having whether it has results in time or not," Athene said.

"Then why didn't you build it on Olympos, outside time?"

"That wouldn't have been possible." It really wouldn't. It wasn't even imaginable. Athene cast another furious glance at me, only too aware who must have told Sokrates that Olympos was outside time.

"And how do you know it is worth having?"

"It self-evidently is!"

"It may or may not be, but you have established that you did not know everything, that it was an experiment. You did not, could not, know it would be a better life for those you brought here against their will."

"They prayed to be here," Athene said.

"The masters prayed. The children and the workers were purchased and given no choice at all, since we have agreed to leave aside the claims of choices made by souls before birth."

Athene smiled. "The children had as much choice as humans ever do. Every human soul is born into a society, and that society shapes their possible lives. And we have given them lives as good as we could imagine. As for the workers, if they had not come here they might never have developed souls at all."

"Even if that is so, it's worth mentioning that since they came here, the children and the workers have not been allowed to leave. In most cities, as young people grow up they can leave and seek out a more congenial home if they do not like it. They could leave Athens for Sparta or Crete, or if they preferred they could choose to found a new colony, or settle among the horselords of Thessaly. But if your children have tried to leave they have been brought back, even if it damaged them." Sokrates indicated Glaukon in his wheelchair. "They have been flogged for running away." He indicated Kebes. "And did you do this with good intentions?"

"Yes!" she insisted.

"But you did it in ignorance of how it would turn out?"

". . . Yes." I could tell she was still uncomfortable, but she seemed to have regained her calm.

"Did you even believe that it could work, or were you just as interested in seeing how it might fail?" I had never told him that, he must have just deduced it.

Athene bared her teeth. "I wanted it to succeed. I worked hard for it. I have spent my time and efforts here. I brought everyone here to make it succeed."

"Everyone except me. Why didn't you bring me here until the fifth year?"

"So you could teach the children rhetoric." She hesitated again. "You were an old man. I wasn't sure you'd live to teach them at fifteen if you came here at the beginning."

"I am grateful for your consideration," Sokrates said, standing straight and hearty. There was a laugh. "Why did you not extend that consideration to those older than me, or frailer? How about Tullius, or Plotinus, or old Iamblikius and Atticus there, who might well have been even more useful than I am if they'd been allowed to come here later when the work of setting it up was done?"

"You were more important," Athene said.

You'd think that would upset the older masters, but not a bit of it. They agreed with Athene that Sokrates was more important. After all, he was *Sokrates*.

Sokrates laughed. "I'm glad to hear it even if they are not. But I don't entirely believe you. I think you knew I wouldn't approve of this city and didn't want me to have a say in its foundations. I think you knew I wouldn't have agreed, and too many of the others would have sided with me. I did not ask to be here. I was brought here directly against my will. The children and workers were given no choice. I actively refused to come." He looked for Krito in the crowd. "My old friend Krito prayed to you to rescue me, even though I had told him I was ready to die by the laws of Athens. I drank the hemlock. I did not fear death. Nor do I fear it now. I ask you again, why did you bring me here?"

"I can't imagine," Athene snapped. Everyone laughed.

Sokrates looked into the crowd again. "Maia," he said. "Do you truly believe that what Plato wrote is the way to reach excellence?"

"Yes," she said, unhesitatingly.

"And you have dedicated your life to that?"

"I have."

"And when you learned that the workers were people, did you vote for their emancipation?"

"I did. And now I support their education," she said, waving at the workers on the edge of the crowd.

"And if you had known earlier?"

"I would have supported their education earlier. From the very beginning," she said.

"And do you think you have been doing good here?"

"Yes!" she said, passionately.

"And have you never had doubts about what Plato said and following everything he wrote?"

"I—" Maia started to speak, then stopped. "I have had doubts," she admitted. "There was so much he didn't specify and we had to improvise. And then when we first had the children. And now with the festivals. I do think we need to modify some of what Plato said there. But I still believe we're trying to reach excellence, trying to reach justice and the good life."

Sokrates leaned back a little, shifting his weight. "Thank you." He turned back to Athene. "I hate arguments that blame everything on the gods," he said, conversationally. "But it seems that here I have one. The children and the workers are doing their best to pursue the good life. So are the masters, as best they can in their limited way. For the most part they truly believe all Plato wrote and want to implement it as best they can, but even they have doubts. But you are ignorant, and you have great power, and you don't hesitate to meddle with the lives of others."

"What is he doing?" I whispered to Simmea.

"He's baiting her," she said.

"Why?" I really couldn't understand it.

"I expect he's going somewhere with it," she said. "He's leading up to something."

Sokrates looked at Athene in a friendly way. "And is it true that you lie and cheat?"

"No!" she raged.

"Mistake," Simmea whispered.

Sokrates looked taken aback. "I'm sorry. You're not following Plato in that either, then?"

"The Noble Lie isn't a lie, it's a myth of origin," Athene said.

"For those of you who haven't yet been allowed to read the *Republic*, and won't be until you're fifty years old, and only then the golds among you, I should explain that the Noble Lie is the lie about the metals in your soul and that your life before you came to the city is a dream," Sokrates explained.

"She's absolutely right, it's a myth of origin," Simmea said.

"Your children will believe it," I said.

"Good," Simmea said, firmly.

"An origin myth," Athene said again. "Not a lie."

"By the dog!" Sokrates said. "And the cheating on the lots for the festivals?"

Athene was silent.

"It's in the *Republic*. Or is that somewhere else where you're not following Plato?"

There was an unhappy murmur rising among the children in the crowd.

"Ikaros? Is this somewhere that you are following Plato?"

Ikaros just stared at Sokrates for a moment, clearly horrified. It really was too bad of Sokrates, making poor Ikaros betray Plato and Athene together. He could have asked any of the masters. But I suppose he knew that Ikaros would tell the truth. "Yes, it is," Ikaros admitted quietly.

There was another louder buzz in the crowd. Athene scowled. Sokrates looked over at where I was standing with Simmea, and then at Kebes. "And didn't you yourself—" he began, and I really thought he was going to accuse her of fixing the results at the last festival to spite me, which might well have let everyone know who I was. Sokrates would never have mentioned it, but Athene in this mood couldn't be trusted to respect my need for secrecy. But if he had been intending that he changed tack, perhaps realising the risk. "—know this was going on?"

Athene nodded angrily.

"Oh, you did? I thought so. But I just use these as examples," Sokrates said. "Though that one is an example of how the city is giving people a bad life. As we established earlier, the festivals go against human nature and make many people very unhappy indeed. And then there's the way you manipulated the numbers to get precise Neoplatonic fractions of each class, instead of fairly choosing based on the excellence of each child. Also—"

"Stop," Athene said, and as she spoke her owl flew down to her outstretched arm, wings wide, making everyone jump. "You're just attacking me, you're not making any points."

"You are a god, you should be better than mortals, but instead you are worse. We act within our limitations and you within yours, and you choose to take our lives and meddle to amuse yourself, doing what you please with them, against our will and in ignorance of whether the outcome is good or evil. You didn't know about the workers. You didn't give the children a conscious choice. You brought me here against my directly expressed wish. You say that this city is the good life, but how can it be the good life if it takes constant divine intervention to keep it going! It can't be the good life unless people can choose to stay or leave, and can choose for themselves how to make it better. Instead you imprison them on this island, with no legacy and no posterity, and you make them have children here whose souls are bound to this time and who will die when the volcano erupts."

Athene took a breath, as if she was about to speak. I don't know what I expected her to say. But she snapped her fingers in Sokrates's face. He shrank and shifted and transformed, until where he had been there was only a gadfly. He had always metaphorically called himself a gadfly, stinging people out of complacency, and now he was no longer a man but an actual literal gadfly, buzzing around the rostrum. Everyone gasped, myself included.

Athene stood still staring for a moment, and I still thought she was going to speak, explain herself, perhaps restore Sokrates. But she just looked in silence, shaking her head, with the castle crown still sitting on her unruffled curls. She gave no last speech, no farewell, no explanations. She looked at Ikaros, but she did not look towards me, or even meet the eyes of Manlius or any of the rest of her favourites. She simply vanished, and with her at the same instant vanished the workers—not just the ones gathered to listen to the debate but, we later learned, every worker in the city except for Crocus and Sixty-One.

In that moment of shock, Kebes jumped up to the rostrum, though Ficino tried to hold him back. "We've heard enough!" he shouted. "These pagan gods are unjust!"

"I have been trying to become more just," I murmured to Simmea.

"Yes, you really have," she agreed.

"This city is unjust!" Kebes shouted on. "I'm leaving to start my own city, better than this one, in a place that isn't doomed and where we can make a difference! Who's with me? To the *Goodness!*" There was a ragged cheer. He reached out for the gadfly, which buzzed away from him and flew over the heads of the crowd to where Simmea and I were standing. Kebes looked after it and locked eyes with Simmea. After a second she deliberately turned away from him, cupping her hand over the gadfly where it had settled against my chest. I put my hand gently over hers and met Kebes's furious gaze. He bared his teeth as if he wanted to kill me, but just for a second. Then he tossed his head and turned to the crowd.

"Come on!" he roared. He set off down the street of Poseidon towards the harbor, with a cluster of people around him. Other people began shouting their own manifestos. Everyone seemed to want to found their own cities, except those who wanted to stay here and take over this city and amend it on their own lines. Everyone was talking at once. I saw Maia weeping. Ikaros was shouting something about angels.

Now you may well say that at that moment I should have resumed my powers and come out of the machine and sorted everything out. Perhaps I should, even though I would have had to have died to do it. But it never occurred to me. Things did happen after that, lots of complicated things, and I'll tell you about them some other time, but this is where this story ends, the story that began with the question of why Daphne turned into a tree. I just stood still in the middle of the crowd with my hand on top of Simmea's, providing fleeting shelter for the gadfly Sokrates, as factions formed around us, and the Just City came apart in chaos.

On my temple in Delphi there are two words written: Know Thyself. It's good advice. Know yourself. You are worth knowing. Examine your life. The unexamined life is not worth living. Be aware that other people have equal significance. Give them the space to make their own choices, and let their choices count as you want them to let your choices count. Remember that excellence has no stopping point and keep on pursuing it. Make art that can last and that says something nobody else can say. Live the best life you can, and become the best self you can. You cannot know which of your actions is the lever that will move worlds. Not even Necessity knows all ends. Know yourself.

THANKS AND NOTES

I read Plato way too young, for which I'd like to thank Mary Renault.

Although I first had the idea for writing about time travellers attempting to set up Plato's Republic when I was fifteen, I would never have been able to write this book as it stands without the existence, writing, conversation, and active practical help of Ada Palmer. There's not enough thanks in the world; I have to send out to the moon and Mars for more. Buy her books and music. You'll be really glad you did.

Evelyn Walling was an appreciative listener as I worked through plot issues. She made some very helpful suggestions. Gillian Spragg helped immeasurably with references. My husband, Emmet O'Brien, as always, was loving and supportive while I was writing.

Mary Lace and Patrick Nielsen Hayden read the book as it was being written. After it was finished it was read by Jennifer Arnott, Caroline-Isabelle Carron, Brother Guy Consolmagno, Pamela Dean, Jeffrey M. Della Rocco, Jr., Ruthanna and Sarah Emrys, Liza Furr, David Goldfarb, Steven Halter, Sumana Hari-hareswara, Bill Higgins, Madeline Kelly, Katrina Knight, Elise Matthesen, Clark E. Myers, Kate Nepveu, Emmet O'Brien, Ada Palmer, Doug Palmer, Susan Palwick, Alison Sinclair, Sherwood

Smith, Jonathan Sneed and Nicholas Whyte. I want to thank Patrick Nielsen Hayden, Tom Doherty and everyone at Tor for their unfailing support as I continue to write books very different from each other.

I used a vast number of different versions of Plato when I was writing this. Alison Sinclair brought me the Loeb 2013 (Emlyn-Jones and Preddy) facing page edition of the *Republic*, which is a thorough piece of work. Having it at hand saved me hours of effort. She also discovered the existence of Ellen Francis Mason, nineteenth-century translator of Plato, whose life is like a type-example of how difficult it was for women to lead a life of the mind. If you haven't read Plato and you now feel the urge, I suggest beginning with the *Apology* and the *Symposium*, rather than diving straight into the *Republic*. There are decent English translations of pretty much all of Plato and Xenophon free on Project Gutenberg.

Love and Excellence

Plato uses the Greek word "arete" which has in the past often been translated as "virtue" but for which I am following modern usage in translating as "excellence." It doesn't really translate well into our worldview—the idea of arete is also discussed here in terms of becoming your best self.

The one term I have used in Greek throughout this novel is "agape" which of course doesn't exactly mean love. Plato's shades of meaning of this term are discussed in detail by the characters, and the word is kept in the original in order to retain one term and not a whole paragraph every time it's mentioned. Greek culture valorized one kind of love, our own valorizes a very different model. Human nature is always the problem when it comes to living with ideals.

Historical Figures

The masters come from times throughout history, and some of them are historical figures, while others are invented, or amalgams of various people. I expect to put more identifications of minor characters and links to information about all of their lives on my website at www.jowaltonbooks.com.

Adeimantus: Benjamin Jowett, Victorian scholar and translator of Plato, 1817–1893. Aristomache: Ellen Francis Mason, American scholar and translator of Plato, 1846–1888. Atticus: Titus Pomponius Atticus, Roman man of letters, 112–32 BCE. Ficino: Marsilio Ficino, Renaissance philosopher and translator of Plato, 1433–1499. Ikaros: Giovanni Pico della Mirandola, Renaissance philosopher and synthesist, 1462–1494. Krito: Crito, fourth century BCE, friend of Socrates. Lukretia: Lucrezia Borgia, Renaissance statesman and scholar, 1480–1519. Manlius: Anicius Manlius Severinus Boethius, Late Antique statesman and philosopher, 480–524. Plotinus: Neoplatonist philosopher, 204–270. Sokrates: Socrates, Athenian philosopher and gadfly, 469–399 BCE. Tullius: Marcus Tullius Cicero, Roman statesman and philosopher 106–49 BCE.

Maia is made up. She was inspired by contemplating Ethel May in Charlotte M. Yonge's *The Daisy Chain*. Kreusa and Axiothea are also made up. Klio and Lysias, who come from our future, are obviously invented.

Apollo and Athene come straight out of Homer.

Pronunciation

I am always happy for people to pronounce names however they want, but some people always want to know how you "really" say them. With Classical Greek names there are standard ways.

Often they're easy once you know where the syllable breaks are. The most important thing to know is that a terminal "e" is never silent but always pronounced "ee" or "ay." Laodike is Lay-od-ik-ee. Simmea is Sim-ay-ah. (Sim like the computer game, ay like "hay," and "ah" like "Ah, why do people worry about how to pronounce things?") Pytheas is Pie-thi-us, with a theta as in "thin."

English has issues with "C." I've tried to avoid them by trans-literating the Greek kappa as K, hence Sokrates. The only place you're going to find a C in a name is with Ficino, where it is pronounced as an Italian "ch," like finch. Ch is always hard, as in Bach or loch.